THE BONDM

'The Drongos can be yours, at least half of it, when we marry.'

'Mary!' Casey struggled to get out of the chair.

'Hush, Casey,' she said. She sank back in her own chair, her eyes glinting evilly.

'It's difficult for a woman alone. She needs a husband to help with plantation affairs.' She paused. 'A gentleman whose money was spent rescuing The Drongos from creditors and who tried to rescue my brother from a swamp, and who is descended from such an illustrious person as the Bondmaster, would be a perfect husband.'

'Why, he could even become the Bondmaster of the Bayous.'

Casey sank back in his chair and sighed with despair. Now not even liberty was to be his.

He turned to Martha and smiled. 'Why, yes, Martha,' he said. 'Let us be married at once.'

She leaned across to kiss him on his cheek, not noticing his eyes harden with an ugly lust for vengeance.

Also by Richard Tresillian in Sphere Books:

FLEUR
THE BONDMASTER
BLOOD OF THE BONDMASTER
THE BONDMASTER BREED
BONDMASTER FURY

The Bondmaster's Revenge

Being Book Five of the Bondmaster Saga

RICHARD TRESILLIAN

SPHERE BOOKS LIMITED
30-32 Gray's Inn Road, London WC1X 8JL

First published in Great Britain by
Arlington Books Ltd 1983

Published by Sphere Books Ltd 1984

TRADE
MARK

Set in 9/11 Compugraphic Plantin

Printed and bound in Great Britain by
Collins, Glasgow.

For Neel

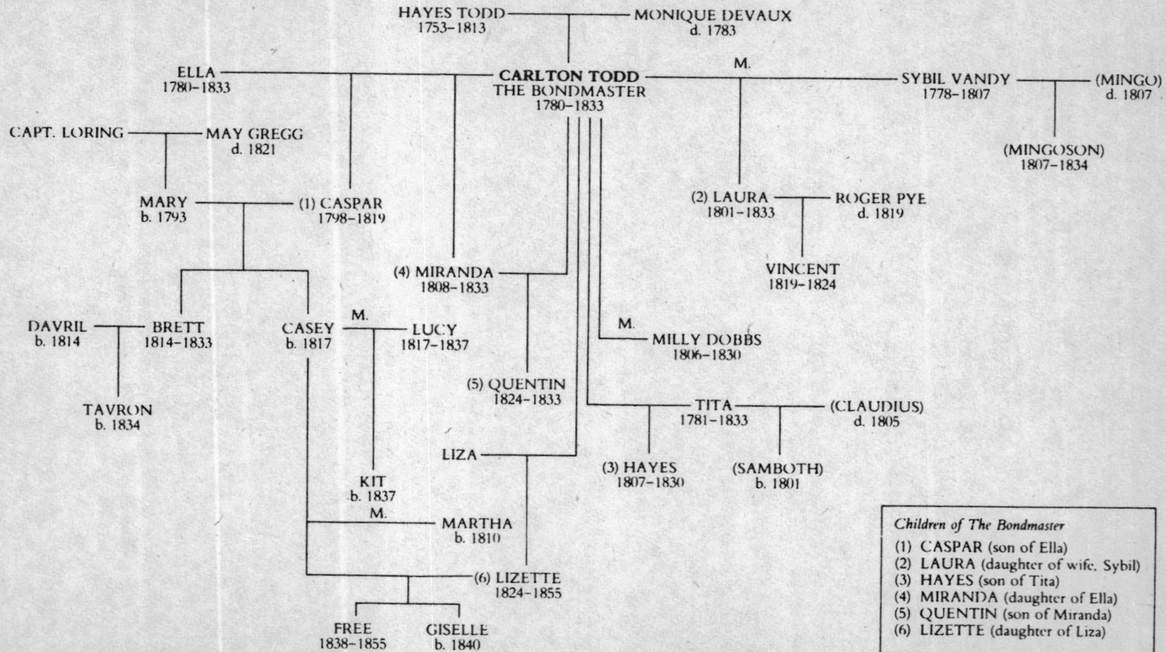

Children of The Bondmaster

(1) CASPAR (son of Ella)
(2) LAURA (daughter of wife, Sybil)
(3) HAYES (son of Tita)
(4) MIRANDA (daughter of Ella)
(5) QUENTIN (son of Miranda)
(6) LIZETTE (daughter of Liza)

CONTENTS

'Roxborough Estate in the Layou Valley was the most productive of Dominica's sugar plantations until it declined at the end of the eighteenth century when the Todd family started the first slave warren in the British West Indian islands.

'The Bondmaster, Mr Carlton Todd, is reputed to have made a considerable fortune by his selective breeding of enslaved Africans for sale to the plantation owners of neighbouring islands.

'With the abolition of slavery in 1834, the Bondmaster's dynasty appeared to have ended. However, a new branch sprouted in Louisiana close to the settlement of Bayou Sara on the banks of the Mississippi where Mr Todd's grandson, Casey Loring Todd, was the executant.'

From: *A History of the British West Indian Islands* by Sir Verne W. Bisset, Bart. Published by Shankland Box, London and Cambridge, 1913.

Prologue

THE BLOOD BOND, 1836

CHAPTER ONE

The creak of bedsprings resounded through the stillness of the plantation house like the crack of a bullwhip. It was night. Downstairs, a light glowed under the door of the library and the drone of voices wavered at the sound. A man, whose somber clothes were covered with a fine red dust from hours of traveling the potholed roads of the Georgia plains, raised his glass in a silent toast.

Leo Singer, his host, scowled. He was dismayed by what was happening upstairs in his own home. He was a man with a passion for beauty and order. His lust for the former, he realized now as he stared sullenly at his dusty visitor, had led him to betray his infatuation with the latter. If he had not been so moved by the boy's beauty to rescue him from drowning, he would not be suffering this intolerable disruption to his routine.

'What a saint you are, Mr Singer,' said his visitor heartily. 'To risk the odium of your neighbors by giving Casey sanctuary!'

Leo Singer sniffed to show his disdain. 'My neighbors care naught for me and I care less for them.'

The visitor, who was British and a retired magistrate, raised his bushy eyebrows in surprise. 'Such an act of charity, Mr Singer. No words can fully express my gratitude. Casey has inherited a fortune. He is not a slave. He is going to be my son-in-law.'

Maddocks, the name by which Leo Singer dignified his plantation house, was precious to the slaveholder for the atmosphere of tranquility in its high-ceilinged rooms and long, shaded corridors. The shattering of this peace by the continued creak of bedsprings from the room above unnerved him.

Leo Singer was in his thirties, a bachelor, lean and rugged with close-cropped dark hair and hooded gray eyes. His mouth was a hard red slit, his manner curt and his voice stern.

'What the devil's going on?' he demanded, forsaking politeness.

'Do you permit your daughter to disport herself so?' He jerked his head at the sound and frowned to show his disgust.

'Hah!' The Britisher cocked his head to listen and at first he appeared nonplussed by the regularity of the harsh squeak, like a door swinging rhythmically on an ungreased hinge. He managed to suppress the outrage he felt at his daughter being alone in a bedroom with Casey Loring Todd, and shrugged philosophically.

'It's been two years since the boy left her,' he said. 'She is overjoyed that we've found him at last.'

'I'll be obliged if you leave my premises at first light!' Leo Singer tried to keep his voice low to contain his fury. 'I do not approve of such license at Maddocks. If the slaves were to hear of it . . .'

'Of course, of course.' The visitor placed his empty glass on Leo Singer's polished mahogany desk and straightened his stock.

'Quite unusual, I agree. Lucy's mother, may she rest in peace, would never have countenanced it either. I've asked myself throughout the long journey here what would be the outcome of Lucy's reunion with the boy. She was his sweetheart, you see, and in view of his inheritance one naturally hopes for marriage.' He glanced at the ceiling and beamed.

'From what we can hear, marriage seems assured now.'

Leo Singer bunched his fists, struggling with himself to control the rage sweeping through him at the Britisher's arrogance. He was angered, too, by the prospect of losing the boy whom he had found eight weeks before, on the night of the uprising at Bullers Park, lying half-drowned by the creek that separated his plantation from Bullers.

There was a quality about the boy, even when he was unconscious, that had moved Leo Singer to hide him instead of turning him over to the patrollers.

With the help of his housekeeper, Mammy Mable,* the only slave he could trust not to babble about the boy, he had carried him into the house and laid him on the bed in the seldom-used guest room. That morning, as the light filled the room, he saw the boy clearly.

His face was beautiful in repose. His hair was long and unkempt, his complexion translucent like precious porcelain. He had reminded Leo of the urchins of the Mediterranean; wild, unbound boys with teasing eyes.

**See Fleur*

Leo had gasped with horror when he pulled back the covers. The boy's chest, abdomen and thighs were scarred with the dark weals of the bullwhip. Stripes crossed his body like the mesh of a sieve.

Leo had put back the sheet in a hurry, and studied the boy's face again. His mixed blood gave him an exotic cast. He looked intelligent, resourceful and, from the scars on his body, obviously had a lively spirit that someone had tried to break. Leo was angered by the senseless mutilation of such a fine physique and resolved to help the boy, at whatever cost to himself.

The boy was Casey Loring Todd. Leo learned how he had been kidnapped in New Orleans and sold as a slave.* At the boy's insistence, Leo wrote to the boy's protector in New Orleans, the artist Gene Cable, and was amazed when the British magistrate and his daughter arrived unexpectedly at Maddocks as a result. Leo had hoped he would not lose the company of his handsome, brooding guest quite so soon.

He rose abruptly from his chair and stalked out of the library in an effort to conceal his disappointment. He crossed the hall and rested his hand on the carved wooden banister that curved up the grand staircase. There was no sound now from the bedroom and he saw, with a start, that the light in the chamber had been extinguished. He sighed. Casey was no longer his.

Lucy shivered with apprehension when Casey moaned; she put her hand out to comfort him. She stroked the broad expanse of his shoulder, gently touching the ridges where the lash of raw leather had sliced into his fine skin.

Casey quietened under her touch and she curled her body around him. His loving had been so gentle. It was the first time and she had waited two years for him. Now he would marry her and they would sail back to Dominica together. The thought of Dominica made her gaze into the darkness around the chamber in wonder. The island was so far from this Georgia plantation.

She slid her hand over the top of Casey's shoulder and clung to him. He was warm to her touch. She marvelled at the strength she could feel, even as he slept. She closed her mind to the loneliness she had suffered since the night of the fire that destroyed Roxborough

*See *Bondmaster Fury*

Hall, the Bondmaster's plantation house in Dominica.

After the fire they had lain together among the casks of Roxborough rum maturing in the mill house. The odor of molasses hung over them, mingling with the smell of the burning house and adding a heady sweetness to the excitement and confusion of the blaze.

'Oh, Casey . . .!' Lucy had sighed then, as she hugged him close.

'You sound so sad,' he had said, touching her face. 'Why?'

'I don't want to lose you.'

He had been silent for a long time. There was no moon that night and the hogsheads in the millhouse deepened the darkness surrounding them. It was impossible to see his face so she touched his lips with her finger and waited. At last, at last, perhaps arriving at a decision that emboldened him, he laid aside her cloak and kissed her bare shoulder. Her body had leaped to life in his hands, and she quivered under his fingers. She had wanted him so much.

'I love you!' she had said, raising her lips to meet his.

The scent of rum filled the air. Beyond the walls of the mill, the river gurgled beneath the water wheel. Above the mountain range in the east, the sky lightened as the gloom of night slipped away.

Lucy felt the tension in Casey's body, as though something was worrying him. He whispered the last word he was to speak to her for two years as he withdrew from her arms.

'Wait,' he had said, and she had waited, unaware that he was leaving her, fleeing out of the millhouse and down to the river.

It was later, when her father, who was the Stipendiary Magistrate, held an enquiry into the blaze which had destroyed Roxborough Hall, that she discovered Casey had boarded a schooner anchored in the Layou River and left Dominica. For two years she had waited while her father tracked him down to the Maddocks Plantation in Paxton County, Georgia.

She cradled him in her arms and smiled triumphantly. The wait had been long and worth every minute. Casey was a wealthy man and, despite his mixed blood, he was bound, now, to be her husband.

Casey stirred again. He felt Lucy's arm around him and he was bemused by her presence. Images of her, of her innocence that he had plundered, and his love for her during those days in Dominica, merged with recollections of the intrigue and greed that had driven him to flee. It was the Bondmaster's cussed fortune that had catapulted him into slavery. The scars on his body and in his mind were his real inheritance.

He rolled over so he was lying on his back. Lucy lay her head on his chest as he drifted back to sleep.

In the village of Layou, where he was born, Casey was popular. He was a considerate child, interested in everything about him. His mother, Mary Gregg, owned the casino and its upstairs bordello and she doted on him. He led an idyllic life, as leader of his gang of friends or in the company of Uraline, his mother's cook, or with Samboth who was his mentor and was once his father's friend.

The inhabitants of the riverine village were a mixed crowd, mixed in blood as well as occupation. The Layou River with its wide mouth and safe anchorage washed all sorts to its shores. Mary Gregg's father was the master of a schooner that had anchored in the bay one day while he tumbled her mother on the mud floor of the very room Casey was born in.* Captain Loring had been a famous seafarer but was regarded as no better than the other specimens of human flotsam and jetsam that littered Layou.

The other inhabitants of the village, Casey's companions, were the unhappy progeny of the liaisons between visiting seamen and the black wenches who accommodated them for a few bits to buy a madras kerchief for their hair. Whites, down on their luck and adrift between ships, added to the population of free blacks and mulattoes who lived off the trade, mostly illegal, spawned by the schooners that anchored in the river mouth.

Dominating the village were the hills, each of them green with sugar cane, that surrounded it. This was Roxborough land, the plantation owned by Carlton Todd, a man known and respected throughout the Caribbean as the Bondmaster.

The Bondmaster, as well as growing cane and making the finest rum in the world, bred slaves. The fame of his breed brought dozens of strangers to Layou in search of new stock to work the canefields of neighboring islands. Casey himself was a friendly boy and he liked to visit Roxborough to see the slaves there, especially Ella, the Bondmaster's cook, who was his favorite. Since his mother disapproved so much of his visits to Ella, Casey could not help being

*See *The Bondmaster*

drawn to the strange house on the hill.

A few days before his tenth birthday in 1827, Casey had slipped away from his mother and followed the trail alongside the River Layou into the Roxborough property. He was curious about a white stranger who had landed by skiff from a schooner earlier that morning and hired a horse so he could ride to see the Bondmaster. The man had swaggered arrogantly, so impressed by his own self-importance he made Casey and his friends laugh as they watched him.

'He come to buy slaves,' Samboth had explained. Casey considered this information. Samboth was a free negro who idled away his days fishing in the river while he recovered, so he claimed, from his nights fishing in darker waters.

'Why does he want to buy slaves?' Casey asked, sitting at the huge man's side and watching the surface of the river for a fish to bite.

'He know,' said Samboth with a shrug. 'I pity de slaves he does buy, dough.'

'Why?'

'Dat man ain' no massa. He want wenches to pester, not cut cane.'

Casey stared at the water. 'How do you know that?'

'I knows.' Samboth shut his mouth firmly, signifying the end of the conversation.

Casey sat with him a few minutes, pondering what Samboth had said. Being Mary Gregg's son with a free run of the bordello, he knew all about pestering. He was puzzled why Samboth thought it was wrong for the white man to want wenches for that instead of to work the fields. He longed for an explanation but the hunch of Samboth's shoulders told him to seek it elsewhere. He crept away from Samboth's side without the negro noticing.

It was not far to where the mill, built of solid gray river stone, loomed out of the trees lining the trail. The water wheel was turning slowly as the river coursed into it. Casey met some slaves on the trail and they eyed him cautiously although none of them spoke under the gaze of their driver.

Casey paused when he reached the wide avenue of tall roystonia palm trees that led to the 'cou', the slaves' name for their master's house. It was an ugly building, menacing the neatly laid out landscape of the plantation. Years later, Casey was to see the fine plantation homes of Louisiana towering majestically above fields bright with cotton. Roxborough Hall, as the Bondmaster chose to call his home, was a miserable hovel compared with the mansions of the deep South.

The lower level of the house was constructed of stone and contained the food store, quarters for the house slaves, and the kitchen. The upper story was wooden, distinguished only by the balcony that girded it on all four sides.

The Bondmaster liked to sit on this gallery observing the activities of his slaves and their drivers in the cane fields stretched out below him.

Casey darted hastily across the avenue to avoid being seen and walked up the slave trail through the undergrowth to the 'cou'. When he reached a thicket by the courtyard near the kitchen, he peeped out cautiously. Neither the Bondmaster nor the swaggering visitor were to be seen although Caliste, the groom, was brushing down the man's horse outside the stable. Casey sidled across the courtyard to the kitchen.

'Lor'!' said Ella in surprise when he tumbled down the step into her arms. 'Yo' does be one troublesome white boy, *oui*?'

He liked the tall woman, who was said by the boys in the village to be a princess and the Bondmaster's bedwench as well as his cook. She always gave him a cake freshly baked from her oven, or a dish of calalloo brimming with fresh water crayfish and thick with dasheen leaves and peppers. Today she held him away from her at arm's length and studied him closely.

'Does yuh mam know yo' here?' she demanded, shaking her head sorrowfully.

'No, Miz Ella,' Casey grinned. 'I left Samboth by the river. He said the white man has come to buy slaves but he ain't a master for wenches because he wants to –'

Ella clapped her hand over his mouth and her eyes rolled upward. Casey lowered his head in apology.

'De Bon' massa go'n cut yuh grain if he hear yo',' she said testily. 'He up dere.' She pointed to the gallery above the kitchen.

Casey squatted on his haunches and looked at Ella, wondering why she seemed so sad when she mentioned his mother. She was tall and imposing even though age had dimmed her beauty, turning the carefree slimness of her youth into gaunt solemnity.

Ella shook her head again and Casey was tempted to ask what was wrong. Her hand dashed down and thrust a biscuit at him. He took it eagerly and grinned his thanks.

'Be off wid yo', fas' nuh, Mas Casey. Dis ain' de place fuh yo'.'

There were other slaves in the kitchen, all of them busy preparing dinner for the Bondmaster and his wife. Although they glanced at him inquisitively, none of them spoke. Casey chewed his biscuit and wondered if Ella would explain the mystery he seemed to have caused, but she turned her back and strode away from him with a sigh.

She began to harangue one of the girls chopping meat on the long wooden table that filled the center of the kitchen. The girl spoke timidly and Ella slapped her into silence. Casey felt that he was somehow the cause of Ella's prickliness so he scurried out of the kitchen into the yard.

'Hey, boy!' a voice called.

Casey leaped at the sound and dived head first into the thicket. He wormed his way into the center of the bushes fearing at each moment that a hand would seize his ankles and pull him back. He stopped, shaking with terror.

Slowly, he cowered down, ignoring the branches that scratched him, and listened apprehensively for the sound of the Bondmaster's boots on the flagstones of the courtyard.

CHAPTER TWO

'Damn the boy! What's he so afeared for?' Carlton Todd smiled ruefully at his visitor and sank back into his chair on the gallery.

'Trouble is,' he said, 'I've got so many young colts and fillies here I don't know them all.' He saw the stranger's eyes light up. 'Don't mean I've got plenty to sell. Needs them, I do. Needs them all.'

Carlton scratched the stubble on his chin, gaining time to make up his mind about the man sitting with him on the gallery. The cut of his clothes, with their exaggerated style, suggested a man of substance, even if his manner was brash. He watched the man snatch the glass of sangaree from Pip, while his eyes looked the houseboy up and down. He seemed to dismiss Pip from his mind in disgust.

'That one's been my houseboy for twenty years,' said Carlton, rankled by the man's attitude. 'I don't put my niggers into fancy trogs. Needs an obliging slave, not a macaroni.' He turned away from the visitor and addressed Pip.

'There's a buck in that thicket there,' he said. 'Came from the kitchen. Root him out, Pip. I don't know that one at all.'

Carlton noted the flicker of doubt in the slave's eyes before the boy turned away. He grinned to himself. It was so easy to see what a nigger was thinking. Pip had the fawning manners and servile smile of a docile houseboy but even at his age, and Carlton knew he must be in his mid-thirties, the boy couldn't hide anything from him.

'Get on with you, Pip,' he called. 'Don't think you're too damn smart for me to send you to the fields. You're gettin' fat and lazy in that kitchen. Catch me that bright-skinned buck and bring him here.'

The visitor, apparently at ease after a few sips of the sangaree, stirred himself. 'Perhaps you don't understand me, Carlton,' he said familiarly. 'I'm not looking for young bucks.'

'Maybe not,' Carlton snorted. 'What did you say your name is?'

'Hardin Calmes.' The man pulled a handkerchief from his sleeve and waved it in front of him.

'Well, *Mister* Calmes,' said Carlton, deliberately emphasising the title, 'I'm the Bondmaster and folks call me *Mister* Carlton. And because I'm the Bondmaster, I have to know what every colt and filly on this plantation is doin'. Right now, there's something mighty odd about the contents of that there thicket.'

Hardin Calmes frowned irritably.

'I'm not aimin' to lecture you on slave management, no sir.' Carlton sipped at his glass of sangaree. 'Maybe in Louisiana or wherever you hails from, you do things different. I tell you, a good house slave is better than an overseer. Just by their stance or a flicker of their eyelids, I can tell if something is amiss on the plantation.' He chuckled and stood up, walking to the end of the balcony.

'My old father could tell by his nose. He stood here every night, sniffing the smells from the slave quarters. He reckoned he could tell if the niggers were out in the dark or if they had shuttered up their shacks and gone to sleep.' He sniffed, shrugged his shoulders, and walked the length of the gallery back to his chair.

'If niggers are sittin' outside when they ought to be sleepin', then they be frettin'. My dad would stop that frettin' by stringin' up a few of them by their ankles and lashin' them.'

'That's what we do in Louisiana.' Hardin Calmes mopped his brow and fidgeted in the heat.

'Is it, now?' Carlton pursed his lips, eyeing the stranger suspiciously. 'Larrups your niggers regular?'

'When we have cause.'

'Oh yes? Some slaveholders do it for sport, I hear.' Carlton drained his glass. 'Too much whippin' ain't good for niggers. Got to keep 'em willin', not scared. Got to treat a nigger well, Mr Calmes, if you want the best out of him. Get good drivers and you'll get good field hands.

'My slaves are content. I give 'em enough feed, and they have their own provision gardens. Even makes a few bits selling their produce in the village.'

He lay back in his chair and raised his legs up so that his heels were hooked over the balcony railing.

'I'm looking for breeding wenches,' said Hardin Calmes impatiently. 'I'll pay well. We want to sail on the noon tide.'

'Noon tide?' Carlton was aghast. 'Today?'

'Yes, yes.' Calmes twisted his handkerchief in his hands.

'That's a shame,' Carlton drawled. 'I reckoned you'd stay a night or two. Likes to know who my wenches are going to, I do. Besides, you haven't met Milly, my wife.' Carlton's face took on a glow of pride. 'She is always pleased when we have visitors. Life can be lonely here for a young lady.'

'Ain't no time.' Mr Calmes didn't bother to be polite. 'Frankly, *Mister* Carlton, my mission is urgent, I've tarried too long. I never intended to sail so far south down islands. Very inconvenient. But at every port and slave factor I visited, I was told to come to you for breeders. Everyone said you have the best breeding stock, prime and fertile.'

Carlton glared, despite his pleasure at hearing of his reputation. 'I ain't never met a man as busy as you,' he grunted. 'We do things more easy in Dominica. That Louisiana you come from must be mighty worryin' for niggers.'

'We drive our nigras hard, Mr Carlton. Have to with cotton. That's why I want breeders. Stock scarce to find these days. I need a few wenches to lay down some suckers for the future.'

Carlton nodded. 'Maybe you knows your business after all, Calmes. You told me when you arrived that your wenches aren't breeding. You ever wonder why?'

Hardin Calmes scowled. 'Of course, of course. Poor stock, old blood. No new shipments to set them with.'

Carlton shook his head. 'I reckon you treatin' slaves too harsh. You got to coddle 'em. It's true! But don't let my niggers know that.' He stifled his smile. 'Ain't a wench go'n drop one sucker if she contrary. You sound like you chivvyin' and brutalisin' your fillies so they all shrunk up inside. A breedin' wench ain't the same as a field hand.'

Calmes looked annoyed. 'We got different methods.'

'Aye.' Carlton pursed his lips then said slowly, 'don't reckon I relish my breedin' stock in some far off country where they ain't happy.'

He stood up and gazed over the acres of cane and forest to the hills above the Layou River. From the fields came the occasional murmur of the slaves and the crack of a whip snapped in the air above their heads. The noise of the children gamboling in the Paddock drifted across to him. His acute eye and ear told him all was well at Roxborough.

'Aye,' he said again. 'Breedin' stock too precious.'

'That's preposterous!' Calmes leaped to his feet. 'You mean you won't sell? Why do you care if your slaves are happy or not when you've sold them? I've never heard the like!'

'Whoa!' Carlton held up his hand to still the man's bluster. 'Ain't sayin' I won't sell, only that my stock is damn precious. Yes, sah!'

'I'll pay your price.'

'Aye, and you will.' Carlton brushed back his silvery hair. He noticed Ella standing in the doorway on to the balcony. She was frowning to indicate her disapproval of something.

'One thing to remember, Mr Calmes,' he said, gripping his visitor by his elbow and walking him along the gallery to where Ella couldn't overhear the conversation. 'My stock has a fine reputation. If you take my Bondmaster breed to America, and they don't give you whelps, my name ain't go'n be worth nigger shit.'

'Yes, yes,' said Calmes hastily, removing his elbow from Carlton's grasp.

'So I want you to guarantee you'll treat my fillies well, and I'll guarantee you'll have breeders who go'n drop you a whelp every spring for half a dozen years.'

'You have my word.'

For a moment Carlton's face showed how little value he placed on his visitor's promise, but he shrugged and turned away. 'Ella,' he called and waited while the housekeeper glided to his side. Calmes appraised her expertly.

'Get me two wenches that's full and one that's ripe but foaled already.' Carlton paused thoughtfully then chuckled to himself. 'And we'll have a female with a whelp. Fetch Liza.'

'Liza?' Ella sounded scandalized.

'Aye. Liza's the lucky one.' He ignored Ella's shocked expression. 'Get 'em all to bathe in the river right quick.' He glanced behind him. 'Get 'em to wait under the gallery. We don't want to disturb Miss Milly.'

'I'm obliged to you, sir.'

Carlton nodded, satisfied that this stranger was playing the game by his rules now. He felt sufficiently pleased to be generous with his advice. 'You got bucks for these fillies, have you?'

'Yes, yes. No shortage of males in my fields.'

'I hope you ain't aimin' to let any rutter that's in heat mount my stock?' Carlton scowled. 'No, Calmes, you must only put your best males to stud. Don't work 'em too hard, and pair 'em off decent. No ruttin' for a stud outside his nest. You got to give a stud a chance to thicken his juice. Like good buttermilk, rich and strong. If you hustle him, his juice ain't go'n stick. It runs back out the wench before she creamed.'

Hardin Calmes pretended a display of politeness to conceal his astonishment at Carlton's theory. 'You've made a fine study of it, sir.'

'Breeding's my life, Mr Calmes.'

The two men sat back on the gallery sipping the fresh glasses of sangaree brought them by Pip. Carlton was irritated by his visitor's impatience but he attributed it to the typical vulgarity of American slaveholders. It was only because he was flattered at the chance of some of his stock going to America that he bothered with the man.

Fertile breeding mares were the most valuable of all now that the trade from Africa had been banned. The life expectancy of a slave working in the fields of cane or cotton was short. The only way they could be replaced was with stock born domestically. It was Carlton's specialized breeding of prime stock, strong and healthy slaves that were tractable and docile, that had earned him his fortune.

Hardin Calmes got to his feet and began striding restlessly up and down the gallery. It was upsetting the rhythm of his household but Carlton ignored the man's bustle. In his youth he would have been keen to oblige this prospective customer but now, nearing fifty and blessed with a new wife* half his age and a fortune in gold, he cared not a jot for the speculators and lickspittles who sought him out.

He wondered if Milly would emerge from her boudoir to meet Mr Calmes. He chuckled. She was probably preparing herself now, trying on one dress after another, harrying her maid to move faster so she could meet the American before he left. Carlton sighed.

His happiness would be complete if Milly herself could have a child for him. Was he the one to blame for her barrenness, he wondered. Was he too old? Impossible! A filly whose virginhead he had broken dropped a whelp for him only a month before. No, it wasn't his fault, there was still juice in his loins. Some day Milly must give him a white heir for Roxborough.

He was disturbed in his thoughts by Ella announcing that the wenches were ready. She hovered at his elbow, anxious to advise him, but he brushed her aside.

**See The Bondmaster Breed*

'You'll want to examine them, I suppose,' he said to Calmes as they hurried down the steps to the courtyard.

'No, no. A quick glance will be enough.'

'Can't tell quality, that way,' Carlton drawled. 'You got to feel 'em. No need to take my word for it.'

There were four women standing naked under the balcony eaves. Their eyes showed their fear. Although the slaves at Roxborough knew that one day most of them would be sold, breeding wenches were seldom disposed of. So Ella's call to the four to bathe and strip down in front of the 'cou' had caused consternation in the quarters. Only one of the four, a lithesome girl with a child at her side clutching her hand, stood confidently.

Carlton made a sign to the women to parade in front of him. Hardin Calmes nodded his head as each passed. There were two women, one black and the other the color of red Mississippi mud, who showed they were full by their round bellies and swollen breasts.

'Finger them, if you want,' Carlton urged. 'Of course, they ain't virgins, but that's not what you want.' He laughed.

The third girl passed nervously in front of the two men. She was sixteen and her body, glowing like burnished copper in the morning sun, rippled as she trod lightly on the flagstones. She was lean, muscular, with a small face and a straight nose.

'Here!' commanded Carlton, settling down on the steps and opening his legs. He pulled the girl by her wrist so that she stood in front of him. 'Open your mouth.'

He seized the girl's jaws in his fingers and twisted her head toward the visitor. 'See, a perfect set of teeth. Good diet and good blood gives you that. Finger her!' He thrust the girl at Hardin Calmes and the man twisted away with embarrassment.

'Go on, she's clean.'

'She'll do.' Calmes' voice sounded strained.

Carlton chortled at his visitor's discomfort. He passed his hands over the girl's breasts, across her belly and down between her legs. 'Got Fulani blood in her,' he said, showing off his expertise. 'That gives her the light color and the straight nose. It's not white blood.' He squeezed her buttocks proudly.

'Niggers like to be fingered,' he said. 'Shows you appreciate them.'

Hardin Calmes' face was reddening and he shifted uneasily. Carlton grinned at the bulge in the man's trousers. 'You aimin' to service these fillies yourself?'

The man spluttered a protest.

'Ain't naught wrong in that. False modesty don't belong in a slave breeder, Mr Calmes. Liza, let's see you.' Carlton crooked his finger at the tallest of the four slaves and the girl strolled over with her daughter in tow. He patted her rump and made her turn.

'Show yourself to Mr Calmes, Liza. Ain't she cute?' Carlton ignored the expression of disgust on the American's face.

'Of course, she's black and maybe you ain't partial to servicing something you can't see in the dark? Believe me, she's a willing filly, a good ride, free from disease and guaranteed fertile. This child is here to prove it.'

The child was three years old and stood silently with her eyes on Carlton. She had a light complexion in contrast to her mother's blue-black hue. Her eyes, almost hidden by locks of long silky black hair, were pale gold.

'You can have the four of them for . . .' Carlton paused at the gleam in the American's eyes and he doubled the figure he was going to suggest. 'Let's say eight thousand dollars.'

'But . . .!'

'Can't speak, young man? Catch your breath!'

'That's too –''

'That's too low for such superb black bitches, ain't it? Breeders all of them, and two of them full. Hope you don't aim to waste my time further by insulting me with a lower bid.' He stood up, offering Hardin Calmes his hand.

'Take 'em or leave 'em?' Carlton raised his eyebrow in a superior manner calculated to arouse the American's ire.

'All right.' Hardin Calmes shook Carlton's hand roughly.

'Fine. I'll tell you what I'll do, since you're so sporting. I'll throw in the chit too.'

'That chit?'

'Mas Carlton!' Ella pulled his sleeve, unable to restrain herself any longer. 'Liza's child, you surely not sellin' her!'

'No, I ain't. I givin' her away.'

'No!'

'Why not, Ella?'

'She yuh own get, Mas Carlton.'

'I know that, Ella. You don't think I'd sell my own off-spring, do you? I'm giving her to Mr Calmes to prove the Bondmaster and his stock are fertile. We're sending our best to Louisiana, Ella. Wenches that whelp every year.'

Ella gritted her teeth to stop her anger and stalked off in a huff so arrogantly that Carlton was moved to upbraid her. As he opened his mouth to speak, he caught sight of a flash of color in the bushes beyond her. He glanced around him hastily. Pip was standing at the top of the back steps, too far away to be any use and he was such a contrary nigger.

'Dale!' Carlton recognized a boy ambling across the courtyard by his African blackness. 'Dale,' he shouted again.

The boy froze and fixed his glance to the ground, too terrified to look where his Bondmaster was pointing.

'A shilling for you if you catch that whelp skulking in the bushes there. Look lively now.'

Dale stared dumbfounded at Carlton. Ella halted her stride and looked from Carlton to Dale and then to the bush where she knew Casey was hiding.

'Dere ain' no whelp in de bush, Mas Carlton,' she pronounced loudly as Dale looked at the thicket. Dale hesitated at the sound of her voice.

'Shut your mouth!' Carlton glared angrily at Ella as bushes in the thicket waved, indicating the frantic progress of Casey to make good his escape. 'Bring that whelp to me, Dale.'

'Yas, massa!' Dale loped across the courtyard toward the copse. Even as he ran, Carlton knew that it was useless. Ella had effectively jinxed his command and whoever was hiding in the bushes would have time to sneak back to the quarters before he was caught.

'Damnation!' he said, ignoring Hardin Calmes and scowling at Ella. 'There was a whelp in that hide and you know it. I saw him coming from the kitchen an hour since.'

'Oh, dat one!' Ella laughed. 'Dat be Tency brat. Yo' know he does be *fou, oui*? He does be too *makak* to know yo' ain' go'n lash he.'

'Hah!' Carlton stomped over the flagstones, back to the grand steps, snapping his fingers at Hardin Calmes to follow him.

'There's something odd going on there,' he muttered. 'That whelp didn't look like one of my stock at all. He looked more like my son Caspar, God rest his soul, than any nigger I own.'

CHAPTER THREE

Mary Gregg was a formidable woman, even to the roistering planters, pompous government officials and tough seafarers who patronized her establishment. Casey, cowering before her in the back room of the tavern, felt every bit as intimidated as her customers when they faced Mary's flashing blue eyes and expressive sneer.

He glanced up at her nervously as she stood with her arms akimbo glaring down at him. Even at that early hour, she was dressed in the opulence for which she was renowned, her wide skirt bedecked with flounces and her bodice tight and revealing.

Casey's pants were torn and his body was scratched from squirming through the cane in his frantic effort to get away from the Roxborough slave who had chased him. He hung his head, stricken with silence. It was Uraline who had caught him when he was skulking outside the kitchen wondering how to slip into the back of the tavern without being noticed. It was no good, for his mother was waiting.

'I tell yew, Casey!' She tossed her head and her blonde tresses bobbed in disarray. 'Yew go'n bring disgrace on me! Where did yew go, boy?'

Casey tried to speak but he was tongue-tied and too exhausted from running back to the safety of the village. Although the slave never gained close enough to catch him, the experience had terrified Casey.

'Samboth was searching all over for yew!'

He gulped. 'I does be sorry, mam.'

'Ah, got yew tongue at last, have yew?' Mary's open palm descended on him and Casey staggered back at the blow, his ears singing.

'I go'n box yew ears till yew learn the lesson good, Casey!' she shouted. Her hand sliced through the air and stung his right cheek.

As he turned, Mary's other hand slapped into his left cheek. He put up his arms to protect himself.

'Mam!' he wailed, dodging Mary's fists when she lunged at him again. 'I ain't done no wrong, nuh.' He ducked and Mary's blow whistled over his head. 'I was be at Roxborough.'

The chastisement ceased as suddenly as it had begun. There was a silence in the room that was somehow more threatening than the bluster of his mother's wrath. Casey peeped through his fingers covering his face. Mary was staring at him, aghast, her mouth open in an expression of such horror that Casey immediately regretted having spoken.

'Is that why yew talking like a slave?' she asked softly.

'No, mam.' He frowned, unaware that in his excitement he had lapsed into the vernacular of the plantation slaves.

Mary was distressed. She sat down heavily on a hogshead lying on its side in the corner of the room and gazed at Casey. He shifted uneasily. It was difficult for him to understand the changing mood of adults. Her sudden despair worried him and he raised his head cautiously. She opened her arms and he fell into her embrace, gasping for breath as she hugged him tightly.

'Casey,' Mary said in a deep voice choking with emotion. 'I've lost one son to Roxborough. I don't want to lose yew too.'

'I'm sorry, mam,' he whispered into her cambric corsage smelling of verbena and powder. He raised his head.

Mary said nothing, only patting his shoulders with a display of affection that amazed him.

'Why mayn't I go to Roxborough, mam?'

Mary regarded him steadily. 'What's yew age, Cas?'

'Uraline say I have ten years next birthday.'

Mary sighed. 'Is it that long since Caspar died?'

From past experience with his mother's tantrums, Casey knew that a way to deflect them was to get her to reminisce about Caspar, his father. 'Am I like Caspar, mam?' he said, opening his eyes wide to pretend innocence.

'Yew!' Mary snorted disdainfully. 'There ain't never go'n be a man like Caspar Todd.'

'I could try.'

'Aye, yew could. First yew must stop going to Roxborough.'

'Why, mam?' He repeated his earlier question and pulled himself away from Mary's embrace. She wiped a tear from her eye and gestured impatiently for him to hunker down at her feet. He listened with rapt attention as Mary told him the full story about Caspar and their affair.*

He learned how Carlton Todd had sired a love child with his slave bedwench, Ella. That child was Caspar, Carlton's first son, and the Bondmaster doted on him. They visited England together and Carlton planned that Caspar should inherit Roxborough with the sobriquet and fortune of the Bondmaster.

The blood that flowed in Caspar's veins was a potent mix: the royal lineage of Ella, his mother, who was a Batutsi princess with a thousand years of selective breeding behind her, blended with the plantocratic pedigree of the Bondmaster himself. He was a lusty, handsome youth and when he was sixteen he and Mary, who was five years older and a whore in her mother's bordello, became lovers.

'Our first child was Brett,' said Mary, unable to keep the tears from her eyes. 'The Bondmaster took him for his own. He was raised in the slave paddock at Roxborough and doesn't know me. When I was pregnant with yew, Caspar made me swear . . .' She paused and gazed at Casey.

'What, mam?' He beat his fists on her knees and she held him tenderly.

'I vowed to raise you in secret, Casey, so that Carlton Todd would never know Caspar had another son in Layou.'

'In secret?' Casey sat back on his heels. 'I'm not a secret. I'm here!'

'Yes, yew are, Casey. Carlton doesn't even know yew exist. If he sees yew, though, he'll suspect something. That's why yew must promise me never to go back to Roxborough. Yew must never let him see yew!'

'Why, mam? If I'm the Bondmaster's grandson, won't he be pleased to know me?'

'Child! Don't yew understand?' Mary's face grew stern and she stood up, putting her hands firmly on his shoulders. 'Yew don't want to be a slave, do yew?'

'No!' He looked shocked.

'Well! If Carlton Todd knows about yew, son, he'll keep yew at Roxborough as his slave for ever. Don't go there again, Casey. Please!'

*See *Blood of the Bondmaster*

'Yes, mam.' Casey nodded his head meekly to hide his curiosity, aware that the Bondmaster had begun to exert a hold on him that he would never be able to shake off.

An hour later, Casey was back in the village street. The demands of her customers soon had Mary bustling around the tavern leaving Casey to ponder his new knowledge. That there was Bondmaster blood in his veins made him proud although he was sensible enough not to let his mother see it. He strolled with a swagger through the village. At the river bank, a crowd had gathered to watch the departure of the slave trader from America.

Hardin Calmes was looking flustered. He had the four slaves he had bought and was anxious to leave Layou quickly. The press of people around him and his small coffle seemed intent on delaying him. The Bondmaster had not given him an escort so he was compelled to stand alone on the bank while he waved frantically at the schooner for the master to send a skiff and some men to help him. The crowd, sensing his discomfort, pushed closer. The slave women, linked together by a long rope bound around their ankles, sensed the sympathy of the free blacks surrounding them and wailed loudly.

Casey attacked the outside of the throng so he could push through. A drunken *mulâtre* struggling to see what was happening was so surprised, he stumbled and let Casey squeeze in front of him. Shouting and shoving, he wormed his way through the crush of people until he was at the river side.

He stared at Hardin Calmes. The man had lost some of his swank but being white and of a masterful mien, to say nothing of the presence of two pistols protruding from his belt, he was still in control. The sight of the skiffs and a party of seamen skulling rapidly against the current of the river to collect him had done much to restore his confidence.

The end of the rope binding the women together was tied around his waist. Casey thought that the women, if they did not want to be slaves to Mr Calmes, could escape very easily with the help of the crowd. Yet the people clamoring around the white man and his purchases were curious, not hostile. Slavery of others was a condition they accepted and to resist it on behalf of those others was out of the question.

The slaves, Casey noticed, were nervous, numbed by the sudden usurpation from the tranquility of Roxborough. They whimpered with fright, not anger. They knew they had been sold and their attitude of meek acceptance had been inculcated in them as part of the Bondmaster's seasoning process.

The little girl clinging tightly to her mother's fingers, was pale with terror. Casey knelt beside her and placed his hand on her shoulder. She flinched, drew away from him and wrapped her tiny arms around her mother's leg.

'Don't be frightened,' Casey whispered in patois. The sound of his voice reassured her and she turned her head. Casey stroked her cheek.

'My, aren't you beautiful,' he whispered. 'Such a pretty girl. You are lucky to be going away with your mam. Oh yes,' he continued, trying to calm the child, 'you have a new master and are going to a new home. There's nothing to be scared of.'

Liza, the girl's mother, regarded Casey haughtily and pulled the child away from him.

'I'm only trying to help, *oui*!'

He stood up, ducking as arms from the gesticulating crowd struck out around him. The skiff had reached the bank and a party of Calmes' men leaped ashore.

They brandished short lengths of rope in their hands and, at a sign from Mr Calmes, began to belabor the crowd enthusiastically. There was a stampede back to the other side of the trail away from the lashing flails and Casey was carried with it. He crawled on his hands and knees taking several blows in the process, to where he could watch.

Mr Calmes swelled in size now he had his henchmen. He snatched a rope from the hand of a sailor and pasted the slave women across their buttocks. The little girl got a lash on her cheek and she screamed. Casey began to run toward her but a hand clamped on his shoulder and held him firmly while the coffle was shipped into a skiff.

'Hush, Mas Casey,' a voice urged him. He squirmed under the fingers gripping his shoulder and looked up at the solemn face of Samboth. 'Yo' ain' got no bus'ness meddlin' wid dem slaves.'

'Did you see?' Casey shouted. 'They hit the little girl.'

'Yas, Cas.' Samboth drew him away gently. 'Dat ain' all dey go'n do she.'

'Why . . .?' Casey was stunned as, for the first time, frustration at the unfairness of slavery hit him. He sat down on the trunk of a fallen palm tree beside Samboth and cradled his chin in his hands.

'That poor little girl,' he said, biting back the tears. 'She ain't done nothing.'

'Yo' got no cause to fret, Cas,' Samboth soothed. 'It ain' yo'!'

'No!' cried Casey overwhelmed with despair. He flung himself across Samboth's lap and shrieked again. 'No! No! No!'

'Hush, hush.' A hand stroked his brow and he opened his eyes in surprise.

Lucy, lying beside him in the bed, snuggled closer. She caressed his chest. 'You were having a dream,' she said. 'Don't worry, you're safe now.'

'Am I?' He stared at the darkness. He didn't want to see her face.

'Yes, you are. Daddy will see we get to New Orleans. We can –'

'You don't know what happened,' said Casey gloomily.

'In your dream?'

'No.' He shook his head, wanting to explain. 'Since I left you that night at Roxborough . . .' There was silence in the room, in the whole house. He sighed, feeling the weight of the atmosphere of the plantation house on his shoulder.

Lucy was touching the wales on his chest, catching her breath with disbelief as her finger traced the length of each ridge swollen in his skin. There were so many.

He wondered what she thought of his sigh of doubt. Could he ever explain why he had left her? Could he describe, and would she understand, the confusion that assailed his mind that last night in the mill at Roxborough? A force greater than his own mind compelled him to flee, yet he had found no refuge.

'Lucy,' he said, gripping her wrist and holding her hand away from his body. 'I was a slave. I was forced to do terrible things . . .' Humiliation caused the blood to rush through his veins and he was glad of the darkness which hid his flush of shame from her adoring eyes.

'I was kidnapped in New Orleans and sold –'

'I know that,' she whispered. 'It's all over now.'

Is it, he wondered. He was nineteen; his youth was spent, crushed by the brutalities and suffering he had endured during the long months of slavery. He embraced Lucy, humbled by her love yet aware that things could never be the same between them again.

'Lucy,' he said, 'I've got to find the man who kidnapped me. To make him pay for –'

'I said it's over now, Casey. Don't let it poison you.'

'I must. For what he did.'

'Isn't it enough that we are together now?'

'I'm not free,' he said. 'The patrollers are still searching for me.'

'No. Leo Singer says they think you drowned. Daddy will escort us to New Orleans. Then we can be married.'

The idea was strangely comforting. It presented images of normality, a respectable way of life as husband and wife in their own home, perhaps a small tavern with a farm and . . . He laughed softly.

'I've still got my gold in the bank. We *could* do it.'

'Yes!' Lucy's happiness was infectious. 'You see, when you consider it, everything will be all right. Casey, I do love you!' She buried her face in the crook of his shoulder sobbing with relief at his renewed hope.

'We can go to England. You can start a new life . . .'

Yes, he thought, but only after I've found that man. He cupped her chin in the palm of his hand and eased his mouth over hers. His tongue dove between her lips and she drew on it eagerly, entwining her fingers in the silky hair curling around the nape of his neck. Her other hand rubbed over the ridges on his back, down to his waist, holding him tightly. He relaxed at her touch and surrendered to the passion engulfing them both.

Lucy remembered the first time she had spoken to Casey two years before, and how he had angrily ordered her to go away. She had followed him from the village through the undergrowth into a secluded glade beside the Layou River. She had watched him bathing naked, and thrilled at the sight of him when he stepped from the river with droplets glittering in the sunlight like diamonds on the gold of his body. His dark locks dripped water down his cheeks and a trickle of moisture ran down the crucifix of hair at his chest to the bunch of curls at his crotch. His thighs bulged with the muscles of an athlete and he strode up the sandy shore with the agility and grace of a young Greek god.

From her hiding place she had gazed on Casey as he stretched out in the sun. He was tall and sleek with a face so kind and handsome it glowed with vitality. His eyes were a pale bronze, startling in the gold of his complexion and giving him an air of profound mystery. He was the same age as her although he seemed steeped in experience she could only guess at. His fine straight nose showed his white ancestry while his small, lobeless ears, like Pan's, were a legacy from his African forebears.

Lucy knew Casey's history; he was the talk of the village and the bane of Lucy's mother who worried constantly that Lucy would succumb to him. Perhaps it was because he was forbidden that Lucy sought him out. She recalled her first words to him, blurted out before she could stop herself, when she saw Casey stretched out on the sand with such indolence she was shocked: 'What a lazy bones!' she had said.

He did not look around when he told her to go away. She had retreated into the bush and waited, overwhelmed by her own temerity in speaking to such a god. After what seemed like an eternity, she moved out from her hiding place and sat carefully on a log, artfully arranging her white dress so that her ankles showed under her skirt. Her hair, bleached fair in the tropic sun, hung loosely from her sensible bonnet.

This time, when she spoke, Casey reacted immediately, covering himself with his breechcloth and staring at her in astonishment. She could not recollect what they talked about that day, all she remembered was the yearning which swept through her as she gazed enraptured at him.

Now, she realized, he had changed. The tenderness in his eyes had been ousted by a lingering hatred, a desire for revenge. His features had toughened and he had grown solemn with maturity. No longer was he a gangling youth; his body was hard and muscular with no spare flesh.

As she lay in his arms in Mr Singer's guest room bed, she sensed the strength not only of his body but of his mind as well. She shuddered, wondering if it would ever really be possible to tame him.

She closed her eyes as he embraced her. His mouth slid from her lips to her neck, biting softly the flesh at her throat. She gasped and he released her, letting his lips trail down to her breasts. She had grown since she had last seen him. Her breasts were rounded, full and eager with the passion that had built up in her during the time she had waited for him.

She quivered under his touch as his fingers explored her body, stirring ripples of emotion surging through her.

She squirmed when his hand lodged between her thighs and his fingers spread her open. She longed for this to be a gesture of love, not a memory of the brutal inspection of slavery. She blew softly into his ear and, with her hands on his buttocks, drew him close.

He took her with a fierceness that seemed to tear her apart, but assuaged her pain with an exquisite caring. She was crushed under him at the same time as she flowered anew and he soared within her. Now, despite the hardships that may confront them, Lucy knew that she was his, bonded to him with a link that could be broken only by death.

He was, she realized as her love gushed to meet his, forever her bondmaster.

Book One

THE DRONGOS, 1837–1839

CHAPTER FOUR

The house was in the street by the old ramparts, close to the Place des Nègres, more popularly known as Congo Plains, on the outskirts of the French Quarter of New Orleans. Casey and Lucy stood hand in hand on the wooden banquette on the opposite side of the street and admired it. The house was painted white; it was small and only one story high. A tub of flowers on either side of its low flight of entrance steps distinguished it from the neighboring houses in the street, all similar in size and color.

This street along the line of the old ramparts exhibited an air of distinct gentility, almost intimidating in its neatness and cleanliness. It was a contrast to the confusion and squalor of the busy streets that led through the French Quarter for the six hundred yards to Levee Street by the Mississippi River.

Thirty-four years before, New Orleans had become officially an American municipality. Then the American commissioners, General James Wilkinson and W. C. C. Claiborne, Governor of the Mississippi Territory who became the first Governor of Louisiana, entered the city. On behalf of the United States, they took possession at a ceremony in the Place d'Armes.

New Orleans, at that time, was a compact if lawless city of about four thousand homes with ten thousand inhabitants, half of whom were white, a quarter free negroes and a quarter slaves. A stockade enclosed most of the town and a palisade was erected where Casey and Lucy now stood. Houses beyond the Rue Dauphin, two blocks behind them, were few in number then.

As the population swelled and the dividing line between whites and free negroes became softened by miscegenation, areas to accommodate the city's cosmopolitan inhabitants had sprung up. Building lots were made available around Congo Plains which, in 1820 at the command of the mayor, Louis Philippe Roffignac, was planted with sycamore trees to bring order to the grass and shrubs of the area. Homes sprung up then, evidence of the growing wealth of those of the city's people whose blood was half white, a quarter negro and a quarter slave.

When Casey and Lucy arrived in New Orleans they soon discovered that the law in Dominica by which a person with mixed blood was equal to a white, was unknown in the city. They were resentful at the restrictions placed on them. Because of his own wealth and the influence of Madame Cable, the mother of his sponsor, Casey could have been immune to society's strictures. But after three months confined to the circle of the eccentric Madame Cable and her artistic set, Casey and Lucy wanted a home of their own. So they chose the very area where their presence would be considered unremarkable: Rampart Street.

The black girl who answered their knock on the door of the little white house looked first at Casey then, with widening eyes, at Lucy. She turned back to Casey, tried to cover her curiosity with a giggle, then bid them enter. Casey handed Lucy up the steps and followed her in to a tiny parlor.

It was a pretty room furnished with exquisite good taste. There were two chairs, in which they sat, positioned next to a small round table of highly polished rosewood. An escritoire poised at the other side of the room. The parlor was as long as the width of the house and, being filled with furniture and knick-knacks, gave the impression of cosy intimacy. It was pleasant when compared with the daunting spaciousness of the Spanish-styled mansions of Madame Cable and the town's elite.

Yvette Lacroix, the owner of the tiny house, swept into the parlor to greet them warmly. She was not one of the elite. She kissed Lucy, held her hand, complimented her on the prettiness of her bonnet, and turned to Casey. She acknowledged his bow, laughed away his praise about the elegance of her dress and seated herself daintily on a stool upholstered in green and gold brocade.

'It's my 'umble 'ome,' she said disparagingly in response to Lucy's words of delight about the house.

'It cost M'sieur plenty but not a cent more than I'm worth.' She tittered again, her dark liquid eyes lingering on Casey. 'I'm so pleased you like it.'

Casey bowed his head again. 'We are indebted to you, Yvette.'

'Nonsense, *chéri*. It is a pleasure to know I can give a couple *so in love* some 'elp.' The emphasis did not go unnoticed by Lucy who blushed.

'My new 'ouse is ready, so you may stay 'ere as long as you like.' Yvette reached for the silver teapot that the black girl placed on the table. She began to pour. 'Jenny 'ere will look after you.'

Casey watched Yvette while she chattered. He had made her acquaintance at one of Madame Cable's soirées. The old lady delighted in breeching the barriers of convention and her house was often the scene of unexpected but entirely pleasurable encounters between the *demi-monde* and the aristocracy of the city.

Yvette Lacroix was from the city's twilight world. She was typical of the women whose beauty had made New Orleans famous and it was her color that precluded her from the echelons of the city's elite to which her grace and charm gave her a natural entrée. She was a quadroon and, as such, could only mix with her legion of white admirers at the quadroon balls, at soirées of enlightened people like Madame Cable, or in the privacy of the house, bought for her by an elderly paramour, on Rampart Street.

It was natural that Casey should have been attracted to Yvette. Her beauty, coupled with her pride in her heritage and color, was striking. They had talked happily together like old friends. Madame Cable, observing their apparent intimacy, hastened to assure Lucy that she need harbor no jealous thoughts about Yvette.

'The lady's sole aim in life is to improve her station,' she whispered too loudly to be discreet. 'She has a gentleman who caters to her every whim and she repays him by doting on him exclusively.'

Yvette herself told Casey how the house in which she lived, bought by a previous protector when she was eighteen, was too small for her and she had a new establishment.

'The aim of every quadroon,' she said with a glance at Madame Cable, 'is the same as that of the creole women; to catch a white man, preferably rich.' She laughed. 'My first gave me the 'ouse when 'e left to marry 'is child'ood sweet'eart.'

'You must have been disappointed,' Casey sympathized.

'Nonsense! We quadroons never expect marriage. When my man left me I settled down in the 'ouse quite content, but I was so young. I went to the quadroon balls to amuse myself not to meet someone to replace 'im. My new gentleman found me there and fell 'elplessly in love with me. What could I do but accept the new 'ouse he bought me!' She patted Casey's arm and smiled.

'Why! You and your bride may 'ave my old 'ouse if it amuses you.' She glanced at Lucy. 'I 'ope the neighbors – they are like my sisters, you understand? – will grow accustomed to the novelty.'

Casey had not asked what she meant and now that the three of them were sitting in the parlor of Yvette's house, he was so overwhelmed at the prospect of having a home of their own in New Orleans that he quite forgot to ask again. Lucy, he saw, was enchanted by the cottage and seemed to have no doubts at all about living there.

The house was neat, as befitted a single lady of good taste, with a boudoir leading off the parlor. This was furnished with all the accouterments of a lady of quality although the presence of a massive fourposter bed large enough for two belied the modesty apparent from the other furnishings. There were no other rooms. Jenny, the slave girl, slept on a mat in the parlor, and she was to stay as part of the house. The kitchen was in the yard where Jenny's mother lived in humble gratitude as the cook.

Casey and Lucy, without further ado, accepted Yvette's invitation to live in the house. Three days later they moved in and Yvette left to begin her new life in a much grander mansion in the Rue Chartres. It was there, many years later when her paramour died, that she opened and managed with strict propriety, a high class boarding house for white bachelors.

Yvette's tiny house and the close intimacy into which living there plunged them added an unexpected tension to the relationship between Casey and Lucy. When they had lived in Madame Cable's house, their moments together were limited to the bedroom. Casey was too relieved then by his escape from slavery and so enraptured with Lucy that he did not consider the possibility of their incompatibility. Only now they were together all day and all night in the confines of the house did Casey begin to find flaws in Lucy's company.

A feeling of dissatisfaction, of having been rushed into a marriage that was not as rewarding as he expected, began to trouble Casey. He tried not to show his feelings. He curbed his wild nature and lived meekly as Lucy's husband, tending her as a doting lover, obliging her, and taking part in her charades of husband and wife. He sat dutifully with her in the parlor, joined in her small talk and pandered to her desires.

Despite his attempts to play the part of a housebound husband, the only happiness Casey had in the marriage was when he and Lucy were in bed. The tensions increased until one day, five weeks after they had moved into the house, Casey was slumped in the parlor's only comfortable chair, his legs stretched out in front of him.

Lucy was busy with a sampler, embroidering it with elaborate care. Her blonde hair was brushed back from her face, the result of forty minutes of Jenny's labor that morning, and she was frowning with concentration. Casey watched her sullenly and was alarmed to feel an inexplicable anger.

The sound of women's voices energetically gossiping in the street droned through the open louvers. Casey twisted in his chair and glanced out. Two quadroon women, both breathtakingly beautiful, were standing outside the next-door house. They nattered happily, unaware of Casey scowling at them. This was their street, the street where white planters housed their quadroon mistresses. Casey and Lucy were the interlopers.

'By the devil!' he said, striking his thigh and sitting up.

Lucy raised her eyes from the sampler and stared at him. Her lower lip trembled. 'What's wrong, dear?'

'Don't "dear" me like I'm some kind of pet!'

He pulled himself out of the chair and walked the length of the parlor. It took only two steps before he came up against the escritoire and had to turn. The furniture shuddered under the weight of his boots on the floor as he strode five paces back to the opposite wall.

Lucy dropped the sampler in her lap, tears glimmering in her eyes. He strode another length before he turned and saw them.

'Oh, Casey!' She dabbed at her eyes but the tears increased. Her shoulders shook and Casey paused in astonishment.

'Why are you crying?' he demanded, his anger subsiding slightly. 'Stop it.'

'Yes.' Lucy took a deep breath and raised her head, composing herself obediently. 'I'm sorry.' She twisted her handkerchief nervously.

'*Mon dieu*!' Casey smacked his fist into the palm of his hand. 'Why these tears?'

She blinked at him. 'I don't know.' She paused and Casey felt the familiar surge of lust at the loveliness of this white girl who had sought him out and claimed him for her own.

'I was frightened,' she said. 'You see, you're so strange sometimes, so restless. I'm frightened you'll leave me.'

'Leave you?' He was startled that an idea that had barely begun to form in his own mind had already occurred to her. It frightened him too and he stepped over to Lucy's side and put his hand on the nape of her neck. He caressed her.

'Don't fret,' he said. 'I've got to get used to marriage, that's all. I'm accustomed to being alone in the open fields of a plantation or running wild in the streets of Layou.' He scowled as he gestured around the parlor. 'This domesticity . . . well, it's a bit confining.'

Lucy frowned and reached for him. 'Are you sure that's all? Sometimes I think you'd rather be with your own kind.'

'By the devil!' he said, feeling his anger returning. 'Aren't you my kind? You came from Dominica to find me. What the hell is my own kind?'

'I mean –'

'I know what you mean, Lucy.' He spun around and walked the length of the parlor. 'What worries you is what other people think, isn't it?' he said, turning his own misgivings onto her.

'We came to this house so we could lead our own life and ignore other people. It's our refuge so what does it matter what they say about us. It doesn't bother me that my grandmother was black, so why should it concern them?'

Casey suddenly realized that the very reasons that had driven them to Rampart Street could also drive them apart. He had seen the amazement in the eyes of white women when he walked out with Lucy on his arm, and noticed the shocked glances of blacks. It seemed their relationship was of great concern to everyone they encountered. The attitude of others had made him see Lucy and himself through their eyes; a white woman with a quadroon man.

That was why Casey had brought her to the house in Rampart Street so close to the negro preserve of Congo Square. Yet even here, among the mulatto mistresses of wealthy white men, they were misfits.

'If we have a child, Casey,' Lucy said, interrupting his thoughts, 'I want him to have a proper home.'

'Huh?' He stared open mouthed.

'Yes. Somewhere he'll feel secure. Not in New Orleans where he'll be chased from one place to another because he's neither white nor black.'

Casey's anger soared at Lucy's perception. He was upset that her thoughts had raced so far ahead of his own. He snorted. 'If that's the problem,' he said loudly, 'leave that to me!' He patted his coat pockets.

'I've enough money from the Bondmaster's gold to send him to the best places to be educated like a white man. He'll be a gentleman no one can fault. He'll be secure.'

'And if we have a daughter?' Lucy's eyes flashed. 'Do you think she'll be allowed to find a husband here? No! She'll be the octoroon plaything of some white man in a house just like this!'

The fury in Casey exploded blindly. His hand slashed out across Lucy's cheek before he could control it. 'You're wrong,' he shouted, knowing she was right.

Lucy stared at him defiantly, seeming satisfied that she had managed to provoke him. Then she hastily lowered her eyes and buried her face in her hands. She tensed and held herself away from him.

He reached for her. 'I didn't mean it . . .'

Lucy's cheek was reddening rapidly. He put his finger to it and stroked her face, murmuring his apologies. When she remained unyielding he was puzzled.

'Fancy saying that,' he said. 'How could you even think such a thing?' He frowned. 'Oh, you're distressed, I suppose. Don't feel alone, Lucy, I'm with you.'

He waited but when she didn't respond, he released her and stood up in bewilderment. Still she didn't look at him. 'Can I get you something?' he asked moodily.

'No, no,' she said, her voice dry. 'I think I'll lie down.'

'Yes, yes, that's it. I'm sorry, Lucy, please forgive me.'

'Of course,' she said, standing up and walking away from him into the boudoir they shared. 'It was a wicked thing for me to say. I'm sorry too.' She let the door swing closed quietly behind her and Casey watched it for several minutes feeling ashamed and wondering if Lucy wanted him to go to her.

A cackle of laughter outside the house decided him. He cursed impatiently, misunderstanding Lucy's need and thinking she was rejecting him. He straightened the stock at his throat, checked the fall of his coat over the creases in his trousers, and the gloss on his boots. Satisfied, he pulled open the front door and stepped swiftly into the street, ignoring the two women who abruptly stopped their yakking to watch him.

He was livid about the disagreement with Lucy and felt doubly cross because the fault was his. How could he have been so stupid? He stomped angrily along the banquette away from the house, not caring where he was going.

How he longed to find the man who had seized him that night two years before. Everything that had happened since then was the fault of that one man. His anger with Lucy was because of that man who had ruined his youth, and robbed him of the power to love, to be tender and caring. One day, he knew, he would get his revenge.

'Oy! Oy!' A voice sang in his ear. 'Yo' too uppity to bid a lady how d'ye do?'

He glanced warily to his right. The front door of a tiny white house, identical to his own, was open and a woman sat on a chair in the entrance. She was laughing at him.

'Oh, Casey, you look like you have all the troubles of your sex on your mind.'

The remark made him halt. Angelique was a friend of Yvette's – a quadroon, an octoroon, he didn't care which – who lived alone in the house provided by her white admirer. Casey shook his head to clear it and bit his lower lip so he wouldn't snap at the girl.

Her laughter changed to a smile of concern at the glint of anger lingering in his eye. 'Why, *doudou*, have you had a tiff?'

'Forgive me, Angelique. I was thinking and didn't see you.'

'That's a fine thing to say to a lady after I've spent two hours deciding which dress to wear and my girl brushed my hair for another hour.'

'All of it quite unnecessary, Angelique.' Casey grinned roguishly. 'You are beautiful enough without such pains.'

'Good.' She smiled. 'A touch of your flattery is always welcome. Come, sit here on my little porch and let's give the street some scandal. The sisters love it.' She nodded her head at the two women now gaping in their direction.

'I've given our neighbors enough scandal already.' He settled down on a chair on ths step beside her, calmed by Angelique's devil-may-care attitude.

'Ah, yes, you *mulâtres* from down islands always were different from our own.'

'What does that mean?'

'A free man of color in New Orleans knows his place, Casey. He has his vocation and keeps to it. He becomes a barber, a tailor or an upholsterer. He becomes wealthy, marries a girl darker than himself, and becomes a pillar of mulatto society.'

'So I'm breaking the rules?'

'You bet you are! It's we quadroon princesses who are permitted by society to pleasure with whites, not you.'

'I thought bringing Lucy to live here would make her feel comfortable.'

'Did you feel at ease when you lived at Madame Cable's and mingled in her white society?'

He felt suddenly very guilty.

'Of course, you didn't. There are rigid class rules here in the French Quarter, Casey, and you have flouted them. You're a stranger and you have gold in the bank so you can be forgiven. But never try to take Lucy to a quadroon ball because that's for white gentlemen and colored ladies only. And don't take her to the Orleans Theater because no white person of either sex can enter there.'

Casey scratched his head. 'What am I supposed to do? I feel trapped, Angelique, and I take it out on Lucy. It's not her fault.'

Angelique sniffed. 'Whose idea was it for you to get married?'

'Hers . . .'

'Exactly. She knew the difficulties.' Angelique patted his hand. 'Why don't you send her away from here?'

'We've only been here a few weeks!'

'That isn't important. It will always be the same here, however long you stay. Send her back to Dominica, Casey. She doesn't belong here. Neither do you.'

Casey turned unexpectedly and caught the smirk of mockery in Angelique's eye. She raised her fan to hide it, but it was too late. He cursed her under his breath for laughing at him and for reminding him of Dominica.

There wasn't a day that passed without him yearning to return, despite his vow to stay away forever from the evil he associated with Roxborough Hall. The lushness of the Layou Valley, the sunlight filtering through the trees moist after a passing shower, the rainbows haloing the hills bordering the Roxborough plantation; all were visions he longed to see again. Dale at Roxborough, Uraline and Samboth in Layou, and his mother, dear Mary Gregg with her firm hand and rough tongue. What were they doing now?

The thought of his mother brought back the distinctive odor of the women in the bordello above the tavern. There was a genuineness in those whores that he missed in the hypocritical divisions of society in New Orleans.

'My!' said Angelique, forming a moue with her full lips. 'If I knew you were going to sulk I wouldn't have asked you to keep me company. My gentleman will be here shortly so perhaps you should go. He mustn't meet you here.'

It was Casey's turn to mock. Angelique was attractive although Casey found her carefully-coiffured hair, beeswax face paint, manicured nails and elaborate costume ridiculous. Although they were reputed to be faithful to only one man at a time, to Casey these colored kept-women with their pretensions were worse than the two bit whores of Layou.

'You want me to go?' Casey sneered, feeling his temper returning. 'Perhaps I will. Perhaps I won't.' He stood up and gripped Angelique by her wrists, forcing her to rise with him. 'Step inside.'

'How dare –'

Casey cut off her protest by locking his mouth on to hers and forcing her to him with his hands firmly placed in the small of her back. He swept her up off the step and carried her into the house.

She pounded his back with her fists. 'The neighbors!' she gasped.

'They can wait their turn,' he said grimly, kicking the door closed behind him. Angelique was cradled in his arms now and he was not surprised when her token resistance ceased as soon as the front door was shut. He marched with her through the parlor into the bedroom.

The bed was identical to the one in Yvette's cottage and Casey wondered which carpenter, certainly a mulatto, had the contract to furnish the *bijou* love nests of Rampart Street. He loathed her, himself and what he saw as the whole mulatto conspiracy.

He dumped Angelique on her bed and she regarded him with horror. 'My hair!' she cried. 'My dress!'

'Ah, yes,' he grunted, his lips pulled back in a snarl of rage. 'Your hair!' He reached down and ran his hand through the carefully combed creation, leaving the girl's hair in disarray.

'Your dress!' He placed his hand on her bodice between her breasts and pulled. The lace fabric that cost her paramour a small slave, ripped open in his hands. He pulled downwards, tearing the dress until Angelique lay in the midst of a pile of rent garments. She watched him breathlessly.

Casey bit his lip as the urge to punish her, and all those like her, surged through him. He was confused by the raging desire swelling in him, nothing like the tender love he felt for Lucy. He saw Angelique's sylph-like nakedness below him, her brown rounded limbs and the anxious rise and fall of her bosom.

He tore open the front of his trousers and fell on her.

Casey lay exhausted on the bed, still deep within the woman, when there was an urgent hammering on the door of the cottage. He yanked himself off roughly, pulled up his trousers and sauntered to the door. He flung it open in the face of a white man who stepped back in astonishment at the sight of Casey calmly buckling his belt.

'Come in,' said Casey.

The man had a mustache and was in his late twenties, dressed as a planter. He carried a pistol at his waist. He was not the man Casey sought.

'She's yours,' he said with a leer. 'I've finished with her.'

He pushed past the man and stepped down on to the sidewalk, whistling jauntily as he walked off to Congo Square.

CHAPTER FIVE

Casey was grateful for the canopy of oak and sycamore boughs shading Congo Square. At that hour of the afternoon there were few people in the park and he was able to stroll around the perimeter without being disturbed. The *vendeuse* on the sidewalk, old negresses with spruce beer, coconuts and popcorn, regarded him suspiciously as they sorted their wares and awaited their evening clientele. Casey ignored them and walked, lost in thought, puzzling about the reasons for his own strange behavior.

The Square was officially known as Circus Square, a name bequeathed to it by the presence, when it was a large open space with a cypress swamp wilderness on three sides and the expanding city on its fourth, of Monsieur Cayetano's circus and menagerie. The circus had slipped from the memory of the inhabitants and been replaced by the name of the African slaves who gathered in the Square to dance.

Congo Square was situated at the end of the Rue d' Orleans. At the other end was the Place d'Armes with the army and navy on its right and left; the courthouse, the council hall and the church at its back. That was the rendezvous of the wealthy; the master, the military officer: the whites.

Congo Square was the preserve of the negroes and riffraff of the city; the outcasts of white society who would gather in their own milieu and enact the prejudices of the white elite on each other.

Sunday evening was the highlight of the week when slaves gathered from all over the city to dance to the beat of the *bamboula*, a bamboo drum. They were watched by the city police and by well-heeled white spectators who were regarded as interlopers. At nine o'clock, the evening gun would boom out from the Place d'Armes and the black men and women who wanted to keep out of the Calaboose had to hasten back to their slave quarters.

The Square provided an escape valve for the frustrations of the blacks because of the opportunity to dance and socialize, and also to get their revenge by mocking in song and dance their masters and the conventions that governed them. Casey, rambling in bitter melancholy beneath the trees, had no song to dispel the frustration poisoning his mind.

Congo Square was the only public place in the city where whites, colored and blacks could mix and actually converse. Although he had tried hard to resist the truth spelt out by Angelique, Casey knew he was deluding himself if he supposed life with Lucy in New Orleans would ever be without tensions.

By Louisiana law, the letters *f.m.c.* denoted his status: a freeman of color. It was a title that did not even rate capital letters. Where the three letters (including *f.w.c.* for a free woman of color) were shown, he was welcome, but Lucy was not. Where she could go, if not already excluded by the censure of white society for marrying him, he could not.

He was trapped, he knew it, and it riled him. He gazed around the field wondering how to vent his frustrations before returning to the cottage in Rampart Street to seek Lucy's forgiveness. He thought nothing of Angelique; she had been a temporary relief that had not solved anything. The confusion he had brought to her own domestic arrangements was not his concern.

He spied, beyond a clump of sycamores, where the pale green willow undergrowth had not been cleared, some men in the frock coats of prosperity gathered in a secretive circle. He glanced across the square and saw that this group was being ignored by the blacks who had begun to promenade around it. There were no *gendarmes* in attendance as was customary. Whatever the group of whites were planning, Casey had a feeling it was against the city's ordinances. Perhaps he would find his erstwhile captor there. His anger and the desire for revenge made him bold and he sauntered toward the group, defying them by his swagger to order him away.

No one remarked on his presence and it surprised him. The men were moving in groups of twos and threes into a clearing behind a screen of foliage. He followed them. One man, trailing two others, glanced at him, seemed to approve his looks and nodded casually. Casey dipped his head in return, curious as to what manner of white society had apparently accepted him so easily. The man himself was dressed respectably in the dull colors favored by tradesmen, but some of his companions sported more dashing attire.

Behind the thicket were some negroes, a score or more white men and some mulattoes, although they appeared to be functionaries rather than spectators. One of the mulattoes was speaking earnestly to a negro who stood, like a black Hercules, in the middle of an admiring circle of whites. Another negro was annointing this muscular giant with oil, rubbing it vigorously across his shoulders and down his back. At a word from the mulatto, the negro stepped out of his breechcloth and stood naked while the other black massaged his buttocks and thighs and applied the oil to his penis.

Some of the white men approached the negro and tried to squeeze his biceps without success. They murmured approvingly among themselves. The mulatto spoke to the negro and he flexed the muscles of his stomach until they formed hard ridges the size of mangos. The mulatto invited the whites to punch the giant's stomach and those who did so chortled enthusiastically.

Casey spun away in disgust. Some exhibition was being planned and he wanted no part of it. He cursed his curiosity for leading him to that place. Someone caught him by the elbow.

'You don't care to join us?'

The man who spoke had sandy hair and eyes that seemed unaccustomed to brightness. His nose was squashed to one side, splayed close to his face. He blinked at Casey and grinned, revealing a row of teeth with the upper two missing. His clothes, or the man himself, reeked of stale tobacco and rum. He was a short, sprightly character in his thirties. Casey sensed that beneath the man's bedraggled exterior, he had the strength of a fighter. He regarded him warily.

The man pulled a flask from a pocket in the tail of his coat and offered it to Casey.

'Good tafia,' he said.

Two years before, in a New Orleans tavern by the levee, Casey had accepted a drink from a stranger only to wake up a day later shackled in the hold of a ship bound for the slave market of Mobile. He backed away as politely as he could.

'Your loss,' said the man, holding the flask to his lips. He tilted back his head and drank with obvious relish.

Casey waited, unwilling to offend the man further by moving off abruptly.

‘Take ten to one on the griffe,’ the man said.

‘What?’

‘Congo’s strong, oh yes, you can see that.’ The man gestured at the negro who was prancing on the spot, lifting his legs high, his eyes bright as he basked in the admiration of the whites around him. The man spat on the ground and his spittle splashed Casey’s boots. Casey pretended not to notice.

‘But ask yourself, young feller, is he cunning?’

Casey shrugged his shoulders and wondered how he could extricate himself from the man’s apparent friendliness. He noticed two of the whites were watching him speculatively, and again he shuddered at the recollection of the misery he had suffered because of the man who sold him into slavery.

Another white man walked up to the pair and pressed some money into the hand of one of them. The man scowled and Casey sensed they were speaking about him.

‘You should do it now,’ his new companion urged him hoarsely. ‘Before the odds change.’

‘I’m grateful for your advice,’ said Casey, moving away. ‘I don’t gamble.’

The man clutched his elbow again. ‘This isn’t a gamble. I saw the griffe this morning. He’s mean. Do you think a griffe would let a *bossal* as black as that one beat him? No! Think on it, feller, you can’t lose.’

He pointed at the pair of white men Casey had noticed. ‘It makes the bile rise,’ he said, ‘When I see how much money Saunders and Baker will make out of them fools.’ He waved at the whites surrounding the naked negro. ‘I’d take bets myself but I don’t have a banker.’

The man squinted at Casey in concern. ‘I can see you’re a prosperous young feller. I don’t want you to stake me. Back the griffe and give me a share when you win. Fair’s fair, ain’t it?’

Casey’s anxiety cooled now he knew what the little man wanted from him. He was intrigued that the white man had accepted him as a fellow human being and not as a social oddity. He was a friendly character and Casey warmed to him, taking a swig from his flask when it was proffered for a second time. He was delighted to find that the tafia was good, a rich rum and not the cheap liquor he had expected.

‘Present from a grateful friend,’ the short man explained with a wink. ‘I see you know good rum.’

Casey grinned. There was no rum that would ever compare with

Roxborough's. He handed back the flask. 'Thank you for your kindness, sir. Now I must leave.'

The man looked crestfallen. He smiled shyly at Casey then shook his head. 'I thought you was a sensible young feller. See it in your eyes. Independence, wealth . . .' He sighed.

'Look, everyone is backing the *bossal.* Ten to one on the griffe. Don't let Saunders and Baker get so rich!'

Casey was amused by the man's persistence and lack of pretension. He glanced around the clearing again and saw that more whites had arrived. They were a mixed crowd. Judging by their dress, some were merchants, perhaps a school teacher or two, some clerks, some ne'er do wells and, by their bearing and hearty voices, some were soldiers in mufti.

Dusk was gathering and slaves had been positioned on the outskirts of the clearing with flambeaux in their hands to light the proceedings. Casey was intrigued to see in the glare of the torches that there were several mulattoes and quadroons among the spectators. Several men were making bets and the rumble of talk was growing louder indicating that the fight was soon to begin.

Casey slyly considered his new companion still waiting at his side. The man seemed honorable enough; his face was pleasant and it was easy to see him as a man temporarily down on his luck. The jovial mood of the crowd and the lack of any animosity to him from all the whites surrounding him, lifted Casey's spirits. He shrugged aside his mood of misgiving and patted the man's shoulder.

'All right,' he said. 'I'll wager.'

The man beamed and led him over to Saunders and Baker, two lugubrious men whose small eyes glinted greedily at the sight of a new customer.

'Ten to one on the griffe,' the man said excitedly.

'Might as well,' Saunders nodded gloomily while Bake sucked his lips. Casey pulled out his purse to search for a coin.

'Not a small bet, is it, Hollis?' Saunders sneered at the sight of Casey's purse.

'No, no,' said Hollis, reaching up to clap Casey on his back. 'My friend wants to back his choice properly.'

Casey's mood made him sensitive to the slight implied by Saunder's sneer. He winked at his new companion. 'So you're Hollis, are you? Well, I do believe you're right, Hollis.' He glared at Saunders.

'Twenty dollars on the griffe.'

'Is the griffe a friend of yours?' drawled Saunders.

'Must be,' sniffed Baker. 'Lot of money to lose.'

'Make it fifty,' said Casey, handing over the money. Both men regarded him dolefully and even Hollis fell silent. Baker checked the coins and nodded to Saunders who scratched his crotch unhappily.

Hollis pulled Casey away. 'Your money's safe,' he said. 'Saunders and Baker are taking so much on the negro they can afford to pay you. They won't skip.'

Doubt struck Casey too late. 'If they abscond with my winnings, Hollis, I'll hold you responsible.'

'Oh aye.' Hollis seemed unconcerned as he turned his attention to the crowd. He passed his flask to Casey who took a swig to steady his temper. He became aware of people glancing in his direction as news of his large wager spread among the whites. Some of them hurried to place new bets.

'You see,' wheezed Hollis happily. 'The odds have dropped, like I said.'

'Where is this griffe?' Casey peered around the glade. The dusk was beginning to give way to the evening darkness. 'I can't see my champion.'

'Nancy, she's the owner, don't care to show him until the fight's about to begin.'

'Nancy! A woman! Have I backed petticoats?' Casey spluttered, the tafia rising in his throat.

'I know fighters, young feller. She's got the best.'

Before Casey had time to regret his rashness, there was a shout from the center of the glade. The spectators closed in followed by the slaves with the flambeaux moving closer. A space was cleared in the crowd and two slaves moved to the center with their torches to throw light on the fighters. For the first time, Casey had a glimpse of the boy he had backed, and he realized he had been fooled.

The griffe, the Louisiana word for the offspring of a mulatto and a negress, was almost hidden behind the cloak of his owner. She stood in front of him with her arms open wide and the cloak shielding him from the gaze of the spectators. No wonder, thought Casey. From the sight of him it was obvious that there could be no contest. The boy's head showed above the rim of the cloak when he jumped, and those in the crowd who saw him seemed to share Casey's poor opinion of the fighter. There were groans of disappointment everywhere. Some of the men nudged each other, pointed at Casey and laughed.

Casey glanced at the griffe again. The boy's face was scarred and his head was narrow at the top like a pointed stake; with his hair cropped so close his skin showed through scabrous and gray. He was scrawny and a lightweight who looked as though he needed a decent meal not a contest with a negro twice his size. In dismay, Casey looked around for Hollis, expecting his new acquaintance to have disappeared. Strangely, Hollis was still at his side.

He was tapping his nose with his forefinger. 'I said he was cunning, didn't I?' He winked.

At a shout from the burly white man who was the umpire of this uneven match, the woman cosseting the griffe let her arms fall and stepped aside. The sight of the griffe full length sent a murmur of disappointment through the crowd and did nothing to restore Casey's confidence.

'He's a runt,' he said, gripping Hollis's arm tightly in disgust at being fooled. 'How dare you trick me like that!'

The man tapped his nose again and smiled so blithely Casey immediately regretted his accusation.

'He'll win,' he said, touching his mane of sandy hair confidently. 'I used to be a fighter myself. I know.'

'The black will pulverize him! I'm fifty dollars down.'

'Not yet, you ain't.' Hollis grinned. 'See, the boy's wily. A nigra don't have to have big balls to win.'

The griffe danced out into the center of the circle and taunted the black fighter like a matador with a bull. The more the Congo boy charged and tried to seize the griffe in his huge hands, the more the smaller boy dodged and weaved around the circle. The crowd grew impatient for them to connect.

'I'd say he's scared, not wily.' Casey glanced at the Congo's supporters. They were chortling with pleasure at the thought of their winnings. Saunders and Baker watched dourly.

There was a roar. The Congo slave caught the griffe and lifted him clean off the ground. He prowled around the ring holding the scrawny boy above his head for the spectators to see.

'Break his neck,' shouted a gruff voice behind Casey, showering spittle on to his cheek.

Casey spun around to remonstrate and found he was looking into the steely gray eyes, cold as a slaveholder's, of the man he had insulted at Angelique's door. 'Break the yeller rat's back.' The man's mustache curled upward as he leered at Casey.

The Congo giant swung the griffe around and all of them saw the boy's fear. He bellowed loudly, flung the boy high into the air and prepared to throw himself on him when his body spattered on the ground. The griffe's reaction was as unexpected to the crowd, who saw it first, as it was to the negro, who didn't see it.

The boy twisted his body in the air and landed lightly on his feet. As he touched the hard mud, he leaped up and charged the astonished giant with his head down, butting him so forcefully in the crotch that the negro collapsed onto his backside and howled.

The griffe, sensing the advantage, hurled himself at the negro while he was down and smashed his chin with his shoulder blade. There was a crack and the negro toppled backward, his jaw dislodged and fractured. The griffe danced away and looked proudly at his mistress.

'By the devil!' explained Casey, momentarily forgetting the mustachioed planter blustering behind him. 'The griffe has the tricks, not you, Hollis.'

The little man beamed with pleasure.

Sensing that they had a fight worthy of their interest, the crowd pressed forward and Casey felt the breath of the planter on his neck and his fists hammering his shoulders. He edged aside so that the man could step up to the front but he remained behind Casey, a constant threat.

The Congo fighter was in superb condition. It took seconds before he was back on his feet, looking slightly groggy. The griffe leaped again, only to fall into the trap set for him. The Congo negro wasn't dazed at all. He stepped aside, the griffe smashed to the ground and the negro jumped on him with both feet. The crowd yelled and the negro rolled over and pounded the boy with his fists.

'Serves the rat right for being so fresh,' muttered the planter, jabbing Casey.

'Who is this man behind me?' whispered Casey to Hollis. 'He's annoying me. On purpose.'

Hollis stretched up to reach Casey's ear. 'That's Jed Barrow. Don't meddle with him, my friend. He's trying to provoke you.'

It's too late now, thought Casey as the fight progressed.

The griffe's display of nimble bravado had served only to increase his punishment at the hands of the Congo giant. The negro was angry, puffing in fury as he bashed the boy's head on the ground. There seemed no hope for the rawboned fighter.

With his money surely lost, Casey decided to edge away from Hollis so he could avoid an encounter with Jed Barrow. He no longer felt as cocksure as he had done when he left Angelique's.

The planter seemed to have other ideas. He clapped Casey on the shoulder and held him firmly. 'See that,' he exclaimed. 'Why doesn't he kill the rat and be done with it?'

The griffe slipped from the negro's grasp and stood in the center of the ring, panting. The negro turned savagely and charged until he was checked by the boy's foot cracking his damaged jaw. He grunted with pain and reached out to clench the boy in his huge fists. The griffe, showing how tired he was, sidestepped. He neglected to protect himself and the Congo's second lunge bowled him over to the ground where the giant easily pinioned him with the weight of his massive body.

'Bully for you!' shouted Jed Barrow. 'Slit his guts, crack his head. Finish him off!' The planter had his hands on Casey's shoulders now and was using him as a support as he jumped up and down.

'No, sir!' shouted Casey shaking him off. He thrust himself forward to escape Jed's clutches.

'Kick his crotch!' he shouted above the roar of the crowd, surprising himself. He was angered by Jed's manhandling of him. 'Squeeze his grain!'

The plucky griffe must have heard Casey for suddenly the giant rolled off him, howling with pain.

'Bah!' cried Jed Barrow. 'Yeller rat!'

'It's a fair fight,' said Casey unable to restrain himself. 'Anything goes.'

'Is that so?' The planter sounded amused and stroked his mustache.

Casey realized the excitement of the fight was getting the better of him. He wanted to leave before he was tempted into coming to blows with Jed Barrow, but how?

The Congo was on top of the griffe now and seemed to be twisting the boy's neck around. Each turn he made, the boy flipped around his entire body causing that giant to pause, perplexed. The crowd, except for Casey and the planter behind him, laughed.

'Kill the rat!' screamed Barrow.

Casey, his eyes livid with anger, clutched Hollis's arm. 'Why doesn't he keep away?'

Hollis was uncertain whether Casey meant the griffe or Jed Barrow. He blinked and shrugged his shoulders. 'It's a fight to the death,' he said.

His words hung ominously in the sudden lull.

CHAPTER SIX

There was an eerie silence while the two boys mauled each other desperately. Casey wanted to ease himself away from the frontline of spectators so he could avoid the confrontation with Jed Barrow. Hollis was clinging to his left arm and on his right stout planters stood in the way of escape.

They could be Jed Barrow's cronies, reflected Casey, acutely aware of the awkward position he was in if Jed Barrow decided to exact the revenge he was entitled to. Had Casey been white, he would be challenged to a duel for cuckolding Jed. The best he could hope for in the circumstances was a beating from Jed and his henchmen.

Why, Casey wondered in a moment of despair, hadn't he fled from Angelique's cottage through the back door? He knew! He was tired of running. He was a man again, not a yellow rat.

'Get the grain!' he yelled frantically at the griffe. 'Don't let him kill you.'

'Shit on the yeller rat,' responded Jed close to Casey's ear.

The crowd laughed and the fighters stirred. The grease on the negro's body was mixed with mud and sweat but his lumbering size made him easier to hold than the griffe who slipped unexpectedly from his grasp. Leaping to his feet, the griffe crouched in the center of the ring of spectators. He was muttering curses in patois, reviling the negro and his masculinity. The giant bellowed with rage and charged, hoping to flatten the griffe. The boy stepped aside, ramming his knee into the negro's crotch as he passed.

The giant bent double with a sigh of pain, winded but not beaten. The griffe attacked from the back, pitching his head into the negro's buttocks and sending him sprawling, face down, in to the mud. The boy's fingers flicked out and tore at the giant's testicles as he fell. There was a roar of disbelief from the crowd as the griffe edged away from the negro pulling at the black's scrotum held fast in his left hand. The skin of the pouch stretched and the negro howled and kicked.

Hollis tugged at Casey's sleeve, slobbering with rapture.

Casey swallowed the bile in his mouth. He was sickened by the mutilation of the negro, and ashamed at his own encouragement of it.

'Forgit ya ballocks and git his throat!' shouted Jed.

Casey wriggled his shoulders and tried to ignore the pushing and provoking from behind.

The oil on his body saved the giant. As the skin stretched, his scrotum slipped out of the griffe's clutch, but the boy was ready. When the negro rose slowly to his feet to swing at him, the boy butted him with his head, catching his broken jaw.

The pain was too much for the negro. He swayed, momentarily stunned. The griffe butted again, this time smashing into his throat. The negro gurgled and went down.

'He must be quick,' whispered Casey, despite the disgust he felt at himself. 'The Congo's hurt but he could still crush the boy in his arms.'

'Hold him,' shouted Jed. 'Squeeze his lights out.'

The negro winced at his pain, stunned as the griffe leaped at him and landed with both knees pounding into his testicles. He reached up to grasp the boy's shoulder in a bear hug, but the pain in his crotch and the pressure on his throat drained the strength from him. He fought for breath as the boy's sharp fingers closed about his neck and began the grisly process of throttling his life away.

'Damn, damn, damn!' Hollis tugged Casey's elbow with excitement. 'Didn't I say he was wily!'

'Toss him off, you great black ape!' Jed sounded furious at the failure of his favorite.

'It's not over yet,' said Casey, watching the negro writhing under the boy who was perched on his chest like a bantam cock. The boy was alternately pumping his knees into the giant's crotch and pressing his thumbs into the slave's windpipe. Blood spurted from the negro's penis and testicles, smearing the bantam's thighs. The boy kept up the pressure relentlessly, waiting for the negro to die.

Casey turned away. 'What a waste!' he muttered.

'Aye,' said Jed. 'I've wasted twenty dollars.'

Casey glared, surprised that Jed should address him. 'I mean the man's life is wasted,' he said angrily.

'That's good sport! He's a slave ain't he?' Jed stroked his mustache and his eyes gleamed. 'He's won his owner enough in fights already to pay back his purchase price and upkeep. No loss at all.'

Casey felt Hollis's warning tug on his sleeve and he looked at his new friend gratefully. He was embarrassed to be facing Jed directly yet the planter showed no sign of recalling the incident at Angelique's.

'The griffe's won,' said Hollis, claiming Casey's attention. 'I told you! Come on, friend, let's collect your winnings.'

The crowd was dispersing. Even those who backed the negro were satisfied with the fight's excitement.

'You won't get ten to one on that boy again,' said Hollis as he led Casey to Saunders and Baker. 'I've got a nose for a winner, haven't I?'

Casey's heart was heavy. He loathed himself for the thrill he had experienced watching the two slaves fight. It could only have been his anger at Jed Barrow's taunts that made him encourage one against the other, he reasoned.

'You look as miserable as Saunders and Baker,' chided Hollis. 'Ain't you pleased you won? The griffe's made you rich.'

Casey wondered what the boy would get out of it. Probably an extra piece of bacon in his food. He glanced to where the boy was standing by his owner. He was panting, heedless of the negro's blood smeared over his scrawny body. The woman in the cloak was laughing as a man congratulated her. It was Jed Barrow. Casey looked beyond Jed to the man with him.

In that instant, Casey's heart seemed to stop beating. The clamor of the crowd, the shouts of those who had won their wagers, the incessant gabble of Hollis, all ceased. Casey's guts churned over, and the blood in his veins seemed to chill. He stared, oblivious of everyone except the man speaking to Jed Barrow.

Casey could hardly believe it. At last! He stood as though rooted to the ground, gaping at the man's face; matching every line, the eyes, the nose, the cruel curl of the lips, to the image he had stored in his mind since the night he first saw it. The man turned and Casey saw the gold band in the lobe of his left ear. Yes, it was the same face; the one that had haunted Casey for two years. Here was the man who had drugged him and sold him to be a slave.

Casey watched the man nod as Jed Barrow spoke to him. The light from a flambeau fell across his eyes. They were pale and evil, unflickering as he watched Jed Barrow intently. His jowls were dark with stubble just as Casey remembered him; his clothes were drab and his boots old and scuffed. He scowled, gave a final nod to Jed and left his side hastily.

Casey sprang to life. He shook off Hollis's hand and pushed through the groups of men lingering in the clearing.

'Hey!' cried Hollis. 'What about your winnings?'

Casey no longer heard. He reached the rim of the circle of light thrown by the flambeau and scanned the glade. The man wasn't there. He hurried down the path through the undergrowth and burst out into Congo Square. Flambeaux blazed where hawkers sat on the sidewalk but in the Square it was almost too dark to see. The promenading slaves had gone, chased home by the threat of the nine o'clock cannon.

Casey paused, wondering what to do. He had no plan in his mind. The hatred harbored for two years was enough reason for chasing the man. Because of him, his liberty had been stolen and his pride ruptured. He had changed from being a carefree, unbound youth to a man soured by suffering and torture. He studied the indistinct shapes as men strolled across the Square after the fight. Most of them were in pairs or groups. Some shapes moved singly, ambling in no particular hurry across the grass. Only one dark figure hastened across the Square, his shoulders hunched with purpose. Casey slipped into the night to follow him.

The man left the Square and entered the Rue d'Orleans. At this end of the town, the street had none of the opulence it exhibited where it joined the Place d'Armes. This was the road's disreputable end. The garret houses of stuccoed brick and wooden doorsteps concealed a variety of intrigues behind their humble facades.

Standing in the shadows at the end of the street, Casey peered at the man hurrying down the sidewalk. He slackened his pace and appeared to be looking for a particular door.

A negress with a tray of costards thrust it at Casey and bawled at him, but he didn't hear. His eyes marked where the man had disappeared and he strolled after him. There was a gap between two of the houses and a narrow alley led down it to a cabaret.

Casey knew the establishment. It was a favorite haunt of robbers, cut-throats, picklocks and all manner of rogues who inhabited the area. An *f.m.c.* was tolerated there if not too well dressed to attract derision or the professional attention of the thieves.

Casey was uneasy about going into the place in his present garb. The cabaret combined a grocery, a dram shop, a gambling garden and rooms for its whores all under one roof. So far as Casey knew, there was no back exit. He squatted down on the stoop of the house opposite to await the emergence of his quarry.

That there was a relationship between Jed Barrow and the man who had kidnapped him did not surprise Casey. He had sensed it. Taking Jed Barrow at his face value, he seemed an unscrupulous planter who would have no qualms at buying or selling a slave without a clear title. He considered himself lucky to have got away from the Square without Jed challenging him directly. Yet Jed was limited in what he could do in public. He couldn't accuse Casey of making love to his mistress without being exposed to ridicule by his cronies.

Casey smiled grimly at Jed's predicament, and kept his eyes on the entrance to the alley.

The only illumination in the street came from the lanterns hanging in houses that still had their louvers open. There was no light in the passage leading to the cabaret except for a dim glow from its open doorway. A trio of men stumbled out of the alleyway and Casey scrutinized them. He expected his erstwhile captor to be alone, for the shiftiness of the man did not indicate that he was of a gregarious disposition. Casey stretched his limbs, resigned to a long wait.

A movement in the alley puzzled him. He stared, uncomfortably aware that someone was watching him from the darkness. He peered closer and saw the dark shape concealed against the wall of the alley. The shape moved across the dim light and Casey saw the silhouette of hunched shoulders and a scowling face.

He rose quietly to his feet and crossed the road, slipping into the darkness under the eaves of a house. He crept stealthily up to the gap as the man peered out. He pounced.

The man fell at Casey's onslaught, cursing gruffly. His shoulder cracked against a step. He lay still while Casey tightened his hold on his shabby coat.

'What yer want?' the man demanded.

Casey's face was in a shadow and the man hadn't seen him properly. He was proving to be a typical coward and offered no resistance. Casey maneuvered so his knee was across the man's chest, pinioning him to the brick sidewalk. This brought him within the circle of light from the house opposite.

The man swore at the sight of Casey's face. 'A nigra!' He spat angrily which was a silly thing to do because the phlegm fell back on his own cheek.

'Yes,' said Casey. 'Not a slave, though! Look well. Do you remember me?'

'Never seen yer before. Let me go. I got no money.'

'You think I want your money!' Casey ground his knee into his chest in anger. The man flinched and began to whine.

'Yer hurt my shoulder. I can't breathe.' He clawed desperately at Casey's leg with his fingers.

Casey was silent, watching him squirm. The blood drained from the man's heavy jowls and his eyes dilated. The menace in Casey's own eyes had triggered off a memory. The man blanched.

'I . . . know . . . yer.'

'I suffered two years of hell because of you!'

The man coughed and specks of blood spattered Casey's trousers. 'What . . . are yer . . . goin' to do?' He choked again.

'What I did . . . it were a mistake.' The man's eyelids flickered and he seemed to be close to passing out.

'I'm sick,' he moaned. 'Let me up. Yer'll kill me. I won't run . . . I can't.'

The urge for revenge drained from Casey as he gazed down on the pathetic figure. He felt soiled at having touched him. It only then occurred to him that his own impatience and naivety was why he had been hoodwinked by such a miserable and obvious crook.

'Release me,' the man begged, coughing again. 'I . . . can't breathe.'

Casey slowly eased up his weight off the man's chest. For two years he had wanted to kill this man but now he had no stomach for it. He wondered if he should turn him over to the authorities. There were probably other free negroes he had sold into slavery.

'What's your name?' he demanded.

'Rick,' the man grunted. 'Release me, son. I can't live long. It's me lungs.' He seemed to shrink as Casey watched him.

'Stand up!' Casey lifted his leg off the man's chest and gripped him by his shoulders, pulling him to his feet. The man moaned.

'My collar bone!' he said, his face twisted with pain. 'Yer broke it.'

'Not all I'm going to do!' Casey swung the man in front of him, keeping one hand on his injured shoulder and the other on his left wrist. 'Now, walk!' He pushed him forward.

'Where're yer takin' me?'

'Lots of questions for a kidnapper. I reckon you need a taste of your own medicine.'

The man shuffled forward slowly, whining every time Casey thumped his back to make him walk faster.

'My shoulder!' he cried. 'Yer hurtin' it.' He raised his free right hand feebly in front of him. 'Let me stop. Let me catch my breath.'

Casey found the man tiresome, and the smell where he had defecated in his pants, obnoxious. He ought to throw him into the refuse in the gutter where he belonged. He jerked him to a halt in a dark part of the street and swung him around.

'You ain't fit to live,' he said, 'for what you did to me. You ain't even worth the trouble to snuff out.'

Casey held the man's shoulder and wrist securely. All he had to do was punch his jaw and the man would collapse to stew in his own filth. Casey scowled, upset by the man's funk and amazed at himself for having been taken in by this snivelling scoundrel.

The man's free hand patted his own chest and passed down to his waist. Casey saw the movement but he took no notice. Then suddenly a knife was driven into his side. Rick's hand, previously limp from his supposedly broken collar bone, twisted the knife viciously.

Casey, overcome with surprise rather than pain, released his grip. The man jumped back, pulling out the knife and crouching in a fighter's stance. A second blade appeared in his left hand from the tail of his coat. He pointed both at Casey.

'Stupid nigra!' The man spat, directing the phlegm with accuracy at Casey's eye. 'Think yer can lick a white man, do yer?' He gesticulated with the knife in his left hand while he wiped the blood off his other knife on his coat.

'Come on, now, nigra. Let's see yer take me.'

Casey stepped back in confusion. Two knives in the hands of an expert required smart thinking, something Casey seemed to have been lacking so far. He cursed himself for letting the man fool him yet again. He deserved the cut in his waist to remind him never to underestimate the guile of a white man.

He laughed aloud at his predicament.

Rick looked disconcerted. 'Yer find it funny?' He waved his knife in front of Casey's face.

Casey feinted with his hand to grab Rick's wrist but brought up his boot instead. His foot smashed into the man's right arm and the knife clattered to the sidewalk.

'Aha!' said Rick, dancing back as Casey moved forward to pick up the blade. 'Wants a fight, do yer?' He lunged at Casey who was forced to drop back before he could get the knife. Rick swooped down and grabbed it.

'I got yer now, yer fancy nigra! Mayhap I'll cut yer or sell yer again for a fancy price, seein' yer in such pretty duds an' all.' He advanced on Casey flashing the twin blades up and down in front of him. Casey had no choice but to retreat.

'Wonders where to cut first, I do,' Rick gloated, his eyes glinting with blood lust. 'In yer heart or in yer throat?'

Casey raised his left arm to defend himself while the other hand held the wound at his waist to staunch the bleeding. His fingers latched on to the buckle of his belt. Swiftly, he unfastened it with a gesture of unleashing a sword. He snapped the belt in Rick's face. The buckle crunched across the man's nose.

'Yet shouldn't a' done that,' said Rick blinking. His voice was thick with pain and anger. He darted at Casey who backed and tripped against a wooden step. The knife slit through Casey's worsted coat and sank into his flesh. He reached up his hands to protect himself.

Rick snarled, and drew back to plunge the second blade into Casey's heart.

CHAPTER SEVEN

Casey toppled backward and Rick tumbled down with him. There was a peaceful calm in the night. The quarter moon was visible through a haze and as Casey gazed at the sky he was surprised at the absence of pain. There was a minor irritation, like gas, at his side, but otherwise he felt nothing except for a weight on his chest.

He tried to move and found the weight was pinning him down. His coat was wet and blood was spilling over him in globs. There was a raw deafness in his ears and they sang loudly as though he had been clobbered with a thunderclap. Casey blinked and bit his lip. He realized that not only was he alive, there was someone lying on top of him who was very definitely dead.

The sound that caused his ears to reverberate with such intensity had been that of a pistol discharged at him from close range. The bullet had lodged in Rick's head, severing his skull, and it was Rick's blood and brains that were soaking into Casey's brocade vest.

Although he was anxious to separate himself from the embrace of Rick's corpse, Casey remained motionless. The man who had fired a pistol with such effect had probably aimed for him and, in the confusion of the melee and the darkness, killed Rick by error. He held his breath and waited.

'Pull him off!' a voice commanded although it sounded no more than a whisper through the shrieking in Casey's ears. He felt Rick's body being dragged off leaving a trail of blood, filth, and the stench of the sewers all over him.

'Not a pretty sight, is he?'

'What about the dead one?'

'Leave him. He's at home in the gutter.'

His ears were clearing and Casey noticed something horribly familiar about the gruff voice giving orders. He half opened his eyes and found himself being scrutinized by the dark shape of a man with broad shoulders and long locks of hair who held a pistol in his right hand. The man was crouched over him and began to pat his cheeks with his free hand. Casey chose to remain as though unconscious.

'He dead too?'

'It will take a lot to kill this one,' the gruff voice spoke with a dry chuckle. The man's hand was on his chest, pressing against it to feel the rhythm of his heart beat.

'Piss on him, Hollis. He'll soon wake up.'

Casey opened his eyes immediately and pulled himself so he was sitting with his back against the step. The two men standing over him both laughed.

'What happened?' he demanded.

'Jed shot the scoundrel,' said Hollis, his leathery face beaming with pleasure. 'The rat didn't know that I've got your winnings here.'

'Lot of footpads in these streets, boy,' said Jed, holding out his hand to help Casey rise. 'You must be more careful around here.'

'I'm Casey Todd, not your boy.' He scrambled to his feet without Jed's assistance.

'You hurt, son?' Hollis gazed at the gory mess on his coat.

'No.' Casey shook his head. It was not far to his home. He could walk it and let Lucy tend to his wounds. There was the cut at his waist and one under his arm, that's all.

Jed reached over and plucked a knife from his torn coat. He eyed him suspiciously. 'I heard you were stubborn,' he said. 'You look hurt to me.'

'It's nothing. I'm grateful.'

'The name's Jed Barrow.' The planter grinned without mirth.

'Yes, I know.'

'Call me Jed. We have a wench in common and now it seems we're bound by a corpse, so we should be friends.' Jed's gray eyes glinted and he held out his hand again.

Casey took it reluctantly. 'I owe you an apology . . .'

Jed squeezed his hand and put his arm around Casey's shoulder, hugging him. 'You done me a favor, Casey. I returned it.'

Casey frowned. 'Why did you kill that man?' He nodded at the body.

'Because he was going to kill you.'

'Do you know who he is?'

Jed seemed unconcerned. Hollis bent down and peered at the corpse.

'He was at Congo Square,' said Casey, puzzled by Jed's offer of friendship.

'I told you,' said Hollis. 'The bastard was after your money.'

'He was speaking to you when I saw him, Jed Barrow. You know him, don't you? His name was Rick.'

It seemed to Casey that Jed Barrow looked at him with new respect, but his voice gave no hint of what he was thinking. 'Really? I think we should get a carriage to help you. You must come with me to my hotel. It's a discreet place and you can clean up there.'

'Oh no!' Casey withdrew himself painfully from Jed's embrace. 'Rick kidnapped me once and sold me as a slave. Maybe he was a partner of yours?'

'Maybe.' Jed tossed his head back nonchalantly and placed the pistol in his waistband. He fastened his coat and looked around him. 'No witness, eh, Hollis? We're quite safe but it makes no sense to hang around here gossiping.'

Hollis picked up Casey's belt from the sidewalk and handed it to him. 'Nice buckle,' he muttered. 'Silver.'

'I can go by myself,' said Casey. 'I don't need your company.'

'See how he treats a friend, Hollis?' Jed smirked. 'Why, I have so much in common with you, Casey, I can't leave you until you're safe. I don't kill men every day, you know.' He laughed, a cruel grating sound devoid of merriment.

'Besides,' he added, 'Hollis has your winnings. I may have to protect you both!'

They reached the junction with Rampart Street and to Casey's surprise, Jed Barrow turned right toward his cottage.

'You know where I live?'

'My dear Casey, you are famous in these parts. I knew all about you long before our little contretemps over Angelique. By the way, you won't see her for a while. She's, er, retiring. Toothache. Quite a swollen face, in fact.' He laughed sourly again.

'It wasn't her fault . . .' began Casey, but Hollis interrupted him.

'When you dashed off, Casey, I got your money from Saunders and Baker, a miserable pair those two, for all they'd won off the Congo's backers, and came after you. Mr Barrow said you were a devil and came too.'

'Thank you, Hollis,' said Casey. He was weary and the wound at his waist was aching. Fresh blood oozed on to his fingers as he pressed it.

He was appalled by Jed's callousness and alarmed by his company, but he was too tired to resist. He stopped by the flower tubs at the steps to his cottage and turned to say goodbye to the men so they would go. Light poured from the open louvers of the parlor. Poor Lucy, he thought, she must have been driven to distraction by his long absence.

She was waiting in the parlor and heard the sound at the step. She called nervously.

'Casey, is that you?'

'Yes,' he whispered, feeling the strength ebbing away from his leg, 'Good –'

She opened the door. He raised his face to smile reassuringly at her, and collapsed at her feet.

'It's an invitation,' Lucy said, 'to a soirée at Madame Cable's. We have to go.'

'I don't see why.' Casey was sitting in the parlor with his legs up on the ottoman. He tossed the paper Lucy handed to him on to the table. He grinned mischievously. 'In your condition, perhaps I don't want you to socialize.'

Lucy blushed. She had told him she was pregnant only two days before. His pleasure had brought a new warmth to their relationship.

'I'm not sure that I want people ogling you.' He swung his legs off the ottoman and leaned over, patting her stomach gently. 'You want to introduce our son to *béké* habits early, *oui*?'

'No.' She sounded whimsical. 'To civilized behavior.'

'Aye,' he said with a sigh. 'I know what you mean.'

'As long as we're in New Orleans, Madame Cable represents the most cultured society we can aspire to.'

'You don't like it here, do you?' It was the familiar theme to their conversations. Casey had thought about Lucy's feelings for a long time when he was laid up recovering from his wounds. 'We could go back to Dominica.'

Lucy sniffed.

'I'm willing to go back,' he said. 'At least I'd feel at home there. Instead of wearing these fancy togs and wondering if I'm doing the right thing all the time. Being three initials, *f.m.c.*, isn't easy. In Dominica I could claim Roxborough and grow cane again. We'd have free labor and . . .' He sat back, wondering what it would really be like to return.

'You don't want that life any more than I do.' Lucy picked up the invitation, toying with it in her hands. 'The soirée's tomorrow night. We've not been out anywhere together since we came to this cottage. Let's go?'

He looked hard at her. She had changed in the six months since she and her father had rescued him from Leo Singer's plantation. The radiance of approaching motherhood showed in her eyes but beneath that contentment there was a lingering doubt. It showed whenever she glanced at him and thought he wasn't looking.

Casey, too, had his doubts, and they were much deeper than hers. The suspicion had begun the afternoon he woke in the bed with his wounds bandaged and saw Lucy sitting in a chair beside him. She was weeping.

'What's wrong?' he had asked, putting out his hand to touch her. It was stiff and he withdrew it painfully.

'Nothing,' she said, wiping her eyes hastily and busying herself in pumping his pillows.

She had told him how Jed Barrow and Hollis had helped to undress him after he had passed out, and had bandaged his wounds.

'Mr Barrow was so kind,' she said. 'He stayed with me the whole night, watching you.'

'Why did he do that?' The doubts were beginning.

'For when you got restless. Mr Barrow was very kind, Casey. He told me I should ask him for anything we wanted.'

Casey frowned and Lucy bathed his brow with a handkerchief soaked in bay rum. 'You mustn't fret,' she had said. 'It's all over now.'

Casey had two wounds, a slice into the flesh above his hip and a nick under his left arm where the knife had been deflected by the padding in his coat. He had healed rapidly. Hollis visited twice and spoke of new fighting nigras he had discovered, but Casey wasn't interested.

He saw nothing more of Jed Barrow although he thought about him constantly. He learned that Angelique had left the district and her cottage had another occupant, a haughty octoroon maintained by a young banker.

To still his growing suspicion, Casey asked Lucy again about the night Jed had spent in his home while he was unconscious.

She was evasive. 'He was so concerned about you,' she said nervously. 'He asked me lots of questions . . . He seemed to know most of the answers already.'

'What sort of questions?'

'About who your parents are. About Dominica.'

'I suppose you told him everything. Lucy! Didn't you realize he might have some evil in his mind?'

'No.' She stared at him in surprise. 'He was so charming and friendly. He told me to nurse you properly and to keep you at home because you are such a hothead.'

'How does he know how I am?' Casey began to lose his temper.

'I don't know. He said you and he shared a mutual friend, that's all.'

Casey calmed himself in time, in case he became obliged to tell Lucy how he had met Jed. His thoughts, while he recuperated from his wounds, returned again and again to the night Jed had spent in the cottage while he was unconscious. It was Jed's idea, he discovered, that he should be given laudanum.

'He said it would ease your pain,' explained Lucy. 'He told me he uses it all the time on his plantation.'

'I'm sure he does,' muttered Casey. 'To question troublesome slaves.'

'That's why you slept so long,' Lucy explained, seeming so innocent. Was she?

The more he probed about Jed's presence that night, the more he wondered if Jed had taken his revenge swiftly and sweetly by making love to Lucy while he slept. It seemed the kind of thing that Jed Barrow would do. Lucy's announcement that she was pregnant only confounded him more.

'You're quite better now, Casey.' Lucy interrupted his thoughts. 'Can we go to the soirée?' she repeated.

Casey sighed. 'Why not? If it gives you pleasure.'

'Now you've spoilt it.' She puckered her lips into a moue that reminded him of Angelique.

'I thought you would like to get out and meet some people. You've been so chafed at having to stay at home with nothing to do while your wounds healed. You should see how vexed you've looked.'

His smile was condescending. 'Is that what's wrong between us, Lucy? Are we too much together with nothing to do?'

'I have plenty to do. Caring for you, making things for the baby.'

'I can buy everything the baby needs.'

'Oh yes.' Lucy twisted the invitation in her fingers and looked wistful. 'Casey . . .?'

She hesitated at the sight of his handsone face with his chin cocked defiantly, waiting for her to speak. 'Could we go to England?'

'England?' He was taken aback. 'Will it be any better there?'

'Of course it will, Casey. You're three-quarters English.'

'I'm not. My mother and Carlton Todd were island born. I'm three-quarters creole.'

'Oh! Those stupid labels you've picked up in America! Does it matter what people call you as long you're true to yourself?'

'It matters here, and I expect it will in England. I might not be an *f.m.c.* over there but the English will find some nickname for me. When Caspar was there he was known in London society as "The Darling Black".'

'It's changed since your father was there as a boy. England isn't a slave society.'

'It's people got rich on slavery.'

'Some of them. The majority are ordinary people like you and me.'

Casey scowled. 'I'm not ordinary.'

'Don't twist my argument!' Lucy's eyes were bright. 'If you won't think of yourself, or me, then think of our child. He'll have a better chance, a fair one, in England. Daddy says he could get you almost any post you want.'

'So that's it!' Casey clenched his fists. 'You and your father have decided my child's future already.'

'No.' Lucy trembled to control her anger. 'I thought you'd like to know Daddy's concerned about you even though he's retired from Dominica. Goodness knows,' said Lucy sounding exasperated, 'you don't need to rely on him! Your share of the Bondmaster's fortune in the Louisiana Bank is enough to make you independent for the rest of your life.'

Casey relaxed. 'That's for our son.'

'Then use some of it for us to go to England. For our son's sake. Wouldn't you like to have him born there, away from . . .' Her gesture of defiance took in the parlor, the street, the whole of New Orleans. 'Away from all this!'

Casey stood up and crossed the floor. He saw Lucy's lower lip tremble as though she feared he would strike her again. Instead, he reached down and caught her hands in his, squeezing them gently. He pulled her up to stand close to him searching her eyes with his own.

'You really want to leave here? To forget everyone you've ever met? Never to see any of them again? To put your past here right behind you?'

'Yes,' she said softly, puzzled by his tone.

'To start a new life, Lucy? To start again?' He put his hands on her waist and drew her toward him. Her eyes widened at his touch and her trembling stopped. She became aware of a warmth spreading through her. Her lips parted to meet his.

He held her tightly, close to his body. His blood stirred and he slipped his tongue into her mouth. He lingered inside her, lost in the need overwhelming them. When he withdrew, she clung to him and with their arms around each other, they drifted to the boudoir.

'It's the afternoon,' giggled Lucy as she sat on the edge of the bed and he stretched out beside her.

He grunted and reached up to unlace her bodice. 'No matter, no one will call. No one ever does.'

He stroked the swelling of her tummy and raised his head to lay his ear against it. 'He'll be an English boy.' He smiled up at Lucy and saw her eyes were moist with joy.

'Thank you,' she said.

Later, when they lay entwined in each other's arms, breathless and united, they chatted as lovers do about their plans for the future.

'Madame Cable,' said Casey, 'has connections with shipowners. Her husband was one. That's where her wealth came from.'

'Then she'll help us to find a ship for England.' Lucy was excited.

'If you ask her.'

'Why!' said Lucy happily kissing Casey's cheek. 'We could be sailing away from here within days.'

They were like honeymooners for the rest of that day and the next. The warmth of their pleasure with each other, inspired by their new plans, stayed with them until they stood, hand in hand, outside Madame Cable's door in the Rue Toulouse. The suspicion and boredom of the previous weeks had vanished and their eyes and bearing showed the difference.

Casey felt fit again, eager for the new challenge of life in England, and Lucy was blissfully happy at the thought of going home. They kissed at the door of the house, oblivious of the scandalized glances of people standing in the street.

Madame Cable's house was built in the old Spanish style. The brick frontage was graced at its upper windows with small balconies of wrought iron, forged with the delicacy of Spanish lace. The noise of the party in progress had attracted spectators who stood on the cobbles of the Rue Toulouse to gaze at the guests enjoying themselves.

Casey ignored them confidently as he raised his hand to bang on the front door.

'Not ignoring me, Casey, are you?' a rasping voice spoke at his side.

'Hollis! By the devil!' Casey shook his friend by his hand. Lucy smiled wanly. 'Are you coming in?'

'If I'm invited.'

'You're invited. Madame Cable won't mind, will she, Lucy?'

'I don't know . . .' Lucy regarded Hollis in his bedraggled suit with dismay.

Casey's expression tightened when he sensed the old question of status and propriety passing through Lucy's mind. He seized the lion's paw door knocker and rapped loudly.

'If Madame Cable welcomes me, then she'll welcome Hollis!' he said.

Judging by Lucy's crestfallen face the mood of serenity they had been enjoying together was shortlived. It made him cross. 'Don't worry, Lucy. You find us a ship. I'll take care of Hollis.'

The door swung open and Madame Cable's negro butler faced them disdainfully.

'Sambo!' said Hollis pushing forward and glaring up at the slave. 'Don't you see it's M'sieur and Madame Todd? I'm their guest. Make way now!'

Lucy gripped Casey's arm. 'You did this to spoil my evening,' she hissed.

Madame Cable waddled toward them. She was a creole with wealth reputed to be as ample as her girth. Her vast fortune nourished her eccentricities. She posed as an artist, dabbling with oils to produce paintings of no merit whatsoever but which gave her enormous fun. Her convictions, although unconventional, were genuine and founded on a zest for life and beauty. She greeted Casey and Lucy with delight.

'*Chéri*,' she said to Casey. 'You grow more divine day by day, doesn't he, *doudou*?' She seized Lucy by her hand.

'This is a friend of mine,' said Casey. 'I met him outside. I hope you don't –'

'Mind Hollis! *Chéri*, why should I? Hollis is welcome here any time. He always has such interesting information.'

Casey grinned triumphantly at Lucy and she blushed. His heart opened then and he longed to hold her and tell her that he loved her.

'There's someone dying to meet you, Lucy,' Madame Cable prattled on, unaware of the unspoken message passing between them. 'He's been waiting for you all evening.'

She steered them into the throng of people gathered in the courtyard. Lanterns hung around the cloisters. Stewards in black coats with gold breeches, white shirts and white gloves, circulated through the crowd with silver salvers laden with goblets brimful with champagne.

'Ah, *voilà*!' said Madame as a man emerged from behind a pillar and strode toward them. He was smiling at Lucy and to Casey it looked like a leer.

'May I present the owner of The Drongos,' Madame Cable said with a flourish. '*M'sieur* Jedediah Barrow.'

CHAPTER EIGHT

Lucy's face was radiant as Jed Barrow took her hand and raised it to his lips. He seemed to hold it there moments longer than convention demanded, pressing it with his mouth so that the hairs of his dark mustache were flattened when he released it and turned to Casey.

He thrust out his hand and, for Madame Cable's sake, Casey took it but released it quickly. Jed's hard eyes were unwavering as he drew closer to Casey.

'Good to see you are fit, Casey. You have your *devoted* wife to thank for that, I'm sure.'

Casey had no time to reflect on the sarcasm in Jed's voice before a liveried slave was hovering at the side of the group and Jed took up a goblet of champagne and handed it to Lucy.

Madame Cable was aquiver. 'Jedediah's such a charmer, Casey,' she warned, her plump hands fluttering in the air like a bulky Spanish flamenco dancer. 'He'll sweet talk Lucy into dancing the whole evening with him, if you're not careful.'

'Eugenia, I share with you a predilection for creatures of grace and beauty,' Jed patted Madame Cable's outsize bottom. 'Since Lucy and her husband are undoubtedly the most handsome couple here, apart from you and I, I shall undoubtedly seek to monopolize their company.'

Madame Cable wobbled with pleasure. 'You're the terror of the bagnios, Jed,' she tittered. 'A lady isn't safe with you standing close to her.'

Jed beamed at the insult.

Madame Cable waggled her bottom happily and glanced toward the door where the butler was ushering in a new arrival. 'Forgive me. I must greet my guests. I'll leave you young things to enjoy yourselves.'

Casey and Jed nodded politely as she left them. Hollis seized the tray of champagne from the slave.

'Leave that here, boy. And get another.' He proffered the goblets to Jed and Casey.

'Like seltzer, this stuff. Give me good tafia any day.' He put the tray on a side table, drank two goblets in quick succession and held a third in his hand.

'Madame's put on a regular fete tonight. I must see what I can learn.' He winked at Casey and plunged into the throng of guests milling around the courtyard.

Casey was impressed by the way Hollis seemed completely at ease in the presence of so many grandly dressed people. In his stained frock coat and torn breeches, the diminutive tipster was a shabby figure beside the ostentatious elegance of the guests. Casey envied his ability to move with a complete lack of self-consciousness among his betters.

'Your, er, husband is thoughtful this evening.' Jed's whispered remark spoken close to Lucy's ear roused Casey.

'Not so thoughtful that I'm unaware of my manners,' he retorted, gripping Lucy by her elbow. 'Shall we meet some of the other guests, dear?'

Lucy bridled. 'What for? You're the one who likes to remain quietly in a corner. I want to talk to Mr Barrow.'

'Very well.' Casey scowled.

'It was so kind of you to help Casey that night,' Lucy smiled coyly and Jed arched his eyebrows. 'He's had so many misfortunes, he rather distrusts certain people.'

'Quite right too.' Jed's laughter was hollow and his eyes glinted as he twisted the ends of his mustache. 'Don't trust certain people myself. Especially with women, eh, Casey?' He dug him in his ribs with his elbow and Casey winced.

'Sorry, old chap. Was that your wound?'

'No.' Casey held his breath. If he spoke he would say something scathing and Lucy would accuse him of sulking.

Jed turned back to address Lucy and Casey listened half-heartedly while he studied the slaveholder. He knew Jed's strength and ruthlessness from their first meeting. From the look of him, his powerful shoulders could wield a sword, or a whip, with ease.

His clothes, Casey noted with interest, were not as well tailored as his own. Jed's coat was cut badly and hung like a sack from his broad shoulders. His breeches were baggy and his appearance gave the impression that he was either a man who didn't care about clothes or was somewhat strapped for money.

Jed's face was square, and from the cast of his prominent jaw, he was a man used to getting his own way. His mustache, as dark and as luxurious as his bushy eyebrows, gave him a raffish air that was obviously attractive to women. Lucy was giggling at his remarks which to Casey seemed quite asinine.

That Jed Barrow had a high opinion of himself was already known to Casey yet when he looked at Jed closely, he couldn't see the reason for it. The man was tough, undoubtedly cruel to his slaves and women and, thus, was exactly like any other profligate Louisiana planter.

Lucy laughed, a sparkling sound that set Jed preening his mustache triumphantly. Casey narrowed his eyes.

'Your wife is utterly charming,' said Jed. 'What a lucky chap you are.'

'Oh, Casey, don't be such a sourpuss! You should see your face.' Lucy laughed again. 'I'm afraid that Casey doesn't enjoy these gatherings very much.'

'You must give him time. Lucy. We're not all of a gregarious nature. I suppose where he comes from, life is rather different.'

Casey ignored the innuendo. 'I don't need time, Mr Barrow.' He took Lucy's hand and he felt her fingers stiffen.

'We don't plan to stay in New Orleans very long.'

'Oh really? Buying a plantation, are you? Several of your kind are doing so, I believe.' Jed smiled sardonically. 'I wonder if Lucy would like the life of a planter's wife, away from all this.' He gestured at the party in progress around them. Couples had begun to dance and, as the champagne took effect, the laughter and shouts of enjoyment got louder.

'We're going to England,' said Lucy.

Jed was startled. His face tensed and he shot a glance at Casey then turned back hastily to Lucy.

'It's for the baby,' she explained.

Casey wondered why she was trying to win Jed's approval. It was odd, he thought, the way Jed looked at them both. There was almost a kind of anger in his eyes, as though he realized he was about to lose something he wanted very much.

Lucy was blushing and he wondered if she felt it too. 'The baby will have more opportunities in England,' she said hesitantly. 'You know . . . it's a different society . . . and Casey's ancestors were English.'

'Creole.' Casey's voice had an edge to it.

Jed frowned. 'Is England the best place for you, young feller? Surely you would have more opportunity here? With your experience you'd be better suited with a plantation.' He stared challengingly but Casey refused to be intimidated.

'Are you suggesting that I'm not capable of anything else?'

Jed's brow darkened and he spoke slowly. 'I'm a planter, Casey, and I'm proud of it.'

'Casey didn't mean anything personal, Mr Barrow.' Lucy glanced sharply at him. 'He's very sensitive, you see.'

'By the devil, Lucy!' Casey squeezed her fingers. 'You don't have to apologize for me.' He turned to Jed and drew himself up to his full height, his eyes level with the planter's.

'We've made up our minds to go to England. Lucy won't be sorry to leave here.' Casey hoped Jed would get the point. 'She wants to put all this behind her.'

Jed sniffed. 'So we're not good enough for you, is that it?' He paused as he stroked his mustache again. 'Have you judged your wife properly, Casey? From what little I know of her, she doesn't seem to share your view.'

Lucy was blushing, twisting her fingers to release them from Casey's hand. 'We'll be better off in England, Mr Barrow.'

Casey noticed the shakiness in her voice and the specter of jealously began to haunt him again from that night Jed had spent in their cottage when he was unconscious. He released Lucy's hand as he watched her eyes lingering on Jed's face. He guessed then that Jed was taking a malicious pleasure in the rupture he was causing in their relationship.

Was he deliberately goading him into doing something rash? Casey glanced around the courtyard for some distraction to relieve his tension. Hollis was leaning against a pillar with a goblet of champagne in each hand. He was talking to a raven-haired woman in a wine-red gown and cut a dashing figure.

A lantern reflected the highlights of the woman's hair and it shimmered in the glow. Her tresses, covering her bare shoulders, were jet black against the ivory of her skin. She was smiling at Hollis with such an intimate manner, Casey envied his friend's success.

'I shall be sorry if you go,' Jed was saying. 'Especially as our friendship is just beginning.'

Casey turned back in time to see Jed's fingers brushing against Lucy's as he took the champagne glass from her.

'Would you like another?' Jed asked.

Casey drained his own goblet and thrust it at Jed. 'I would, if you don't mind.'

Jed smirked at Lucy as if sharing a private joke about Casey and moved off in search of a steward.

'How could you be so boorish!' Lucy spoke softly so no one else could hear. 'First you bring in that stinking rascal Hollis, and then you go out of your way to insult Mr Barrow. He could knock you down if he wanted, and I wouldn't blame him.'

'That's surely what Mr Barrow is goading me to do to him,' said Casey thoughtfully. 'Lucy, can't you see, he's just making fun of us? He can't stand it that I've got what he hasn't.'

'I suppose you mean me! How ridiculous. He's just being charming.'

'It's not you he wants, Lucy. His desires are deeper. He can't stand it that a mulatto like me can have a fortune. Look at him. He's weighed down with debt. I should think that there's a mortgage on his property and on every one of his slaves. If his cotton crop fails, he'll be finished.'

Lucy gasped. 'How can you accuse him of such a thing! He's a true southern gentleman.'

'Is he?' said Casey. 'Watch his eyes. They're hard and ruthless. He's a scoundrel, not a gentleman.'

'You don't know him.'

'I suppose you do? I forgot you spent a night with him.'

The accusation stung Lucy and she flushed brightly, her cheek twitching. Casey immediately felt contrite. He closed her trembling fingers in his hand and drew her close.

'I'm sorry, Lucy,' he said. 'Sometimes there seems to be a devil inside me.'

'It will go when we leave this city,' she said, trying to regain her poise. 'You can only remember your bad experiences here. I forgive you, Casey. I know you didn't mean it.'

She spoke softly, anxious to cool his temper and that only added to his suspicion. He stared beyond her to where the raven-haired woman was standing.

Hollis had left her and he was surprised to see she was talking to Jed. Hollis was hidden behind the pillar and from his stance with his ear cocked, Casey realized he was eavesdropping on Jed and the woman.

Casey grinned to himself and wondered what they were saying that was so interesting. Had he known, he would have been even more wary of Jed Barrow. But Hollis didn't tell him what he overheard that night until years later and by then it no longer mattered.

'You'll have to do it,' Jed hissed at the woman. 'He's suspicious of me. Rick got him once, he won't be fooled again.'

The woman considered for a moment and shifted her position against the pillar so she could observe Lucy unnoticed. She patted her hair. 'If I invite that smug wife of his, she's too polite to refuse. Then he'll have to come. You pretend that you're not keen on the idea.'

'Very well, but you must get them to The Drongos soon. She said they're going to England.' Jed was anxious.

'Have they got passage yet?'

'No.'

'Then leave it to me. I'll see they don't.' The woman's voice was thick with menace.

Jed leaned over and kissed her lightly on her cheek. Casey saw the surreptitious kiss and wondered who she was. Lucy was speaking to him.

'Yes,' he said without thinking.

'You haven't been listening to what I said!' she challenged.

'I was . . . thinking.'

'What about?'

'Us.'

Lucy pouted. 'Now I know you're lying.'

'I hope I'm not intruding?'

Casey and Lucy turned together. The woman he had been watching was standing beside then now. His first impression was of an expanse of white flesh looming from a low corsage of lace and deep red ruffles. He blinked at the smoothness of her rounded breasts at the rim of her bodice.

The woman was amused at his obvious display of interest. Lucy hurriedly slipped her hand back into his.

'This is Mrs –' began Hollis before he was elbowed aside by the woman extending her hand to Casey at chest height.

'I'm Martha,' she said in a husky voice.

Casey shook off Lucy's clinging fingers and grasped the hand held in front of him. He bent to kiss it, feasting his eyes on her bosom. She had an extraordinary figure with a waist so petite he could clasp it between both hands. Her perfume roused him, stirring memories of the lazy intimacies with the casino girls at home in Layou. Her eyes were dark and sultry and met his gaze without false modesty.

'This is Casey Todd and his wife Lucy,' said Hollis brightly, determined not to be ignored.

Martha acknowledged Lucy with a brief nod then faced Casey. 'Hollis here has been telling me you have a keen eye for fighting nigras.'

Casey swallowed quickly to relieve the sudden dryness in his throat. He was acutely aware of the effect this extraordinary woman was having on him. He wondered if she felt it too.

'I only did what he advised,' he said meekly.

'He says you're such a sporting man.' The woman's eyelashes lowered provocatively.

Casey tried to conceal the excitement rising within him. 'My wife here would hardly approve,' he stammered.

Lucy sniffed.

'Ah, yes . . .' The woman heaved a sigh that made her bodice seem in danger of being breeched.

'What Casey does is his own affair,' Lucy snapped. She gazed around the room in an attitude of studied boredom.

'Indeed?' Without warning, the woman swooped on Lucy and seized her hand. 'Please, don't let me start off on the wrong foot with you, Lucy. I was married once. My husband left me because I didn't care for him enough.'

Lucy's mouth dropped open and she blushed. 'I didn't mean any offence.'

'Martha, call me Martha.' The woman beamed. 'I'm so glad, Lucy, because I want us to be friends. Jed's told me so much about you and Casey.'

'Jed Barrow?' Casey feigned interest. 'You know Jed?'

'Everyone knows Jed.' Martha smiled sweetly. 'Now why don't you two sporting gentlemen chat together. Lucy and I have a lot to discuss. In private.' She took Lucy's arm and let her away toward the drawing room.

Casey gazed after her in amazement.

'Take care,' said Hollis. 'I just heard –'

'Here's more champagne!' Jed pushed between them. He was followed by a slave bearing a tray. They each took a glass from it.

Casey sipped slowly then turned back to Hollis. 'Who is that woman?' he asked. 'Quite a piece! Damned attractive.'

Jed glowered at Casey. 'She's my sister.'

Casey felt himself flush with embarrassment. He took a step backward to hide his face. Jed chuckled and Casey was relieved to see that he seemed genuinely amused.

'We always seem to be at loggerheads, Casey, you and I. You're right, of course. Martha is damned attractive and I'd kill any man who takes advantage of her. She's a kind woman, Casey. Full of spunk.'

There was silence between the two men. Casey got the impression that Jed wanted to ask him something but was hesitant to do so. Hollis took advantage of the lull to regale them with a story to which neither of them listened. They were both relieved when Martha and Lucy rejoined them.

Lucy was bubbling was excitement and Casey was anxious to know what she and Martha had talked about.

'Your lovely wife says you are going to England soon.' Martha sounded disappointed. 'Isn't that a shame! I wanted you both to stay with us at The Drongos. Wouldn't that be nice, Jed?'

Jed nodded dourly. 'If they are leaving soon, it won't be possible.'

Casey thought Jed sounded as relieved as he was himself.

'When are you leaving?' Martha asked.

'We don't know yet.' Lucy sighed. 'We haven't arranged anything but we want to be in England in time for the baby's birth.'

'Then it must be soon!' exclaimed Martha. 'I do hope you find a ship. It's very difficult.'

'Why is that?' Casey was puzzled.

'Cabins get reserved simply months in advance.'

'Oh dear.' Lucy looked anxious.

'Jed has some influence, Casey. He ships sugar to England, you see.' Martha turned to her brother. 'Couldn't you get Casey and his wife a passage?'

Jed grunted, apparently annoyed by the suggestion. 'I could try,' he said grouchily.

Lucy clapped her hands. 'That would be wonderful.'

'We can't impose on you,' Casey said hastily wanting to avoid any obligation to Jed Barrow and his sister.

'It's no trouble at all,' Martha gushed. 'You certainly won't get passage without help. You could come to The Drongos and stay until it's arranged. The house is huge. It will be such fun to have you.'

That conversation with Jed and his sister reoccurred in Casey's mind several days after the fete. The party had degenerated into the usual French Quarter frolic with much sprightly dancing, fisticuffs and general mayhem by the time they left.

Casey had been surprised at the friendliness shown to him by Jed and Martha. Jed's mocking manner disappeared in Martha's presence and he seemed to be restrained under her influence. Casey suspected that she was the one who controlled the purse strings.

'Why don't we go to The Drongos?' Lucy pleaded when they lay in bed one night discussing Martha's invitation a few days after the party. 'You've tried all the shipping agents and haven't got passage yet. Martha was right. We need someone's influence. If we stay with her, she's sure to help us.'

'There are ships,' Casey mused aloud. 'At first I thought it was my color that made every agent say all cabins are taken. There's something else.'

'You're imagining it.'

'Am I? Usually a tip has a way of overcoming people's prejudices. Not with those agents. It's as though they have instructions to refuse me.'

'Then we'll *have* to ask for Jed's help.'

'It's Jed now, is it? You called him Mr Barrow to his face at the party.'

'You call him Jed. Why shouldn't I?'

'I do it to annoy him. He doesn't relish an *f.m.c.* treating him as though he's equal to him.'

'Oh!' said Lucy, exasperated. 'You annoy me with such talk. The sooner we get to England . . .'

Casey ignored her. He was pondering why Jed had offered to help them get a passage. What was his motive? And why couldn't he find a ship by himself? 'We're almost being forced to take Jed's offer.'

'It wasn't Jed who offered,' said Lucy. 'It was Martha. She invited us, not him.'

'That's why it's so odd. If Jed had invited us, I'd believe it's because he fancies you.'

Lucy laughed. 'Then shouldn't I be worried in case Martha's plan is to lure you into her bed?'

'Why's that so funny?' Casey felt himself stirring at the thought of Martha, and moved away from Lucy's side so she wouldn't notice.

'Martha's wanton behaviour is all show, that's why. She's lonely and miserable under that vulgar manner.'

'Funny. Jed said something like that as well.'

'It must be true.'

Casey slipped his arm under Lucy's head and stroked her neck. 'I doubt it. There's something odd about those two.'

'Are we going to go to The Drongos to stay with them while we wait for a ship?' Lucy nudged his cheek with her nose.

He sighed. 'I don't want to go to The Drongos.'

'Casey,' Lucy murmured, 'I know you dislike plantations but you don't have to worry. Jed and Martha are two very kind people and they will help us. We can't refuse after they've been so kind as to invite us. Besides, I'd like to go there. It will be a chance to get away from New Orleans and to relax before the voyage.' She squeezed him playfully. 'Think of the baby. He wants me to rest.'

Casey sighed again, knowing he was beaten. 'I think it's strange, that's all.'

'You're imagining things, Casey.' Lucy raised her head and bit his ear.

'Maybe I am,' he said drowsily. 'We'll go if it will make you happy.' He turned and touched her breasts, wondering idly how it would feel to hold Martha Barrow in his arms. He was roused by the thought. Lucy noticed and wriggled closer to him.

He made love to her without feeling, to satisfy her, while his mind tried to ignore the misgivings stirred by the idea of a trip to The Drongos.

CHAPTER NINE

They lingered over their coffee. Doing things at an easy pace was one of Casey's pleasures since he had come to the Rampart Street cottage. He luxuriated in this life of indulgence after his months as a slave. Lucy, too, enjoyed the unhurried moments when she had Casey to herself. She watched him possessively at he sat at the table in his silk under-breeches and cradled the dish of coffee in his hands.

Beyond Casey, as he sat steeped in thought, the louvers were open to let the morning breeze into the tiny parlor. Rampart Street, because of the sybaritic nature of its residents, was slower to wake than the trading areas of the Vieux Carré by the levee. So the harsh squealing of the wheels of a carriage juddering over the ruts as it raced along the street was a disturbing sound.

Lucy peeped through the louvers behind Casey's shoulder, curious to know which of her neighbors was receiving her patron so early. The horses snorted as the carriage clattered to a halt.

'Casey,' she cried in alarm. 'It's stopping here.' She was wearing only her night dress and backed away from the window in panic. 'We're not dressed. I can't let anyone see me like this.'

Casey gazed at her approvingly. 'Why not? You look wonderful.' He patted her stomach. 'Doesn't she, son?'

'Oh!' Lucy stamped her foot. 'Put on your breeches and shirt quickly. You'll have to tell whoever it is to come back later.' She waited impatiently for him to stir until the voice of the coachman at the step drove her into the boudoir with a shriek.

Casey grinned and stood up lazily, stretching himself. His body, clad only in the thin silk of his under-breeches, bulged. The muscles of his chest rippled. The stripes scarred across his skin had softened and he was no longer ashamed of them. He threw open the door to the street, unconcerned about his appearance.

'Ah declah!' The exaggerated whoop of the woman shattered his contented lethargy. He blinked.

'Martha! I didn't expect you.'

'I'm so glad.' She stood on the sidewalk and gloated up at him. 'You look much better like this than when we first met.'

'Wait,' he said, dodging behind the shelter of the door. 'I'll dress.'

'Here?' Martha gazed up and down the street wtih distaste. 'I can't wait here.' She started up the step. 'Are you going to let me in?'

'Of course,' he grinned. 'I'll take the risk if you will.'

'Casey,' she simpered when he closed the door behind her. 'I'm surely not at risk?' Her eyes rested on his breeches. 'Is Lucy at home?'

'Yes, she's dressing. I'll call her.'

'Oh no, don't disturb her on my account.' Martha gazed around the tiny room with disapproval. She sat on the edge of a chair and loosened her cloak.

Casey glimpsed the ruffles of her high corsage and realized with disappointment that this morning she was dressed with the severity of a maiden aunt. He remembered those lovely breasts that were now concealed beneath the strictures of her bodice.

'You must be wondering why I've come,' she said.

'Oh yes.' He sat quickly and crossed his legs. It was six weeks since he'd seen her.

Martha's hair was piled high under her bonnet, revealing the firmness of her profile, a softer version of her brother's. Her eyes, instead of having the glint of evil that he associated with Jed, were flirtatious with a hint of humor twinkling in them. By her busy manner, Casey sensed that she was a formidable woman and he found the combination of her beauty and strength very appealing.

'Well,' she said without hesitation. 'I've found you a ship.'

'How –?'

'Listen, Casey, and I'll tell you. Jed's so busy that I didn't rely on him. I had a chat with an acquaintance of mine at Pritchards, the shipping agents, and I've booked you a passage for next month.'

'I don't believe it! Yesterday, Pritchards told me there was nothing available for six months, at least.'

'There are ways,' she said, fluttering her eyelashes.

'After all this time! Lucy will be thrilled.'

'And you?'

'I'd like to go to England . . .'

'I think you'd like plantation life more, Casey. You aren't the type for society.' She shifted her legs so that her skirt rose above one ankle.

'Can I get you something?' Casey gulped. He wasn't sure how he could stand in his undergarments without causing offence. Martha, he decided, was the kind of woman he liked.

'I'm not staying,' she said brusquely. 'The ship sails in four weeks so why don't you and Lucy come and stay at The Drongos until then? This place doesn't really suit you, does it, Casey?' She gazed around the room in mock horror.

'You need the space of a big house, and the open fields. That's what I mean about plantation life. You'll love The Drongos.' Her smile was warm and inviting.

Casey considered the situation. There was an implication involved, he was sure, especially when he saw the gleam in Martha's eye. He thought of Lucy, wondering if she was listening behind the door. 'Lucy would like to come,' he said.

'Good. Can you be ready for three o'clock?'

'Today?'

'Yes. We'll go on the steamboat. It's a hundred and seventy five miles to Bayou Sara. Jed's in New Orleans too so he'll be with us. Do say you'll come!'

Casey stood up in confusion. 'It's very sudden.'

'You don't have much to take, do you?' Martha gestured at the contents of the parlor. 'These things aren't yours, are they?'

'No.' He grinned at her disapproval. 'I mean, there are arrangements to make.'

'Nonsense. You have to return to New Orleans to get the ship for England so you can arrange everything then. Come, Casey, at least for a couple of weeks. Think of Lucy; it will do her a power of good to get away from this tainted atmosphere.'

He hesitated. 'I must ask Lucy.'

'Of course. Perhaps I'm selfish,' Martha smiled demurely. 'I long to have Lucy's company. She's so delightful. And you'll find The Drongos much less formal than New Orleans!' Martha stood up, pulling her cloak around her.

'Now don't see me out,' she laughed, sweeping her eyes the full length of his body. Her lips puckered wistfully. 'I'll send the carriage for you at three.'

Lucy burst into the parlor as soon as Martha had gone. She peered through the louvers at the carriage heading away to the fashionable part of the city. She was still in her nightdress and the sight of her body, plump with the rounded curves of pregnancy outlined against the sunlight, stirred Casey even more.

He stood behind her and held her guiltily, hoping she wouldn't realize that it was Martha who had begun the desire pulsing through him.

'Casey,' she said laughing. 'I'm so excited!'

'Come here.' He tightened his grasp around her waist when she tried to move away. 'Kiss me.'

'No, no, we've got no time.' She tickled him playfully under his arms and he let her go. 'I'm so pleased. We'll have a lovely time at The Drongos, you'll see.' She paused and giggled.

'Why, Casey Todd! You're shameless! Fancy receiving Martha like that.'

'You were here. What's wrong with it? You yourself said she's not what she seems. I think you're right. Martha Barrow is a hard, scheming female, determined to get what she wants.'

'I don't care! She's my friend and I like her.'

'Hmm.' Casey grunted, not willing to admit that he liked Martha too, although in quite a different way. He caught Lucy in his arms and kissed her. She danced away.

'We must prepare everything. Shall I write to Madame Cable?'

'Why?'

'To tell her we're going to The Drongos. She might find it strange if we don't let her know.'

'No,' said Casey, irritated by the thought of having to inform the old woman of his whereabouts just because she considered herself his protector in the Vieux Carré. 'It's only for a few days.'

They were ready when the carriage came for them at three. Their possessions were few; some dresses for Lucy and two suits for Casey. He had never hankered to own more than was necessary for his survival and had not got accustomed to having sufficient funds to buy whatever he needed, and didn't need.

His tastes were simple. In fact, it was the suggestion of the informal life that Martha had promised at The Drongos that had swayed him to accept her invitation. He would have liked to have seen Hollis before they left to find out more about The Drongos from him. From Jed's casual remarks, he knew he shipped sugar and cotton, but that was all.

Martha was waiting for them on the steamboat. Casey boarded the huge craft with trepidation. Although by that year steamboats had been in operation for a quarter of a century, some people still called them 'swimming volcanoes.'

There were over two hundred engaged in the Mississippi trade and the best of them could steam the distance up river from New Orleans to the falls of the Ohio at Louisville in six days. Races between the steamboats to reduce the time were frequent. Steamboats had displaced flatboats and other craft that were dependent on strong men to pull them up river.

The opulence of the boat intimidated Casey and he trailed moodily after Martha as she escorted Lucy along the narrow gangway that ran outside the saloon on the upper deck. He refused to enter the saloon, conscious of the offence he might unwittingly give the well-heeled passengers, and unable to face yet another put down. Instead, he peered through the windows at the elegant carpets, magnificent furniture and grand pianos that contributed to the fame of steamboats as the ultimate in luxurious travel. Ladies had their cabins below deck and as soon as the steamboat chugged away from the quay to begin its journey up river, Martha took Lucy below. Casey was left to brood.

He was leaning on the rail, contemplating the sad vastness of the Mississippi when Lucy joined him an hour later.

'Isn't it splendid, Casey? My berth has an enormous feather bed and pillows with the softest down. The furnishings are so plush it's just like an hotel. What's the gentlemen's cabin like?'

He shrugged his shoulders. 'I'll sleep on deck.'

Lucy bit back the words she wanted to say, and regarded him curiously. His face was turned to the low river bank facing the thick vegetation that grew to the water's edge. His eyes blazed in the reflection from the dying sun and the sunlight dappling his face gave him an exotic beauty. Lucy slipped her arm under his and squeezed him lovingly.

'I know you didn't want to come,' she said in a rush. 'Martha was so insistent, wasn't she? It's so good of you to agree just for my sake. I know you'll like it.'

'On the contrary.' He lifted his arm and draped it around her shoulders, drawing her closer to him. 'I am pleased we are going. See that!' He nodded at the water. 'The Layou river in Dominica is a silly little girl compared with this wide wicked woman of a waterway.'

Lucy giggled. 'You can't call a river a woman.'

'Why not? In Dominica we have male and female rivers.' He sighed. 'This Mississippi . . . she's a woman all right. What depth! See how she moves, isn't she glamorous and sultry and deceptive, like a woman.'

'You don't like Martha, do you?' Lucy clenched the rail with her hands. 'You're making up this nonsense about rivers to tell me something.'

He shrugged and turned to face her. 'I like this river, Lucy. Already I feel different. Do you remember how I used to sit for hours gazing at the waters of the Layou. It was so clear and sparkling in the sun. This is deep, sluggish; a tough man's river. It suits me.'

'You'll make me believe you don't want to go to England.' She pouted.

'If that's what you want, Lucy.' He put his hand under her chin and raised it, leaning down to kiss her.

'No, Casey,' she said, pulling away. 'People will see.'

A flicker of surprise at her reluctance hovered in his eyes. He brushed at his brow and laughed his doubts away. 'I haven't seen Jed yet,' he said, changing the subject meaningfully and returning to gaze at the wide sweep of the river.

'Martha says he's in the saloon gambling.'

'That's not very courteous of our kind host, is it? Where's Martha?'

'She's resting.'

'Then perhaps that's what you should do. Don't worry about me. I like to watch the water. It's very restful.'

Casey spent the hours of the voyage, when he wasn't curled up on a hatch cover asleep or swallowing coffee brought to him by Lucy, staring enraptured at the Mississippi. Lucy sensed his mood and wisely left him alone, spending her time instead with Martha.

Casey had fallen under the spell of the river, allowing its incessant flowing to inspire thoughts in him that swelled then vanished, borne away like debris on the current.

Jed, who watched him unobserved from a seat in the saloon, noted how Casey bore the tedium of the journey with patience. He did not know that Casey was enriching himself from the river, drawing on it for strength in the same way that he did during his youth in Layou.

The arrival of the steamboat at Bayou Sara was a noisy, frantic affair. It was dusk. The blare of the steamer's whistle startled sleeping birds into shrieking and the drifters milling on the bank into shouting at the passengers. There was an air of urgency that Casey couldn't understand because of its contrast with the placid water. He noticed with relief from his vantage point on the upper deck that Bayou Sara resembled Layou, just as he had expected it would.

The hamlet was large and extended into the rising hills behind it the way Layou did. The wooden buildings had the appearance of having grown faster than their owners intended. The largest, with gaps for windows and doors facing on to the river, was built in five parts, each nailed to the other. Two second stories, like second thoughts, had been raised aloft so that one had a door that opened on to the night, fifteen feet above the ground.

'That's the hotel,' said Jed who had come out of his hide in the saloon to join Lucy and Martha at Casey's side. 'We don't have long to unload.'

'What a real pioneering town!' mused Casey. 'I feel at home already.'

'I thought you would!' Jed's voice was spiteful.

'Are we going to stay here?' asked Lucy, too worried to notice Jed's venomous tone.

For Casey, the serenity he had gained from the tranquil voyage was soured by the sound of Jed's harsh tongue. He realized then that any peace he hoped to find at The Drongos would be won only when he and Jed settled the differences between them. He sensed the time for that was approaching.

Martha drew Lucy close to her, 'Come, child, Bayou Sara's not a place for ladies.'

The men on the river bank began to shout Jed's name. There

were raucous comments in a river patois that Casey didn't understand.

'Take no notice,' said Martha. 'Wharfside rats of no consequence.'

Jed was answering the men's banter with a torrent of abuse in a dialect that matched their own. Casey was surprized at the impact he made although his words were unintelligible to him. The drifters on the dock fell silent and slunk away as a party of negroes shouldered them aside.

Casey watched the performance with interest. The negroes, five in all, were broad, muscular men clad only in breech cloths. They formed a line at the waterside and waited silently for the boat to tie up. When the gangplank was lowered, Jed shouted at the negroes and three of them trotted on board while two remained keeping watch.

'Are they your slaves?' Casey asked.

Jed spun around on his heels without bothering to answer and hurried to the companionway where he disappeared below deck. Martha ushered Lucy along after him without another word so Casey turned back to the rail to watch the unloading. He resolved not to let this odd brother and sister think they could treat him like one of their slaves.

The negroes were carrying out their baggage from the ship. Jed stood at the gangplank shouting at them to move faster while the other passengers who wanted to disembark tried to push their way ashore. At the same time, people were struggling to get on board. The two negroes posted on the bank as watchers, guarded the heap of baggage being dumped in front of them. They threatened anyone who came near and the white men skulking in the shadows snarled back at them like angry dogs.

In the midst of the melee of landing, with people pushing to get on meeting the stream of people fighting to get off, while Jed's slaves barged through them, Casey saw Lucy being propelled along the plank by Martha. She clasped a riding crop in her hand and was using it to belabor people scrambling around the two of them.

Casey raced along the deck and down the companionway to the lower deck where Jed was standing at the head of the gangplank directing his negroes. 'What the devil are you doing, Jed?' he shouted. 'Lucy's in the middle of those cut-throats without an escort.'

Jed laughed. 'Ain't no worry, boy. It's everyone for himself now.' He aimed a kick at the backside of one of his negroes rushing past with a bundle on his head.

'Got to move fast now, Casey. The ship ain't stayin' more than a few minutes.'

Casey looked down and saw that Lucy had reached the dock and was being sheltered by Martha and one of the big blacks. She collapsed on the pile of baggage and began to fan herself. Martha was shouting.

'Why didn't you help her?' Casey grabbed Jed's arm to get his attention.

'Take ya hands off me!' Jed pushed him aside angrily and kicked another negro down the plank.

'Come on,' he shouted, grabbing his arm and trying to drag Casey with him. 'Can't fool around now. Got to get off the ship.'

'Let go of me!' said Casey softly. 'I'm not your slave.'

'Ya damn well won't be free either if ya don't get off now.'

The ship's whistle howled out and the commotion on the gangplank increased as more people struggled to get on board. Jed made another grab for Casey. He hesitated. Lucy was on the dock so he had to go ashore yet he was determined not to be treated like a recalcitrant slave. He put up his fists.

Jed shook his head and sniggered. 'If you want, you can swim ashore, I'm not forcin' ya!' He spun around and dived into the throng beating his way through the crowd with his fists.

Casey cursed himself for his foolishness and flung himself after Jed. The ship's whistle gave a final flourish and the plank began to shake. Men were casting off the ropes. Casey leaped off the plank moments before it slipped from the ship and fell into the water. He landed on the bank beside Jed.

'What an ass!' Jed was laughing. 'Ya nearly had us both in the river.' He looked at Martha. 'Nigras all off?'

'What about Lucy?' said Casey, clenching his fists in anger. 'If she's hurt –'

'I'm all right, Casey. It was fun, wasn't it. Martha says the ship is trying to save time so it can race that other steamboat to Natchez.' Lucy pointed to a second ship, its lights blazing, that was steaming at full speed trying to overtake the one they had just left.

'That's madness.'

'That's how we live out here,' said Jed, still chuckling. 'And you wanted to fight me!'

Casey sat on his haunches, his fine breeches and coat torn and dirtied, and he wondered what hell he had come to in Bayou Sara.

CHAPTER TEN

Bayou Sara was an outlaw town. The burly negroes who formed a circle guarding the four travelers and their possessions, were a necessary precaution. Dusk was thickening and the gloom of night blended with the murkiness of the river to create a half light in which crime and evil flourished. The atmosphere was forbidding and it made Casey as wary as Jed. He drew Lucy close to him while Jed, his pistol prominent in his belt, dispatched one of his negroes for a boat. They both peered alertly into the gathering darkness over the shoulders of the other slaves.

Bayou Sara had grown without the permission of any planning authority, and it remained beyond the law. The town did not even have a proper name; Bayou Sara was the creek that flowed into the Mississippi on its northern shore.

It had sprung up from nothing at the end of the century when the crew of a flatboat anchored in the creek and erected a rough shelter. The boatmen of those days were a tough breed. They survived on a diet of raw whisky and bad food and when they were not working the boats they were drunk or fighting. In summer they wore only trousers of coarse linen and wool, and in winter they wrapped themselves in furs. They were used to rough living and the temporary shelter they established soon attracted others.

Their craft, the flatboats, were sometimes as long as a hundred feet, and twenty-five feet wide. They were made of massive timbers and planks like a barge to float tons of freight, livestock and families down the Mississippi through territory infested with pirates and hostile Indians to the anchorage in front of Tchoupitoulas Street in New Orleans.

More than a thousand boats a year made the hazardous voyage from the north and since they had no means of returning, they were broken up and sold for lumber at their destination. Some of them never reached New Orleans. They were taken over by their crews for the flatboaters' own township. The captured cargo fed the mutineers, and the timber from the boats was used to build the makeshift cabins that gave Bayou Sara its ramshackle appearance.

The town grew slowly and without hindrance. The flatboaters were a wild bunch and as long as they kept to themselves, no authority saw fit to intervene. They were soon joined by the keelboaters, an even tougher set of men whose strength and fiercesome reputation as brawlers matched their jobs to provide the power to get keelboats upstream.

This was done by bushwacking, the method by which a boat was steered close to the bank and the crew pulled it along by hanging onto the bushes. Sometimes they used a cordelle, a five-hundred feet long rope tied around the boat's mast and pulled by the keelboaters as they walked along the shore. Another means of ascent was for forty men to stick long poles into the river bed and punt their boat forward in unison.

With the advent of steamboats, the town's population increased as the crews of both the flatboats and the keel boats took to the easier life ashore. These men were ruthless and the township expanded in a rough and ready fashion under their influence. No one was afraid to work, as long as they had rye whisky.

Gradually women were attracted to Bayou Sara. They were mostly rejects from the brothels and streets of New Orleans and Natchez, and were as bellicose as the men. Their tough spirit stood them in good stead. Families grew and Bayou Sara developed into a regular anchorage and river port.

Twenty years before Casey's arrival, the town attracted public attention when it was the starting point for a race between two steamers. The captain of the *Constitution* challenged his old rival, the captain of the *Washington*, to a race. Both boats stoked up their furnaces and started off from Bayou Sara. A few minutes later, the cylinder head of the *Constitution* blew up in a cloud of steam. Ten passengers and a notorious river boat gambler were killed.

Casey listened to the brief history of the settlement with curiosity, his nerves tense. It reminded him so much of Layou. The four of them were waiting for Jed's negroes to bring the boat that was to take them up the creek to The Drongos.

'Of course,' said Martha in a belated attempt to allay Lucy's fears, 'all that happened a long time ago. Bayou Sara isn't such a bad place now, dear, when people know you.'

Casey frowned. 'Why do we have these negroes guarding us, then? It doesn't seem very safe to me.'

'Oh, it's not for you and Lucy.' Martha's laughter was nervous. 'It's to protect the provisions and your baggage.'

'Why do you live here if it's such a wicked place?' Luch shuddered as she cast a glance at the darkness that now surrounded them.

'The Drongos is quite far from here, Lucy.' Martha smirked in a way that made Casey realize the extent of their isolation. 'This is where we land, not live.'

'Don't you have any neighbors?' Lucy was beginning to have her doubts too.

'A few poor whites. The other planters live in St Francisville.'

'Where's that?' asked Casey.

Martha waved into the darkness. 'Behind Bayou Sara. Actually, it's to the forefront in respectability. It's the main social center for hereabouts. It's got churches, a court house, a library, a Masonic lodge. I don't care for it at all.'

Casey was about to ask why when the boatmen and some negroes appeared. They began transferring the cargo to the small boat for the trip up the creek. Another boat was brought alongside and a negro helped Martha and Lucy into it while another held a flambeau aloft. At the edge of its glow, Casey saw the bedraggled whites who had been crouching in the darkness. They were drawing in to see what they could seize.

'You said the whites aren't afraid to work?' challenged Casey as Jed jumped into the boat beside him.

Jed didn't answer at first; he was counting his negroes. When he was satisfied that they were all there, he gave the order to proceed. The cargo boat went first, disappearing almost immediately into darkness. Their own followed, with a negro in the prow as look out and the man with the flambeau in the stern. The oarsmen began to row with a practised skill before Jed relaxed.

'So many questions!' said Jed mockingly. 'It's the old generation who don't mind work. These young whites don't have the spirit. They say that's what nigras are for.'

'Surely they don't have slaves?' Casey was aghast.

'That's right. Too poor.'

'Then how –' Casey stopped speaking as he noticed the different rhythm of the oarsmen.

The boat had entered the bayous, that area of sluggish streams and creeks and marshland adjoining the Mississippi. In the darkness it was impossible to see the trees crowding down thickly on both sides of the bayou but Casey sensed the lush vegetation. The air was oppressive, humid and heavy with the atmosphere of the wilderness.

Casey understood that this was nature's territory where the intrusion of man was tolerated but not accepted. The feeling, which frightened Lucy clinging to Martha in the seat in front of him, was reassuring to Casey. His blood tingled with excitement at the familiar mystery of the bush, the undergrowth and the dark places of the unexplored.

Casey trusted the negroes to pilot the boats safely along the bayou even though his own eyes could hardly see the water. The moon was not yet high enough to give light, and the trees hanging over the bayou kept out the stars. He grinned to himself in the darkness and admitted some respect for Jed. The man was quiet now, aware that no cursing of his could change the fact that their lives depended on his slaves' competence.

They progressed in silence for many minutes. The deep breathing of the negroes and the splash of their oars in the water were the only interruptions to Casey's thoughts.

'This is our highway,' Jed said softly. 'The negroes know their way in the dark.' He chuckled. 'You wouldn't.'

That truth stated so bleakly ought to have alarmed Casey. Instead he was lulled by the nostalgia the journey was evoking and so missed the menace in Jed's words. He spotted a light far ahead in the north bank of the bayou but kept the knowledge to himself.

The negroes rowed tirelessly and Casey supposed that if the bayou was the only thoroughfare to Jed's plantation, it would surely be kept clear of fallen trees and other obstructions. It was wide and the lookout would soon know if they had strayed too close to the bank.

There was a sigh from Jed as he spotted the light. 'The landing's ahead. We have to walk from there.'

The slaves maneuvered the boat easily to the shore. Casey

jumped out first to help Lucy and Martha. Jed turned his attention to the small party of slaves who stood mutely awaiting them. Two held flambeaux and were instructed to escort them up the trail to the house. The other slaves toted the bags on their heads, trotting along the trail in front of them. Through the trees in the distance, lights glowed at the top of an incline.

'That's our house,' said Martha with pride. She held Lucy close to her. 'We'll soon be there, dear.'

Lucy's silence caused Casey concern. He glanced at her in the pale glow from the torches and saw her face was set with an air of determination. He wondered if she, too, was sensitive to the atmosphere of their surroundings. In the glare of the flame as they progressed along the path, Casey noted boughs had been lopped off trees and a ditch to drain out water dug alongside the trail. Its good repair was a welcome sign to Casey that the plantation was well run.

The negroes holding the torches were dressed in the standard plantation issue of osnaburg short trousers and loose cotton shirts. They were silent and Casey was relieved at the absence of fear in their attitude. They showed respect and ability, responding to Jed's instructions so promptly it was obvious they were accustomed to off-loading boats and escorting guests up the trail in the dark.

The path was rising and Casey took Lucy's elbow to help her up the slope. He was hurt when she drew away from him with a start.

'What's wrong?' he asked, baffled.

'Casey!' She sounded bemused and slipped her arm under his. 'I must have been dreaming.' She was trembling and Casey squeezed her comfortingly.

'Not far now.' Martha tried to sound happy but it was plain that she too was tiring.

'It's hot toddy then bed for both of you as soon as we arrive,' she said. 'Plenty of time to look around tomorrow.'

There were more lights visible through the trees and Casey was getting an impression of The Drongos plantation house. He was disappointed because he had expected a grand brick mansion with columns and wide patio. The Drongos house, or what he could see of it through the panoply of live oaks that surrounded it, was a low wooden construction of two stories.

Instead of white columns there were iron posts with elaborate friezes of cast iron to the roof. Dormer windows were outlined against the roof and lanterns hung in some of them. The main door was open on to the wooden gallery and inside a chandelier blazed with candles.

Lucy was leaning heavily on him when they reached the edge of the gallery and she trod the six steps wearily. A large negress in a blue cotton cap and a red checkered dress that scraped the floor, bustled over to her.

'Hilda!' said Martha with obvious relief. 'Take Mistress Lucy upstairs to the guest room. I'm sorry I don't have a maid for you, Lucy. Hilda does everything here. She'll look after you.'

Casey recognized Hilda instantly as a proud and competent housekeeper, typical of her kind who were the mainstay of southern plantation homes. He surrendered Lucy gratefully to Hilda's care, amused at the glance of disapproval the housekeeper gave him.

'She's my wife, Hilda,' he said pointedly. 'You take good care of her, now.'

'Master Casey and his wife will be staying in the house together, Hilda.' Jed's tone was stern. 'You see they have everything they want.'

Hilda's frown was so brief, Casey would not have seen it if he hadn't been watching her face closely. A lot could be learned about a master from a slave's expression. It was reassuring when Hilda smiled broadly.

'Why dat sure, sah. Welcome Miz Lucy an' Mas Casey, sah an' ma'm. Follow me, nah; ah take y'all to de bes' room in de Drongos.'

'I'll retire with Lucy if you don't mind,' Casey said to Jed and Martha. He peered off the gallery into the darkness of the plantation. The negroes had vanished but he sensed the presence of slaves lingering in the shadows waiting to be summoned.

'It's so kind of you to invite us to stay.'

'The bags have been taken to ya room.' Jed was curt. 'If there's anything missing, that's too bad. It's those varmints at the river, not my nigras.'

'Sleep as long as you want, Casey.' Martha attempted a provocative smile but Casey could see her heart wasn't in it. 'Goodnight.'

Lucy was alone when he reached the guest room. His instinct was to explore the house but he was worried about her. A single candle burned in its holder. She was sitting on the bed, too tired to rise.

'I told that slave to go,' she said. 'She was too bossy.'

'Oh dear.' Casey pulled off his coat and flung it on a chair. 'Hilda runs this place. I hope you didn't offend her. She's the one you've got to keep on your side.'

'No, no.' Lucy gazed wearily around the room. 'I told her you were coming and we wanted to be alone.'

'Just so.' Casey closed the door. 'How do you feel? I swear we wouldn't have come here if I knew the journey was so difficult. You in your condition.'

'My condition's fine.' Lucy revived and began to unfasten her clothes. 'I need to rest, that's all.'

'All right,' said Casey glumly. 'I can take a hint.'

'You don't mind?'

'Not at all. I'll sleep on the floor.'

'Perhaps it's better. The bed's nice, isn't it?' It was a fourposter with a tester covered with red velvet. The posts were octagonal, roughly hewn and sturdy.

'Typical plantation furniture,' Casey said, trying the mattress. 'Hard as a board but better than the floor.' He grimaced, annoyed by Lucy's casual rejection of him.

'Martha does so hope you'll like it here.' Lucy sounded anxious. 'It was rather strange coming along that bayou in the dark. I felt quite frightened, I don't know why.'

'That's the spirit of the woods.'

'Don't be mysterious, Casey.' She let her dress fall to the floor and Casey picked it up.

'Hilda will scold me if I let you do that.' He laid the dress over a chair.

'I wonder if we'll feel lonely here.' Lucy sounded doubtful. 'I mean with only Martha and Jed in this big house. They have plenty of slaves, though.' She slipped into bed, looked at him thoughtfully, then shifted to one side and patted a space for him to join her.

Casey grinned, stripped off his clothes down to his drawers and snuffed out the candle. He got into the bed and nestled down beside her.

'That's why Martha wanted you to come, for company.' He held her gently. 'We won't stay long. A few days for politeness sake, then we'll go. I know these places. They have a way of claiming visitors so they never leave.'

Lucy shuddered. 'Don't say that, Casey.'

'I mean that it's easy to get used to slaves doing everything, of being a king in your own castle.'

There was a knock on the door and it opened before Casey could say anything. A girl with a candle walked in followed by Hilda bearing a tray on which stood two large mugs with steam rising from them.

'Ah declah! Y'all plumb tuckered fuh sure. Why! Y'all in bed a'ready!'

Hilda chuckled and put the tray on the table by the bed. She bustled around the room collecting up the clothes Casey had laid out on the chair.

'Ah gwine launder all dese t'ings,' she said. 'Get rid ob dat city stink. Nah y'll drink yah toddy an' sleep tight. Mistress made it herself an' bid me sure to see y'all drink it.' She winked at Casey, beckoned the girl to follow and swept out of the room, closing the door behind her.

'My goodness!' said Lucy who had drawn the covers over her. 'What a fusspot.'

'No, she isn't,' said Casey. 'She means well.' He passed a mug of hot toddy across to her. 'Sip some of this.'

Lucy took the cup and drank, feeling the warmth of the whisky seeping through her. She wriggled comfortably. 'I wonder how many slaves he has?'

'It must be plenty.' Casey was thoughful. 'They seem to be well cared for, strong too. Did you notice how none of them said anything all the time they were with us. Very respectful.' He sipped at the drink. It had a curious taste that he attributed to the local rye whisky.

'Yes.' Lucy yawned. 'I spoke to one when we were waiting for you to get off the ship. Martha said they can't talk.'

'What?' Casey yawned too. 'Why not?'

'They're dumb.'

'All of them?' He finished the drink and put the mug on the table.

'Yes . . .' Lucy was almost asleep. 'They've had their tongues cut out.'

She closed her eyes and the cup fell from her fingers to the floor.

Casey gazed at her in horror as her words penetrated his befuddled brain. He tried to rise but it was too late.

'The toddy . . .!' he gasped before he became unconscious. Too late, he realized what the curious taste was: laudanum.

They had been drugged.

CHAPTER ELEVEN

Pain racked Casey's head. He was neither asleep nor awake but suspended in a drugged dream state. He struggled to rise but the pain knocked him back and a weakness paralyzed him. He was filled with an insatiable desire for water. His lips were parched and he dreamed of the bayou, the Mississippi, and the sparkling rock pools of the Layou River where he had bathed as a boy.

Thirst tormented him so much he yearned for cool water to be splashed on his face from a gourd. He longed to stand under the waterfall coursing down the side of the hills in the Layou Valley, and to gulp down water in gallons to revive him.

He put his lips eagerly to the glass of water held against his mouth. He tipped back his head and drank it all. Another was pressed to his mouth and he gulped it down. He fell back on the pillow and moaned.

'He'll sleep properly now,' the woman's voice said. 'Belladonna brings on a thirst.'

'I thought you'd used laudanum.'

'Both.'

There was silence as someone left the room. Casey couldn't open his eyes nor move. He fought sleep but it crept over him. He was lost.

Jed nodded his head. He placed the girandole with its lighted candles on the table so his hands were free. He ignored Lucy lying on her side and pulled the covers away from Casey. He stood above the bed and stared at the sleeping body stretched below him on the mattress. He held a knife ready in his hand.

When Casey didn't stir and, by the regular rise and fall of his chest, Jed judged he was really asleep, he replaced the knife in its sheath. He stared for several minutes at Casey's body, naked except for the silk drawers that seemed inadequate for his manhood. He studied him from head to toe, assessing the proportions, the muscles and the skin tone. He was relieved to see that, apart from the blemishes of the whip scars, the boy's body appeared to be perfect.

He leaned over and touched his chest tentatively. Casey didn't stir. He pressed down his palm firmly over the heart and counted its beat. His eyes lingered on Casey's bulging pectoral muscles and on the wilderness of hair that curled across them. He squeezed his flesh and noted how tight it was against his breastbone.

Satisfied with the heartbeat, Jed began a minute examination of Casey's body, pinching folds of flesh between his thumb and forefinger, searching for weak spots. He fingered his throat and slid his fingers over Casey's face and squeezed his nose. Casey remained motionless so Jed put the blade of his knife between his teeth and forced open his mouth. He peered inside, checking his teeth, upper and lower jaw; they were faultless. He measured the size of Casey's forehead with the span of his thumb and forefinger.

Next Jed turned his attention to Casey's arms. He felt them carefully and noted the muscles that were flabby and could be toned up with labor. He held his hands and examined the long fingers, checking the color of his fingernails for blemishes. He turned the hand over to look at the palm and was pleased to see it was well marked with firm lines.

Jed turned his attention to Casey's stomach. It was flat, scored with muscles and showing no excess fat. He placed his hands under Casey's buttocks and eased him off the mattress so he could slide his drawers down over his thighs. His penis stirred as the silk slid over it. Jed caught it in his hand and squeezed it. He fingered Casey's testicles, feeling them carefully for defects, then bounced them in his hand.

Casey was hardening under his touch and Jed scowled. He prodded the thatch of hair for weaknesses and peered closely for lumps, scabs and lice. He took Casey's swollen penis in both hands and felt it pulsing. With one fist on top of the other, he measured its length. It was prodigious and made Jed feel angry and ashamed at his own inferiority.

He let the penis go and kneaded Casey's thighs and calves. He pinched his ankles, counted his toes and scratched the sole of his foot, amused at the way the foot suddenly sprang to life in his hand. Then he gripped Casey's hip, ignoring the rigid penis, and heaved him over on his side.

He brushed his shoulders slowly, feeling the muscles and bones. He traced his fingers down his spine to the trim waist and on to the muscular buttocks. He inserted his finger into the anus and probed until Casey groaned and twisted in his sleep.

Jed nodded with satisfaction and stood back from the bed to survey the whole length of Casey's naked body. With his bronze skin, muscular torso, thick thighs, strong legs and long, firm penis, Casey was blessed with the splendor of his negro ancestors. White blood had given him perfect proportion and good looks; his intelligence and cunning he had inherited from both sides. Jed was impressed. Casey was perfect; even better than he had dared to imagine.

There was only one thing left to do. Jed unbuckled his belt and walked back to the bed. He slapped Casey's buttocks and although he stirred, he didn't wake. Jed climbed on to the bed and straddled Casey, reaching over his hips to grasp his penis.

The crack of a whip snapped by his ear and he leaped off the bed, turning in surprise toward the open door. Martha stood there frowning, the whip poised in her hand ready for another blow. Jed stumbled and tried to fasten himself.

'You're supposed to examine him, that's all.'

Jed shrugged. 'His seed?'

Martha was in her nightdress. She strode into the room, took up the girandole and prodded Jed with the whip handle. 'Come on,' she said. 'You can see he's fertile from that.' She glanced with distaste at Lucy lying curled up at the other side of the bed.

'You could have hurt me.' Jed rubbed his crotch.

'How is he?'

'Perfect.' Jed sighed. 'Can you credit it, Martha? Not only have we got one of the Bondmaster's breed, at last, we actually got one that's descended from the Bondmaster himself!'

'But he ain't a slave,' said Martha.

'No.' Jed followed her out of the room, shaking his head. 'He ain't a slave, but he sure is a man.'

'Oh lor'!' exclaimed Hilda when she opened the door and walked into the bedroom. 'T'ank de Lor' ah made dat chil' stay in de hall.'

She bustled over to the table, set down the tray and stood with her arms akimbo, staring down at the bed.

Casey was naked, lying on his side, facing Lucy with his drawers at his ankles.

'Dat sure de greates' beauty ah eber see,' Hilda muttered to her herself. 'De po' boy! He done get some big lashin' somehow.' She leaned over to touch the wales on Casey's back.

'Aie!' she screamed as Casey caught her fat wrist in his hand. 'Let me go!' she squealed in a softer voice.

Casey's eyes blazed at her.

'Yo' gwine rape me an' yo' wife dere beside yo', Mas Casey?' Despite her surprise at the sleeping body coming to life so suddenly, Hilda couldn't overlook his manliness pointing right at her.

'Hilda!' Casey's voice was taut with anger. 'What did you put in that toddy last night?' He sat up in bed and used both hands to hold the large housekeeper so that her eyes were level with his.

She tossed her head proudly. 'Today, Mas Casey? Ah only carry dat to yo'. Mis Mart'a done prepare it sheself.'

Casey released her and patted her bottom as she turned away. 'I believe you, Hilda. Sorry for frightening you.'

'Dat t'ing don' frighten Hilda, sah, Lor' no. An-y-time, oh yas!' She sauntered toward the door, swaggering her hips with exaggeration. 'Ah sure glad yo' here, sah,' she said as she reached the door and turned. '*May, sha* , yo' an' me got one big understandin'. If!'

Lucy took the cup of coffee from Casey's hand without opening her eyes. 'I've such a headache,' she said.

'No pain there?' He touched her stomach.

'No. I was so tired, Casey. I fell asleep straight away.' She drank her coffee eagerly. 'I'm thirsty this morning. It must have been the toddy.'

Casey said nothing. If he told Lucy that Martha had drugged them she wouldn't believe it. As far as he could make out. they were both all right. He guessed, from his own torn drawers around his ankles, what had happened. He wondered what Martha had done to him and he to her. How odd not to know.

He swung himself out of bed and stoop up, kicking off the drawers. His head pounded with pain but the coffee soothed him. He tasted it again carefully, realizing that he would have to be on his guard all the time in case Martha tried to drug him again. He wanted to be conscious for the next encounter. He wrapped the bed cover around his waist and walked to the window.

The view from the dormer was staggering. Casey opened his eyes wide and felt the sleep being shaken out of him. The Drongos House was built at the top of a hill and that gave it a commanding vantage point over the surrounding countryside. Casey had a clear view over the tops of the live oaks, dripping with a screen of Spanish moss, to the canefields below.

A feeling of homesickness surged through him when he gazed at the waving green ribbons of sugar cane. He shrugged it off. The cane fields were bounded by trees which thickened into woods and wild bush that stretched as far as the eye could see. And then, almost on the horizon, was a muddy line drawn through the green of the trees: the Mississippi.

Casey opened the window and leaned out to see the position of the sun. It was shining from the right side of the house and as their bedroom was at the rear, he was looking north. The prospect pleased him.

He was drawing back his head when something in the distance caught his eye. He leaned out again as far as he could, looking to the east into the sun. A creek meandered its way through the overhanging trees and there was a clearing far from the house in the depths of the woods. Casey scanned the thick vegetation looking for a trail but couldn't see one. In the clearing there was another house, much smaller than The Drongos, and a long, barn-like structure with a stockade built around it.

Within the area of the stockade there were a few people either standing and facing the palisades or squatting on the ground. It was too far away for him to see more but the sight of the compound, presumably where Jed housed his slaves, appalled Casey. He withdrew from the window.

Lucy was lying back on the pillows with her eyes closed. He groped under the bed for the chamber pot, relieved himself into it, then poured water from the jug on the dresser into a basin and splashed it over his face. A soft pain still lingered in his head and it made him angry.

Why, he wondered, had Martha gone to such lengths?

He dressed rapidly, in breeches and shirt, but remained barefooted, carrying his boots in his hand so he could move silently about the house.

'I'm going for a walk.' He leaned down over Lucy and kissed her on her lips.

She turned her head away. 'I'll stay in bed for a little longer.' She didn't look at Casey and that increased his feeling of annoyance.

'If Hilda thinks you're sick, I won't be able to keep her away from you.'

'Tired,' said Lucy into her pillow. 'Just tired . . .'

Attributing her moodiness to the drugged toddy, Casey bit back his impatience and strode out of the room. He found himself in a parlor in the centre of the house with a door on his left and one on his right. The carpet was worn on the approaches to the two doors, which he assumed were bedrooms. The parlor was furnished functionally with sturdy pieces and a plain brass spittoon. Casey guessed the room was used more as a thoroughfare to the bedrooms than a salon in which to relax. He crossed the floor to the couch under the window and mounted it for a better view.

Outside were more live oaks and beyond them, about a hundred paces from the house, was a stream. It was slow moving and appeared to be deep. A trail led from it through the trees to the house. It was too close to be the Bayou Sara so Casey surveyed the rest of the landscape.

The long trail up which they had walked the night before veered diagonally off to the right down the hill. It, too, was shrouded in trees. There were some small cane pieces close to the trail but the general vista was one of impenetrable forest with The Drongos house isolated in the middle.

No one moved in the yard in front of the house, and it puzzled Casey why not. It was the hour for slaves to be doing the morning chores. He eased himself down from the window and sat on the couch. Opposite was the door to his own chamber and on the left was the top of the wide staircase that curved down to the entrance hall below. He listened carefully.

Was everyone still asleep? Where were the slaves? He expected them to be cleaning the house, chattering and singing to each other as they went about their work with the maximum of discreet noise to show they were busy. The Drongos was silent and because at that time of the morning there should have been activity, it disturbed Casey.

He got up and walked to the stairs, intending to find Hilda. He began to descend, quietly, affected by the soundlessness of the house. He was halfway down when a door creaked open and he froze.

He heard voices in the parlor he had just left so he peered around the curve in the stairs to see who was there.

Martha stood at a door with her back to the stair well. She was wearing a light colored nightdress of a thin material that did nothing to conceal the luscious curves of her body. Casey stared at her with a pleasure only dimmed at not knowing what Martha had done to him while he was drugged.

He mounted a step to call her, then stopped. Martha was reaching up to the man standing in the doorway. His eyes were on her face and he didn't see Casey. Martha held him in a tight embrace as the man, Jed Barrow, kissed her passionately on her lips.

Casey moved down the stairs to the entrance hall, stunned by the sight. There was no one around so he wandered through the rooms considering what he had seen. Strangely, as he thought about it, he found Martha's involvement with her brother was a challenge. It was nothing to him and yet . . . and yet . . .

On his right, with its double doors open to the hall, was a parlor, elaborately furnished, with a gaming room behind it. To the left of the hall was another parlor, a mirror image of the first, with the dining room adjoining it. The table was set with four places. Floor to ceiling casement windows overlooked the back veranda.

Casey peered through them in the hope of seeing Hilda or some of the other slaves but there was no one in sight. He strolled back to the hall just as Jed descended the stairs.

'What! Creeping about like a prowler?' Jed waved at Casey's boots which he still clutched in his hand. 'You're our guest, Casey. No need to pad around barefoot . . . like a slave.'

'It's so quiet here, I didn't want to disturb anyone.'

'Won't disturb me. I get up at dawn . . . to rouse the nigras.'

'Martha?' He deliberately ignored Jed's jibes.

'She rises early too. Checks the books.' Jed walked across the hall out to the front veranda, expecting Casey to follow.

'Come, Casey. Sit here and put your boots on. I want to show you something while we're alone.'

Casey sat in the chair that Jed indicated and pulled on his boots. Jed stood at the wrought iron rail with its decorative patterns and stared out across the shadowed courtyard. His hands were clasped behind his back and he was opening and closing his fingers nervously.

'I'm ready,' said Casey, stamping his feet on the deck of the veranda. 'Are we going far?'

Jed shot Casey a glance of annoyance, the kind of look more suited to a querulous slave than a house guest, and walked down the steps.

Casey reacted by refusing to be hurried and sauntered after him at his own pace, pretending great interest in the vegetation. Actually, he was intrigued by the atmosphere of the house. It was so enclosed in deep shade from the profusion of trees surrounding it that, even with the sun up, it aroused a feeling of mystery and awe in him.

He paused to gaze at the long veranda, over a hundred feet of it, that stretched the length of the house. It was broad and threw further shadows over the windows and walls of the house. He wondered what tales of plantation life that veranda could tell.

'You'll see the house later!' Jed was impatient for him to follow. 'Come this way.'

A path led through the trees to another building shielded from the house by a screen of bushes. It was hexagonal in shape, its lower story accessible through an archway built in each side, six arches in all. There were no doors. A flight of stone steps were visible through the arches and from where he stood, Casey could see the casement windows of the upper story. It reminded him of a jail.

'What is it?'

'My *garçonnière* ' Jed sounded proud. 'My father built it. It was for my privacy. You know . . .' He nudged Casey in his ribs with his elbow. 'For when I wanted to ride a slave wench so I wouldn't disturb the whole household.' He leered, his mustache bristling. 'You can use it any time.'

'Me?' Casey faltered, hating Jed.

'Sure,' Jed sniggered. 'With Lucy swelling up you'll need a few wenches yourself.' He draped his arm around Casey's shoulder but Casey cringed and ducked away.

'I can find special wenches for you, Casey, my boy. Don't be shocked. It's bayou tradition. A guest stays, the host must provide for his needs. You can use my *garçonnière* any time.' Jed touched Casey's chest lightly then slid his hand down and squeezed his crotch.

Casey stepped back sharply and swung his fist up into Jed's face. Jed, taken by surprise, took the blow full in his jaw and staggered back.

'What the hell!' he gasped, rubbing his chin.

Casey put up his fists ready for a fight.

'No, no, Casey.' Jed looked rueful. 'T'ain't nothing to get riled at.' He moved out of Casey's reach and considered him warily.

'You're mighty lively, dammit! Quick with your fists. I don't forget a blow, you know. But you an' me's friends.' Jed stuck out his hand.

'I mean no harm, Casey. You sure are hot like a wild stallion. Spoiling to fight me, same as on the steamboat.' He chuckled. 'Casey, you need a wench to drain that juice out of you. If you want to mount any of my fillies, you go right ahead!'

Casey swallowed the bile rising in his throat and checked his impulse to lambaste Jed Barrow once and for all. The white man, at that moment, represented all he hated about the slaveholding plantocracy.

Instead, he slapped away Jed's hand and stalked back up to the house. Jed hurried after him.

'What's wrong with that, Casey? I've got some fine fillies, light skinned or dark, clean too. I'm only being polite, dammit.'

Casey tried to close his ears to Jed's remarks, but he couldn't. 'Politeness, be damned. Do you forget I have a wife?' he shouted. 'I'm not a stud to mount your wenches!'

Jed smirked. 'You forget how I met you, boy?'

'By the devil!' Casey clenched his fists in frustration. 'I'm going to get Lucy and we're leaving here!'

Jed's eyes, suddenly hard and threatening, narrowed. His fingers rested on the handle of his pistol. He smiled cruelly. 'No you ain't, Casey,' he said softly through his teeth.

'You ain't never leavin' The Drongos. Never!'

CHAPTER TWELVE

The Drongos, Lucy was told by Martha as they sat together in the upper story parlor on the couch under the large dormer window, dated from 1796. It was in that year that General David Barrow, fleeing from George Washington's army, arrived by boat at Bayou Sara. His confrontation with the flatboat riffraff led him to seek to build his homestead away from that lawless landing place.

General Barrow, although a wealthy judge and business man from Pennsylvania, was an independent cuss and played a prominent part in the Whisky Rebellion of 1794. On his arrival in the bayous, he obtained a Spanish land grant of 650 acres of land from Baron de Corondelet on which to build his home.

The General chose the design best suited to the climate. The rain, the numerous bayous, lakes, swamps and rivers all contributed their moisture to make the area very humid. With short winters and summers that were long and hot, an airy house was needed with comfortable outdoor living space. He built a veranda with a steep, hipped roof of cypress shingles. Inside, there were doors and windows that were interchangeable; on hot days the windows of the downstairs rooms could be removed for breeze to circulate. He planted trees to shade the house.

'The General, my grandfather, was a determined man,' Martha said. 'It took him four years to build The Drongos in this wilderness. It killed him in the end. He died before I was born and my father who had come from Pennsylvania with him, inherited the plantation and the wealth. He bought more land, more slaves, more furniture, married mother, who was a Creole, and gave the house life.'

'Mother landscaped the gardens. She wanted shade but she wanted the wildness of the forest kept away from the house. The Drongos is surrounded by blooming shrubs and flowering magnolia trees because of her. The walk up here from the Bayou Sara is along an avenue of cedars, magnolias and live oaks that she planted.'

'How lovely,' murmured Lucy distractedly. She was still weak from her drugged sleep and had to struggle to match Martha's vivacity.

She had dressed hurriedly in a dress of white jaconet with a loose waist and a corsage finished with a tucker of fine lace. Her stomach seemed to bulge and she felt shy about her shape beside the elegant Martha.

'Daddy loved The Drongos,' Martha said, unaware of Lucy's discomfort. 'He found European craftsmen to improve the decor. They added the plaster frieze work.'

Politely, Lucy raised her eyes to the ceiling where delicate patterns of flowers edged the room.

'The chandeliers are French,' Martha said proudly. 'Crystal.'

'I had no idea your house was so beautiful,' said Lucy uncertainly. 'Only . . .'

'Only what?'

'Don't you feel cut off from everything? It's so isolated.'

Martha smiled and laid her hand on Lucy's. 'No, *sha* ! I grew up here so I'm used to it. We are on the bayous and it's a short way downstream to the landing. From there we have the steamboats to New Orleans or Natchez.'

Lucy was caught up in Martha's enthusiasm. She lost her nervousness while Martha told her of her childhood at The Drongos and how her mother educated her while her father sent Jed to neighboring plantations to learn about cotton, cane and slaves. She heard how Martha's mother had died of the black vomit and how her father had gone into a decline and was drowned in Bayou Sara soon after.

'They say it was an accident,' said Martha, a tear glistening in her eye. 'Maybe it was. But daddy had lost the will to live. That was seven years ago. I came back here three years later to help Jed. 'That's when my husband, the worthless brute, got himself killed in a duel.'

'How exciting! I mean, I'm sorry.' Lucy blushed.

'I wasn't sorry, I can tell you. Not then. Sometimes I miss having my own man . . .' Her voice dropped and Lucy wondered what to say.

'That's enough of me,' Martha said suddenly, her brightness returning, 'What about you? Tell me about that husband of yours. How did you ever meet him?'

'It was in Layou – '

'Yes, I know that. But, I mean, marriage! Imagine!'

'We love each other.' Lucy was puzzled by Martha's tone.

'I can understand that, dear. Don't fret.' Martha squeezed Lucy's hand. 'How many times have I seen a strong, handsome man and longed to possess him!'

'It's not like that with me and Casey.' Lucy withdrew her hand and blushed.

'You are so lucky, my dear. To have such a man as your very own. Do tell me, does it make any difference?'

'What?' Lucy was on the defensive.

'Oh, I don't mean his color. I know about that and the problems you've got. I mean well, you are rather small, aren't you? He's so big, more my size really and one has heard so many things about the *size* of quadroon men.'

Lucy stared with disbelief.

'Is he brutish to you, dear?' Martha's eyes gleamed. 'Isn't he just too passionate and demanding? Not like a white gentleman at all. However do you cope?'

'I don't know . . .' Lucy was close to tears. Martha's remarks had exposed something to her that she had never dared to think of. She caught her breath, deeply ashamed that Martha could speak of such matters.

'You don't know Casey. He's not like that. He's kind and gentle. I've never thought of him as being 'different'.'

'Nonsense, my dear!' Martha moved closer and Lucy saw her cheeks were flushed with excitement. 'I've heard the story of how you and your father found him. It does you credit. Not every woman would do what you did to get the man she's set her heart on. I admire you for it. Oh,' she sighed, 'the *demands* you must suffer.' She shuddered as though thrilled.

'Really! I must go!' Lucy began to rise. 'I feel quite faint. The journey . . .'

There was a loud commotion in the entrance hall. Lucy was grateful for the interruption. She heard the veranda door pulled open and shut with a crash and then someone climbing the stairs, two at a time.

'Oh dear,' said Martha reaching for Lucy's hand and holding it firmly. 'It sounds like Jed is in one of his moods.'

It wasn't Jed who rushed up the stairs into the parlor, but Casey. His eyes blazed with anger and he faltered at the sight of Lucy huddled together with Martha on the couch. He swallowed hard as Martha said good morning and fluttered her eyelashes demurely.

'Casey!' Lucy recovered her poise and rose from the couch, pulling her hand away from Martha's. 'I'm so glad you're here.'

'Why, yes,' said Martha with a smile. 'We were talking about you. Lucy was telling me how gentle you are as a husband.'

Casey's face darkened. He turned from Martha and watched Lucy suspiciously. 'Lucy, I'd like to see you in the bedroom.' He opened the door to their chamber and stood by it.

'Well, I'm sure I don't – '

'Lucy!' His sharp voice cut her off.

'Oh, do as he says,' Martha whispered, gloating. 'Husbands!'

'Will you excuse me?' Lucy was distraught, 'I'm so ashamed.'

'Don't worry , *sha*. I know how it is. We'll talk later. I'm absolutely fascinated.' She turned to Casey. 'You mustn't let Jed upset you, Casey. Don't take what he says too seriously.' She patted her bosom.

'He's a bit stupid sometimes, I know. It's his way. If you have any, er, problems with him, just come to me.' She walked over to him and lowered her voice.

'I'm the one who's responsible for The Drongos, you see. Jed's a little hasty and doesn't always see things in the same light as a sensible person like you or I might do.'

Casey bowed his head curtly and ushered Lucy into the room. He turned back to face Martha.

'You can tell your *brother* ,' he said contemptuously, 'that I'm a man too, and a hot-blooded one. I get my temper from my mother. She was white, you know.' He closed the door, shutting Martha out.

'That's an odd thing to say.' Lucy sat on the bed and covered her eyes. 'What a disgraceful way to behave. You must apologize – '

'Stop that, Lucy!' Casey paced the floor, cracking his knuckles. 'There's something odd about this place. We're going to leave.'

Lucy stared at him. 'When?'

'Now.'

'Don't be silly.'

'We must leave, Lucy. At once.' He strode across to the window and turned back. 'Are you going to get ready?'

'No, I'm not. Even if we have a good reason to go, I'm much too tired. Do you forget the baby?'

'What!' He struck his head with the palm of his hand.

'Casey, what is wrong?' She stood up anxiously. 'What happened?'

He sank into a chair and sighed. 'It's Jed. Now I know why he wanted us here.' He told Lucy about the *garçonnière*. 'He said I can have a wench there. He wants me to be a stud so he can get children out of me by his slave women.'

'Why should you be so rude to Martha?' Lucy sniffed. 'That's traditional planter hospitality, isn't it? Even in Dominica. Daddy told me that whenever he stayed at a plantation for the night, he was offered a slave girl to sleep with him. It's the way slaveholders increase their stock.'

'Lucy!' Casey was shocked. 'How do you know such things?'

'Why shouldn't I know?'

'It's not . . . it's not ladylike.'

Lucy sat at her mirror and touched up her hair. 'I suppose I should be flattered that you've taken umbrage over that. A white man wouldn't, I'm sure. If he had a wife in my condition, he'd be expected to . . . well . . . do something else.'

Casey shook his head. 'I didn't know . . .'

'Well, now you do, so that's that. I want you to apologize to Martha for your boorish behavior. You disgraced me in front of her. I don't know what she'll think.'

'By the devil! Why should we care?'

'Because we're her guests!' Lucy pushed his hand away from her shoulder.

He bit his lip. 'I'm sorry if I want you too. Are you tired of me?'

'No!' Lucy was surprised at the passion in his voice. She lay down the brush and turned to look at him. 'You are my husband. Casey, and I adore you. You must understand that there are times when . . .' She raised her eyebrows seeking help. She patted herself.

'Well, it's obvious, isn't it? I can't feel romantic all the time. Oh!' She decided that tears were the best solution and put her hands to her eyes. 'Oh Casey!'

He backed away and sat down on the bed. 'I'm confused too,' he said. 'It's not so simple, is it?'

'Let's not talk about it any more.' Lucy stopped sobbing and peered into the mirror. 'Martha must be wondering what has happened.'

'Martha!' Casey was about to curse Lucy's perpetual concern for what Martha thought, when another piece of the jigsaw fitted into place.

'Forgive me, Lucy,' he said. He began to see her in a different light. 'I'll conform to the planter's way. No, I don't mean I'm going to service Jed's slaves. I'm going to have proper respect for you. You should have told me before. In your condition . . . I didn't realize.'

'Men don't,' said Lucy, turning and smiling at him.

Casey began to play the part of a gentleman. He apologized for striking Jed who shrugged off the incident under the watchful eye of Martha. He was extra solicitous to Lucy, trying to please her whims, waiting on her at times like a servant, not a husband. He flirted politely, and always in company, with Martha and wondered if the game would become serious. After the first week, when nothing untoward had occurred, he put aside his misgivings stirred by their first night at The Drongos.

He decided to conform to please Lucy. She was enjoying her stay, living in the grand manner with Hilda in constant attendance. So he behaved the way she wanted him to behave. He refused to be provoked by Jed. He was puzzled by the man's changing moods. At times he was morose and at times full of good nature and bonhomie. Casey refrained from comment, although he could not ignore the fact that under the surface of his host's conviviality, there was tension waiting to break out.

As Casey grew familiar with The Drongos house, it lost its air of mystery. The interior, especially the twin parlors, was luxuriously furnished and he found it a pleasure to relax in the deep couches in the evenings. The exterior, whether he was sitting on the veranda gazing out at the trees, or walking in their shade, was cool and peaceful.

The absence of slaves that had so puzzled him on his first morning was explained by Martha. Hilda, she said, had been instructed to keep the slaves, there were only two of them anyway, out of the house so as not to disturb them after their journey.

Hilda, as Casey surmised, ran the house. She commanded with an exemplary firmness the two girls who worked under her. They were quiet, well trained, and a tribute to Hilda's own qualities. The only males Casey saw were a taciturn old man who tended the lawns and a sulky boy who ran errands. The heavy work in the house was done by Hilda who was proud of her strength.

Remembering their first night in the house, Casey was prepared to refuse anything suspicious that Martha offered. No offer was made, either of a nightcap or of intrigue. The four of them spent an abstemious and proper existence, passing days in idleness on the veranda and the evenings in reading to each other or in playing cards for buttons instead of money.

To Casey, it seemed that Jed was making as much effort as he was to conform to a behavior he found unnatural and detested. Casey wondered who would crack first.

Martha controlled them. She suggested what they should do, and Jed always followed her wishes although his enthusiasm depended on his moods. Casey assumed that Martha had reprimanded Jed about the incident at the *garçonnière* because the bachelor retreat was never mentioned.

After adjusting to the social life of a bayou country house, and conducting himself the way Lucy wanted, Casey began to get restless. He noticed that whenever he attempted to walk to the nearby stream, or even to stroll under the trees surrounding the house, either Jed or Martha hurried over to accompany him. It became irksome but he kept his feelings to himself in case Lucy accused him of being surly and ungrateful.

Casey was told that the stream close to the house was the Bayou Celeste and it flowed into the much larger Bayou Sara. When he walked to the banks of the Bayou Celeste with Martha and Lucy one day, he observed a small boat moored there. He was relieved to see it because it was big enough to carry himself and Lucy if they needed to escape.

'Whose boat is that?' he asked.

Martha looked vague. 'Jed's, I suppose.'

'Is it possible to row down to the Bayou Sara from here?' He tried to make the question sound conversational.

'Oh, no! It's too shallow and overgrown with weeds.' Martha was excited. 'There are alligators too,' she added, pretending horror.

Lucy shuddered and Martha changed the conversation, leaving Casey with the impression that she was trying to scare him off. He persisted and asked about the stockade in the forest that he could see from their bedroom window.

Martha shrugged. 'There are a few slaves living there, that's all. The ones who work in the cane.'

'I'd like to go there.'

'It's really of no interest.' Martha's eyes narrowed.

'I could go by myself one day. Where's the path?' Casey was surprised by the hard expression on Martha's face. It made him uneasy, without him knowing why.

'No path,' said Martha too hastily. 'Jed uses the bayou to get there, rowing upstream.'

'I can row. I'd like to go.'

'Ah, unfortunately the boat is being repaired.' Martha fluttered her eyelashes which Casey had come to recognize as her usual reaction when she was lying.

'How can that be? The boat tied up there looks fine.'

'That pirogue would sink under you,' said Martha, eye lashes fluttering again. 'You wouldn't like the alligators to get him, would you, Lucy?'

'Casey, why must you be so . . . so . . .' Lucy sighed in exasperation. 'Oh, I do think I have a headache coming on.'

'I'm sorry, Lucy.' Casey was at her side immediately, as he always was when Lucy complained, which seemed to be often. 'Would you like to lie down?'

'Yes, yes, that would be nice. Take me back to the house.'

When they were in the bedroom and the door was closed behind them, Casey asked Lucy if he could get her anything.

'No, of course not. Stop fussing, for heaven's sake.'

'I thought you had a headache.'

'Well, I don't! But I ought to have with all the trouble you're making for Martha. Fancy questioning her like that. As though you think's she's not telling the truth.'

'Well, is she?'

Lucy stamped her foot. 'I had to say I had a headache to stop you being so rude. Don't you know it's not polite for a guest to ask white folks if you can see their slave quarters? Martha was trying to put you off tactfully without causing offence, but you barged on regardless.'

Casey stared at her. Lucy's criticism was that of a stranger to him. Was this Martha's influence on her? The two of them spent hours each day together in Martha's boudoir in a cosy tête à tête on the couch in the parlor, or gossiping and giggling on the veranda. At first, Casey had been grateful for Martha's interest in Lucy but now he realized it was causing him to lose touch with her.

'I wasn't thinking, Lucy,' he said, advancing toward her and holding out his arms to embrace her. 'I was curious, that's all.' He expected her to put her arms around his neck when he apologized.

Instead, she clucked her tongue irritably, brushed his arms aside and walked away from him to the window. 'Don't you ever think of anyone but yourself?' she said. 'Why do you want to hold me all the time? How do you think I feel?'

Casey shook his head. 'I can't believe what I'm hearing.' He gulped. 'Am I repulsive to you?'

'No,' she said. 'That's typical of your arrogance to misunderstand me. I just don't want you pawing and grasping me all the time. It's . . . well, it's not how white folks behave.'

'I'm not white folks, Lucy. I never have been.'

'Yes, yes you are. Most of you, anyway. If you wanted to behave like a respectable white gentleman, you could. You know that! Instead, you want to shame me with your lust and your curiosity about other people's slaves. It's all so . . . so humiliating!' She burst into tears, holding her head in her hands.

'Damn!' she cried, shocking him. 'I do have a headache. You've made me feel wretched, Casey.'

He looked at her from the centre of the room, wondering what to do. If he tried to hold her, she would condemn him for being too passionate. If he walked out of the room she'd say he was selfish in leaving her. Her peevishness baffled him. And where had she got all those new notions and language from?

The door opened. Maybe he didn't hear the knock. Martha swept in.

'Oh, Lucy , *sha* ! Don't cry.' Martha hugged her to her bosom, glancing over Lucy's head at Casey and giving him a sympathetic, conspiratorial wink. 'The baby,' she mouthed by way of explanation, then she waved him out of the room.

Casey wandered down the stairs. Jed was nowhere to be seen and the vast parlors offered no comfort for his mood of dejection. He avoided the open door to the front gallery and headed, instead, for the back of the house. The veranda at the back overlooked a lawn and a pond surrounded by willows. It was a soothing sight for his troubled mind and he stepped off the veranda to cross the grass, conscious that it was the first time since his arrival at The Drongos that he had been alone in the grounds.

The sun was low in the sky at his left and cast long shadows from the willows over the three wooden cabins at the eastern side. The aroma of baking wafted over the grass from one of them, and he changed his course to see who was there.

'Lor', Mas Casey!' said Hilda when he put his head through the open door of her cabin and sniffed hungrily. 'What yo' doin' here?' She rubbed her hands on her apron and challenged him with her eyes.

'Please don't scold me as well,' he said with a rueful grin. 'I've had enough for one day.' He looked around the cabin and realized it was The Drongos kitchen.

'I remember how I used to visit our cook when I was a boy and had troubles. She wasn't as good as you, Hilda, but Uraline sure knew how to cheer me up!'

'Fie, Mas Casey! Yo' axin' fo' dat!' Hilda moved toward the door and stood with her arms akimbo facing him. She only reached up to the shoulder and her bulky face shook with indignation.

'Ah bin watching yo', Mas Casey, an' ah wonder what yo' is?' Casey sighed and turned away.

'No! Yo' come back here an' listen to what ah hab to say.' Hilda glanced across the lawn to the house. 'Mas Jed down by de bayou.' she said, putting her hand out and holding Casey by his arm and pulling him back into the cabin.

'Yo' sit dere,' She said, pushing him down on a stool. 'Now ah bigger dan yo' so ah don' wan' no lip.'

Casey smiled warily. 'Is this the way you bully the slaves?'

'Slaves!' Hilda threw up her hands. 'Don't yo' know what de Drongos does be?'

'No, I don't.' He sat up, alert now.

'Yo' don' care?' Hilda was flummoxed.

'Yes, I care, but I don't know what you're talking about.'

'Yo' come here actin' like a white man, but yo' ain'. Yo' got yourself a white woman an' fine clothes but yo' got good niggah breedin' in yo', boy, ah know dat. An' yo' ain' happy!' Hilda held up her hand in case he protested. 'Ah see yo' strike Mas Jed an' he ain' done yo' not'in'. Dat ain' right.' Her jowls quivered and she shook her fists in his face.

'What are you trying to tell me, Hilda?'

She snorted. 'Yo' done strike Jed, but where yo' spunk? Yo' ain' neber ax yo'self'bou' yo' own kin at de Drongos?'

'My kin?' Casey shifted uncomfortably. 'I've got no kin here.'

Hilda grunted. 'Yo' see, yo' done fo'get yo' blood. Why don' yo' ax 'bou' de Drongos slaves?'

He shrugged his shoulders. 'When I do, my wife says I'm being troublesome.'

'Yo' scared yo' wife? Yo' scared Jed Barrow?' Hilda turned away from him contemptuously but her question made him sit up and square his shoulders.

'No,' he said tentatively. 'No, I ain't.' He spoke bolder the second time as some of his old confidence seemed to rush back to his veins.

'Dat good, dat good!' Hilda bent down and opened the door to the brick oven. She peered in.

The aroma of freshly baked bread filled the kitchen and stirred a feeling of yearning in Casey. It took him back to the days of his youth in Dominica when he was the boy every one admired, when he walked through the village with the swagger of a man who was heir to the Bondmaster. When he was afraid of no one.

He rose to his feet and gripped Hilda by her shoulder. turning her around so she faced him. He gazed at her careworn face and her rheumy, yellow eyes.

'What is it I must do?' he asked, sensing destiny.

Hilda smiled, satisfied. 'Be here at midnight.' She took a cleaver from a hook on the wall by the fireplace and pressed the handle into his hand.

'If Jed follows you, kill him.'

CHAPTER THIRTEEN

The Drongos at night was as somber as a sepulcher. There was no sound, no flambeau; and no slaves sleeping on the floor across the threshold of the veranda door. The very silence of the house was intimidating; no one snored, no bed creaked, no rats scurried across the polished boards of the wooden floor.

Casey had no difficulty in leaving the bedroom without waking Lucy. Since he slept on the floor, she wasn't disturbed. He walked carefully through the house, feeling his way in the total darkness. The cleaver he clutched in his hand gave him assurance against the unknown.

The door to the back veranda was open and he wondered at the folly of Martha and Jed in sleeping in an unlocked house. Insurrections of slaves had occurred throughout the South and many slaveholders lived in fear. He left the door ajar and stepped lightly across the deck of the veranda where he paused.

The moon was almost full, adding to the ghostly appearance of the house by casting shadows over it from the surrounding trees. Casey sniffed the night air and sighed with relief. It was humid and musty with the odor of the undergrowth and creeks. There was no scent of humans.

Casey was barefooted and wore old breeches and a silk shirt. He stepped onto the lawn and gazed up at the moon. He was at ease in darkness and moved swiftly, keeping to the shadows, toward Hilda's kitchen.

For the first time in months he felt completely free; no Lucy to tend, no slave whip to fear, no social pitfalls to avoid. He was bursting with enthusiasm when he reached the kitchen. The door was closed and it was in darkness. He stood silently at the side of the cabin and listened.

He heard the rasp of heavy breathing and grinned. Hilda was

outside the cabin too, waiting for him. 'I see you,' he whispered.

A dark shape that could have been a shrub in the dark beside the cabin lumbered to its feet. 'Dat good, dat good,' Hilda said hoarsely. 'Ah don' see yo' til yo' get here.'

She opened the door noiselessly and ushered him in. The cabin was in darkness except for the glow of embers from the hearth. She shut the door.

'Shuck off yo' britches.' Her voice was soft, close to his ear.

'What?'

'Cas,' she said, touching his hand and taking the cleaver from him. 'Yo' got to do what ah tell yo' dis night, o' we done fo'.'

'Why do you want me naked?' he whispered back to her.

'Don' ax no questions!' She slapped him on his buttock. 'Come on, boy!' She sounded impatient.

Wondering if he had been lured to the cabin by Hilda as a ruse to get him to pleasure her, Casey reluctantly rolled down his breeches with Hilda fumbling to help him. He kicked them off and stood naked in front of her. She brushed her hand up his thigh and her fingers closed over him.

'Ah declah!' she said, slobbering. 'Dat good niggah breedin' in trut'.' She released him and thrust a piece of material in his hands. It was osnaburg, a species of coarse duck worn by slaves.

'Slip on dis pant,' she said.

Casey pulled on the slave garment. He had been roused by the touch of her warm, moist fingers and was oddly flattered by her remark. It was a contrast to the put-downs he had been accustomed to from Lucy. The rough material of the pants served to aggravate his condition.

'De shirt,' said Hilda, chuckling greedily when she touched him again.

He exchanged his silk shirt for one of the same material as the pants. It was torn and dirty and stank of another's sweat. He saw Hilda move across the cabin to the fire and crouch down in front of it. She put her hands into the ashes under the grate, then crossed the cabin back to him. Reaching up, she wiped her dirty palms over his face and into his hair, ruffling it. He felt the warm ash sticking to his skin.

'Dere, now, yo' does look like a Drongo's buck,' she said proudly. 'Dirty like one, an' ranky too.'

'These are slave clothes, Hilda . . .'

She clucked her tongue impatiently. 'Sure dey are. Dat's what yo' does be.'

Casey flinched. 'I ain't –'

'Hush yo' voice, boy, an' foller me.' Hilda opened the door carefully so it didn't scrape on the floor, and peered out. She waited, her hand on Casey's chest to halt him, then relaxed when she judged it was all right to move. She waddled into the night and Casey followed, his mind burning with questions.

The dark under the trees was complete. He was forced to take Hilda's hand so as not to lose her. She moved with an easy familiarity, guiding him behind the cabins and through the ornamental trees into the forest. They entered a path too narrow for them to walk side by side. Brambles snagged Casey's body, scratching his bare legs. Branches caught in his hair while mosquitoes buzzed in his ears. After fifteen minutes forcing their way through the undergrowth Hilda paused.

Casey sighed with relief and realized how out of condition he was.

'Yo' come too soft,' Hilda whispered astutely, nudging him in his waist. He noticed the tension had gone out of her voice. 'Fancy livin' ain' no good for a niggah.'

He nodded his agreement but she couldn't see his face. 'It's nice, though, Hilda,' he said, squeezing her hand.

'Lor'!' Hilda was hoarse. 'Now ain' de time!'

'Where are we going?'

'Yo' see. Hush now.' She started off again, walking at a slower pace. The path was leading down an incline and Casey guessed they were going to the bayou. He wondered if this was Hilda's secret path or a regular one. Judging by the obstructions, it wasn't used very often. Hilda stopped again.

'Don' speak to no one, yo' hear,' she said sternly.

'Hilda, why don't you tell me what this is all about?'

'Yo'll see soon enough!' A thought occurred to her. 'Lor', ah fo'get. Yo' don' tell yo' mistis yo' comin'?'

'No, of course not.'

'An' no one see yo'?'

'I doubt it. The house was so quiet and I made no noise. The veranda door was open and I left it that way.'

'Dat good, dat good,' Hilda grunted with relief. 'Ah done leab de door open. It does squeak awful an' yo' got to go back de same way.' She thought again. 'Miz Mart'a does be sleepin'?'

'How should I know? I don't even know which is her chamber and which is Jed's. She seems to use both.'

'Aye.' Hilda was quiet, the silence feeding Casey's imagination. Gradually, he realized that Hilda had left him. He was impresed how she had moved away without him knowing. Did she want him to wait, or to follow?

He listened carefully, his ears sharpened by the danger. The ground was squelching under his feet and he hunkered down to relieve his discomfort. As his ears became accustomed to the burble of the night creatures in the trees around him, he picked up the sound of the bayou's languid flowing. There was a muffled voice and he tensed, wishing he had a weapon.

Hilda was at his side again. 'One ob de drongos is at de end ob de pat'. Don' worry, ah tell he yo' ma buck from Rosedown an' he gwine let yo' pass.'

'What's a drongo?' Casey couldn't resist asking. 'I thought it was the name of the house.'

Hilda seized his face in her fingers and squeezed. 'Yo' sure is mighty white wid yo' q'estions. De drongos is de black birds what guard de slaves. Dey can't talk an' dey strong like ox so dey gwine kill yo' if yo' say one mo' word. If!'

Casey recalled the mute blacks with the superb physique who had accompanied them from Bayou Sara. He had not seen them since, nor had he been able to find out anything about them from Martha and Jed.

He crept along behind Hilda, his curiosity overcoming his annoyance at the damp, the mosquitoes, and the way he was being treated by the cook. She stopped again, and he became aware of another shape beside her.

Suddenly, hands wer on him, feeling his own hands, his chest, his waist and touching his crotch. Now he knew why Hilda had taken the cleaver from him. He smelled the stench of the man and was about to protest when he moved away and let him pass.

They were at the bayou. The creek was narrow and the water moved sluggishly. Casey took a deep breath, relishing the freshness of the night air after the confines of the bush trail. He peered around him and became aware of other shapes squatting on the bank.

Hilda tugged at his pants and he sat down on his haunches beside her. She placed a warning finger on his lips and he grinned, nodding his head to show he understood. If all the men around him had their tongues cut out, Casey did not intend to draw attention to himself by speaking. He had a feeling that his own tongue might be sliced out if he did.

It was obvious that the slaves were waiting for something. There was a clearing in the bank below them where a boy stood holding a flambeau. It was shaded by the bushes and only a flickering light shone on the scene. Casey and Hilda were outside its glow. The boy was about sixteen and naked, his dark body glistening under the torchlight. His eyes were on the bayou, staring intently downstream.

A collective sigh and a rustling sound of expectancy passed through the waiting slaves when the boy dipped the flambeau to the water and raised it again. Twice more the torch flamed and fell, and then Casey heard the sound of oars. There was another noise too, and it made his heart lurch. He reached for Hilda's hand and clung to it fiercely, praying he wouldn't shout.

Hilda sensed the chill of horror that gripped him. She raised her free hand to the back of his neck and stroked him soothingly. He calmed under her touch.

The tongueless blacks rose up like swamp birds at the dreadful sound. They surrounded the naked boy at the bayou side. Hilda eased back into the bush that concealed the two of them, drawing Casey with her. The blacks touched their flambeaux to the boy's torch and the bayou was ablaze with light. The sound swelled.

It was the desperate whimpering cry of humans in bondage; of men and women wailing helplessly. It was a noise that Casey had hoped never to hear again, the cries of men and women captured and tortured into slavery, rooted from their homes and families and plunged into nights of terror on a journey to a strange land.

It was the chilling scream of the newly enslaved, shocked and disoriented, that resounded along the bayou. It echoed in a long, low moan of raw fear, from bank to bank in the tunnel of overhanging trees and thick undergrowth.

Casey looked at Hilda in astonishment as first one pirogue, then another and another, floated into the glare of the torches. The naked boy lodged his torch in the fork of a tree and pulled the first canoe to the shore. The oarsmen rested while the drongos slaves swarmed around and hauled the boat's passengers to their feet.

They came slowly, terrified and confused. Iron chains clinked as they were hustled onto the shore. They cowered down with fear but the slave guards kicked and punched them back onto their feet. The first negro in the coffle was slapped by a slave until he understood that he should move along the trail by the bayou bank. He moved slowly, dragging his leg shackled to the chain that bound him to the others.

Casey felt the fear of the negroes as the coffle filed past the bush where he and Hilda were hiding. He longed to rush out and thrash the drongo guards for beating these new slaves but the helplessness of it restrained him. He could only gape at the horror, made more hideous by the callous way the dumb drongos did their job. They pushed and punched with ruthless efficiency, their animalistic grunts mingling with the cries of the slaves.

Casey counted thirty captives, women and men. They all wore loose shifts sticking to their bodies in the humid night heat, stained with mud, blood and excrement. They were thin, pitiful creatures, stumbling along the path chained to each other.

As each of the pirogues discharged its slave cargo, the oarsmen turned it skillfully in the narrow bayou and paddled downstream with the current. Casey recalled how Martha had said this bayou was impassable. He watched dumbfounded with anger while the last captive was beaten along the path by the drongos and all the torches, except one, were removed by the guards.

He sighed heavily, realizing now how completely he had been deceived by Martha and Jed.

The naked boy at the bayou bank removed the last flambeau from the crotch of the tree and held it above his head, looking up the path carefully. Satisfied that no one remained, he spat into the creek, scratched himself, then squatted on the ground to pee. He gazed around the glade, his eyes falling on the bush that sheltered Casey and Hilda.

'Hah!' he grunted without fear. He stood up and sauntered over to the bush.

'Who dere?' He thrust his torch forward, waving it to indicate that he had seen them. 'Come out, yo' bossal!'

'Lor', Parry, we ain' no bossals.' Hilda kept her voice low and calm. She tugged Casey to his feet.

'Hilda?' The boy was puzzled. He glanced briefly at Casey then back to the cook. 'Wha' yo' dwine here?'

His voice was shrill and it was a relief to Casey that this boy wasn't dumb like all the other guards. He was well built, with the thick thighs of a bush negro and the burgeoning chest of a warrior. His skin gleamed and his youthful face was pleasant and friendly.

'Come to see de new stock, Parry. Dis be Casey.'

Hilda hesitated, perhaps wondering if she could trust the boy. 'He avistin' me from Rosedown.'

The boy's eyes widened. 'Rosedown? Dat de bigges' plantation in St Francisville! Yo' famous, Hilda.'

She chuckled, cuffing the boy none too gently on his cheek. 'Yo' go on now, Parry. We got something to do.'

The boy grinned knowingly and his penis danced in the torch glow.

'Come to de kitchen tomorrer an' ah gib yo' clabber.'

'Oh yeah, Hilda! Ah's yo' man when yo' tire ob de Rosedown niggah.' He pulled himself to show her his length, whooped with delight, and took off along the track after the coffle.

'Yo' can t'ank de Lor' dat Parry de marker tonight. He ma sister's get, born an' bred in de bayou. Mas Jed ain' tongued he yet.' Hilda moved along the trail behind the youth without waiting to see if Casey was following.

The path was wide and well cleaned although the mud was slippery after so many people had passed along it. Casey kept close to Hilda wishing she had told him about Rosedown in case someone else questioned his presence.

Ahead, through the trees, was the glow of the flambeaux staked out in a circle and the noise of white men shouting directions. Casey was relieved by the sound of voices after the moans of the captives and the monstrous grunting of the dumb drongos. Hilda stepped off the trail and pulled him with her.

They were in a thicket outside the stockade he had glimpsed from the bedroom window. The stakes of the fence were tall so he shifted his position for a better view through the open gates into the compound.

A white man stood by the gate tallying the slaves as they were ushered through by the drongo squad. Flambeaux had been placed around the palisade and Casey saw clearly the thirty slaves hunkered down in a dejected group in the center. They were tired and drained of resistance but the drongos circled them watchfully.

'Dey come from Baratarie,' whispered Hilda. 'Smuggled ashore and brought here by night along de bayous. Second shipment of bossals dis year.'

'What's a bossal?'

'Ah,' Hilda chuckled softly. 'Wondered when yo' begin axin'!' There was a lot of activity in the compound so there was little danger of them being overheard, yet Hilda kept her voice low. 'A bossal be a slave from Africa.'

'They can't be from Africa!' Casey was almost shouting and Hilda held up a warning finger. He lowered his voice. 'The slave trade's been abolished for years. No slaves come from Africa now.'

'Does do.'

'How?'

'Ah tellin' yo'. Dey ship dem to Baratarie an' Mas Jed buy dem when he goes to Nuorleans. De drongos lead dem here t'rough de swamps an' bayous an' nobody don' know. Mas Jed smart.' She sounded proud.

'What does he do with them? I haven't seen many slaves around the house or in the yard.'

'Do?' Hilda rolled her eyes up in exasperation. 'He season dem den sells dem to de factor. Dis ain' a sugar plantation, Casey. It does be a slave station to supply de sout' wid niggahs.'

The boy Parry was going through the coffle telling the slaves to stand up. Those who didn't were dragged to their feet by the drongos. The white man who had counted them in, strolled over to the house that dominated the stockade. Another white man came out at his call and stood on the gallery and gazed across at the slaves.

'Mas Jed,' breathed Hilda, crouching lower although it was impossible for her to be seen in the dark.

Casey stared, his eyes on someone standing behind Jed. The person was keeping in the shadows and wore breeches and a wide frock coat that did not quite conceal the splendid curves of its very feminine shape. Casey blinked and stared again.

'That's Martha!' he said in surprise. 'What's she doing here?'

Hilda ignored his question and dug him in his ribs to keep khim quiet.

Jed strolled over to the slaves and began to inspect each one, accompanied by the white man and Parry. He had a whip in his hand and used the handle to lift the penises of the men, or to thrust between the legs of the women.

He seemed leery of getting too close to the slaves and his examination was cursory. He issued instructions to the white man and sauntered back to the veranda. Parry walked at his side and Casey saw Jed put his hand on the boy's shoulder. He rubbed his hand slowly down the boy's back and patted his bare buttocks.

Casey stirred angrily.

'Don' worry 'bou' de boy, Cas. Parry smart. He gwine do what Mas Jed tells he so he can keep his tongue. If he don', he become one mo' dumb drongo.'

Jed whispered something in Parry's ear, tweaking his penis as he did so. The boy nodded and trotted off, out of the compound toward the bayou.

'He gwine bade.' Hilda stood up. 'Yo' better come wid me nuh, befo' Mas Jed return to de house.'

Casey glanced at the stockade again. Martha was leaning against the balustrade surveying the slaves as they were unchained. They were being escorted one by one by the drongos to the windowless huts that formed one side of the compound.

He shook his head in sorrow. 'What's going to happen to them?'

Hilda sighed. 'Ah tell yo' dat a'ready, Cas. Mas Jed gwine bran' dem, an' Ruffin, he de oversee', gwine to season dem. Some dey neuter, some dey tongue, an' some dey 'pregnate wid de breedin' bucks.'

Casey shuddered, seeing there what Jed planned for him. 'What's Martha doing here?' he asked again. 'Is she involved too?'

'Mistis Mart'a?' Hilda cast a glance of pity at him. 'She de owner ob de Drongos, de house, de guards, de slaves, Parry, me, every-t'ing.' She paused and looked him straight in his eyes.

'She gwine own yo', Cas boy, 'less yo' 'scape befo' she 'duce yo' too.'

CHAPTER FOURTEEN

Casey's impulse when he returned to his bedroom was to wake Lucy and tell her what he had seen and get her to flee with him. Yet as he stood over her in the darkness, he hesitated. He would need to plan their escape properly; he would need a boat and help to evade the drongos. So, instead of disturbing her, he lay down on the floor where he had become acustomed to sleep, and spent the rest of the night considering what he had seen and what he should do. He slept fitfully. When the gray light of dawn filtered into the room, he awoke. His first task was to remove the filthy slave garments Hilda had made him wear, and clean off the mud from his body. He pulled off the shirt and torn breeches, wrapped a piece of towel around his waist, and padded softly from the room.

For white people, he had discovered, bathing was not a frequent occurrence. Lucy was content to have a bath in a tub filled with buckets of heated water about once a month. He liked to bathe every day, not in a tub of hot water like the whites, but in a free flowing stream, cool and clean, or with a pail of water hauled up from a well and tipped over his body from head to toe.

The house was still when he made his way down the stairs to the veranda. He did not know if Jed and Martha had returned from receiving their new slaves. He moved stealthily so as not to disturb them if they were at home. He usually bathed in the late afternoon in the waters of the Bayou Celeste where it passed close to the house.

The vague light was strengthening slowly when he eased open the door onto the front veranda and slipped out. He stood by the wrought iron balustrade and stretched, forcing his arms upward as high as they would go, closing his eyes and yawning deeply. He relaxed and peered out at the gray morning.

One of the live oaks, a massive tree whose boughs spread almost to the house and were draped with festoons of Spanish moss like a lady in a fringed lace shawl, moved. He looked at it again. Its huge trunk was still in darkness and for a moment it seemed to be breathing as its dark silhouette expanded slightly then assumed its normal shape.

Casey sniffed. His acute sense of smell picked out the odor of a man mingling with the bog smells of the bayou and trees. Hilda had told him, to support her contention that he was himself a captive of Martha and Jed, that the drongos guarded the house at night. The opening of the front door must have alerted one of them.

Now was a good time to test whether Hilda was right. If it came to a scrap with a drongo guard, Casey was ready. He swung off the veranda and strolled easily across the grass toward the bayou. He was aware of a black shape, darker than the rest of the dawn, shadowing him. He breathed deeply as he walked, tasting the air of freedom. He had been a captive before and now he valued highly what previously he had expected would always be his by right.

For all his bravado, Casey had no doubt that Jed and Martha, if they were determined, could hold him. The Drongos plantation was too isolated. There were no neighboring plantation house and the nearest town was the lawless Bayou Sara. Furthermore, he realized with an unhappy insight into his situation, no one in New Orleans knew that he and Lucy had gone off with Jed and Martha.

He stood in despair on the bank of the bayou, aware that the drongo who was trailing him would have an opportunity to see what he was doing. The water looked black and uninviting; he knew it would be cool and would dash the fatigue from his body. He longed for a clear head so he could plan what to do. He loosened the towel and let it fall to his ankles. He stepped carefully into the water, testing his footing in the soft mud and leaves of the bed of the stream.

His presence worried the birds in the overhanging trees and they shrilled with alarm. He dived, luxuriating in the water chilling his body. When he surfaced, the birds had calmed and a dark figure stood on the bank, his naked body outlined against the rising dawn.

The black youth – Casey couldn't see his face – was watching him curiously. Then he was in the water, swimming with powerful strokes toward him. Casey stood in four feet of water when the negro emerged behind him.

The youth placed his hands on Casey's shoulders. He began to rub vigorously, using his fingers to massage his back and splash water over him. Not a word was spoken. The youth took Casey's arms in his firm hands and scrubbed them thoroughly. He rubbed his chest clean, murmuring at the lash scars, and made Casey raise his legs so he could wash them too. Finally, he ducked Casey's head under the water, scrubbing the ash from his hair and face.

Casey bobbed up, grinning and relaxed. The youth smiled back at him.

The surface of the slow moving stream was shining in the dawn light. Casey had recognized the boy when he slipped into the water after him. He put his hand on his shoulder, splashing water on to his chest. The boy shook his head and moved away.

Casey understood. He had been washed and groomed by the boy as a vestige of an African tradition they both knew by instinct. The boy was showing his subordinance to him; Casey could not reciprocate.

They waded together to the bank. The youth scrambled up and then held out his hand to help Casey. Casey took it and climbed on to the bank. He shook himself and wiped the water off his body with his hands. The boy did the same thing.

'Ah knew yo' weren' no Rosedown niggah!' The boy laughed softly.

Casey shrugged his shoulders, content to let his new friend explain.

'Hilda tell me 'bou' yo'. Ah come to de house to watch fo' yo'.'

'Jed didn't do anything to you . . .?' Casey wasn't sure how to ask such a delicate question. He liked the boy. His blackness was that of a thoroughbred with a skin that shone like dark velvet. His face was eager, his smile dazzling and his eyes blazed with a fervor that his existence as a slave hadn't dimmed.

'No!' The boy chuckled again and thumped Casey on his chest in a gesture of scorn.

'Hilda tell me yo' burstin' wid anger when yo' see Mas Jed touch me.' It amused the boy. 'He can touch me all he wants but Mistis Martha ain' gwine let him do mo' dan dat!'

Casey reached for his towel but the boy was quicker. He picked it up and passed it to him.

'Mistis Martha powerful possessive,' the boy said.

'Of you or of Jed?'

'Me?' The boy was baffled. 'She a virtuous lady, Casey. She don' pester wid slaves. Only Jed.'

'He's her brother.' Casey tied the towel around his waist. 'That's not virtuous.'

'He's white.' The boy picked up his own breech cloth and wrapped it around his loins, fastening it with a piece of cord. He glanced toward the house and was evidently satisfied. He turned back to Casey.

'Hilda say yo' not happy here. She t'ink Jed got some plan to sell yo'. Ah don' know. If yo' need help yo' can trus' me an' Hilda. No one else. De swamp niggahs don' like outsiders.'

'Why should you help me? You're Jed's favorite. If you cross him he'll cut out your tongue.'

'Ah wan' yo' to take me wid yo'.'

The boy's eyes, so full of trust and faith, held Casey's. The effect was devastating, making Casey feel ashamed at his lack of faith and confidence in himself.

'I'll try,' he said, inspired by the boy's childlike trust.

'I'll be yo' slave,' the boy grinned. 'As long as yo' want me, an' when yo' don't, yo' can gib me to yuh chil'un.'

It was Casey's turn to laugh. 'I haven't got any yet.' With a pang of guilt he thought of Lucy alone in the bedroom. If she woke and found him gone from his place on the floor, she would be alarmed.

'How can I meet you again?' he asked, glancing at the house.

'Tell Hilda yo' wan' Tissa an' ah come.'

'I thought your name was Parry?'

'Dat ma slave name, Parry Barrow, 'cause Mas Jed has my title deed. But ma real name, ma Afycan name, is Tissa.'

Daylight filtered through the trees and Casey was worried about getting back to the house. He didn't want to meet Martha or Jed on the stairs. He gripped the boy firmly on his shoulders.

'I must prepare Lucy, my wife. I'll tell you when. Can you get a boat?'

Tissa nodded.

'Then leave the rest to me,' Casey said, more confidently then he actually felt. 'Thank you, Tissa.' He squeezed the boy's arm.

Tissa shrugged his shoulders. 'Go in through de back door an' up de back stairs,' he said as Casey moved away. 'Dey be sleepin' still.'

Despite Tissa's friendship and Hilda's good nature, Casey wondered if he was caught in an elaborate attempt to dupe him. Lucy's reaction when he returned from the creek and told her what had happened, was scornful. She sipped the coffee the slave girl had brought her, sitting up in bed and staring at him.

'What does it matter if Jed has a slave farm?' she said. 'That's what Roxborough was. It doesn't involve us.'

'He and Martha might try to keep us here.'

Lucy grimaced and put down her cup. 'Jed and Martha? Don't be silly!' She frowned at the taste of the coffee, and maybe at him.

'Look, Casey,' she said, sounding tired. 'I'm having a lovely rest here. When our ship is ready, Martha will tell us and we'll go back to New Orleans and get on it and sail away to England. Why can't you relax too and enjoy yourself?' She yawned and turned her head to the wall while he gazed anxiously out of the window.

Heavy storm clouds, gray with menace, were bunching up on the horizon, threatening the weak sun. The stockade was barely visible in the distance. It was in shadow, and there was no sign of movement. The vast Mississippi lay like a ribbon wrapped around the package of swamp and forest waiting for the rain to fall. A feather of smoke drifted across the darkening sky from the kitchen where Hilda was baking biscuits for breakfast.

Casey finished dressing but Lucy didn't stir. He left the room without speaking to her, trying not to show that he was offended by her ridicule. It struck him as ironic that he seemed to have a greater rapport with his new friend, the boy Tissa, and with Hilda, than he did with his own wife.

He was surprised to find Martha in the parlor downstairs. She was dressed in a rose-colored gown, her long black hair tied up in a chignon. She smiled at him brightly.

'Don't go away, Casey.'

'I don't want to disturb you.' In actual fact, Casey didn't want to speak to Martha at all. He backed out of the room.

'Wait, Casey. This is a perfect opportunity for us to have a little chat.' She smiled again, her face radiant. She showed no sign of having spent half the night in a slave barracoon.

'It's about Lucy,' she said.

Casey returned slowly. Outside, the sun had given up trying to shine and retreated behind the encroaching clouds. The parlor was plunged in gloom. He sat, not in the couch as Martha suggested, but in a chair opposite her on the other side of the room. He studied her warily.

The slimness of her neck was startling and she held her head at such a graceful angle that he gasped at her beauty. The loveliness of her delicately pale complexion was accentuated by dark eyes that glimmered at him with a measured sultriness. Her lips, the light red shade of a hibiscus flower, were slightly parted. Her hands were clasped in her lap, showing the fine bone structure of fingers that could be regarded as exquisite. Her bosom rose and fell with a slight exaggeration that monopolized his attention.

He sat straight backed, his hands clenched and resting on his thighs. 'What about Lucy?' he asked, his voice cracking.

'Oh, Casey!' Martha laughed. 'I know you don't like us very much. You've had a stupid disagreement with Jed and you seem to regard me as some kind of the worst wanton.' She fluttered her eyelashes to convey how wrong he was.

'I want to be a friend to you, Casey, I really do. I think you're absolutely charming, sensitive and intelligent and know you're wealthy. What a devastating combination! Lucy is lucky to have such a wonderful husband.'

Martha paused and leaned forward. The heart-shaped corsage of her low-cut gown opened to reveal the brim of her firm, inviting breasts. Casey swallowed nervously.

'Please don't think I'm prying, Casey. I'm talking as a friend of Lucy's, if you won't accept me as your friend.' She rose from the couch and walked toward Casey. She stood behind his chair and laid her hand on his arm. 'My dear, is everything all right between you and Lucy?'

He shifted in his seat, uncomfortably aware that Martha's bosom was level with his left ear and pressing down.

'No, don't answer!' she said, suddenly sweeping away across the room to her couch. She had succeeded in disconcerting him and he sat wondering what was coming next.

'You have to excuse Lucy. If she seems off-hand one minute and loving the next, it's only a phase she's going through. Try to be kinder to her, Casey, more considerate. Be patient until the baby is born, then she'll be like the Lucy you married.'

'Thank you.' He stood up, not giving her the satisfaction of seeing how annoyed she had made him. He was tired of hectoring women, especially one masquerading as a lady but who controlled a barracoon of smuggled slaves.

He turned away from her as the rain began to fall with a roar, its fury drawing a curtain of water across the front of the veranda. It streamed down relentlessly, bringing relief to the oppressive atmosphere in the house.

'Damn!' said Martha. 'I hope Jed doesn't get wet.'

'Where is he?' Casey kept his voice steady, curious as to what lie she would use in reply.

'At the barracoon. Some new slaves arrived last night.'

Casey spun around as though she had hit him. 'You admit that?'

'Why ever not?' She looked at him oddly. 'Thirty head. Not bad stock after we've fed and trained them. Cost a packet of money with the price rising every day.' She paused, misinterpreting his expression of astonishment.

'I'm sorry Casey, you wouldn't want to hear about my business.'

'I do, I do.' He scratched his head. 'So The Drongos is a stock farm, is it?'

'Well . . .' She smiled in a deprecating way. 'I'd like it to be but I can't get the nigras to breed. Jed's tried everything, even studding them himself.' She stood up.

'I don't want to bore you with such matters, Casey. You and Lucy are here to relax before you go to England. You'll soon be away from our silly ways where we think the price of a slave is more important than literature or politics.'

'What . . .!' Casey was stunned. Where he had suspected he was a captive in the midst of mystery and intrigue, there was none. He decided to test Martha's sincerity.

'We want to have two weeks in New Orleans before we sail,' he said blandly. 'I think we should leave here right away. Tomorrow at first light.'

'Oh dear,' said Martha. 'So soon?' She walked over to the escritoire and opened it with the key she kept on a silver chain around her waist. 'Let me see where I put that sailing notice.'

She delved through the papers rolled together in a pigeonhole. 'Ah yes.' She read quickly. 'My goodness, the sailing is in ten days' time. You certainly must leave tomorrow.'

'That's all right?'

'Why do you sound so surprised? Of course it is.' Her eyelashes swooped up and down like the fluttering wings of a humming bird. 'I'll arrange my nigras to row you to Bayou Sara in the morning.'

The rain drummed on the veranda steps, splashing on to the deck. Hilda bustled into the parlor and began to close the windows as the curtains billowed in the wind. One of the slave girls helped her.

Martha stared out at the rain, her face puckered in a moue of disappointment. 'Jed will miss breakfast,' she said.

'Mas Jed gwine be stuck a' de 'coon 'til noon,' Hilda said emphatically. 'Dis rain settlin' in fo' de duration.'

'Will you go for Lucy?' said Martha. Casey was lost in thought. 'Or shall I? She must be frightened all alone upstairs in this storm.'

Casey raised his head hastily and left the room, leaping up the staircase two steps at a time. He flung open the door to the bedroom. 'Lucy!' he shouted. 'Everything is all right!' He looked at the bed. It was empty.

He glanced around the room. 'Are you there, Lucy?' he said, advancing on the brocade covered screen behind which she dressed. There was no answer.

'Come on, Lucy, don't play games. It's breakfast time.' He peeped around the screen expecting to find her giggling as she crouched behind it. She wasn't there.

He frowned and checked the rest of the room, even behind the door. When they were first married she sometimes teased him by hiding, but recently such games seemed to bore her. He bent quickly to look under the bed but only the chamber pot and dust were there.

'Lucy!' he called again, standing at the doorway in case she was in one of the other rooms upstairs. The only answer was the heavy beating of the rain falling on the roof.

He raced downstairs to where Martha was waiting. 'She's not there!' He glanced around. 'Isn't she down here?'

Martha looked blank, raising her eyebrows with concern. 'Hilda!' she called as Casey pushed past her to look in the parlors.

The cook bustled in from the dining room. 'Have you seen Mistress Lucy?'

'No, ma'm, she ain't down here.'

Casey returned to the entrance hall. 'I've checked all the rooms.' He was anxious now. 'She's disappeared.'

'Nonsense,' said Martha, clapping her hands. 'She's probably on the veranda watching the rain. She can't hear us calling with all this noise. Take a look, Hilda. Send one of the girls upstairs, in my chamber, and the master's. She might be there reading.' Martha turned to Casey.

'Was she dressed?'

'Of course.'

'What was she wearing?' Martha's coolness was a contrast to

Casey's panic. 'Try to think. Was she dressed to go out walking?'

'I . . . I don't know.' He cursed himself. The last time he had seen Lucy she was in bed sulking with her back to him and her face to the wall.

'She not on de piazza,' Hilda reported with a doleful glance at Casey. 'An' she not upstair.'

'Then she must have gone out for a walk!' Martha led the way to the front veranda. The rain was gusting across the deck in wind flurries. It streamed into the house when Casey opened the door.

'She couldn't have noticed the rain coming on. These storms blow up so suddenly.' Martha clutched her hand to her hair and kept away from the doorway as Casey peered out.

It was as dark as dusk outside with the rain hurtling down and drenching the Spanish moss on the live oaks until the branches bent.

'Shut the door, Casey!' Martha had to raise her voice to be heard above the hammering of the rain.

'I'm going out,' he shouted. 'She must be trapped somewhere under the trees.'

'No!' said Martha, clinging to his arm. 'You'll never find her in this. She'll be safe, there's so much shelter. When it eases up, she'll come back.'

'But she's six months pregnant!' shouted Casey. 'She'll be frightened.'

He pulled away from Martha and ran across the veranda out in to the rain. The fierceness of the storm made him stumble. Drops hit his neck and beat against his shirt soaking it in seconds so it stuck to his skin.

He wiped his eyes as he wondered which way Lucy could have gone. She wasn't in sight under the live oaks in front of the house. Rain streamed down his face, it was cold and stung his eyes. He was angry and worried. Something terrible must have happened to make Lucy venture out of the house alone.

He ran to the shelter of the trees but the rain was so intense it followed him there, the leaves giving way under its weight and dripping down in torrents. He peered into the gloom of the copse behind the oaks and magnolias. The rain and the darkness made it impossible to see clearly. If Lucy was there, she was well hidden.

He was puzzled and tried to think what she would do. If she had left the house for a walk, where would she go? The afternoons they spent together by the side of the Layou River flashed into his mind. He raced back across the lawn to the trail leading to the creek. Branches pulled at his shirt as he rushed along, shouting her name.

'Lucy! Lucy! . . .' He stopped at the water's edge and stared. There, in the middle of the bayou, with the rising water swirling angrily around it, blown up like a bladder and trapped in the fork of a fallen tree, was Lucy's white nightgown.

CHAPTER FIFTEEN

Casey plunged into the raging water and half-swam, half-stumbled to the spot. He raised the nightdress tenderly, groping underneath for her body. The nightdress tore loose from the branch and fluttered in his hand.

Rain smashed down through the trees with a fury matched by the raging of the bayou. Its red mud water swirled around Casey threatening to throw him off his feet and sweep him away. He steadied himself against the tree that had fallen from one bank across to the other, its branches acting as a dam on the debris borne along by the surging torrent.

He wiped the rain from his eyes with Lucy's nightdress, and peered into the whirl of water spuming at his waist. Carefully, he waded the length of the tree's trunk, feeling with his legs for any obstruction that could be her corpse. When he reached the opposite bank, he dragged himself wearily out of the water and sank down on to the squelching mud.

His boots were filled with water and he pulled them off. His clothes were soaking wet and his shirt clung coldly against his skin. He ripped it off, preferring the cold sting of the rain on his shoulders to the clammy dampness. He wiped his eyes again and looked around.

The bayou was not deep and if Lucy wanted to cross it, she could have done so. Why did she shed her nightdress? Perhaps for the same reason that he had removed his own shirt?

Casey pulled himself to his feet and looked around him. There was an indentation through the undergrowth that he hadn't noticed before and it could be a path. The thought of Lucy wandering naked through the swamps in the rain appalled him. Yet it was better than having to fish her body out of the bayou.

He pushed his way through the brushwood, stumbling in his bare feet on the rough ground until the path broadened out into a glade. Instinctively, he stepped behind a tree to keep out of sight while he surveyed the scene. In the clearing was a small cabin, its steep-pitched roof covered with worn cypress shingles that were being severely beaten by the rain.

Its tiny gallery was awash with pools of muddy water. Broken shingles and rough cut, unpainted boards sided the cabin to protect its mud-and-Spanish-moss walls from the hard rain. Even so, the old cabin appeared to be in danger of collapsing under the onslaught of the storm. There was one door off the gallery and it was closed.

Casey ran across the glade on to the gallery and flung open the door.

The inside was in darkness with all the wooden shutters closed against the rain. The faint light from the open door revealed one room that filled the tiny cabin. Its floor was made of boards laid over mud. Rain was splashing on the boards from holes in the roof and at first Casey could see nothing more. He expected a family of slaves to be crouched for fear of the rain under the bed platform in the far corner of the room.

Instead, a movement by the door caught his eye. A woman in a shift soaked and begrimed with mud, squatted on the floor staring up at him. Across her lap she cradled the naked and swollen form of Lucy.

'By the devil!' Casey reached down. 'What have you done to her?'

The woman shrank back at his voice, offering Lucy to him with a gentle pride in her bearing. Casey lifted her in his arms and carried her to the door. In the faint light he stared at the cold, wet body in his hands. Lucy's eyes were closed and her face was frozen in a mask of fear.

Casey lowered his lips to hers. Her breasts quivered with life. He sighed.

The woman was at his side, holding a sodden old blanket. She draped it over Lucy without a word. Casey blinked and rain from his hair fell on Lucy's face. She opened her mouth.

'Water . . .' she breathed.

Casey frowned and looked at the woman. He was astonished, in the daylight from the open door, to see she was white. He glanced back in confusion at the chaos and poverty of the cabin.

'The bed,' he said. He carried Lucy to the corner where the bed was a shelf suspended from the wall of the cabin, supported by two squared cypress posts. He placed her on the weaved mat of dried grass laid on the shelf to serve as a mattress.

'Water . . .' Lucy moaned again.

Casey assumed that she was having a bad dream about crossing the bayou.

The woman understood her need. She held a cup filled with rainwater to Lucy's lips and they both watched her drink thirstily. When she had drained the cup, her face lost its tight expression of anguish and she fell back in sleep. Casey held her hand and massaged it while he thought.

'Third cup of water,' the woman said glumly, breaking the silence.

Casey glanced at her again. She was wearing an osnaburg shift, the blue uniform of slavery. Her hair, as wet as his own, hung limply down her cheeks. She was thin with eyes, a startling gray, that knew the despair of hunger.

She had a disdainful mien that conveyed her contempt for Casey. Her bearing, more than her eyes and features, convinced Casey that she was genuinely white and not a pallid octoroon.

'She's my wife,' he explained and watched the woman's expression change from contempt to something less stern. In doing so, she assumed a lean beauty of her own that reflected hope despite the disappointments etched around her deep sunk eyes. Casey put her age at no more than ten years older than himself.

'What happened?' he asked softly, stroking Lucy's face to remove the strands of hairs.

'She was in the bayou.' The woman shrugged. 'She was acting like she wanted to drink it. I pulled her out, brought her here.'

Casey nodded. The woman's quiet authority impressed him. 'I thought . . .'

The woman sniffed. 'T'ain't nothing to what I thought.' They smiled at each other.

'I'm Rhoda,' she said. 'Don't ask Martha about me. She'll blacken me until her teeth drop out. I'm her half-sister, you see, by my father's swamp-woman mistress. I'm allowed to live here on sufferance.'

Casey peered out of the cabin. The sky was lightening and the rain easing up. He wondered if Lucy would be safer in Rhoda's care. No.

She was cold. He had to take her back to The Drongos. A fire would warm her, and a long sleep.

'Do you think the baby –?'

Rhoda glared at him and turned away. 'I don't know anything about babies,' she said with a bitterness that made Casey abandon his question.

'I'll take her back,' he said hastily. 'The rain is easing off.'

'If you wish.'

'Will you come?'

'No.' She turned back to him. 'I vowed four years ago when Martha took over my father's home, that I'd never cross the bayou.' She walked to the door, indicating that Casey was to leave.

He lifted Lucy off the shelf, wrapping her right arm around his neck. She clung to him.

Rhoda seemed to relent. 'I'm here if ever you want me,' she said, wiping her eyes.

It was then that Casey realized the moisture glistening on her cheeks was tears, not raindrops. He carried Lucy out of the dilapidated cabin and down the track towards the bayou.

The fuss Martha made over Lucy when he returned with her to the house appeared to be born of genuine concern for her welfare. She followed Casey up the stairs to the bedroom offering advice. She ordered a warming pan for the bed, and brandy for Lucy.

'No brandy,' said Casey firmly. 'She's resting now. Let her sleep it off.'

Martha protested that she knew best how to stave off the swamp fever she was certain Lucy had caught. 'The swamps,' she said, wringing her hands. 'All that rain. The poor child might die.'

'Not Lucy.' Casey was adamant. 'She's tough.'

'De baby?' It was Hilda who voiced Casey's real concern. 'Yo' boun' to physic she.' Hilda pumped the pillows of the bed and smoothed Lucy's hair. She was in a deep sleep that no touch could disturb.

'Later, when she wakes. I want to hear what she has to say. We'll wait.'

'Very well!' Martha left the room in a huff. Casey closed the door sharply behind her. He spun around and advanced on the old housekeeper.

'Hilda!' His angry voice startled her and she let go of Lucy's hand

and looked up in surprise.

'Did you make Lucy's coffee this morning?'

She frowned. 'No, Cas, ah didn'. Mistis Mart'a done dat an' gib it to de gal to bring she.'

Casey nodded sadly. 'Leave us alone now, Hilda. I'll stay with Lucy.'

He spent the day in thought while Lucy slept. Once she half-roused and he held a glass of water for her to sip. In her sleep she seized it eagerly then lapsed back into a fitful doze.

She woke in the afternoon, dazed and with a pain in her head that made concentrating difficult. Casey was at her side and held her hand tenderly. She had no recollection of her strange walk in the rain.

'Thirst,' she said. 'I fell asleep and I had such a terrible thirst.'

She attributed her sleepiness and craving for water to her pregnancy. Casey was worried. He could not ignore the trembling of her lips and hands. He wondered if she would be fit enough to travel the next morning when he wanted to leave The Drongos for good.

She slept again while Casey wiped away the sweat that dampened her brow. She woke once and complained of the cold so Casey called Hilda to bring another blanket.

'How can she feel so cold when she's sweating?' he asked.

Hilda nodded knowledgeably 'De miasma,' she pronounced. 'Ah bin waitin' for it. Ah gwine physic she now, fo' sure.'

She laid the extra blanket on Lucy and left the room. In minutes she was back, during which time Lucy threw off all the blankets to the floor.

Hilda clicked her tongue against her teeth in a sound of rebuke. 'Jes' what ah say!' she muttered, pushing Casey aside.

'What's that?' he demanded when Hilda held a cup of steaming, pungent liquid to Lucy's lips.

'Lor', don' yo' trus' Hilda?' The slave shook her head sadly. 'Herb tea. Ah know some secrets too, Cas. Don' worry 'bou' Lucy. She gwine be well when she lick dat miasma.'

'You made the tea yourself?'

'Sure did. Ah don' hol' no light by Mistis Mart'a's remedy. Spoon of laudanum she use fo' everyt'ing.' She fed Lucy the tea and she seemed to calm under her care.

'Now dis,' she said, holding another cup. 'Brandy an' peppers.

We gwine rub dis po' chil' wid brandy an' peppers to chase 'way de miasmas.'

Casey left Hilda with strict instructions that on no account was she to let Lucy have any nostrum prepared by Martha.

It was nightfall. The rain had ceased, leaving a landscape adrip with moisture and the air cool. He used the slave stairs to the back veranda to get out of the house without encountering Jed and Martha. He needed to think. He was convinced that the sooner he and Lucy left The Drongos, the better.

He took the path to the *garçonnière* . He was accustomed to the murkiness of plantation trails and he loped along lost in thought. Leaves shook water on him and drenched his hair, but he didn't care.

He was almost at the *garçonnière* before he noticed the light shining from the upper story. He watched the windows carefully. No one moved in the room upstairs so he walked quietly across the open space in front of the hexagonal building and went inside. He sat quietly on the flight of steps leading to the room and listened.

There was a scraping sound followed by a bump. He wondered who was up there when he saw Jed striding along the path. Jed was whistling and stroking his mustache. He smacked his whip against his thighs as he walked and gave the impression of being very pleased with himself. Casey slipped into the darkness behind the stairs as Jed entered the arched precinct.

Jed dashed up the stairs to the room without hesitating, his boots clumping loudly on the wooden steps above Casey's hiding place. He pushed open the door and Casey heard him greeting the person inside.

'Aha!' He sounded excited. 'Now I've got you, you young scamp.'

'Ah done 'range de bed like you' tell me, Mas Jed.'

Casey frowned at the sound of the slave's voice. It was not the dulcet tones of a wench but the cocksure speech of a boy. Casey held his breath and listened. Jed walked across the room, then his footsteps stopped and he sighed, probably sitting down.

'Help me off with my boots, boy.'

'Yes, Mas.'

It was Tissa's voice. Casey recognized the underlying inflection of pride, even as the youth pretended to be subservient. A boot fell to the floor and Jed groaned with pleasure.

The darkness outside the *garçonnière* was complete; the only light was the glow from the open door above his head. There was another thump as the second boot hit the floor.

'Rub ma feet, boy!'

'Yessah.'

Jed sighed loudly with contentment. 'You have fine hands, boy.'

'Yes, sah.'

'You're a pleasing nigra, Parry.' There was silence.

Casey pictured the scene of Tissa forced to rub Jed's feet while he lolled back on the bed. He was sickened by it.

'How would ya like to be ma body servant, Parry?'

'Yes, sah, if yo' please, sah.'

Casey detected the sarcasm in Tissa's reply and was impressed by the slave's spirit.

'You must do everything I require of ya, Parry.'

'Yes, sah.'

'Ya'll have to tend me in the big house. Sleep in ma chamber, serve me every way I wants.' There was the sound of a slap and Tissa yelped.

'Ah ain' done not'ing, sah!'

'I don't like ma nigras to be uppity. Maybe I should cut out your tongue?'

'Oh no, sah! Please, sah! Ah serve yo' good, sah. Like what yo' want.'

'That's better. Now shut that door, pull down your pants and come here.'

Casey was stunned. Tissa would not be able to escape. He either did what Jed wanted or had his tongue cut out so he'd become a grunting black ape, like the drongos.

The door banged shut above Casey's head and there was no further sound from the upstairs chamber. Casey pondered what he should do. The youth had boasted that he was safe from Jed but it didn't seem so. His happy innocence and the trust he placed in him shamed Casey into action. He dashed up the stairs to the door, flung it open and hurtled into the room.

Tissa lay spreadeagled face down across the mattress of the four poster bed. His arms and legs were stretched out and shackled by heavy iron manacles to the bed posts. His naked body, with its taut muscles glistening with sweat, was rigid on the white silk of the counterpane.

Jed was bent over Tissa's leg, fastening the last manacle. He was naked and swung around in alarm as Casey rushed at him.

Casey's first punch landed squarely on his jaw, the second to his solar plexus doubled him up in agony. He dropped to the floor and grabbed his whip which lay by the bed. Casey stood back waiting for Jed to rise. The slash of the whip in the air startled him. He ducked.

Jed flicked the whip again from the floor and caught Casey across his nose. The blow stung and brought water to his eyes.

Jed rose up and advanced, snapping the whip rapidly in front of Casey's face, forcing him back. Jed sneered. Even in the confines of the small room, he was adept at manipulating the whip so the thong struck its target every time. He parried Casey's attempt to grab it.

'Aha! You want to fight, do you, boy? I'll show you!'

Jed stepped back to the bed and lengthened his stroke. The tongue of the whip was sharp with the cut of a razor. It sliced through Casey's shirt into his skin.

The pain made him blink. Another stroke cut into his cheek. Casey could not face a whip and he was ready to bolt down the stairs. He glanced at Tissa twisting helplessly in chains on the bed. The sight filled him with rage and gave him courage.

He charged at Jed, wincing as the whip cut a flurry of blows across his face. He was blinded and lunged at Jed hoping to knock him down.

Jed sidestepped with the arrogance of a matador and Casey sprawled across the bed on top of Tissa.

'Aie!' shouted Jed with relish. He lashed at them both with a fury of passion, his mouth slobbering and his face red with excitement. 'Aie!'

'Get his grain,' hissed Tissa, in an unconscious echoing of the advice Casey himself had once given a fighter. 'Befo' he get yo'n.' Tissa heaved his shoulder and tossed him off the bed.

He fell badly, cracking his knee on the floor. Jed's whip sliced into him again, finding the soft flesh of his crotch.

'Boy, this is better than I dreamed!' Jed spluttered, dancing back for another stroke. He was an expert. The tip of the whip tore open Casey's breeches, exposing him. Tissa snorted with disgust.

The boy's ridicule snapped Casey's restraint. He rolled across the floor as the whip lashed him, catching the thong with his body so it wound around him, pulling the handle out of Jed's grasp. He was now entangled in the whip but his hands were free. He dived for Jed's waist, smashing into his stomach with his shoulder and toppling him backward over a couch, falling on top of him.

Jed squealed with delight.

The merriment disconcerted Casey and he hesitated. Jed seized the advantage and wriggled away, kicking out at his crotch with his foot. Casey retaliated by grabbing Jed's ankle. He stood up and pulled Jed on to the floor.

Jed tried to twist out of his grasp, panting with exhaustion. He lay still and Casey, suspecting a feint, dragged him backward on his bare stomach across the floor boards. Jed howled with pain as his penis snagged on the splinters in the wood.

Casey flung him down with contempt. He unwound the whip and flicked it over Jed's body, careful not to let the lash strike him. Jed whimpered.

'Get up!' ordered Casey.

Jed scrambled to his feet; his body was dusty from the floor and his penis was swollen. He held it gingerly. There was a look of adoration in his eyes, like that of a whipped cur for its master.

Casey was sickened by the man's perversity. 'Release the boy!' he shouted, to hide his own feelings.

Jed plucked at his mustache, keeping an eye on Casey and the whip, as he moved to the bed.

Sensing Jed's fear of the lash, Casey cracked it angrily and Jed hurried with the padlocks. Tissa leaped to his feet and grinned his thanks.

'Make him dance, Cas!'

'Go!' Casey nodded his head to the door. He was disturbed by Jed's whimpering and Tissa's enjoyment of it. 'Don't tell anyone of this, do you hear? Not even Hilda.'

Tissa picked up his osnaburg pants and pulled them on hastily. 'Yes, Mas Casey,' he said, winking.

He scuttled down the stairs. Casey guessed he would lurk in the shadows to see what happened next.

'Well,' said Jed, straightening up and stretching himself. 'That was a real bust!'

'What?' Casey drew back, ready for another of Jed's tricks. The white man sat on the edge of the bed and began to pull at himself.

'That was a fair fight. I enjoyed that.'

Casey stared at him, unable to hide his loathing.

'I like you, Casey,' Jed said with a leer. 'You're a good sport.'

CHAPTER SIXTEEN

Lucy recovered slowly. Her sleep pattern returned on the second day but the fever made her delirious, red-eyed and weak. Casey fretted at the time she was taking to get better because the sailing date of the ship was drawing near. Hilda assured him she was making proper progress and maintained the strictest watch over her treatment. The precaution was unnecessary. Martha showed no attempt to meddle in Lucy's care, as Casey suspected she might.

No mention was made of the incident at the *garçonnière* but to Casey it was ever uppermost in his mind. When he sat at dinner he was conscious of Jed watching him slyly. If Casey caught his eye unexpectedly, Jed would preen his mustache and smirk. To his horror, Jed took to clapping him frequently on the shoulder, squeezing his elbow, and using every opportunity to indulge in displays of intimacy that he found distasteful.

Casey's loathing for Jed increased with each squeeze and leer. He could not understand how Jed could ignore his open dislike of him. His relationship with Martha was tense too. He was no longer fooled by her flirtatious nature and wondered, instead, what part Martha had played in Lucy's odd behavior.

Whatever Martha may have done, she seemed as concerned as Casey about Lucy's recovery. It soon became apparent that Lucy would not be able to travel to New Orleans in time for the sailing to England. Martha provided the solution.

'I will write immediately to the agents,' she said as she and Casey sat on the veranda one afternoon. Jed was on the plantation and they were alone. Lucy had begun to spend periods on the couch in their chamber. She had not yet found the strength to descend down stairs.

'Give Lucy another week, and you can get the steamboat.' She laid her hand lightly on Casey's arm as he sat in a rocking chair next to hers. 'You must be so careful, Casey, because of the baby.'

'I know, I know.' He could not hide his impatience.

'You shall sign this letter too. We'll explain the delay and request them to assign you a cabin on the next sailing as a matter of priority.'

'Is there any chance of that?'

'Of course, Casey. My name means a lot. With your signature and perhaps a draft on the Louisiana Bank, they will do whatever is necessary.'

He stopped rocking the chair backward and forward and regarded her steadily. The idea made sense. A token payment in advance should ease any obstacles. They might only be delayed a few days as a result.

'Yes,' he said with an air of relief. 'Please write something. I'll sign.'

'I'll do it right away.' Martha stood up.

'How will you send the letter?'

'That's easy. One of the slaves will take it to Bayou Sara and give it to the steamboat captain.'

'Bayou Sara?' Casey was thoughtful. 'I'd like to go with him.'

Martha was at the door, about to enter the house. She turned abruptly. 'That's not necessary, Casey. My slaves are quite capable of delivering the letter. They've done it before.' Her smile was cold and commanding.

Casey grinned back, unabashed. 'I'd like to visit Bayou Sara anyway.'

'It's a shocking place, Casey, You wouldn't like it.'

'Maybe not. I have to decide that for myself.' He paused. 'You sound as though you don't want me to leave The Drongos?'

'Fie on you, Casey!' She laughed. 'Go to Bayou Sara if you wish. Jed will accompany you.' She disappeared into the house and Casey returned to his seat, aware that Martha had once more gained the upper hand.

In the event, he did not make the trip. Martha wrote the letter and he signed it and the bank draft. Hilda called him to sit with Lucy as she had her chores to do. It was their pact not to leave Lucy alone. He stayed with her until the evening. When he came down, Martha told him she had already sent off the letter to catch the evening steamboat.

'I didn't want to delay,' she said. 'It was the right thing to do, wasn't it?' She patted her bosom, her lips parted in a blatant appeal for his approval.

'Oh yes,' he muttered, resigned to her trickery. Martha, it seemed, always got her way.

Perhaps because he was obliged to remain near the house because of Lucy's illness, Casey noticed he was allowed to roam over the plantation without being escorted by Jed or Martha. Every morning, after he had entrusted Lucy to Hilda's care, he called up the dogs and strolled along the trails leading from the house.

The dogs were vicious animals and it took him time and the judicious use of scraps from Hilda's kitchen to get them to obey him. When he was out of sight of anyone watching from the house, he beat the dogs thoroughly with a stick. They were intelligent animals, although fierce, and after several beatings, he had them trained to the point where he would only have to raise his stick and they would cringe in front of him in fear.

Casey wanted to visit the barracoon. He had not seen Tissa since the extraordinary affair in the *garçonnière*. Hilda advised him to stay away from the slave quarters. She said there was an overseer there, Ruffin, who would not take kindly to Casey's curiosity.

'Tissa be all right,' Hilda assured him. 'He does be 'prentice to a drongo boatman. Mas Jed won' trouble he no mo.''

So Casey's walks were devoted to intimidating the dogs and to exploring the layout of the plantation. The house had been built at the highest point of a rolling landscape that descended to the swamps behind the barracoon. On the higher, firmer ground were the canefields and beyond them, in land cleared in the woods, the gardens where the slaves grew produce of their own.

The plantation slaves were housed in cabins adjoining the barracoon compound. Because the dogs had a natural antipathy for slaves, Casey had to keep away from the areas where they worked or lived.

The plantation was surrounded by impenetrable undergrowth and forest that had never been cleared. It was bordered by the Mississippi on the west and by the Bayou Sara to the south. The smaller Bayou Celeste was the eastern boundary with alligator swamps beyond it.

Casey was keen to visit Rhoda in her cabin on the other side of the bayou and to learn more about her. He had told Lucy how he found her in Rhoda's care.

'I'd like to go there,' Lucy said when they talked about it a few days after he had signed the letter to the shipping agent. 'I'd like to thank her.'

'When you are well. You mustn't tire yourself.'

'We'll go tomorrow.'

For once, Casey was pleased by Lucy's refusal to heed his advice. The next morning, she insisted she was better and descended the stairs for breakfast. It had been two weeks since her crazed walk in the rain.

Martha was cool toward her, showing none of the friendliness of the previous weeks. Jed was curt, winked at Casey and left for his rounds of the plantation.

Lucy pecked at the ham and grits, swallowed her coffee nervously, and showed signs of being ill at ease. Casey had never disclosed his suspicions to Lucy about the cup of coffee she had drunk the morning of her "attack". However, it was evident from Lucy's changed attitude to Martha that she had enough doubts of her own now.

They were both relieved when Martha announced she had plantation ledgers to attend to in her office. This was located in the nook under the main staircase off the entrance lobby, and she hastened there leaving her own breakfast half-eaten.

'Something seems to be worrying her,' said Casey when they were alone.

'Yes,' Lucy's voice was flat. Casey waited for her to elaborate. She didn't. 'Can you take me to see Rhoda now?'

He rose from the table, puzzled by the intensity of her expression. 'Are you sure you're well enough? You don't want to risk having a relapse. We can't delay the departure any longer.'

'I want to try.'

'Walk around the veranda today. Build up your strength first. We can go another day to see Rhoda, before we leave.'

Lucy stood up and moved to the door. 'Are you coming?' she asked testily. 'Or do I have to find the way myself?'

She leaned on him as they walked the path to the bayou. She had lost weight while she was in bed and to Casey she seemed so frail and light. He prayed that what he was doing was right for Lucy. She had to get well quickly so that they would get the next sailing for England.

She was a determined girl, and he was bound to help her. In another two months, their son could be born, so they had to get that next sailing. Even so, as he supported her frail body, he wondered if it was already too late to think of going. How could she stand such a voyage?

'Let me rest,' she said when they reached the bank of the bayou. 'It's quite beautiful here.'

Casey gazed at the tangle of vegetation and brushwood with the tall trees blocking out the sun and the muddy stream flowing sluggishly at their roots, and disagreed. The bayou was a dank, mosquito-filled, gloomy spot and he urged Lucy not to linger.

'There's a boat,' he said, surprised to see the pirogue tied to a branch near where they stood. 'I'l take you across to Rhoda's in that. You can rest again there.'

He helped her into the craft and she sat without moving in the prow while he poled it across the water. The under current was stronger than he expected so he had to push upstream to get the pirogue to drift to the clearing on the opposite side. He made the boat fast to a stake in the bank and guided Lucy carefully up the narrow overgrown path.

In the sunlight, the exposed grain of the cabin's unpainted boards gave the old place a mellowness less depressing than when Casey had first seen the cabin in the rain. The gray shingles hung lopsided on the roof and the veranda had canted over to one side as though sliding away from the rest of the shack. As Casey stood at the edge of the glade staring at the cabin, he heard Lucy catch her breath.

'You remember, don't you?' he challenged.

'I thought it was in my nightmare.'

'Are you scared?'

'No.'

Rhoda was in the shade of the veranda, waiting for them. She kept out of the sun as they crossed the clearing and remained by the door as Casey helped Lucy onto the tilting gallery. Lucy hesitated before greeting Rhoda and then took a step forward and fell into her open arms, laying her head on Rhoda's bosom. She began to weep as Rhoda patted her shoulder tenderly.

'I've been expecting you, dear,' she said. She ignored Casey.

He saw that Rhoda's hair, now it was no longer lank with rain, had the same dark sheen and silkiness as Martha's. Her features had softened. She still wore the coarse blue shift of a field slave, and Lucy's cheek was reddened by the rough material when she withdrew from Rhoda's embrace.

'Come inside.' Rhoda stared defiantly at Casey.

'It's all right,' he said. 'I'll wait here.'

'I've got nothing to offer you.' It was a statement not an apology.

Casey shook his head. 'Take care of Lucy. She needs a friend.'

Rhoda nodded. She put her arm around Lucy and led her into the dingy interior of the shack.

Casey waited a moment and then turned away. His eye caught a movement in the bushes surrounding the house. He peered carefully in time to see a dark shape retreating into the thicket. He sniffed. There was a confusion of scents, with the mildew smell of the old cabin combining with the aroma of rotting corncobs, trash, and the odor of the swamps behind Rhoda's cabin.

The distinctive stink of a hulking drongo slave hung over it all. Casey resisted the urge to chase the man. He was sorry he hadn't brought the dogs with him. He squatted down on the sloping veranda, keeping his head out of the sun, and waited.

Lucy's recovery had been slow. From what Hilda said, swamp fever had that effect, leaving the victim melancholic and debilitated. Her visit to Rhoda's cabin was encouraging, and the presence of the drongo guard confirmed that even if Martha and Jed let them wander alone, they were being watched all the time. He wondered if Rhoda was aware of the drongo skulking on her property.

It was an hour before Lucy emerged. She seemed happier. 'Rhoda is very kind,' she said. 'She's been crocheting a shawl for the baby.'

Rhoda scowled. 'T'ain't nothing.'

'You're very kind,' said Casey. 'Don't you find it hard living here alone?'

Rhoda said nothing.

'Don't you long for company sometimes?'

'I mind my own business,' she snapped. 'And you mind yours.'

Lucy laughed. 'Casey's always asking silly questions.' She grimaced. 'I've got used to it now.'

'Do you ask Martha questions too, young man?'

'Yes . . . ' Casey was wary. 'What kind of questions should I ask her?'

'You know!' Rhoda nodded her head and said nothing more.

Casey noticed that Rhoda glanced frequently at Lucy's waist. She seemed fascinated by her pregnancy. He wondered why.

'There are many things I'd like to ask Martha,' he said. 'We are leaving The Drongos as soon as Lucy feels fit, so I won't.'

Lucy smiled and put her hand into his. 'Rhoda wants me to stay. She says she'll help me with the baby if I do. She says she has land here. We could build a house here and drain the swamps and grow cotton.'

Casey was astonished. 'Do you want that?'

Lucy avoided his eye and faced Rhoda. 'We planned to go to England.'

'Yes, yes,' said Rhoda crossly. 'Don't wait, don't wait. Go at once. Go tonight.'

'Rhoda, dear, what's wrong? Has Casey upset you?'

Rhoda's lips twitched as though she was going to speak. Instead, she beamed. The wrinkles at her deep-set eyes spread with her broad smile and the gloom lifted from her face like a shadow passing away. She took Lucy's hand and crooned happily.

'Perhaps you stay . . . visit me here . . . such talks we'll have. We'll sew for the baby and do all manner of things . . .' She squeezed Lucy's hand then let it go reluctantly.

They crossed the clearing to the path. Casey felt Rhoda staring after them. When he turned to wave, she darted nervously back to the cabin.

'She must be very lonely,' he said. 'Maybe that's why she acts so strangely.' He was puzzled by Lucy's gaiety.

'What did you talk about that's made you so chirpy?' He squeezed her hand. 'She's a tonic for you, even if she's *folle.*'

'She's not mad! She's very wise. These women are, you know.' Lucy stopped chattering and stared. 'Casey! Look, there's someone in the bushes.'

Casey peered through the trees where Lucy pointed. Leaves shook in the breeze, a bird cried, and from the distance the angry shout of a slave driver drifted over to them. He saw no one in the undergrowth. Lucy trembled and drew closer to him, her bright mood gone.

'Don't worry,' said Casey, trying to restore her good spirits. 'Probably Rhoda's slave hiding until we've gone.'

'She doesn't have a slave. She's too poor to have one.'

'Then one of Jed's.'

'Why was he watching us like that?'

'Forget him, Lucy. Let's hurry back to the house so you can rest. You must be tired, surely?'

'Perhaps I am.' She smiled and he put his arm around her. She gave a little sigh and her body stiffened, then went limp as she toppled against him.

He caught her before she fell to the ground, scooping her up in his arms. Her head lolled back and her bonnet fell off, sending her long fair tresses drooping downward.

'Lucy!'

She didn't answer. He glanced into the undergrowth that pressed in on the narrow trail. 'What did you see?' he asked, wondering what had caused her to faint.

'The poor darling, she's so tired,' he muttered to himself as he carried her to the bayou bank.

The pirogue had vanished. He stepped into the water, holding her as high as he could so she didn't get wet, and felt his way carefully across the soft bottom of the stream. She was heavy and his arms ached.

When he climbed up the opposite bank, he set her down gently against a tree trunk and patted her hand. She didn't revive so he scooped up water into the palms of his hands and splashed it into her face. She moaned and rubbed at her chest.

It was then he noticed the small tear in her bodice, and the sliver of wood, no thicker than a needle, protruding from it.

He knelt down and hurriedly unlaced her bodice, pulling it back to bare her bosom. A dart had penetrated above her left breast, at the side. Its impact had been deflected by the cambric of her bodice and it quivered loosely in her flesh.

He held the thin shaft of the dart in his finger and thumb, close to the skin, hoping it wouldn't break. He pulled sharply and the dart sprang out.

He lowered his head and placed his lips over the wound, sucking desperately.

CHAPTER SEVENTEEN

Casey laid Lucy on her bed and stood back while Hilda applied a herb compress to the wound. He had sucked out the poison, and spat it into the bayou, but Lucy had not recovered from her faint. Martha, who watched her housekeeper and one of the slave girls fussing over Lucy, was skeptical.

'Nigra medicine ain't fitting for a white lady,' she said reprovingly to Casey. 'I have quinine.'

He looked at her askance and said nothing.

'She's your wife,' she said with a shrug. 'Such a pity. I thought she was going to be well enough for the next sailing. It's in four days' time. Doubt she'll make it.'

'By the devil!' Casey shouted, giving way to his disappointment. He flung himself on the couch and covered his eyes with his hands. 'Why? Oh, why?'

'Hush now, Casey.' Martha rushed to his side and put her arm around him. 'She's not dead. She can have the baby here. We'll get the best attention. There's a white midwife in St Francisville . . .'

'No!' He gritted his teeth and breathed deeply to control himself. Martha's proximity resulted in him inhaling the odor of her perfume, a musky scent of verbena and vetyver. It roused him, as did the touch of her fingers on his neck, brushing lightly against the long curls of his hair.

It was odd; how could the woman he suspected of causing Lucy's distress have such a profound effect on his emotions. He wanted to seize her in his arms, crush her to his body and devour her lips with his own: to overwhelm her evil intrigue with the wild passion bursting for release within him.

'The rogue drongo done that,' Jed announced sharply. He had been standing at the chamber door unnoticed by anyone. Martha shifted away from Casey and stared at him.

‘Where have you been, Jed?’ she demanded. ‘You could have helped carry Lucy upstairs.’

‘Looking for the drongo, dear,’ he said. ‘The chit in the kitchen told me Lucy got the dart. Obvious who done it.’

Casey looked from Martha to Jed. ‘What’s this all about?’

‘Damned if I know!’ Jed stroked his mustache, pleased to have Casey’s attention. ‘One of my slaves broke loose about a year ago. Fang, we call him. Would have got him with the dogs, of course, but he’s no trouble. He lives wild in the forest, hunts with his blowpipe. Remembers how from Africa, I suppose.’

‘What does he use for poison?’

‘Oh, some leaf, or snake venom. All the nigras know about poisons, don’t they, Hilda? It’s part of their voodoo.’

The housekeeper raised her eyes for the first time since Jed had come into the room. She kept her hand on the poultice held against Lucy’s breast. ‘Ah don’t know ’bou’ no voodoo, Mas Jed.’

‘Damn, you do! Hilda, ain’t you the biggest conjure woman in Bayou Sara?’ He winked at Casey. ‘The nigras are scared of Hilda because of her powers. What she doesn’t know about snakes and poisons ain’t worth knowing.’

‘Stop that nonsense, Jed. Hilda doesn’t know anything of the kind.’

‘Oh, very well.’ Jed sulked, then said, ‘Beats me why Fang should want to blow dart Lucy.’

‘Casey took her across the bayou.’

‘Did he, by jove!’ Jed looked at Martha in astonishment. ‘Then that’s the reason. His hide is on Rhoda’s patch. Maybe she told him to do it.’

‘Someone tell he, dat fo’ sure.’ Hilda straightened up and glared across the bed at Jed, challenging him to stop her speaking. ‘Fang ain’ harm no one befo’. He ain’ got no tongue an’ he ain’ got no wicked t’ought in his soft head.’

‘That’s enough, Hilda.’ Martha rose imperiously. ‘I think we can leave Lucy to let nature take its course.’

‘Ah ain’ finish, ma’m.’ Hilda was seething with anger and no one was going to stop her having her say. ‘Ah done see Fang dis mornin’. He came by de kitchen. He tell me somet’ing an ah don’ un’stan’ cause he grunt an’ point a’ de house an’ make blowin’ noises. Den he run off to de bayou.’

'Indeed?' Martha swept across the room, her dress rustling on the floor boards. 'Come, Jed, that's enough slave talk.'

She turned and beamed at Casey. He saw then a worrying similarity between Martha and her hermit sister. Their eyes held the same manic gleam.

'I'm sorry about Lucy, I really am,' Martha said. 'If it's a snake poison, Hilda may be able to cure her. I've got medicines, too, when you want them.'

Casey shook his head. He was sickened by the smirk on Jed's face and Martha's gleam bothered him too. He turned his back and waited until the two of them had gone. Hilda gave the slave some instructions and the girl hurried off down the back stairs.

"Ah gwine gib yo' a wongah, Cas. Too much bad conjure in de Drongos fo' 'nocent folk like yo' an' Mistis Lucy. Yo' need protectin'.'

'I have no fear of black voodoo, Hilda. I need a charm against white chicanery.'

'Yo' right, boy.' Hilda nodded her head and drops of sweat from her brow fell onto Lucy.

'She gwine be 'lerious fo' a few days. Ah tell Tissa pick de leaf ah need from de bush an' ah gwine mix de an-te-dote. She ain' gwine die.'

'The baby?'

Hilda shrugged. 'No harm.' She paused. ' 'Cept mayhap he get might' anxious to see dis wicked world.'

Casey sighed and Hilda bustled out of the room, leaving him to his thoughts. He pulled a chair up to the bed and sat beside Lucy. Her fair hair was spread out around her like a halo and with her eyes closed and her hands resting on her breasts, she seemed to be praying.

Casey blamed himself for her suffering. This was the second time an 'accident' had happened to Lucy. Was it part of a plan to keep them at The Drongos? Jed knew that he would never leave the plantation with Lucy. But why? Why did they want to keep him at The Drongos?

He would probably never know the answer to that question. Escape was the only solution and it had to be soon. Martha and Jed, whoever was the one who planned the attack on Lucy, relied on her weakness to keep her in bed. Casey knew her better than that. If

Lucy was determined to do something, she would do it, even if she was drugged or poisoned.

He squeezed her hand and leaned forward to whisper in her ear. 'We're going to get away from here, Lucy. For the baby's sake. We'll go as soon as you're well. We'll go by boat at night and we'll be quite safe.

'Get better quickly, dear, and we'll go to England. I promise.'

For a week, Lucy stayed in bed tossing and turning with the effects of the poison, taking her meals in a crazed state, dependent entirely on Casey and Hilda. Casey's sucking of the venom from the wound had helped and Hilda's ministrations also assisted her recovery. It was the baby who really saved her.

To Lucy, in her delirium, the baby became a real person. He was a boy, of that there was no doubt in her mind, and the boy urged her to recover. It was imperative that he be born, he insisted with the obstinacy of his father.

Lucy was enchanted with him. She talked, in her mind, for hours with the child. He told her what he looked like – handsome and strong like his father, with his mother's complexion and sense. Yes, he was white, he insisted; his skin would be white like hers but he would have his father's eyes. He was fit and lusty and they both agreed they were longing for the day when he would be born.

When Casey watched Lucy, unaware of her dreams, he was alarmed to see her twitch as though the baby was punching and kicking to get out. He understood now that there would be no time to get to England. It would be enough to get Lucy away from The Drongos. They would go to Madame Cable's. He could entrust Lucy's confinement to her care.

He made his plans. With the help of Hilda, he arranged to meet Tissa that night under a live oak tree that grew beside the back veranda. He told no one his plan, not even Hilda. He suspected that Jed would exact vengeance on the housekeeper if she helped him.

Tissa confirmed his view. 'Yo' don' know 'bou' Mas Jed, Cas,' he whispered when they were hunkered down together on the bole of the oak.

'He get de overseer to beat dem niggahs every day. Dey call it seasonin'. It rippin' de hide off every black mens and womens 'til dey drop. When de bossals ready to die, Jed stop de overseer an' gib dem feed an' sweet talk. He tell dem he de master an' dey prime an' dey got to breed to gib he whelps.'

Casey seethed with anger in the darkness.

'He tell me to rut wid any niggah. He say he gwine gib me a gol' piece fo' every one dat drop a male.'

'You did that?'

'Naw, Cas! I ain't coverin' no filly fo' Jed to sell de foal from out its dam's titty.'

Casey clapped his arms. 'Keep down your voice, Tissa. The guards.'

'Dere ain't no drongos here.' Tissa waved at the house. 'De slaves all lock up in de compound. Jed know yo' not gwine leave here widou' Lucy an' she sick an' dying.'

'Dying? She's an' dying.'

'De niggahs say she is.'

'What does Hilda say?'

'She say she ain't gwine let Lucy die. It bad fo' her fame as a conjure woman.'

'Lucy will get better.' Casey paused, a thought entering his mind. 'Hey,' he said. 'If Jed knows she is fit, will he put the drongos to guard us again?'

'Sure t'ing. An' she gwine get sick 'gain, too.'

'In that case, Lucy must pretend that she's still sick to fool him. As soon as she's fit enough, we'll escape by the back stairs. We'll walk through the forest to the landing on the Bayou Sara, where the bossals came. Can you get a boat there for us?'

'No.' Tissa shook his head. 'Too far fo' Lucy to walk. She'll be weak an' she carryin'.'

'I hadn't thought of that.'

'Ah can get de p'rogue to de Bayou Celeste.'

'By the landing near Rhoda's cabin?'

'Ah gwine try. De overseer, he chain de boats a' night so de bossals don't 'scape. Ah gwine loose one befo' he chain dem.'

'Be careful, Tissa.' Casey gripped his hand. 'I know what it's like to fall foul of a lash-happy white man. If there is any danger, don't do it.'

'Ah hab de way, only waitin' fo' yo' to tell me de when.'

Casey released the boy's hand and smiled. 'You're a good man, Tissa. I'll send word by Hilda that I want to see you by the bayou. You'll know that means to bring the boat at midnight.'

'Yo' gwine write a pass fo' we all?'

Casey was surprised. 'Why do we need a pass?'

'If de paddyrollers stop us. When Mistis Lucy hab a pass for we all, no one gwine dis'gree wid dat.'

'You want me to pretend I'm a slave?' Casey didn't like that idea.

'Only way to 'scape. If yo' say yo' is Mistis Lucy's husban', de Bayou Sara trash gwine lynch yo' fo' coverin' a white lady.'

Confronted with that logic, Casey agreed to write the passes so Lucy could pretend she was their owner. On some days there was a boat departing from Bayou Sara at dawn. Providing they weren't missed at The Drongos until the girl brought in the morning coffee, they could be on board and steaming down the Mississippi before Jed or Martha would know they had gone.

Casey promised Tissa that he could accompany them. 'As soon as we reach New Orleans,' he said, 'I'll make a draft in Jed's favor for your market value. That way I can't be accused of stealing you. You'll be freed in front of a notary and have papers to make it legal.'

Tissa's eyes dropped. 'Ah don' wan' to be free. Ah wan' to be wid yo'.'

'We'll see.' Casey was touched by the boy's trust. 'We'll see.'

They parted then, Tissa slipping soundlessly into the forest while Casey cautiously made his way back into the house.

There was a glimmer of light showing under the door of Martha's bedroom. The sound of Jed's voice in conversation with Martha made him hurry to his own chamber and dart inside. Lucy was sleeping peacefully. He watched over her for a few minutes, willing her to get better. He lay down on the floor and stretched out to sleep.

The next day, Lucy showed signs of improvement and by afternoon she was clamoring to leave the bed, at least to sit on the couch. Casey explained his plan to her as briefly as possible. Lucy considered it for a long time, startling Casey by moving her lips as though she was talking to someone else.

He left her side to stride around the chamber, trying to control his impatience.

'Yes,' she said softly. 'I'll do what you say.'

'Good. That means you must pretend to be very weak and confused. Don't even tell Hilda that you are better.'

'Don't you trust her?'

'Of course, I do. She cured you. That's the problem. She'll want to boast around the plantation that her potions stopped you dying. She'll find out soon enough when we've gone.'

'When will that be?'

'As soon as you think you're strong enough.'

'I must exercise. Can't I walk around the chamber like you?'

He stopped pacing and came to her side. 'As long as no one sees you. If someone does come in when you're out of bed, just drop down in a faint. We can't risk Martha or Jed knowing you have recovered.'

The ruse worked well. Color returned to Lucy's cheeks and Hilda was baffled how she appeared to be better yet remained delirious or asleep all the time. Casey took his meals with her, partly to keep away from Martha and Jed, and partly to share his own food with Lucy who had developed a tremendous appetite.

'Our son needs to build up his strength too,' she explained.

Casey humored her although he was puzzled by her childlike state of mind. Often she lapsed into periods of silence moving her lips and apparently conversing with herself. He knew there was no time to lose in getting her away from the mad atmosphere of the bayous and swamps back to the sanity of the city. He decided to risk it. He told Hilda he wanted to see Tissa that night by the Bayou Celeste.

'Dat easy, Cas.' Hilda beamed. 'Ah gwine visit ma sister tonight an' ah tell Tissa maself.' She shook her head sadly at Lucy's prostrate form on the bed. 'Ah don' un'stan' de mistis. Ah gwine ax ma sister any oder cure she know.'

'Don't worry, Hilda. I'm sure your remedies are the best.' He patted her outsize bottom and she gurgled with pleasure.

As soon as Hilda left the room, Lucy threw back the covers with obvious relief. 'Is it tonight?' she asked. 'I'm ready.'

'Yes.' Casey sat down at the escritoire and wrote out the two passes, signing them with Jed's name. He explained to Lucy that she was to say that he and Tissa were her slaves and to show the passes if anyone stopped them.

Lucy walked across the room with her nightdress billowing out in front of her and stood behind his chair as he sat at the desk. She touched him gently on his ears.

'We love you, Casey,' she said.

His heart melted and he stood up and took her in his arms. 'Oh Lucy,' he said. 'That's the first time since we came here that you've said that.'

'It hasn't been easy for me, Casey. I've had to learn, too. Now we are going to be all right, and we love you.'

Casey frowned. 'That's wonderful. Tell me, who is "we"?'

'My son and myself.'

'He's my son too, Lucy.'

'Yes, he is. He really is.' She turned away with a tear in her eye. 'I must pack some things.'

'Don't take too much.' He folded the passes and put them in her reticule.

That evening he stayed in the chamber instead of joining Martha and Jed. Lucy was excited and her face glowed as she sat on the bed and hummed a lullabye softly to herself. They had eaten and he placed the tray outside the door so that the slave girl wouldn't disturb them when she came for it. Casey hoped Hilda would remember to leave open the veranda door when she closed up the house, as she usually did when he was to meet Tissa.

He was impatient for midnight to come and sat on the couch drumming his fingers on its arm. He tensed when he heard the heavy footsteps of Jed bounding up the stairs. Lucy lay down in the bed and pulled the covers over her. There was a knock at the door and it opened immediately. Casey stood up.

'Is she all right?' It was Martha. She looked around the room carefully and noted Lucy was lying with her eyes closed. Casey walked over to the door to prevent her coming right in.

'She's been restless. No change otherwise.'

'Oh dear. It must be so tiresome for you. I could have sworn I heard voices here earlier on?'

'Maybe I was talking to myself.' Casey grinned sheepishly.

'No, you wouldn't do that. You were talking to Lucy.'

He swallowed guiltily. 'That's right. I was. Trying to get her to understand. No good. She's still very sick. I hope you don't mind. We might have to stay for a few more weeks.'

'I'm pleased to have you.' Martha's eyelashes fluttered and she edged closer to him. He drew back. 'Well,' she said with a final look at Lucy. 'Goodnight.'

She turned to go and then glanced back quickly just as Lucy moved.

'She seems flushed. I don't believe she's asleep at all.'

'Oh, she isn't.' Casey blocked the doorway. 'She's hot. She'll sleep soon.'

'Hmm.' Martha walked across the landing. At the door to her chamber, she turned back. 'If you need anything, call me. Jed is going out tonight. He's going to New Orleans on the dawn boat. He won't be back for a few days.' She nodded her head at Jed's chamber.

'He's getting dressed now,' she added softly. 'Perhaps after midnight . . .?' Her eyes glinted in the light from the candle and she smiled.

Casey bit his lip and closed the bedroom door.

He wore the foul-smelling osnaburg pants and the torn shirt Hilda had given him weeks before. Lucy dressed in her loosest gown, and they were both amazed at how large she had become.

Casey toughed her tenderly. 'Can you feel it moving?' he asked.

'Oh yes,' Lucy smiled at his silly qustion. 'He is very excited tonight. To be going on a steamboat . . .'

'Hush!' said Casey, holding his fingers to his lips. 'At least he can't cry and wake every one.'

'No, he'll do as he is told. He won't cry.'

Casey went first, holding Lucy's reticule in one hand and leading Lucy with the other. They crept down the stairs carefully and there were no creaks to alert Martha. The door to the veranda was open and they slipped out quietly.

Casey paused on the veranda and sniffed. The moon was vivid and its pale light lengthened the black shapes of the trees and forest. Lucy tightened her grip on his hand.

'Come,' he whispered very quietly into her ear.

He held her firmly, guiding her down the steps on to the flagstones set into the grass. She hesitated, and he had to urge her forward with a gentle push. She seemed to go into a trance and followed him without a murmur. When he quickened his pace, she quickened hers. When he slowed as they gained the shelter of the undergrowth surrounding the path, she slowed.

They reached the bayou with ease and Casey felt more confident. He found the tree where she had lain the day the dart pierced her, and he told her to sit and rest by it.

She emerged from her trance. 'No,' she said. 'I'll stand.' She was holding herself and although she was out of breath, she was trying to hum.

'Are you in pain?' he asked in alarm.

'No, no.' She closed her eyes.

'Tissa will be here with the boat,' he said to encourage her. 'I'll look.'

'Don't leave us!' The cry was poignant and the hackles at his neck tingled when he heard her. 'We're frightened.'

'It's all right,' he said, patting her cheek quietly. 'Tissa will be here.'

There was silence, and he listened carefully. Water lapped the bank and the night insects warbled in the forest. He glanced back at The Drongos. A light flickered in their own chamber and he was surprised to see lanterns burning at the front of the house. They had been lucky to get out without being challenged by Martha or Jed. He peered into the dark ribbon of water, wondering when Tissa would come.

'Why are we waiting?' Lucy said with a moan. 'We must hurry.'

'Yes, yes I know.'

'Where's the boat?'

'Don't get anxious. He'll come.' Casey tried not to show the doubt he was beginning to feel. What if Tissa had been caught? His worry increased as the minutes passed. He held Lucy in his arms and listened to her keening softly to herself. She wouldn't sit down so they leaned together against the trunk of the tree.

Tissa came silently. Casey sensed his presence before he saw him. He stood beside them in the dark and Casey reached for his hand.

'Thank god you're here, Tissa, Let's go.'

'No, Cas, not tonight.'

'What! Come on, we must go now. Hurry!'

'Ah fail yo', Cas. Mas Jed done take de p'rogue.'

CHAPTER EIGHTEEN

'No pirogue.' Casey repeated the words to himself, scarcely comprehending. Lucy stirred beside him.

'De drongos done go fo' a new passel of slaves an' Mas Jed gone to Bayou Sara. Dere ain' no boat.' Tissa was close to tears. 'It ain' ma fault, Marse Casey.'

Casey drew a deep breath, his mind racing.

'Go back, Cas,' pleaded Tissa. 'Marse Jed gwine see y'all. We try nex' moon.'

Lucy slipped her hand into Casey's and squeezed it. 'We can't go back, it's too late for that.'

'Jed will be on the steamboat,' said Casey. 'That's if we manage to get to Bayou Sara in time.'

'It makes no difference if Jed sees us. You're not his slave.'

'By the devil, Lucy!' Casey almost shouted and turned to Tissa. 'Tissa, we're going! We have every right, but you can't come. Jed can stop you because you'd be a runaway. He can't stop us, though. Now, can we get another boat from somewhere else?'

Tissa thought. 'Upstream Bayou Sara itself. 'Cross de swamp.'

'Which way's that?'

Tissa pointed across the creek into the forest. He pulled at his ear. 'Where de sun come up, de swamp folks lib. Dey hab p'rogues. Yo' pay an' dey take yo'.'

Casey patted Tissa's shoulder. 'You're a friend, Tissa. I'll never forget you. Can you hold Lucy's reticule while I carry her across the bayou?'

Tissa took the bag from Casey and stepped down the bank into the stream, looking back as Casey bent to lift Lucy.

'I can walk,' she said. 'If you help me.' She scrambled down the bank beside Tissa before Casey could stop her.

Tissa caught her hand and with Casey holding her other hand, they escorted her across. She gasped a few times as the chill of the water struck her thighs and her feet sank uncertainly into the feathery bottom of the leaves and sand.

When they were safely on the opposite bank, Casey turned to Tissa. 'Go now. We'll be all right.'

'Mayhap ah will, mayhap ah won't'

'You must go, for our sakes.' Casey was grim. 'You mustn't be seen with us in Bayou Sara.'

'Y'all ain't gwine see Bayou Sara widou' me to guide yo' t'rough de swamp.' He set off up the path that led toward Rhoda's cabin. Casey and Lucy followed him without a word.

The moon was shining brightly when they reached the glade. Lucy paused at the sight of the cabin, glowing out of the darkness like an apparition. Tissa tugged at her hand.

'We pass 'round' dat,' he said. 'Dere ain't no dogs gwine scare yo', so don't fret.'

'I want to see Rhoda,' she whispered.

'There's no time.'

They moved silently around the cabin, keeping to the edge of the glade. The shutters were closed and the skewed veranda was in darkness. Lucy tugged at Casey's hand trying to free herself. Suddenly, a cackle of laughter shattered the silence of the clearing.

The three of them stopped and stared at the cabin. A solid shadow detached itself from the tilting edge of the veranda and glided toward them.

'You've come at last,' a voice said excitedly.

'No, Rhoda. We are going through the swamp. You can't stop us.'

'I can take you!' Rhoda stood close to them, her eyes searching Lucy's. She put out her hands and touched Lucy's huge waist.

'You'll need me to get through. I know the path. Wait.' She hurried back to the cabin while Casey crouched on the ground, clucking with exasperation.

'We don't need her,' he said irritably.

'We do!' Lucy's voice was so soft, he barely heard her, but her insistent tone was unmistakable. He did hear the anguish in her voice though and he sucked harder on his lips to still his own anxiety.

Rhoda joined them and took Lucy's arm from Casey. He let go and she seemed to relax with Rhoda beside her. Tissa led them into the forest where a narrow path snaked through the trees.

It was difficult for Lucy to walk. Her dress snagged on the undergrowth and she stumbled frequently as her legs gave way. She was panting heavily and Casey knew she could not go far without resting. Rhoda was almost carrying her, crooning softly in her ear with words of encouragement. Their progress was slow and the ground gradually softened beneath them as they got deeper into the swamp.

As the moon rose higher, its mild light crept through the overspreading branches. The trees were enormous; sycamore, gum, cotton wood and cypress, and all around them seemed impenetrable to Casey. The bush was alive with the noise of night animals and insects; whoops, growls and whistles that sounded without warning close to their ears.

This was the land of the bear, wildcat and tiger, and great slimy reptiles that slithered away unseen at their approach. Water was over their shoes and they splashed warily from bog to bog.

Lucy sought refuge from her misery and fatigue by leaning on Rhoda and submerging herself in a trance-like state where the pains stabbing her womb were dulled.

Tissa had a stick and probed each step before advancing. If the water moved, he guided them around it. There was no path now, only instinct and memory to get them through a vast expanse of swamp, growing deeper and wetter and more dangerous with each step.

Still they staggered on, with Casey fearing every instant he would hear Lucy's cry at the dreadful sting of a moccasin or Tissa's shout as an alligator crunched his leg in its jaws.

The bark of the dogs broke the spell that bewitched them and drove them on like zombies. Casey called a halt and Tissa and Rhoda stared at him in surprise at the interruption. They had reached a small plateau in the morass where thick palmettoes with leaves interlocking in a barrier blocked their path.

The howl of the dogs was getting closer. It shocked Casey to realize that, despite their efforts, they had not journeyed far from Rhoda's cabin.

'Dey searchin' fo' we all!' Tissa was stunned. 'De dogs gwine get we fo' sure.'

Casey peered helplessly into the darkness around them. 'The water should throw them off the scent.'

"It ain't deep enough. Dey pick up de smell on de place we walk.

We can't go no deeper wid Mistis. She ain't well.'

Lucy slipped out of Rhoda's grasp and sank to the ground. She was murmuring softly and her face was contorted with pain. Rhoda bent down to give her some comfort, making a pillow for her head from her reticule, and drawing up her knees. She wiped her brow which was hot and feverish, and held her hand.

Lucy rolled her head from side to side, uttering short, sharp screams of pain.

Rhoda smiled. 'The baby,' she said, her eyes shining in the moonlight. 'The pains have begun.'

The yelping of the dogs was getting closer. Around them, through the tangle of palmettoes, the swamplands sank to a level underwater where the dogs would lose their scent. If only they could move.

There was a crashing sound in front of Tissa and he stepped back hastily as an enormous alligator tore through the undergrowth and hurtled off the plateau's edge into the stagnant water. The barking of the dogs grew louder.

'What we gwine do, Mas Cas?'

Casey hesitated, shocked with the realization that they were all depending on him for survival with alligators in front and killer dogs behind. He glanced down at Lucy who was clutching herself, bravely trying not to scream again.

'Do you know what to do, Rhoda?' he asked, fearing the worst.

'Oh yes!'

Rhoda's eagerness surprised him. He knelt down and peered closely at her. She was slobbering, her eyes blazing wildly and her face, mottled by a patch of moonlight seeping through the palmetto leaves, had the glare of madness.

He rose heavily to his feet at the sound of the dogs bounding through the trees behind him. He turned to face them when suddenly a shape burst though the forest and rushed toward him from the swamp.

'Lor'!' a voice shrieked. 'Ah done, ah done.'

'Hilda!' Tissa caught the cook as she tumbled in a heap at Casey's feet. The dogs yowled close behind. Casey stiffened with resolve.

'I'll lead them off,' he said. He broke a branch off a tree and plunged with it into the marsh.

His feet squelched in the mire. The dogs, who had been chasing Hilda and only hesitated when her scent got confused with the stench of the bog, heard him coming. Their barks changed from the excitement of the chase to yelps of pleasure as they recognized a smell that was familiar.

They leaped at him, spraying him with mud and making him stumble. He raised the branch above his head and cracked it down. It smashed the lead dog on his nose and he howled with pain and surprise. The other dogs recognized his anger and fell back, cowering at his feet.

Thank god, Casey thought, for the beatings he had trained them with.

Hilda was regaining her wind. She sat up and stared in the gloom about her. 'Lor',' she said, 'ah don' believe dis. Mistis Lucy here-ah!' She thrust her pudgy arm at Tissa for him to help her to her feet.

'De dogs chasin' all we, Hilda,' Tissa explained eagerly. 'Ah leadin' de folks to Bayou Sara dis slave way. Mistis Lucy droppin' she chil' an' she can't walk no mo'.

Hilda brushed herself down and glared at Tissa. 'Dem dogs achasin' me, boy, not yo'. Dey done take ma scent when ah does be walkin' to de conjure meetin' swampside. Dey huntin' wildcat an' 'scape from dat *makak* drongo what runnin' dem.'

She drew herself up to her full height, having caught her breath and her pride, and stared around, shaking her head again.

'Miz Rhoda!' she called sternly, walking over to where Rhoda squatted beside Lucy.

Rhoda blinked nervously, waiting to be scolded.

'Look like we got one big job tonight. If!' Hilda said, taking charge.

Rhoda relaxed. 'I'll help you, Hilda,' she said, eager to please.

'Dis po' white girl gwine need de help,' Hilda said, lowering her face to peer closely at Lucy. She pressed her palm under Lucy's nose to test her breathing.

'She strainin'. De babe ain' gwine be long nuh. Cock up her legs some mo', Miz Rhoda.' Hilda surveyed her surroundings.

'Ah done birt' full niggahs in de canefiel's,' she announced to Tissa who was hovering as close as he dared without touching off Hilda's temper. 'Ah s'pose ah can birt' a half-niggah in de swamp.'

Lucy stirred. Her eyes were glazed and she saw only the hulking outline of Hilda between her and the dark sky. She was frightened and the pain throbbing alive inside her, was demanding all her concentration. She spoke softly and Hilda hitched up her skirt around her waist and got down with difficulty on to her knees in the mud to listen.

'He's white . . .' she whispered. 'Not half . . .' Her attempt to speak was cut off by a new pain that ripped through her. She grabbed Rhoda's wrists and locked her hands around them as she screamed and screamed.

'Eh! Eh!' clucked Hilda. 'Dat good, dat good. Tissa, get a piece ob clot' fo' she to hold. She gwine snap Miz Rhoda wrist in two like dat.'

Tissa pulled off his shirt and offered it. Hilda nodded at him to wait. When the pain eased and Lucy relaxed, her screams dying on the breeze, Hilda prized open her hands from Rhoda's arms. Rhoda fell back with a smile of pleasure.

'I took her pain,' she cried. 'I felt it.'

'Dat good!' Hilda murmured without thinking. 'De clot',' she said to Tissa. 'Tie she hands to de tree wid it.'

Tissa was aghast. 'Hilda, she white . . .!'

'Do it, boy, befo' de pain get she rollin' again.'

Tissa held Lucy's hands gingerly and lifted them behind her head, placing them together so that the fingers touched behind the trunk of the palmetto tree. He wrapped his shirt around both wrists and bound it into a knot.

Lucy lay limp until the pain began again and she struggled to free her hands, straining against the tree as she fought the agony striking through her.

'Make sure she tie firm, Tissa. Dat gwine gib she strengt'.' Hilda looked at him sharply, considering something. 'Yo' know de way to St Francisville?'

'Ob course. Yo' wan' Doc Yarrow, don' yo'?'

'Not me, boy!' Hilda straightened her back. 'Ah ain' lose a whelp yet an' ah ain' gwine lose dis one! Miz Lucy white. Mayhap she wan' de white doctah.'

Tissa pulled at the reticule under Lucy's head. Rhoda held the other side and pulled it back. Lucy groaned as her head was bumped about.

'What yo' doing', boy?' Hilda knocked his hand away.

'Ah need ma pass. Miz Lucy does hab it in she bag.'

Hilda slapped his ear. 'Dat yo' pass. Yo' ax de doctah come quick. An' Mas Jed too.'

Hilda stared after him as he disappeared into the swamp. Now she was alone with two white women, one half-witted and the other half dead, and only alligators and snakes for company. She prayed Casey would come back soon.

Lucy screamed again. Rhoda dabbed at her brow with a handkerchief, muttering gibberish to herself.

Hilda sighed with exasperation and wiped her hands on the side of her shift to remove the swamp mud from them. She placed her fingers between Lucy's thighs and probed gently. Lucy screamed again.

Casey heard the scream and winced. He wanted to run back to Lucy if only the dogs would let him. Every time he turned, they slunk along at his side. When he pointed in the direction of The Drongos and told them to go, they refused to leave him. He thrashed them, they ran off then came crawling slowly back with their tails wagging.

It was vital that he keep them away from Lucy so he began to walk back along the swamp trail. The dogs knew the route better than he did and he followed them easily avoiding the marsh mud. They made such a racket with their joyful yelping, he wondered why their handler didn't come for them.

At last he reached Rhoda's cabin and sank exhausted on the veranda. The dogs fell to the grass around him and panted, their eyes watching his own. He stood up, and the dogs were on their feet. He shouted at them to stay, waving his stick at them, and stepped toward the path. They followed. He was perplexed.

If someone had wanted to keep him there, it couldn't have been done more effectively. The only solution, it seemed, would be for him to return to The Drongos and tie the dogs where they belonged. He pushed open the cabin door to look for some rope. The dogs waited impatiently on the veranda. One of them, bolder than the rest, smelled meat and poked his nose into the cabin.

'Come on, boy,' said Casey, luring the dog inside. 'Come on!' he shoulted at the others, holding open the door. Some of them hesitated until they heard the commotion of the other dogs that had discovered Rhoda's salt pork store. Then they dashed in too.

Casey stepped outside, slammed shut the door and fastened it.

After he had caught his breath he set out to find the trail back through the swamp. He was tired and at a loss to know what to do.

He stumbled along blindly in the darkness, thinking only of rejoining Lucy.

His haste made him careless about the route. He walked until the water rose up to his knees and he had still not found her. He stopped and listened but there were no human sounds, only the appalling cackle and shrieking of the swamp creatures. Reluctantly, he accepted he was lost and turned back.

Lucy's scream, a long high-pitched wail that floated over the swamp, guided him to her. Her cry came from his left, when he expected it from the right. He fought his way through the vegetation, cursing himself for his stupidity in walking round and round in circles so close to where Lucy lay.

He listened once more to get his bearings. Lucy's scream had died; there were sounds of anxious voices not a hundred yards from him. He pushed on, splashing through the dark pools of moving water, not caring if he disturbed alligators or deadly snakes, only desperate to get to Lucy. He knew she wanted him.

'Rhoda!' It was Hilda's voice he heard calling again and again, not Lucy. 'Rhoda!'

The shout directed him to the plateau and he emerged on to the firmer ground from the opposite direction, with the wall of palmetoes between him and Lucy. He rushed into the trees, pulling the undergrowth and intertwined leaves apart with his bare hands.

'Lucy!' he shouted. 'Lucy, I'm coming.'

Hilda raised her eyes to the heavens and prayed. She heard him fighting his way through the palm brush and she waited, kneeling at Lucy's side. He burst through the trees close by Lucy's head and dropped on his knees, cradling her to him. He pulled her hand from Hilda's grasp.

'Lucy!' He stopped abruptly, suddenly understanding her silence. 'Lucy?' He lowered his voice to a shocked whisper. She was lifeless. He squeezed her hand then shook her shoulders frantically. There was no reaction. He turned to face Hilda.

'She gone, Casey,' Hilda said sadly. 'She gone.'

Somehow it wasn't a surprise. He peered into the darkness around Lucy, missing something. 'The baby?'

Hilda began to sob. She lay her head on Casey's shoulder. He twisted and let Lucy fall back to the mud, taking Hilda in his arms and hugging her. The cook's sobs grew into a howl of anguish that echoed through the trees and over the swamp waters.

'Tell me!' Casey said, shaking her gently. 'Tell me. Was he dead?'

Hilda choked and her sobs died. 'No, not dead.' She braced her shoulders and raised her head proudly. 'He born 'live.'

'A son?'

She nodded.

'Where is he?' Casey thrust Hilda from him and leaped to his feet. 'You must tell me, Hilda!' he shouted, pulling her up by the bodice of her shift.

'Rhoda . . .' Hilda began, choking again.

'Rhoda? Where is she? Has she got my son?'

Hilda sank back to the blood-stained grass by Lucy's thighs and flung herself across her body. 'Rhoda done take de chil'', she said between sobs. 'Ah try to stop her . . .'

'What happened, what happened?'

'She done loose de chil' . . . in de dark'

In his desperation, Casey pulled Hilda off Lucy and slapped her face. 'Tell me, damn you!' he said.

Her eyes widened with fear at the white rage in Casey's eyes.

'Miz Rhoda loose de chil',' she repeated slowly, terrified of this new side of Casey.

'In de swamp. Ah hear Miz Rhoda scream an' say de alligator get de baby. Den she run, oh she run . . .'

CHAPTER NINETEEN

Casey ran. He splashed into the swamp, the spongy mud sucking at his feet as he yanked them out and plunged in again; running, stumbling, falling into the water, scrambling to his feet and running on again. He crashed through thickets thick with thorny bushes that tore at his flesh, rushed into mires that squelched loudly and where leeches latched on to his skin; and he dashed through stagnant marshes stirring deadly snakes that flicked their tongues at him after he was gone.

Casey ran until his chest burst and his legs collapsed and he could run no more. He threw himself to the ground, burrowing his face into the sodden soil and clawing at the mud with his hands. He wallowed in the slime, his mind keening just as Lucy had hummed a dirge as she let him lead her to her death in the swamplands of the bayous.

He thrashed at the slush and it slurped as he pounded his fists and arms into its sickly ooze. Then he lay exhausted and confused, covered with black stinking mud as dawn approached and he wanted to die.

The muffled sound of dogs barking penetrated his self-pity. He listened, wondering if he could hear a baby's cry, or Lucy's joyful laughter as she held her son to her breast and suckled him. The barking continued. He raised his head from the mud and stared about him; at the bright green plants that shrouded him, at the shrubs and at the herbs that grew in profusion under the tall, moss covered trees where creepers waved dankly in a whisp of breeze.

He peered through the pall of vegetation as the gloom lightened into a gray dawn revealing the ramshackle cabin in the forest glade ahead.

The dogs were calling him. He dragged himself to his feet and staggered out of the morass. He lurched from one tree to another, leaning on them for support and catching his breath. The insistence of the dogs gave him strength. He groped his way out of the bush to the clearing. The tiny cabin shook with joy, the dogs leaping against the door making the walls shudder as they yelped with excitement at his approach.

He stumbled across the grass and pulled himself on to the veranda causing the rail to tilt further to the ground. He reached up to turn the wooden clamp that held the door closed. He was thrown to the floor as the dogs bounded out.

They hared off across the clearing and down the path to the bayou, heeding a call Casey couldn't hear. He dragged himself into the cabin and lay on the hard floor, oblivious to the upturned cooking pot, the rifled food cupboard and the filthy chaos left by the dogs.

He drifted into a long, deeply troubled sleep from which nothing disturbed him, not even the rats playing around his ears nor Rhoda creeping into the cabin to get the cache of money she had hidden behind a loose brick in the chimney piece. She left silently, a bundle under her arms, her jet black hair dishevelled and her eyes wild with crazy determination.

It was still. The light he gazed at in wonder through the open cabin door was as somber as when he fell asleep. Casey lay long, watching the gloom grow darker instead of bright with day. The damp air creeping in through the door made him shiver. Gradually his mind cleared and he understood that he had slept through the whole day, maybe two days, and dusk was replacing the dawn.

His limbs ached. His legs were ribboned with lacerations, blood and black mud coagulated together in stiff strips. Moving was painful and he dragged himself wearily to his feet, using the edge of an upturned chair for support.

The interior of the shack was a mystery to him as he groped around it. The bed shelf where Lucy had lain weeks before contained a pile of rags. A chair with its string seat in tatters, where Lucy had been nursed by Rhoda, was in a corner. An old dresser stood on rickety legs against a wall, its mirror cracked and its drawers open with clothes hanging out. The hearth was cold and bricks from the chimney-breast had fallen to the floor.

He sighed deeply, trying to establish a plan of action in his mind. Nothing would come. Lucy and his son were dead. That was all.

He sauntered, without being aware of it, down to the bayou. His pants and shirt, what remained of them, were stuck to his body by the thickened mud. He jumped into the water and let it swell around him, rubbing himself briskly to moisten the caked mud and blood. The scratches stung and he cleaned his wounds roughly. He plunged his body under water and pulled off his shirt and removed his pants, letting them drift slowly downstream into the night. Only when he had cleansed himself thoroughly from head to toe did he emerge from the bayou. He wiped himself dry with his hands and looked around.

He was standing on the eastern bank, Rhoda's side, and night had fallen. He walked slowly back to her cabin relishing the night air on his wet, naked body. His skin rasped and prickled where the flesh had been torn and it irritated him to activity.

He fought the stiffness in his joints by walking faster along the trail. When he reached the cabin, he fumbled around in the interior until he bumped into so many things he was forced to give up his attempt to tidy the shack. He righted the upturned rocking chair and carried it out on to the veranda. He flung himself in it with such despair that the tiny frame wobbled under his weight.

Slowly, he rocked backward and forward, gazing at the night. The sorrow that wracked him swelled to anger as he traced back the events that had led to Lucy's death and the baby's loss in the swamp. He narrowed down the blame to himself, for being so malleable. Never again, he vowed, would he let others control him.

His thoughts blurred as the rhythm of the chair provided a gentle motion that had his head drooping. As the moon rose above the trees and filled the glade with its soft light, Casey nodded off to sleep.

He woke with a start and immediately tensed, ready to spring out of the chair and defend himself. A light glowed within the cabin but there was no one on the veranda or in the glade in front of it. He listened to the sound of a person moving around inside the cabin, shifting furniture, closing drawers, and then sweeping the floor.

Dust and dirt flowed through the door then a broom worried it out, followed by a black leg, bare foot on the wooden floor. The dust was pitched off the edge of the veranda onto the grass and the person sweeping withdrew into the cabin. Casey clambered to his feet and walked inside.

'Ah disturb yo', Cas?' Tissa smiled uncertainly across the room. He had set the furniture back in its place, lit a fire in the grate where a blackened pot was bubbling and filling the shack with an appetising aroma, and cleaned the floor.

'Dis place sure was a mess.'

'I didn't hear you.'

'Don' worry, Cas. Ah know yo' down.' He poured a ladleful of liquid from the pot into a mug and handed it to Casey. 'Drink it,' he said.

Casey sipped the scalding soup slowly, standing in the center of the room regarding Tissa as he worked and wondering how he could have slept without knowing the boy was there. He shook his head as his senses were roused and he saw the danger he would have been in if Tissa had been Jed . . .

He carried the mug of soup back to the chair on the veranda and sat, shivering more with shock than the cold. Tissa noticed and came out with a damp-smelling woolen blanket that he draped around his shoulders. He sat on the top step of the veranda, dangling his legs over the edge, sharing the silence while the moon climbed slowly up into the sky above the glade.

Casey wanted to speak but when he tried, his mind reeled with sadness and anger and he was forced to bite his lower lip to keep from shouting out with despair.

He reached over and touched Tissa's shoulder. The boy edged closer to him and rested his head on his thigh. The physical contact helped Casey to control his bitterness. He sighed.

'Well . . .'

'Don' speak, Cas. It a'right. Ah stay wid yo'.'

Casey shook his head. 'Where's Rhoda?'

'She gone. Swamp women crazy like dat.'

'Why? Why did she run?'

'She know she done somet'ing bad. She scare' Mistis Mart'a gwine lick she.'

'Where did she go?'

Tissa shrugged. It was of no importance to him. 'Into de swamp, de bayou. She gone.' He raised his face and smiled at Casey. 'You can stay here now. No one gwine know.'

'You knew I was here. You caught me sleeping. No one's ever done that before.'

'Of course ah knew. Ah was lookin'. Ain't no one else lookin'.'

Casey straightened up. 'What do you mean?'

'Hilda tell Doc an' Mistis Mart'a dat yo' gone t'rough de swamp to Bayou Sara. She say yo' quit de Drongos fo' ever now dat . . .' Tissa hesitated.

'It's all right,' said Casey, knowing he must face up to it. 'Now that Lucy is dead.'

'Ah sorry 'bou' dat, Cas. Was she time . . .'

'Yes.' He sighed again then bucked up as a thought struck him. 'So Martha's lost interest in me? What about Jed?'

'He in Nuorleans. Don' 'spec' he come fo' days.'

Casey sank back into the chair, and Tissa shifted his head as the rocker rose up and fell back to the deck. Casey laughed strangely, an ugly sound contrasting with the burble of the night noise from the swamp around him.

'Somet'ing funny, Cas?' Tissa moved away, worried by this sudden change in his mood.

Casey stood up abruptly, towering over Tissa. The boy gazed up at his nakedness and frowned. Casey's shoulders were shaking with silent laughter and the rest of his body jerked in spasms.

Tissa jumped to his feet in alarm. Hilda had warned him that Casey's mind could have been turned by the shock. She had given him a potion for Casey to drink if that happened. Tissa had it ready by the fire.

'Ah get yo' a coolin' drink, Cas,' he said, moving into the cabin.

Casey followed the boy into the center of the cabin where the glow from the candle and the embers lit up his body. 'Look at me,' he said, flinging off the blanket. 'I'm free! No one owns me, no one even knows where I am. No one cares. I'm nobody, and I've got nobody.' He shrugged.

'Yo' got me, Cas. I care.'

'You! You're a Drongos slave. I don't even have any clothes to wear. The only thing I've got,' he said, pulling his penis viciously, 'is this!'

'Dat de bigges' ah ever see,' said Tissa proudly. 'Yo born to be a breeder.'

'Stop that slave talk, Tissa!' Casey flung himself on the bed shelf. 'I'm not a stud!'

'We be what we be, Cas. Dat what Hilda say.'

Tissa snuffed out the candle with his fingers. 'Yo' gwine sleep, Cas? In de mornin' ah gwine come wid britches fo' yo'.'

He untied his own pants and rolled them down his thighs to the floor. He was naked now and hung them on the back of Rhoda's chair. He climbed on to the bed shelf beside Casey and wriggled so that Casey's arm was around him.

'Yo' safe here, Cas. Ah gwine care yo' good.'

Casey lived undisturbed in Rhoda's cabin for three weeks. If Martha knew of his presence within half a mile of The Drongos, she gave no sign of it. Tissa came every night with food from Hilda's kitchen and stayed with him until dawn. Jed was in New Orleans during that period and the routine of the plantation slackened.

Martha kept to the house leaving the compound to be run by the overseer, Ruffin Calmes. Tissa was able to move freely at night, although by day he was forced to labor on boat repairs under the watchful eye and ready whip of Mr Calmes.

The regular slave complement of The Drongos was around thirty, according to Tissa. In addition there were the occasional consignment of bossals who filled the stockade until they were ready to be shipped to auction in Bayou Sara, or New Orleans. A new consignment had arrived recently and they were being seasoned by Ruffin Calmes and by what Tissa described as 'white trash', white men from Bayou Sara.

Casey let Tissa speak about the plantation but his thoughts were on other things. During the day, he was preparing himself. He prowled through the forest for miles around the cabin. He traveled far up the Bayou Sara, across the heights beyond the swamps to the outskirts of St Francisville with its grand houses and orderly cotton plantations.

He roamed further each day, pushing himself to the limits of his endurance, testing his strength. He felled trees, carried great logs, ran without stopping for miles through the lowlands, and swam the bayous and even the wide Mississippi itself.

He was careful not to be seen by either slaves or white men. He wore only the osnaburg breeches Tissa had stolen for him. He had no pass, nothing to prove his identity. In fact, he did not exist.

The Drongos slaves knew he was staying in Rhoda's cabin, but it was no concern of theirs. Occasionally, he came face to face with Fang, the mute black who lived in the forest. Fang would grunt with fear then shy away and flee like a startled bear. Casey didn't bother to chase him; he held no hate in his heart for him.

Each day, he felt himself getting stronger. He expected in time that

Rhoda would return from her wandering in the swamps, and he left her possessions untouched. He replaced the worn shingles on the roof, fixed the rotten posts supporting the veranda so it no longer sloped, replaced boards in the walls and on the floor, and dug a garden in the clearing, pulling up weeds with his bare hands and readying it for planting.

Each night, he was exhausted when Tissa came. He welcomed the young chap's company and eagerly ate the food Hilda sent him while he pretended to listen to Tissa's prattle.

'Hilda sen' yo' white folk's vittles.' Tissa sounded reproachful. Casey proffered the dish to him.

Tissa shook his head. 'Yo' eat. Hilda says yo' workin' yo' troubles out yuh mind an' body so yo' got to eat good.'

Casey nodded with his mouth full of ham.

'Mas Jed comin' soon. Hilda don' know what yo' gwine do den 'cause dat his ration yo' eatin' every night.'

Casey stopped chewing and swallowed. His eyes brightened. 'Jed . . .?' He was thoughtful. 'When will he be here?'

'Yo' gwine go when he here, Cas?' The boy was worried. 'Ah don' reckon he gwine let yo' stay in dis cabin. If Miz Rhoda gone, he gwine take it fo' heself. He put his virgin here fo' sure.'

Casey wiped the dish clean with some bread and stuffed it into his mouth. 'He's got to put me out first,' he said, leaning back, satisfied. 'I'm sure going to miss Hilda's cooking.'

'Yo' gwine go back to Dominica?' Tissa frowned. 'Take me wid yo'.'

'I'll go if I'm ready,' he said then lapsed into silence, considering something Tissa had said. 'Who is this virgin?'

Tissa's eyes sparkled. 'Ah glad dat int'rest yo'. She right pleasin'. Yo' ain't never see a wench like dat. She cost Mas Jed four t'ousan' dollar from Mas Ruffin's uncle. He had she since she were three years, so she a virgin guarantee.'

Casey snorted. 'These southern gentlemen don't worry about virginity. They don't know what it is.'

'Dis one sure a virgin, Cas. Mas Jed inspeck she good. Her maid ain' break an' she 'bou' fifteen. Hilda finger de girl too an' she know!'

'Why is this girl so special?' Casey was mildly curious. The meal had made him drowsy. He had traveled more than thirty miles of bush country during the day, running hard to sweat out his lusts and to toughen his limbs. He reckoned there wasn't a man, black or white, in the country who could beat him now. Tissa's words floated over his head until something suddenly attracted his attention.

'. . . down islands.'

'What?' Casey sat up. 'Say that again.'

Tissa pouted. 'Yo' always fallin' asleep when ah talk. She does come from some special slave stock down islands. Mas Ruffin's uncle wanted to burst de girl himself but he got de ven'real so bad he too soft. 'Sides, his wife kept de filly by her side day an' night' cause she raise de girl an' . . .'

Casey nodded off.

'Eh, eh! Casey.' Tissa slapped him on his back. 'Yo' t'ink ah'm 'gerating. Yo' come to de barracoon an' yo' see she de sweetes' chil' yo' ever saw. Skin like gold an' wid eyes like yo' own, an' a body dat rousin'.'

'You sound like you want to taste her yourself, Tissa.' Casey stood up and stretched his arms above his head. He yawned. 'I must sleep now.'

'Will yo' come?' Tissa was dancing from one foot to another. 'Will yo' come to de compound tomorrow befo' Mas Jed 'rive? He settin' big store by dat virgin. He say he gwine break she when he come from Nuorleans. She well guarded by Mas Ruffin.'

'I don't want to tangle with your overseer.'

'He won' be dere tomorrow night. Marse Ruffin 'companyin' de Mistis to Bayou Sara to meet Jed.'

'All right,' said Casey wearily. 'If you like.' Then he paused thoughtfully. 'Perhaps that will be the time.'

'De time fo' what, Cas?'

Casey didn't answer. He swung himself up on the bed board, stretched out with his hands behind his head, and began to plan his revenge.

CHAPTER TWENTY

When Casey had first seen the slave stockade, it had been lit brightly with dozens of flambeaux as Jed received his consignment of new stock. Now, it was in darkness except for the torch that burned in its holder outside the long buildings that Tissa identified as the barracoons. In the darkness, as he followed Tissa, he was confident that he would not be noticed by the two whites who were in the overseer's house.

The slaves called the stockade their compound. It was circular in shape and fenced with stout pickets. There were two gates, one near the Bayou Sara and the main one that gave access on to a well used trail to the house and plantation lands.

The overseer's cabin was located close to this gate. The barracoon for males was on one side of it while females were housed in an identical long building on the other side. Directly opposite the overseer's cabin, across the center of the compound and bounded by the palisades at the rear, were the slave huts. There were ten of these in varying sizes and states of repair. Behind the huts, unknown to the overseer, was a third gate, the slaves' own.

This was so carefully disguised that even in daylight, it looked as sound a part of the fence as every other solid picket. The slaves used it only at night, when the main gates were closed and the whites thought the slaves were sleeping in their huts.

Ruffin Calmes would have been astonished to know how many of his charges were abroad each night. Just as the bayous were the highways of the plantation, so was darkness the day of the slaves. They moved freely out of the stockade, replacing the tiny gate each time so that any over-zealous white on patrol would not see it.

They visited friends on other plantations, consulted Hilda in her kitchen, hunted, fished, or attended religious meetings held in the depths of the swamp. The more reckless slaves were known to spree in the taverns of Bayou Sara. Before dawn, absent slaves would slip back into the compound, sleep for two hours in their cabins, and then wake with the six o'clock bell calling them for work.

Casey watched while Tissa deftly removed the gate. He bent his head and stepped through the gap into the compound. Tissa cautioned silence, leading him toward a cabin at the end of the line of huts, next to the barracoon for women, and close to the ring of light cast by the flambeau. From the light, they could see the shape of a drongo stretched on the ground outside the cabin. Tissa gestured to Casey to wait.

He stepped out into the hard mud plaza in front of the cabin and sauntered toward the hut giving the drongo a chance to see him. The negro raised his head and tensed until he recongized Tissa. He relaxed and waved him inside.

A faint shaft of light struck across the darkness when the cabin door opened. Casey drew deeper into the shelter behind another hut. Tissa had been inside the cabin for a few minutes when the door opened and a woman peered out. She had a pail in her hand. She thrust it at the drongo who rose reluctantly to his feet, grunting angrily. He took the pail and shambled off to the river gate. The woman peered in Casey's direction and beckoned.

When he stepped in the hut, he blinked twice, first to adjust his eyes to the candlelight, second to make certain that the girl standing in the corner was real and not a trick of the shadows. She was tall, his height, with hair, black and straight, that cascaded around her shoulders. Her face had the pure loveliness of a classical madonna with almond shaped eyes that shone like gold, and a complexion the warm glow of honey.

Her cheeks wore the delicate blush of a tea rose, and her lips, parted slightly in surprise, were full and passionate. She tossed her head nervously and her hair shimmered in the glow from the candle.

Casey gasped. Her shift, a poor slave garment, could not smother the incredible perfection of her body. Her breasts looked exquisite, firm and beautifully rounded, yet quivering with excitement as her chest rose and fell under the rough osnaburg cloth. Her legs . . .

Casey flushed when he saw the girl's bold eyes sparkle with amusement at his obvious interest.

A slave who was a genuine virgin was a highly valued creature among the fraternity of white men who traded in negroes. On some plantations, the slaveholder himself seduced his pleasing females at the age of twelve. Sometimes his overseer beat him to it. An unscrupulous trader who chanced on a virgin would be expected to deflower the girl himself and then sell her as chaste.

However, on most southern plantations the emphasis was on work, not breeding, and the slaves lived under a regime that was designed to preserve them for work, not for a white man's lust. On such plantations, few young females wanted to be left out of what little enjoyment slaves were permitted. So they succumbed to the plantation's randier bucks almost as soon as they could hold a hoe.

Rarity was the reason why Jed Barrow, having had the luck to find a virgin slave who had been sheltered by her mistress since she was three, had paid so much for her. Her almost white features and her beauty tantalized him even more and induced him to spend over the market rate. He had posted a drongo to guard her and put her in the care of a trustworthy female slave to preserve the girl intact until his return.

'Ain't she jes' like ah say?'

Tissa's exuberance shamed Casey. He glanced reluctantly around the cabin, taking in the crude furniture, the bundle of rags in the corner which was the bed for the girl and her keeper, and the single candle burning low.

He swallowed nervously and nodded his head in agreement. Tissa introduced him to Hannah, Hilda's sister, who was the cook for the overseer and the other whites in charge of the compound.

'Yo' look mo' 'ndsome an' spunky dan Hilda say!' Hannah shrieked with laughter. The girl, Casey noticed out of the corner of his eye, blushed a deep *café au lait* color. She was enchanting!

'I . . .' His voice squeaked unnaturally high with his nervousness. He coughed and began again. 'I've heard a lot about you, Hannah. Thank you for your help when Lucy was ailing.'

'Accep' ma sympat'y.' Hannah grabbed the hem of her shift and pulled it between her legs so she could hunker down on the floor. Casey and Tissa squatted opposite her. The girl remained standing without speaking a word.

Casey felt the girl studying him. He found the air in the cabin stifling.

'Mas Ruffin 'rive in Bayou Sara,' Hannah said in answer to a question from Tissa. She sniffed disdainfully. 'De two whites at de house wan' wenches so ah gwine sen' dem Becky an' Dido.'

'Seems like you run this compound,' said Casey to please her.

'Aye.' She nodded her head. 'So did our mam befo' we. Hilda keep de house an' ah keep de slaves.'

'Do you have children yourself?' Casey struggled to make conversation when all he wanted to do was gaze at the girl.

'Ten or so. Dey all dead or sold, 'cep' fo' Tissa here. He t'ink he smart but he gwine lose he tongue if he sass Marse Jed 'gain.'

Tissa rolled his eyes at the ceiling and Hannah laughed loudly. Casey stole another glance at the girl. His eyes met hers; she stared at him boldly and then lowered her head before Hannah noticed.

Casey pursed his lips. He wanted the girl, oh yes he did, but how to go about it? He sighed and stroked his chin.

Hannah rose up from the floor and regarded Tissa and Casey carefully. She seemed to be satisfied, for she announced that she had to go to the overseer's house to organize their two bedwenches for the night. She opened the door and peered out.

'Dat darn niggah ain' back wid my watch,' she said, glancing into the cabin. She looked from Casey to Tissa and then at the girl still standing in the corner with her eyes lowered modestly to the floor.

'Tissa!' she said with a note of warning in her voice. 'If dat drongo tries to get in here while ah'm gone, yo'jes' holler fo' me an' ah come an' bite off his balls. If!' She chuckled at the thought.

'Yo' an' Casey guard de chit well, nuh, yo' hear? Marse Jed gwine die of 'poplexy if she lose she maid befo' he burst it himself.'

Casey joined in Hannah's hearty laughter, pleased that the old woman was delighted at the thought. He held the door open for her and she bustled down the steps, her shoulders still shaking with mirth.

Casey was gripped with tension he had never felt before. His stomach was fluttering and he was forced to grip his fists to stop his hands shaking. His feet tingled and his thighs seemed to be melting. He closed the door quickly and stood with his back to it, trying to keep out of the candle glow. He was too tense to speak.

Tissa sensed the atmosphere that filled the tiny cabin as soon as his mother left. He glanced quizzically at Casey. He saw his neck was stiff and his head held high like a hunting dog sniffing the scent of his prey. Tissa followed his gaze. The girl was starting at Casey, her breasts alive as she panted with her heart-shaped mouth half-open.

Tissa shifted uncomfortably, his own loins swimming with desire. He swallowed.

'Cas,' he said softly, his voice barely breaking the spell in the cabin. 'Ah gwine check de drongo.' He rose to his feet and slid out of the cabin, carefully closing the door behind him.

Casey and the girl knew he had gone, but they didn't hear him. They were locked in a conversation of their own without a word being spoken.

Casey took three strides across the floor of the cabin, the tough cloth of his pants grating against his swollen crotch. The girl, as slender and as graceful as a sapling in the breeze, inclined gently toward him.

His arms enfolded her. Her hands hesitated against his waist then slid around his body grasping him lightly. She raised her head, her eyes sparkling and her lips àpart with anticipation. He brought his mouth down slowly to meet hers and they kissed.

It was a long, tender embrace and she clung to him, her hands clawing at his spine when he tried to draw away. He opened his mouth and hers opened too, and their tongues touched.

At that moment, doubts vanished. Casey felt her lissom body quivering in his hands. She drew on him hungrily as he swelled with desire.

They stood in the center of the cabin while the candle flickered. They were enraptured with each other. Gradually, they sank to the floor. Casey held his arms around her until they were lying side by side and she was nestling in his embrace.

'Hannah come soon,' she whispered. The first words she had spoken to him.

'You're not frightened?'

'I've waited too long.'

'Jed will . . .'

'I want *you,*' she said. 'Now!'

She kissed him on his lips and he felt her tongue probing his own mouth. He drank her in then tenderly parted from her, raising himself on his elbow to gaze at her body. His fingers slid down her thigh to the hem of her shift and he drew it up gently. He moved to a better position so he could cup her breasts in his hands. The girl squirmed under him.

'Hurry!' she said, driven to distraction by the pressure building up deep within her. 'It must be you! You!'

He understood. Whatever would happen to her at the hands of Jed Barrow, she needed someone, anyone, to remember as her first man. That way, Jed would never be completely her master.

Casey's need matched her own. For weeks he had lain on the floor at night beside Lucy's bed, shamed by her rejection of his love for her. Now there was only a great yearning demanding to be satisfied.

He pushed his breeches down to his ankles and then moved his hands to her thighs and spread them apart, raising her knees. He was brutally in control of himself, driven by the weight between his legs. He swung over the girl, placing his hands on either side of her waist, palms down on the cabin floor. He lowered himself on to her and began.

Her hands fled to his waist, holding him off, then yielding, as she herself yielded. He strained and thrust hard, no love softening his approach. She whimpered as he penetrated and then gave way to a scream that he stifled quickly with his fist and drove into her.

Her legs locked around his waist as he bucked with a frenzy which she matched with her fists beating against his buttocks. They hurried with equal speed to fulfil their need before the cabin door burst open and they would have to face Hannah's wrath. Then suddenly it was done. With heavy sighs and grunts and yelps of pain, they completed the loveless act with a rush at the end of vicious satisfaction.

They lay exhausted, clinging to each other until Casey wiped away her tears and withdrew. He kissed her and she kissed him back. He nodded pleased with himself. Revenge was now his and it was sweet.

'I'm bleeding,' she said. 'It's all over the floor.'

'That's what Jed wants to see.' He reached for a rag from the bundle that had served her as a pillow, and pushed it into her hand.

'What about . . .' She was too exhausted to speak. She dabbed at the blood then fell back into the corner of the room. She began to sob.

'Shut up!' Casey hated to hear the sobbing in case he weakened. He wished Tissa would come.

'I'm not crying because of you,' she said.

'Then stop it!'

'I have.'

He knew she wanted him to ask the reason for her tears. He wasn't going to play that game. He stood up and pulled on his pants, forgetting the blood that began to seep through. 'I won't see you again,' he said. 'I'm going at first light.'

'You're gonna run away?' She stopped shaking and stared at him in surprise. 'Because of me?'

'Hah!' he snorted with disgust. 'I'm not a slave so how can I run away? I'm going home.'

There was a scratching at the door. He walked over and opened it. Tissa poked his head around, saw the situation and scurried in, pulling the door closed behind him.

'Mam coming,' he said, trying not to look at the girl although his eyes were drawn toward her. 'She a'right?'

'No.' Casey smirked. 'Jed Barrow bought used stock.'

'I hate you!' the girl said, flinging the bloodied rag into his face. Tissa stared unbelievingly.

'Well, it's used stock now.'

'Yo' didn't!' Tissa picked up the rag and slipped it down the front of his own pants. 'Mam gwine kill me,' he said. 'Mas Jed gwine kill she.'

'No one has to know.'

Casey gazed at the girl, ignoring the helplessness in her eyes. That look threatened to have him seizing her in his arms and begging her to run away with him. 'What's your name?'

'Lizette.' Her lower lip trembled.

Casey turned to face Tissa so he could avoid that beautiful face with its tear-stained cheeks. The ache didn't leave him. 'All she has to do is fake it. Lizette,' he said without watching her, 'you can do that, can't you?'

There was silence and he glanced at her. She was nodding and the sense of pride and bravery in her stance made him feel weak. 'Well, I'm going.' She still said nothing. He faced her squarely across the room. 'Goodbye, Lizette.'

She pretended not to hear, turning her cheek to the wall. Her hair was dishevelled and her breasts protruded from her shift. It was rucked up to her waist and her thighs were exposed as she crouched like a friendless waif. Casey felt himself stirring again.

'By the devil!' he gasped. 'Let me go!'

She shook her head.

He strode quickly across the room to strike her. His hand was raised and the blow was aimed at her face. She didn't flinch. Then someone was gripping his hand, forcing it down.

He let Tissa lead him away, shame burning his cheeks. There was silence in the cabin while he breathed deeply, trying to gain control of his emotions. He loved the girl, he hated her. Just when he thought he was strong, she had revealed how weak he really was.

'I'm sorry,' he said, shaking his head to cover his embarrassment. 'I don't know what came over me. I've been like an animal tonight. It's the hatred I have in my heart for Jed Barrow. I wanted to get at him through the girl.'

'No,' said Lizette softly. 'I think you wanted more than that, that's why I cried. I felt a pain for you, not because of you.'

'For me?' Casey stared at her. 'I'm nothing to you. Jed's your master and you must do whatever he tells you. What we did, how we cheated him, is already in the past.'

'You are running away,' she said, biting her lip to keep back the tears.

'That's not true.'

'Isn't it?' said Tissa, taking her part. 'Yo' sure scared, Cas. Dat why yo' runnin' now, 'cause Mas Jed comin' soon.'

Casey swung around to give vent to his anger until he saw the mocking expression on Tissa's face. He checked himself. 'I want to go home to Dominica,' he said softly. 'You know I'm not scared of Jed.'

'Dominica!' The girl was on her feet and ran across the floor to Casey before he realized it. She wrapped her arms around his neck, gazing up into his eyes. 'I'm from Dominica too!'

'By the devil you are!' said Casey forcing her hands away from him. 'You're not getting me to take you with me by that trick.'

'It's true,' she said. 'Old Mr Calmes bought my mother there. I was only three at the time. I don't remember it but Mam always spoke of Dominica like it was home.'

Casey began to tremble. His strength seemed to drain from him and he stood limply, his head down. Lizette's happy face plagued him and he turned away from her, but he knew he had no control over what was going to happen.

'My father was a white man. He owned the biggest plantation in Dominica.'

Casey swayed and gripped her arms. He stared at her face and looked deep into her eyes. Those eyes. They looked back at him.

He recalled, years before, another time when those eyes had searched his and pleaded mutely for help. 'Who was your father?' he asked, knowing the answer.

'Carlton Todd,' she said. 'The Bondmaster.'

He embraced her, his lips on hers, as the door of the cabin swung open and Jed Barrow stood watching them.

CHAPTER TWENTY-ONE

The sight of the girl who had cost him four thousand dollars in the arms of a strapping yellow slave he had never seen before, made Jed halt. His first thought was that the buck was from another plantation and had followed Lizette to The Drongos. Then, as Casey slowly turned to face him, Jed understood. He gripped the door jamb for support.

'Hurry up, Jed. You're blocking the door.' Martha's crisp tones sounded behind him. 'Let me see this virgin you're so excited about.'

Jed slid along the wall of the cabin, his eyes fixed on the couple in the center. Martha pulled herself inside briskly. She was dressed as a man in wide breeches and a loose coat with her long hair bunched and hidden under a broad brimmed hat. She took in the scene, glanced at Jed and laughed.

'Hah! You've got what you wanted now. If!'

'But . . .' Jed was too furious to speak.

Martha walked over and prodded Casey under the ribs with the handle of her whip. 'Casey!' she said nodding her head at the irony of the situation. 'So this is where you've been hiding. We thought you'd left us for good.'

Casey pushed the whip away and kept his hand around Lizette's waist. 'Don't touch me Martha.'

'I'm sorry, Casey.' Her voice was thick with sarcasm. 'You're dressed as a slave, so I thought you'd become one.' She ran her eyes over his naked chest, down to the blood stained breeches and back to his face.

His eyes smouldered as he glared at her and she stepped back in the face of the energy inside him. At the slightest provocation he could knock her down, smash Jed across his jaw and leap out of the cabin and disappear. She did not intend to let that happen.

'Ah declah!' said Martha, letting the whip fall back to its place dangling from her waist. She put up her hand and touched Casey lightly on his arm. 'You have changed, Casey, dear. Much more like a man.' Her voice swooped with innuendo.

He flinched, but did not brush her hand away. Her eyes glinted and she turned back to Jed.

'What are you going to do, Jed Barrow?' she asked mockingly. 'He's taken up your offer of traditional plantation hospitality.' She laughed again and nudged Casey with her elbow.

He controlled his temper by squeezing Lizette, drawing her closer.

Jed's face was livid with rage. 'I wanted her first,' he spluttered. 'She was pure Bondmaster stock. Think what . . .' He stopped under the force of Martha's glare.

'Yes,' said Martha and smirked.

Jed,' she continued, 'don't you remember what you said about Casey when you got me to invite him here? Pure Bondmaster stock, you claimed. Of course, the fact that he wasn't a slave and couldn't be bought didn't worry you, did it? You wanted him here to cover your fillies. Well, you got your wish.' She snorted with contempt.

Jed tugged at his mustache and glanced from Casey to Lizette. 'Did you mount her, Casey. Was she . . .'

'I want you to free this girl!' Casey hugged Lizette close to him. 'I'm taking her away from here. I'll give you what you paid for her.'

Martha and Jed exchanged a quick glance.

'It's not easy to manumit a slave, Casey,' said Martha sounding sympathetic. 'There are laws about that, even in Bayou Sara.'

'That's not my concern.' Casey was adamant. 'I'm taking Lizette.'

'You could stay here,' Jed offered hastily. 'We'll give you Rhoda's cottage, you can help me with the slaves.'

'I'm going.'

'Why not?' said Martha, putting her hand on Jed's arm to restrain his and winking at him so that Casey didn't see.

'You can buy Lizette. She's surplus stock now. You're free to leave whenever you want. Before that, though, we must see what we can do to give Lizette her freedom legally.'

'What does that entail?'

'I really can't say. We'll send for a notary from St Francisville in the morning. I'm sure he'll find a way around any difficulties.' She fluttered her eyelashes demurely.

Casey frowned, uncertain. He glanced down at Lizette who had kept her eyes on the floor for the whole time. She didn't look up. Tissa, he noticed, had crouched in a corner trying to make himself invisible. Outside the cabin, listening avidly at the open door, was Hannah, torn between curiosity and fear at what might happen to her.

'Can I take Lizette with me tonight? To Rhoda's cabin.'

Martha flushed and the corner of her mouth twitched with displeasure. She had been thrilled to discover that Casey was still at The Drongos. She was equally astonished to see how attractive he was when stripped down in slave togs instead of playing at being a gentleman.

She had contrived, successfully she hoped, to throw on Jed any blame that Casey might feel toward her for Lucy's death. Evidently, with Lizette in his arms, Casey's grief had been short lived. It was this sight of him manfully shielding the slave girl that caused Martha such anguish. She had other plans for him now.

'That won't be necessary,' she said brusquely. 'The girl will be safe with Hannah. It's not that we don't trust you, Casey,' she added hurriedly. 'Think what problems it would cause with the other slaves.'

'You won't harm her?' Casey directed the question at Jed who had a strange gleam in his eye.

Jed was startled. 'What? Oh no, of course not. Why should I do that?'

'Why, indeed?' said Casey. 'And do you swear not to punish Tissa and Hannah? They didn't know I was here.'

Jed glanced at Martha and she nodded. 'Nothing to punish them for,' he said.

'If you do . . .' Casey drew himself up to his full height. 'You'll have me to answer to.'

Martha beamed. The crisis had been temporarily averted. Now she had to explain to Jed that it was all for the best and if he didn't act rashly, he would have Casey, Lizette and their offspring under his control. She was satisfied. Jed had been humiliated and she had Casey within her grasp. It couldn't have turned out better.

'How delicious!' she murmurmed. 'Come, Jed, we must leave these two together. I'm sure they'll want to talk.'

She moved toward the door without waiting to see if Jed agreed with her. She was getting impatient with him. He had bought the virgin without consulting her and she had only found out from the overseer by accident. Jed, she thought, was getting too independent. It would be very satisfying to use Casey to teach him a lesson.

Hannah was waiting nervously as Martha left the cabin. Martha leaned over to her and whispered in her ear. 'If Mas Jed does anything, anything at all, to that slave chit, you must send for me at once, do you hear?'

'Oh yas, ma'm.' Hannah nodded her head vigorously, sweating with fear.

'Good.' Martha smiled. It was really very satisfactory. 'Come along, Jed,' she said without looking back. 'I want to talk to you.'

The tone in her voice escaped none of the slaves. They watched Jed march angrily out of the cabin trailing behind Martha. She strode in her man's clothes across the compound to the river gate where some drongos waited with a pirogue to take them up the bayou to the house.

Tissa was the first to speak. 'Dey say dat Mart'a de one wid de balls.'

'Hah!' said Hannah, waddling into the cabin. She took Lizette out of Casey's arms and hugged her. 'Yo' gwine be free, chil'!'

Casey grinned. 'Look after her, Hannah. She's very precious. She's my family.'

'De po' chil' overtire', Cas.' The big woman scooped Lizette in her arms and laid her gently on the floor of the cabin, bringing up rags to form a pillow. 'Yo' mus' be mo' gentle wid she nex' time, Cas. Ah hope yo' ain' split she. De blood . . .'

Casey bit his lip. 'I was angry,' he said. 'I wanted revenge.'

'Yo' got dat!' Tissa punched him. 'Mas Jed wanted to *kill* yo'! Yo' see de fire in he eyes? He sure gwine draw his pistol if Mistis Mart'a weren' dere.'

'Yes.' Casey was thoughtful. Martha had revealed why Jed had wanted him at The Drongos. It must have been easy for Jed to discover that his grandfather was the Bondmaster. The fame of the Bondmaster breed was known even in Louisiana. What had happened to Lucy must have been Jed's doing to induce him to stay. He was baffled.

'Come on, Tissa,' he said. 'Let's go back to Rhoda's cabin.'

'Yo' not stayin' here wid she?'

'No.' Casey grinned. 'Lizette's better with Hannah than with me. For now. She needs time to recover. I was in too much of a hurry.'

'Dat de way,' said Tissa wisely.

Casey slept long and peacefully that night. He awoke with the sun up and Tissa gone. A dish of coffee, although it was cold, was on the table by the bed. He sipped it pensively. It was odd how things happened without one knowing why, he thought. Jed's machinations had brought him and Lizette together. Martha was sensible. She knew he was a free man and had the fortune to do what he pleased. She would persuade Jed to give the girl her freedom. He sighed with contentment.

Lizette was everything he could wish for. She was young with a lively mind and a most appealing beauty. He tried to recall her mother. The Bondmaster's slaves were well built women, long limbed with fine hips and thighs. He won his reputation because of the quality of his stock. He had covered so many of the wenches himself, he never knew how many whelps were his own. There could even be others in Louisiana. Bondmaster stock had been shipped throughout the islands, to Havana and to New Orleans.

The slaves who left Dominica were the unlucky ones. Slavery had ended there three years before. A slave could build his own cabin on the Queen's Three Chains, the strip of land between the slave plantations and the sea, and work for a wage.

What would his mother say if he returned to Dominica with Lizette on his arm? He smiled to himself. She would be shocked. A white woman was what he should aspire to. He had tried that with Lucy. He had loved her, yes, but he felt a closer bond with Lizette, and he didn't know her yet.

He shuddered, ashamed at the brutal way he had taken her. He would treat her so tenderly from now on. Their love would grow and they would find the happiness destined for them.

He washed out his breeches and put them in the sun to dry. He spent the morning restlessly. There were logs he had collected to chop for the fire, so he toiled in the sun for an hour splitting the wood and stacking it neatly behind the cabin. He hoed the soil in the garden and removed the new weeds.

When the sun was too hot, he wandered about the cabin straightening furniture, replacing plates on the shelves and looking for more things to do. He was on edge waiting for Martha to send for him to discuss the arrangements for freeing Lizette. In the end, he could wait no longer.

After working naked all day, he sluiced himself at the bayou to get rid of the dust and sweat, and pulled on the piece of pant which was now dry. He smoothed down his hair. It had grown long in dark ringlets falling over his ears, and with his bronze color heightened by the sun, he had the rakish air of a Latin. He had no shirt nor shoes and sauntered in a carefree manner along the trail to the stockade.

He planned to see Lizette then go to the house to negotiate her freedom with Martha. He would sign a draft in her favor to transfer the equivalent funds from the gold he had deposited at the Louisiana Bank in New Orleans. Then he would leave The Drongos with Lizette for ever.

His lighthearted mood continued while he waded the bayou close to where the stockade fence bordered its bank. He expected the slaves to be at their tasks and was wondering where he would find Tissa. He followed the fence northward looking for the slave gate he had used the night before. He did not want to enter through the main gate and encounter the overseer or any of the other whites.

Someone was working in the forest ahead of him. He could hear the sound of branches being pushed aside, and the heavy breathing of a man exerting himself. He reached the stockade behind the slave cabins and peered carefully at the stakes to see where the entrance was hidden. It was so well concealed he couldn't see it.

He decided to ask the help of the slaves working in the forest close by him. He pushed through the undergrowth toward the spot where the noise was coming from. Brushing aside the branch that obscured his view, he stopped, appalled.

Lizette was tied to a tree. She was naked. The sun shone through the leave, throwing its gleam on her face. Her eyes were glaring with outrage and she was tossing her head angrily. A piece of cloth was bound across her mouth so she couldn't speak or cry out. Her hands were tied behind her back and a rope was wrapped around her waist, securing her to the tree.

Jed Barrow was facing her six feet away. He had finished tying her to the tree and seemed to be considering what to do next. At his feet there was a whip. It was the type overseers use, with a short wooden stock braided over with leather and loaded at the butt. The lash was about three feet long, made of rawhide strands, and it was curled like a snake on the ground.

Jed seemed to be alone. With the slaves out in the fields, and the whites occupied in supervising them, he must have felt that he was unlikely to be disturbed. At least, he was relaxed enough to sit on the fallen trunk of a tree and contemplate Lizette.

Casey also looked at her. As far as he could see, she had not been harmed and even though bound and gagged, she was holding her head defiantly. He was curious what Jed intended to do to her. He kept his anger under control to watch.

The sight of Lizette, naked and bound to a tree in the sun, roused Casey. He had no idea she was so beautiful. His eyes were drawn to the lush patch of hair, like honeysuckle, curling on her smooth skin glistening in the sunlight. Her thighs and hips had generous curves yet she was lithe and supple. She wriggled under the bond at her waist with a disturbing motion that had Casey grunting to hold his breath.

Jed was swaying slowly backward and forward, murmuring to himself and plucking at his crotch. Lizette watched him haughtily. His murmuring rose to a crescendo, and suddenly he stopped with a groan. Casey leaned forward to see what he was doing.

Jed stood up and without warning raised his hand and sent a knife slicing through the air toward Lizette. She saw it coming and ducked. The knife nicked her upper arm and fell to the ground.

'I'll try again,' Jed drawled, and threw another knife straight for her thighs.

Casey pounced, but he was to late to stop the knife. He slammed his body into Jed, toppling him over. His fist smashed into Jed's jaw as he went down but Jed rammed his boot in a blow under his ribs. Casey flung himself on top of Jed and the two of them rolled, scrapping and struggling to rise, into the swamp at the side of the glade.

Casey was on top of Jed and pressed his face into the mud. Jed slid away, using his boots for leverage, and tossed Casey back onto firmer ground. He leaped at him as he began to rise. His agility took Casey by surprise and he fell under the onslaught. Jed pounded him with blows while he tried to roll and get his hands on Jed's neck. Jed withdrew, scrambled to his feet and kicked at Casey.

Casey caught his foot in one hand and held Jed's ankle with the other, twisting and toppling Jed down again, face first, into the undergrowth. He bent down to grasp him at the back of his neck but Jed butted him in his abdomen and he doubled up with pain.

Jed grabbed Casey around his waist and swung him round so that his head smashed into a tree. The blow stunned him and he fell limp in Jed's grasp. Jed grunted, flung him onto the ground and snatched up his whip. He unfurled it and slashed Casey across his back as he struggled to shake off the effects of the blow and rise to his feet. Jed sprang forward and snapped the whip down with a cruel lash across Casey's eye.

Casey blinked and stumbled, falling down again, his head in the swamp and his body prone in the undergrowth. Jed kicked him viciously in his side, causing Casey to gasp with pain. He kicked him again.

Casey had been dazed by the fall against the tree and found it hard to recover. His face was under the swamp water and Jed realized this. He jumped on his neck, landing with the heel of his riding boot cracking into his throat. Casey rolled away and tried to struggle out of the mud. Jed regained his own footing and the two of them, dripping with foul smelling black swamp mud, faced each other knee deep in the mire.

Casey breathed hard, blinking to clear his eyes. Jed was lunging at him. Casey saw him coming and stepped aside clumsily. It was enough. Jed toppled over his foot and sprawled into the mud. A shadow moved over them as Casey flung himself across his body, pinioning him in the fetid swamp.

The shadow moved, a knife glinted under Casey's nose and the blade sliced into Jed's throat. The hand withdrew the knife and blood dripped off it into the swamp. Casey pressed his hands on Jed's head and held him under the water. He stared at the blood oozing out of the gash in the side of his neck, then raised his eyes to see Lizette staring down at him.

Lizette had used the knives Jed had thrown at her to cut her bonds. The second knife had lodged in the rope and begun the process. Using her teeth to hold it, she had cut herself free. The rope binding her wrist was easy to unfasten, and she had crept up on Jed and Casey as they rolled in the swamp. She had driven the knife across his neck the way she had seen slaves cut a pig's throat. Now, with Jed's struggles growing weaker as Casey held him under water, she smiled.

'I killed him,' she said.

'No!' Casey panted. 'He's not dead yet.'

'Let me slice off his prick.'

'No! Isn't this enough?' Casey pulled himself to his feet, leaving Jed motionless in the dark swamp water. He waited to see if he would rise too. He took the knife from Lizette's hand and bent down, wiping it clean on the seat of Jed's breeches.

'Did he hurt you?' he asked, his eyes still on Jed.

'Yes! He cut my arm. Is he dead now?' She kicked him with her bare foot, splashing blood and swamp water over them both. 'He must be dead now.'

Casey put his arm around her shoulder, acutely aware, despite a throbbing pain in his head, of her nakedness. 'Where's your dress?'

'I don't know.' She put her head on his chest and began to weep.

'Oh, Cas,' she said. 'I was frightened. He was going to kill me, I know it.'

'It's over now.' He raised his eyes and looked around the glade. He continued patting her shoulder while he gazed at Martha Barrow standing in the trees watching him. Behind her was Hannah and a white man he had never seen before. The man had a rifle pointed at his chest and an expression on his face that said he intended to use it.

Casey threw the knife on the ground and pushed Lizette away from him. There was a sharp thud behind his ear and Casey spun at the shock. His head seemed to crack open. His knees buckled under him and he collapsed unconscious across Jed's body.

The sting of water being splashed onto his face brought him round. A familiar voice was calling his name. He stirred, testing the pain in his head. It didn't grow worse but since it was like a needle scratching across his brain, he couldn't imagine how worse it might get. He could move his head, and that was enough. He flexed his fingers and moved his arms, surprised to find they weren't bound. He was sitting in a chair, a rocking chair, and it was daylight.

'Cas! Yo' a'right, Cas?'

He opened his eyes to find Tissa peering at him anxiously. There was a mug of water in his hand and he stopped splashing it when Casey smiled a little lopsidedly.

'My head,' he said, raising his hand to feel the damage. 'Was I shot?'

'No!' Tissa snorted. He leaned closer and said softly, 'One of dem crackers hit yo' from behind wid a picket.' He jumped back and looked up. Casey followed his gaze.

He was sitting on the gallery of the overseer's cabin. A white man sat on the rail at the other end, regarding him with studied nonchalance. There was a rifle cradled over his thighs which he held loosely as though it was of no consequence.

Casey was puzzled. He wasn't bound and his sole guard had an expression of such indifference, he felt he could walk off the gallery and no one would stop him. The pain in his head made him pause.

'What's happening?' he asked Tissa in a low voice.

'Ah don't know.'

'Where's Lizette?'

'She wid Hannah. She cryin' but she ain't hurt bad.'

'Jed?'

'He dead.'

Casey began to nod his head but it hurt so much he kept it steady. There was a bump the size of a mango at the back of it, but the skin wasn't broken. His face was puffy from the blows Jed had given him and there was a dull ache in his crotch. He had been surprised by the strength of Jed's resistance. The white man wasn't as soft as he seemed. He wouldn't make that mistake again, if he had another chance. That's what puzzled him.

He had killed a white man so he was certain to die himself and it would be as agonizing a death as the neighborhood whites could dream up. He knew that; it was inevitable. If he hadn't killed Jed then, it was bound to happen as long as he remained at The Drongos. But why, why, wasn't he tied? Did they want him to try to escape so that they could hunt him like a runaway slave?

Then he understood their problem. He wasn't a slave so they weren't sure how to deal with him. They would have to send for a marshal or whoever represented authority in Bayou Sara. That was impossible. The only authority in that town were the people themselves. They held the law in their own hands, just as at The Drongos. Martha was the one who would decide what would happen to him.

Casey touched the lump on his head and winced at the pain. How did Martha feel, he wondered. Surely she would want him strung up from a branch of a live oak in front of the house. In a way, death would be a relief after his years on the run, not from other people, but from himself.

Tissa was squatting on the floor at his feet, concern expressed in the sadness of his strong face. Casey patted his shoulder.

'What we be, we be, you said to me the other day. Don't worry on account of me, boy. I'm sorry I couldn't help you to get your freedom. I've messed up everything now, haven't I?'

Tissa was about to speak but the door of the house opened and Martha came out followed by the white man who had been with her in the wood.

'Aha,' said Martha sounding pleased. 'You've recovered. Hank hit you too hard, I'm afraid.' She inclined her head slightly at the man sitting on the railing. 'He's not too bright. Another of my father's bastards from the swamp.'

Casey moved in the chair, wondering if he should stand up out of politeness or cower like a prisoner.

'Don't disturb yourself, Casey. Are you in pain?'

He swallowed, ready to speak, but Martha continued. 'I don't think you know Ruffin Calmes. He's the overseer here.'

Casey saw the man wore a twisted expression on his face that seemed to indicate he would rather be somewhere else. He moved away from Martha and went to stand by Hank. The two men gazed out over the compound, still in the afternoon heat.

'Calmes is very reliable.' Martha paused to see if Casey understood. He didn't.

'Martha,' he said in the silence. 'Don't punish Lizette. Hang me if you must, but spare the girl. She did not do anything.'

Martha snapped her fingers and Tissa edged closer. 'The chair, boy, the chair,' she said, pointing to a rocking chair a few feet away. 'Put it next to Master Casey for me.'

Tissa rushed to obey and Martha settled herself in the chair as though at a fashionable fete and they were about to discuss the rising price of cotton. She touched Casey's arm with a gloved hand and fluttered her eyelashes.

Casey noticed how her manner had changed, her usual harassed expression with lines puckering her brow had disappeared. In the afternoon sun she looked the Southern lady, in control and aware of her worth. She also looked excited.

'I don't know what you're talking about, Casey,' she said lightly.

He blinked. 'Of course you do. Jed . . .'

'Say no more.' She sighed. 'He was my brother and, of course,

I'm sorry to lose him.'

'I killed –'

'Such a tragic death and I accept your condolences.'

'But –'

'We live side by side with death in the bayous, Casey, I'm used to it. Why Jed went out in that swamp, I don't know. The alligators there have killed slaves who've tried to escape so many times before. They are better than any guards.'

'It wasn't an alligator, Martha.' He kept his voice firm, fighting the pain in his head, wondering if he was hearing what he thought he was hearing, or was his brain playing tricks with him. 'It was –'

'What do you mean, Casey dear? Of course it was an alligator. We all saw it. Mr Calmes and Hank here tried to save him but the 'gator had his jaws around his throat. There was no hope. It was terrible.'

She raised her handkerchief to her nose and sniffed. 'It was so good of you and that slave chit to try to rescue him.'

Casey sat back abruptly in the rocking chair and it retaliated by pitching him forward. He grasped its arms and steadied the motion, blinking at the pain. He was completely adrift.

'What are you going to do?' he asked, to gain a clue about what she meant.

'I shall carry on as best I can. It won't be easy. It never is for a woman alone.' She smiled at him as he wondered vaguely if he was supposed to offer to help. Instead, he thought of Lizette.

'Will you free Lizette?' he asked. 'I can pay her purchase price.'

'Ah, Lizette . . .' Martha frowned. 'How do you want to pay the price?'

'With a draft, of course.'

'Ah yes.' Martha gloated.

'Is something wrong?' Her expression made him anxious.

'Well, it's like this, Casey. Jed did something quite unforgivable in New Orleans.'

'What?' A horrible suspicion ripped into Casey's mind. The pain in his head vanished and he gripped the arms of his chair firmly, leaning forward and staring at Martha's eyes. They were shining bright with triumph.

'The draft you gave me for your passage, you do remember, don't you?'

He gritted his teeth, fearing the worst.

'Well, Jed owed rather a lot of money to the slave factor and there was a mortgage on this plantation and on the slaves and debts for some other matters and, well, Jed made a little alteration in your draft and . . .'

Casey sighed. 'Go on.'

'He cleared your account at the Louisiana Bank and you haven't got any money.'

'Nothing at all?'

'No, no gold, nothing. Certainly not enough to buy Lizette's freedom.'

'You knew he was going to do that, didn't you?'

'Jed always was a hot head.' Martha smiled. 'There's a consolation, though,' she added sweetly.

'He brought me the last of your gold when he arrived last night. That's been so useful today because I've been able to see that Mr Calmes and Hank are well provided for. I thought you'd want me to do that especially as the gold was really yours.' Her lips parted and she seemed to be begging for his approval.

'Just in case they thought you weren't actually trying to rescue Jed from that swamp. Now they are quite sure you were.'

Casey was stunned. His money, his hope for the future, was gone. The pain returned and he sank back slowly into the chair. All he had now, he realized grimly, was his liberty. The Bondmaster's gold had saved him from lynching and the rest had been swindled out of him by the man he had killed. It was justice.

'Ah, Casey, don't look so gloomy!' Martha chuckled. 'There is a bright side to everything. Look at it another way. Your gold cleared the mortgage on The Drongos and the slaves. The title is clear now and it's in my name. Isn't that wonderful!'

'It's not mine, so how is it wonderful?'

'It's not yours yet . . . Do you want it to be?'

He squinted at her, trying to guess her scheme. It wouldn't restore his fortune, but he grasped at the chance she seemed to be offering.

'The Drongos can be yours, at least half of it, when we marry.'

'Marry!' He struggled to get out of the chair.

'Hush, Casey,' she said. 'You don't want to hurt yourself any more. Mr Calmes and Hank wouldn't like that.' She sank back in her own chair, her eyes glinting evilly.

'It's difficult for a woman alone. She needs a husband to help with plantation affairs. Mr Calmes is not inclined to marriage and Hank is my half brother.' She paused. 'A gentleman whose money was spent rescuing The Drongos from creditors and who tried to rescue my brother from a swamp, and who is descended from such an illustrious person as the Bondmaster, would be a perfect husband.

'Why, he could even become the Bondmaster of the Bayous.'

Casey sank back in his chair and sighed with despair. Now not even liberty was to be his.

Tissa watched him carefully, willing him to accept. Lizette was in the cabin with Hannah, crying for him.

He turned to Martha and smiled. 'Why, yes, Martha,' he said. 'Let us be married at once.'

She leaned across to kiss him on his cheek, not noticing his eyes harden with an ugly lust for vengeance.

Book Two

BONDMASTER OF THE BAYOUS, 1845–1855

CHAPTER TWENTY-TWO

Bayou Sara in 1845 had the air of a boom town but seemed, like a trollop who has married above herself, confused by its new status. The levee, where steamboats used to discharge passengers and cargo and leave as rapidly as possible, had grown into a full size landing with three wooden piers where passenger boats moored overnight. Stores had opened alongside the track that led from the Mississippi; boards had been laid from one store to another until there was a boardwalk on both sides and the track had become the settlement's main street.

The wooden shacks that gave the town its raffish appearance when Casey arrived seven years before, had become modish with architect designed loggias, dormer windows and fresh coats of paint. The main street had sprouted tributaries, avenues through the pine trees with well constructed houses where slaves answered the door and a wagon waited outside.

The original lawless inhabitants watched with the satisfaction of greed as their makeshift township blossomed into a major river port. The boom was unexpected but none of the scroungers and thieves who were the townsfolk hesitated to take advantage of it. They opened taverns, casinos, hotels, bordellos and even chandlers', barbershops, blacksmiths' and notary offices.

Any service that could be devised to extract money from the strangers who came to Bayou Sara was initiated with the cunning that the settlers had inherited from generations of shiftless ancestors. The source of this sudden prosperity precluded the respectability that inhibited other southern towns, and matched the lax morals of the inhabitants. Bayou Sara's boom was slaves.

The demand for slaves throughout the south had become insatiable. Cotton sold at a higher price with each new season and more acres of forest were being cleared and ploughed to grow more cotton.

Planters needed more slaves at the very time the supply of stock from Africa was becoming scarcer. Slaves died young, the average age at death for negroes was 21. Slaves were worked so hard, and fed so badly, they refused to breed so there was no indigenous supply. The shortage of slaves sent the price soaring and anyone who could meet the demand could name his own price.

Bayou Sara, because of its location between New Orleans and Natchez, was an ideal entrepôt for this lucrative trade. Its people were not adverse to double dealing and corruption, and crime was second nature to them so the trade in slave livestock suited their inclination for an easy, dissolute life.

Even though the demand was there and the people of Bayou Sara were willing to meet it, by stealing slaves if necessary, the town could not have boomed without a steady supply of stock. Jed Barrow, when he was alive, had begun in a small way to meet that demand by contracting with the slave importers at the coast for regular shipments. He sold his purchases at occasional auctions outside Bayou Sara's makeshift hotel then drank or gambled the proceeds. He was always in debt and his stock was so inferior the price remained low.

Bayou Sara would also have remained low, a stagnant backwater hamlet, if Casey Loring Todd had not decided to seek his revenge and the people of Bayou Sara had not decided to get rich too.

Casey's plan for revenge was twofold: he would get his fortune back, using any means possible, by exploiting Martha; and he would vindicate the loss of his only child by siring whole litters of whelps.

Casey was cool headed when he arrived at his decision. He had married Martha not out of any desire to accommodate her, nor even to save his own life, but because it was the only way he could get his full revenge.

The marriage had been solemnized at The Drongos by a drunken cleric who had drifted into Bayou Sara and stayed. It caused a brief scandal among the hypocritical gentry of St Francisville while the swamp folk and the riffraff of the settlement reacted with indifference.

Casey's desire for vengeance was overwhelming. It caused him to abandon his principles. He was devoid of passion or love for Martha. He performed as an animal, brutally and without feeling. To his dismay, the more callous he became, the more Martha doted on him.

Martha seemed to find, in their odd relationship, a partnership that pleased her and, provided he satisfied her when required to do so, she was content to let him lead his own life. She refused to relinquish control over the plantation finances. She maintained a daily record of each transaction and expense, watching Casey transform The Drongos into an increasingly profitable enterprise.

Casey bided his time. He was a hollow man. Lizette became his regular bed wench and bore him a son he called, with a touch of irony, Free. More followed by other slaves. He was driven only by his thirst for vengeance, not by love.

Every slave on the plantation was, by virtue of his marriage to Martha, under his command. He used that power to cover any female he found pleasing. As with Martha, there was no feeling involved. He mounted the females coldly, withdrawing and fastening his breeches as soon as he was finished. Sometimes his seed held and the females bore offspring. The slave stock increased.

The changes at The Drongos made little difference to Bayou Sara for the first two years. No one in the settlement cared. Casey stepped up the purchase of slaves from the flesh smugglers in Barataria and soon the stockade at The Drongos was full and a new one was constructed. Martha sanctioned the extra expense, swayed by Casey's insistence that investment in slave stock would be lucrative. She could afford to wait. Casey's fortune had cleared all debts on the property, and he treated her in the robust manner that made her happy with him.

He deployed the new stock in clearing the plantation land for cultivation and, in the process, seasoning them and fattening them up and improving their value. He also, by his more humane treatment, got them to become breeders. Soon, a nursery for the new born offspring was constructed. Expenses increased because Casey insisted on the best quality feed for the slaves. He knew there was money available and regarded it as his own money that had been swindled from him. Meanwhile, Martha recorded every cent he wheedled out of her, and waited for the returns on her investment in a half breed husband.

Casey's concern was not to make money for Martha but for himself. The slaves were Drongos property, not his. In time, he intended to see that he inherited The Drongos and all the slaves on it. Until then, he plotted with his own schemes to exact his revenge and a vast fortune at the same time. He decided to use the settlement at Bayou

Sara, which was beyond Martha's influence, to do this.

He began by making visits to the hamlet accompanied by Tissa. He wore ordinary plantation clothes and no one suspected he was the new owner of The Drongos. To the Bayou Sara denizens he was just another black drifter.

'I don't recall when I first saw him,' said Willard Wadey to his visitor.

Willard was the proprietor of Bayou Sara's biggest tavern, known along the length of the Mississippi as 'Wadey's'. He was a tough, middle-aged man who had been a flatboater in his youth.

'This tavern was a small cabin then. This half breed would come here in the evenings with a black boy at his side. He sat outside while everyone got chockay with whisky. Sometimes he would disappear for a few days and then he'd be back. We thought he was a runaway hiding in the swamp. No one bothered.'

Willard Wadey waved expansively around the bar room to show how it had expanded. The building was nearly a hundred feet long, with a bar running the length of one wall and swinging doors on to the boardwalk at the other. Chandeliers hung from the ceiling, stairs led up to a gallery overlooking the saloon and to the bedrooms.

Wadey's visitor, a short, stocky man with sandy hair and a gleam of curiosity in his eye, glanced around the tavern. He had known Willard during their days together as flatboaters.

'I heard you'd got a partner,' the visitor said. 'I didn't know it was him. What happened?'

'After we'd got used to this yeller feller hangin' around, he come up to me one day with a proposition. My lot was a large one with a track down to the landing. I kept some livestock on it, that's all. Well, this boy says he'll guarantee me twenty head of prime slaves a month, well seasoned, if I set up a slave auction ring in my empty yard to sell them.' Willard grinned at the thought of Casey's cheek.

'It's then that I find out the boy is Martha's new stud from The Drongos. He had a way with him and his proposition made sense. The deal was a bastard and I can see now that he screwed me. He wanted fifty-fifty of every thing. Not just commission on the sale of his own stock, but on every slave sold in my auction yard.'

Willard pushed the bottle of whisky across the bar to his friend who poured it slowly with the air of a connoisseur.

'He always was smart,' the visitor said proudly.

'Smarter than you know!' Willard poured his own drink and swallowed it. 'I agreed with the boy. I had nothing to lose and I hardly expected much business here in Bayou Sara. Do you know, Casey also said he wanted fifty percent of the extra profit I made out of the increased trade the auctions would bring to my tavern!'

Willard shook his head sadly as he recalled what he had agreed with Casey. 'Times were hard then. Even half a share of extra profit was welcome to me, and it wasn't going to cost me extra, was it? I must have done it to humor the boy. He was a nice kid, eyes a bit wild, you know, the way those swamp folks get.'

Willard stared at his visitor, shaking his head in amazement at his own gullibility.

'I suppose it took time to get the project going?' the man said.

'No' Willard grinned. 'Casey's slaves came and built the auction ring while he supervised. He knew exactly what he wanted, and it cost me nothing. Business improved from the first, people were that curious to know what was going on.

'Casey spread the word about selling the finest breed of slaves you ever saw, and it intrigued folks. Planters flocked here for the first auction and, my, we was rolling in money!'

Willard lowered his voice. 'That was five years ago. Casey owns half of everything you see here. But to look at him, you'd think he hasn't got a dollar to his name. He still walks around in an old coat and patched breeches like a swamp nigra. No one knows he's got equal shares with me. I'd be the laughing stock of the bayou if they did.'

The two old friends shared another whisky together then the visitor, who had never been to Bayou Sara before, said he would look around. He left Wadey and walked out of the tavern with a spring in his step that belied his forty years. There was to be an auction that afternoon and he wanted to inspect the stock.

The slaves were penned in picket cages under shade trees in the lot adjoining the tavern. The area was fenced off and the grass of the compound was worn down to smooth, hard mud by the thousands of spectators who had gathered there over the years to buy new stock.

The visitor knew that since that first sale of twenty slaves, the monthly auction at Bayou Sara had become a famous affair. The superb physical condition of slaves from The Drongos plantation and their docility and willingness to work made them prized throughout the state. Other slaveholders sent their spare stock to sell at Wadey's in the hope that they would benefit by the enhanced price a Drongos slave commanded. Planters came from miles around to buy, and some retained agents in Bayou Sara to purchase the best stock by private treaty before the auction began. Business, and the town, boomed, thanks to Casey.

As he stared at the slaves in their cages, the visitor was impressed, not only at the success of an old friend, but at the condition of the slaves themselves. They had a gloss and a pleasing countenance; trim, muscular bodies with thick thighs, and eyes that were not cast down but eager and happy. There was not a lashmark on them.

'Prime stock,' a voice said at the visitor's ear. He answered without looking at the man addressing him, assuming he was the auctioneer.

'Aye,' the visitor said, 'and pricey, too.'

'Cost a packet to season,' said the man. 'The best always cost more.'

The visitor glanced up at the man curiously, then he gasped with astonishment. He whipped off his hat and bowed. 'Casey Todd!' he said in surprise, noting the dirty brown coat he was wearing, the patched trousers and the scuffed boots.

'Don't you remember me?'

The visitor waited while Casey tore his eyes away from gloating at the slaves and gazed down at him. He had a stare that made the visitor feel ashamed of his own grimy clothes and the stench of the tap room. The glance seemed to be calculating his worth.

Casey shook his head and began to move away. He gestured at the auction arena that was beginning to fill, making it obvious that he could waste no more time on a worthless shrimp of a man.

The visitor grabbled his elbow as Casey turned and danced nimbly at his side. 'It's me, Hollis Pickup! Don't you remember, I helped save your life once?'

It seemed to Hollis that as Casey recalled him, his heart sank. He was clearly unwelcome, as through Casey expected him to ask for a handout with his next breath.

'I remember, Hollis.' Casey's voice was hard and without enthusiasm. 'We'll talk later. I've got business to attend to.'

'That's all right, Casey.' Hollis scratched his chin, aware how his breath stank of whisky as it wafted over Casey. He stood back apologetically.

'I heard you got fine bucks,' he spoke softly, overawed by the change he saw had taken place in Casey since he first met him in Congo Square. 'I bet you've got fighters in them, eh?'

Casey raised his eyebrow. 'Fighters?' His voice gave no clue to his thoughts.

'Sure, good stock. You must have something special. There's money to be made with fighting nigras. I could help you. I'll train them, fight them . . .'

Casey's eyes showed no emotion. He glanced around at the people waiting for the auction to begin. Then he moved back to Hollis and dropped his voice to a whisper.

'I don't know why you're here, Hollis,' he said. 'I don't owe you anything.'

Hollis was upset by Casey's attitude. It was not what he had expected. 'You have forgotten me, haven't you, Casey. Unless your nature's changed completely. Did I ever ask you for anything? Wasn't I your friend, your real friend? Casey, I tell you. I can still pick good nigras. I can train them too. Give me a chance with your bucks and I'll make your fortune.'

'After the auction,' said Casey curtly. 'Wait by my boat.' He strode away, hailing a party of prosperous-looking planters who had just arrived.

Hollis watched him talking to them and then became aware that he himself was being watched. He turned and saw a black youth at his side, dressed in the livery of a house slave.

'Yo' know ma master, sah?' the youth asked.

'Yes.' Hollis nodded slowly, puzzled.

'Befo'?'

'Before what, boy?'

The youth gestured vaguely, rolling his eyes in an expression of bewilderment. Hollis chuckled and reached up to rub his hand across the boy's shoulders.

'Yes, boy, I did. I knew Casey when there was no side to him. He was the darndest good feller you could meet. He's changed . . .'

'Yes, sah.' The youth smiled ruefully. 'He ma master an' ah take care him. If yo' his frien' yo' help him too.'

'Teach your grandmother,' said Hollis with a chuckle. 'When I knew Casey he wanted friends. To look at him now, he doesn't need anyone.'

Hollis watched as Casey swung through the crowd, greeting some men with a handshake, others with a brief bow of his head. He whispered to some, joked with some, nodded his head wisely and listened to others. Hollis saw he moved with arrogance despite his ill-kempt appearance. He also saw the reaction of the white men after Casey passed them. One man spat, another wiped his hands with a great show of distaste on his trousers, some smirked, and others shrugged. Yet all the men, even though some hated or were jealous of Casey, seemed in awe of him.

The auction began. There were twenty slaves on offer and all were sold single. Auctions were commonplace in the South with the most famous being held at Hewlitt's Exchange in New Orleans. This one, under an open sky with the sun baking down on the purchasers but not, Hollis observed wryly, on the slaves, was similar to most with one important exception.

The slaves on the block smiled. Their faces glistened, their bodies shone with rude good health, and their muscles gleamed. They posed to show off their strength and treated the whole affair as if it was some sideshow at which they were the stars, not the victims.

'Why do they look so happy?' Hollis asked Tissa, who still stood with him.

''cause they pleased.'

'How can they be pleased to be sold?' Hollis pushed his hat back on his head and scratched his scalp. The slaves were greased but that alone couldn't account for their radiance. They glowed.

Tissa shrugged. 'Dem nigahs does be seasoned for sellin',' he said. 'Dey want to make mo' dan de nex' one.'

'Surely it doesn't matter to them what they sell for?' Hollis had never heard anything like it.

'Sure it does.' Tissa wondered how a white man could be so stupid. 'A t'ousan' dollar niggah knows he better dan a five hundred dollar niggah.'

'Ah yes.' Hollis turned and touched Tissa's shoulder again, squeezing it. He was impressed by the solid stature of the boy and his broad chest under the ruffles of his white shirt. 'And what value of nigra are you?' he asked.

'Ten t'ousand, sah!' Tissa grinned broadly. 'Marse Casey ain't gwine sell me, sah. Never.'

'You sound sure of that.'

Tissa's smile faded when he caught sight of Casey signalling him. 'Yo' got to come wid me now, sah. De a'ction sale does be ending.'

'Indeed?' Hollis frowned. 'Why should I come with you? I want to see my friend Willard Wadey for a drink before I'm ready to go.'

'No.' Tissa put his arm on Hollis' elbow and held it firmly. 'Mas Casey signal me to take yo' to de Drongos an' ah gwine take yo'.'

'All right,' said Hollis, bracing himself. 'I'll go if you take your hand off me.' He pulled his arm away from Tissa's grasp and was pleased that the slave seemed surprised at his strength.

He followed the slave toward the waterfront, reflecting that it must have been seven years since he had last seen Casey at Madame Cable's soirée when he got drunk and fell in the fountain. It had taken him a long time to find him. So many changes seemed to have taken place in Casey's outlook, it made him doubt if his scheme would work.

He reached the landing stage and looked around for Casey. Instead, a group of dark-skinned, monstrous-looking blacks closed in and surrounded him. No one smiled or said a word. Hollis tilted back his hat, not sure whether to be impressed by the fine physiques arrayed before him, or nervous at being made Casey's prisoner.

He followed Tissa meekly into a pirogue and waited.

CHAPTER TWENTY-THREE

Casey laughed when Hollis taxed him with the way he had been escorted from Bayou Sara by the menacing slaves. 'That's the way they're trained to behave,' he said. 'Jed cut out their tongues and made those black birds his guards. I didn't mean to frighten you.'

'I thought I was bound for the calaboose.'

Casey laughed again and finished his whisky. The two men were sitting in rocking chairs on the piazza, watching the shadows of the live oaks lengthen as the sun slipped slowly out of sight beyond the Mississippi to their right. Ahead of them, a lawn of well cut grass rolled down the slope to the Bayou Celeste where it meandered sluggishly to the Bayou Sara visible through the trees.

The old trail to the Bayou Sara, to the right of the house as they sat gazing over the acres of lawns and trees, had been fashioned into a broad, open avenue. It stretched out of sight down the hill to a proper landing stage where that afternoon Hollis had landed with his escort of drongo guards. A wagon had brought him up the hill to the house.

'Have another whisky.'

Hollis tore his eyes away from the serenity of the scene in front of him. He drained his glass rapidly and placed it on the tray of the liveried slave who stood waiting.

'Never refuse,' he said, wheezing. The slave moved silently off the gallery into the depths of the house. 'Don't recall you being much of a drinking man, Casey.'

Casey darted a suspicious glance at the ex-pugilist. Hollis watched his expression change as he scrutinized him. He knew his battered face was more lined, and his fair hair was thinning, but he had a confident look despite his old clothes and stinking smell.

'You find something wrong in my drinking?' Casey challenged.

'Oh no, Cas. Not me,' Hollis shook his head and held up his hand in a gesture of peace. 'Seems to me, you've changed somehow, that's all.'

'We all change, Hollis. I had to, to survive.'

'Yes, I suppose so.' The older man nodded his head, fearful at saying anything that could set off the anger wound up in Casey. He wondered what had caused the change.

Even Casey's face, once so open and appealing, had become twisted. His smile slipped easily into a sneer, and his eyes had an unscrupulous cast where before there was only trust. He had filled out, his waist had thickened and that youthful spring in his step had become an arrogant swagger.

Curiously, Casey seemed to have become a white man, in hue as well as manner. His face was gray, not yellow, and sitting with his legs thrust out, his brown trousers bulging at his crotch, he appeared to be a typical southern slaveholder.

The slave was at his side and Hollis took his glass from the silver tray. He realized that this was the same slave who had escorted him from Wadey's auction ring. He thanked him.

'You've got a fine nigra there,' he said, hoping to get Casey into a better frame of mind.

'Humph!' Casey grunted and slapped the slave's backside as he walked away. 'Tissa is the only one I won't sell. He knows it so he takes advantage of it. A man can't always be a master of his nigras, you know that?'

'Dammit, Casey. You sound just like a white man!'

Hollis knew he had said the wrong thing as soon as the words were out of his mouth. Casey drained his whisky in one gulp, his knuckles whites as he clenched the glass. His cheeks darkened and his lips tightened into a mean thin line in his glowering face.

There was silence as the sun disappeared and a gloom spread over the park. Hollis shivered and drew his coat around him to ward off the chill from the swamps and the blast from Casey's anger. The rebuke when it came was unexpected for the soft, menacing voice in which it was delivered.

'I am white!' Casey said slowly, making an effort to control himself. 'My mother is white. I take her color. My grandfather was white, both of them. One was a sea captain, the other was the first Bondmaster. I am as white as they were.'

'Yes, yes, Casey.' Hollis swallowed his whisky without tasting it. 'That's what I meant.'

Casey hadn't finished. 'You see this plantation?' He waved his hand with a sweeping gesture to encompass the scene in front of them.

'Seven years ago, this was a wilderness. I've made it a plantation a white gentleman would be proud to own. When I came there was only swamp and jungle and a stockade of bossals. Now we have gardens and a park. I grow cane and cotton and raise the best nigras from Natchez to New Orleans.' He paused and lowered his voice, turning to stare directly at Hollis.

'Could I do this if I weren't white, eh?'

Hollis fidgeted in confusion; he ran his hand through his sparse hair and tried to avoid the fervor in Casey's eyes.

'No, don't think I'm mad, Hollis,' said Casey pointedly. He seemed to relax. 'I know exactly what I'm doing. I tell you . . .' He leaned across and tapped Hollis on his knee. 'Life's cheated me far too many times, Hollis. Now I'm the Bondmaster here and I'm getting my revenge.'

Hollis was relieved to hear a woman's voice talking sharply to a slave as she stepped through the front door on to the piazza. He struggled to get to his feet but Casey, who once used to be so polite, restrained him.

'No need,' he said with a shrug. 'It's only Martha.'

'I'm, I'm –' Hollis stuttered, caught half way out of his chair.

Casey interrupted him and spoke to Martha over his shoulder without looking at her. 'I've brought another drunk home with me. Hollis. Do you remember him? You didn't want me to take him into Madame Cable's soirée.'

Martha's smile froze. 'That was Lucy, not me.'

Casey shook his head. 'One bitch is the same as another.'

Hollis was shocked. He smoothed down his coat and attempted a bow. Years of wheedling and eavesdropping had made him a pathetic figure but he knew his place. 'It is so kind –'

Martha sighed loudly at the sight of him. 'You choose your friends with such care,' she said bitingly.

Tissa was beside her with a chair and he placed it so she was able to sit facing the two men.

'Tell Lizette to bring my fan,' she said, wrinkling her nose.

'Hollis is going to stay here,' Casey said firmly. 'In the *garçonnière*.'

'How nice.' Martha grimaced. 'Is he going to cover the fillies and give us some new stock? You could use some help, of the right color.'

'I thought perhaps you might fancy him yourself,' Casey retorted.

Tissa entered with a whisky for Martha which she took without water. She raised her glass at Hollis and said mockingly, 'You are most welcome here, sir. Casey sometimes tires of my company. It will do him good to have a friend.'

'No need to insult him, Martha.' Casey sat upright and glared at her. 'He is my friend, as it happens, and he *is* going to help me with the nigras.'

'Maybe you'll have more time for me then?'

'I fulfil my obligations to you.'

'Oh yes,' she sniffed. 'How much is your friend going to cost for his help?'

Hollis listened to their banter with growing consternation. He found it odd to be caught up in their animosity toward each other, and to be discussed as through he wasn't there. Just like a slave. He drew himself up and placed his empty glass on the balcony rail.

'I haven't raised the matter of recompense, Martha. We're all old friends, after all. You may remember meeting me with your late brother.'

'I don't.' Martha sipped her whisky, her eyes gleaming maliciously. 'I should inform you, sir, that I control the exchequer in this household. If you are to be on the payroll you will have to justify your presence to me, not to Casey here. He is only the manager.'

'Martha!' Casey shifted irritably. 'Hollis used to be a famous pugilist. He's going to train some of the nigras.'

'To do what?'

'To fight. There's money to be made at it. I could organize a bout at Bayou Sara once a week. People would come from miles around.'

'Is this true, sir?' Martha frowned and faced Hollis properly for the first time. She sniffed to cover the fact that her own curiosity was aroused by the idea, and by Hollis. Under his tattered clothes, he could be quite presentable.

'A pugilist, eh? You don't seem to be doing so well at present, Mr Hollis.'

'I need nigras, Martha.' Hollis glanced into the house where lights glowed showing the luxuries of the interior. He shuffled quickly on the spot, poking the air with his fists. 'Casey knows I'm an expert.'

Martha snorted contemptuously. 'My husband is a good judge of nigras, Mr Hollis, on account of his affinity with them. But of white men, I'm not so sure.'

'Hollis is here, and that's that,' Casey shouted.

Hollis backed to his chair and sat down. The relationship between Casey and Martha was no concern of his, he reasoned, wishing he had another whisky. He was ashamed and astonished by it. Yet he sensed beyond Martha's formidable exterior, a certain sympathy, even interest in him. He was, after all, only a few years older than her . . .

A negro woman, slim and graceful, glided on to the piazza. She was wearing a long blue dress under the white apron of a house maid. Her hair, which was straight without the kinks of pure negro, was brushed up under her white cotton cap. Her smile was warm and Hollis was pleased to see such an attractive person to dispel the hatred swirling about the veranda. He wondered if she was Tissa's wife for she was about his age.

The girl curtsied and extended her hand to Martha. 'Your fan, ma'm,' she murmured.

'Where the hell have you been!' Martha glared at the girl and snatched the fan from her. She struck the girl with it then flicked it open and waved it in her face.

'Lizette wasn't a long time,' said Casey. 'Only a minute.'

'She was too long for me.'

Casey shrugged. The girl waited, her eyes lowered. 'Is there anything else, ma'm?' she asked.

'No!' Martha snapped. 'Don't go to your quarters yet. Stay in the kitchen with Hilda. Is Mr Hollis to eat at our table, Casey?'

'Please don't put yourself to any trouble over me.' Hollis squirmed uncomfortably.

'I won't,' Martha retorted.

'Of course he eats with us.' Casey grinned. 'You're not judging a man by his coat, are you, Martha?'

She waved her fan faster. 'I thought nigras stank, Casey dear, not white men.' She gleamed with pleasure at the insult and swung back to the maid.

'Lizette, tell Hilda there is one extra for dinner. And send a boy to the *garçonnière* to prepare a bath. Look in Master Casey's closet for his best shirt and see it's laid out for Master Hollis. Do you understand all that?'

'Yes, ma'm.' Lizette's reply was prompt and obliging.

'Now don't you sulk with me, girl!' Martha fluttered her fan. 'Get along with you. Quickly.'

Casey raised his eyes to the ceiling and said nothing. Hollis, who had suffered too many indignities in his life as a drifter to show he was offended, wondered what calamity had changed Martha into a shrew and Casey into a cad.

He had time to reflect while he was having his bath in the room at the *garçonnière*. Tissa attended him. The boy half filled the tiny bath tub with water that had been warmed by Hilda over the kitchen fire, then added cold water brought up from the bayou in pails by a pair of slaves.

'Help me with my boots, boy.' Hollis sank into a chair and stuck out his legs, delighted to have a slave to serve him. Tissa hesitated. 'Come on, boy, pull them off.'

Tissa sucked his teeth noisily, showing his displeasure. He knelt before Hollis and pulled off one boot roughly then he began to tug at the other.

Hollis leaned forward and laid his gnarled hand on Tissa's collar-bone. He pressed his thumb down at the base of Tissa's neck and squeezed, paralyzing him.

Tissa's eyes popped out and he gasped, powerless to move.

'Now listen to me, boy,' said Hollis. 'I may not look much but that don't mean I'm going to take insolence from a bright young feller like you. There's spunk in me yet, and you remember it. Treat me right, boy, and you'll learn plenty.' He released the slave and sat back.

Tissa rubbed his neck, staring at him stupidly.

'The boot,' said Hollis, waggling his foot in his face.

'Yes, Mas Hollis!' He pulled it off quickly and stood up, backing away.

Hollis smiled to himself as he removed his trousers and stood naked at the side of the tub. His flesh was gray with dirt and his own odor made him wrinkle his nose. Folds of flesh hung loosely on his body where lack of exercise had rendered his muscles flabby. But he was still powerfully built for his age, and size, and a match for any man.

He was amused by Tissa's wide-eyed glance as the boy rubbed his neck and seemed to be puzzled at how he had been made helpless by a man only half his size.

'It's technique, Tissa.' Hollis stepped gingerly into the bath. 'If you know the tricks, you can have the strongest man at your mercy.'

'Will yo' teach me, sah?' Tissa watched him respectfully.

'Maybe.' Hollis lowered himself so his bottom was in the water and his feet stuck out over the end. 'Come and scrub me, Tissa.' He was pleased by the way the slave dashed over and picked up the coarse soap and began to massage his back.

'I ain't had a bath for over a year or so,' he said, splashing himself.

Tissa kept quiet, rubbing Hollis's body with the soap. Hilda had told him to see this new guest was clean and he did his job effectively. He scrubbed Hollis's scalp, stirring scabs and dirt that had lain undisturbed for months. He massaged his shoulders and chest and buttocks and abdomen, and rubbed his sinewy thighs and legs. Then he tipped a pail of cold water over Hollis's head and wrapped him in a large towel.

'You can use my bath water if you like,' said Hollis peeping pink and panting from the towel. 'You're a good nigra.'

Tissa declined with a shake of his head and guided Hollis to the bed where he had laid out one of Casey's shirts and old breeches salvaged from Hilda's collection of Jed's cast-off clothes. Hollis dressed eagerly.

'Now I feel fit to serve your master,' he said. 'How do I look?'

Tissa grunted. 'Fine, sah,' he said with a wink. 'Hilda ax me if yo' usin' a wench.'

Hollis smiled. 'What did you tell her?'

'Ah say ah don't know, sah.'

'Tell her yes!'

Tissa gaped.

'Remember, boy, what I said about technique. Know the tricks and what matter if you're small and floppy down there. I can pleasure a wench with as much gusto as you or Casey.'

It was Tissa's turn to smirk. 'Ah don't t'ink so, sah. Ah does be in comp'tion wid Mas Casey. He hab nineteen gets an' ah got seventeen, sah, wid anoder six on de way.'

'By the devil!' exclaimed Hollis. 'What is this?'

'We raisin' stock, sah. Mas Casey gib de bucks a piece ob gol' fo' ev'ry wench we 'pregnate. Not a wench here ain' in heat an' ain' carryin', 'cep' Hilda. Even ma mam, Hannah, got she self full fo' a drongo. She gwine get clot' an' t'ing when she drop de whelp.'

'It's unheard of.' Hollis strutted proudly in front of the mirror, smoothing back his hair. He was pleased with himself and the prospect of regular meals, a bed and a dusky wench to screw every night. 'The slaves must be mighty content here if they want to breed suckers for Casey.'

'Dat right sah. Mas Casey don't beat de niggahs. T'ings change here since Mas Jed die, sah. It rewardin' to sire a whelp, and the dam get presents too.'

Hollis hunched his shoulders and clenched his hands into fists, crouching like a boxer and watching his reflection. 'What does Casey do with the whelps?' he asked, stabbing the air.

'We build a pen where de old queens what dry raise dem. Mas Casey say when dey hab twelve years, dey ready for de a'ction sale.'

'You don't mind that?' Hollis straightened up, flicked his stock with a flourish and faced Tissa.

'No, sah. Tell de trut' ah ain' sure which get does be mine no mo'.'

At dinner, Hollis saw more of the odd relationship between Casey and Martha. Now that he looked reasonably presentable, Martha stopped insulting him and confined her scathing comments to the slaves, picking especially on Lizette. Nothing the maid did satisfied her mistress. Lizette smiled throughout the abuse, serving in an unruffled manner that only infuriated Martha more.

'When are you going to sell that chit?' Martha demanded when dinner was over. 'She thinks she's too good to serve me.'

'Leave her alone, Martha. She's the best maid you've ever had.'

They left the room for the parlor and Casey sprawled in an easy chair while Martha was perched on the edge of the couch. She wore a full gown of a heavy burgundy color material with a low corsage and a waist skillfully corsetted to conceal her spare inches.

Were it not for the bitterness that showed in the sulky downturn of her lips, Martha would be a very attractive woman. Hollis wondered how much of the blame for her tetchiness was due to Casey's offhand attitude toward her.

Martha ignored Casey's defence of the maid and turned to Hollis. 'My husband,' she said archly, 'cares more for his slaves than he does for me, his wife. When one is sick, he stays in the compound until the beast is better. When I am ill, he tells me to dose myself with laudanum. I suppose that's my penance.'

'Slaves are very valuable,' said Hollis trying to be tactful. 'When I was a young man, we didn't realize that. I remember –.'

'Just so!' Martha cut him off rudely. 'I wonder what the going price is for a good wife these days? A little love and affection, wouldn't you think? A little consideration occasionally? Surely that's cheap enough.'

Hollis tried to make conversation. 'I was married once,' he began.

'Hah!' Martha stood up. 'There are times when I wonder who is this man!' She pointed her finger at Casey. 'He lives in this house but his heart is in the quarters with the slaves. Do you think that's where he really belongs?'

A vein pulsed in Casey's neck but there was no other sign of his reaction to Martha's tirade. He raised his head from contemplating the contents of his whisky glass and smiled lopsidedly at her.

Hollis saw his reddened eyes and swaying head and realized that the whisky had anesthetized him.

'Is something wrong, bitch?' Casey asked calmly.

'Oh!' Martha stamped her foot and swept across the floor, knocking down a small table with the swish of her skirt. She reached the door and shouted for Lizette.

'Bring my cloak, girl,' she ordered. 'I'm going out.'

CHAPTER TWENTY-FOUR

Casey picked up his glass and drained it. Pain throbbed in his head as it always did when Martha taunted him. To answer her caustic remarks would lead to a blazing row followed by an uneasy truce and the laborious process of who gives in first. If Martha wanted sex, she was the first to apologize and begin an elaborate ritual to win his favor.

If he wanted money, and he frequently did in the early months of their marriage when he was buying new slaves or extending the plantation, he was the one forced to make it up by toadying to her. Rows were the currency of their marriage.

'Tissa!' Casey shouted, venting some of his anger on the slave's absence.

'Yes, Mas Casey!' The boy came running in from the veranda.

'Whisky!'

'Yes, sah. Ah sorry, sah. Mistis Mart'a done go to de quartahs, sah.'

Casey dismissed him with a nod of his head. It was a relief. It had taken him a long time to get accustomed to Martha's demands. When he had accepted the odd agreement that bound him, he knew what was expected of him: regular servicing of the white mistress of The Drongos.

It was slavery in a new guise. His only option was to escape across the bayous and try to find his way to New Orleans. He had nothing more than the slave breeches that Tissa had given him. He would have been held as an escaped slave if Martha did not have him arrested for killing Jed. There was no option really. Besides, he had an obligation to Tissa and Lizette.

Marriage to Martha gave him access to his own money and the chance to help his two friends. Truth came after a few months of exposure to Martha's devious ways when he discovered it was all part of her plot to trap him. By killing Jed that afternoon in the swamp, he had unwittingly assisted her plan. So he became her husband, moved into Jed's chamber in The Drongos, and began a masquerade that continued, although its importance lessened for both of them over the years.

Tissa placed his whisky on the table in front of him. He reached for it in a drunken daze. He was vaguely aware of Hollis sitting uneasily in the chair opposite him. He heard him mutter in his whining voice some pointless banter with Tissa. It was no concern of his. Tissa would escort him to bed in good time.

Casey sighed deeply, gazed at the glass in his hand and was surprised to see it full. He downed the powerful draught in a single swallow. The pain was dulled.

It seemed to him that the ache had been in his head since the moment Hank had knocked him out with the picket. Hank had gone long ago. With Casey's gold in his pocket as the price of his silence, he did not survive a week in Bayou Sara. His body was tossed out of a whorehouse window into the Mississippi and no one mourned his loss.

Ruffin Calmes stayed on, a constant reminder that Casey's status at The Drongos depended on his cooperation. Fortunately for them both, they learned to respect one another. Ruffin was the guardian of Casey's secret and it did not take Casey very long to discover Ruffin's weakness. From mutual guilt they built up an acceptable working relationship. Casey gave the overseer the support he never received from Jed and together they perfected the management of raising slaves.

Slaves were the dowry Casey had won with his forced marriage to Martha. He immediately developed his plan to make money for himself through them to make him independent of her. Until that time, though, he succumbed to her blandishments. He was lusty in his youth and it was not unpleasant mounting Martha. She was demanding and he took his time, toying with her. When she was close to distraction, he would thrust at her with a fury that ended only with the discharge of his pent up anger deep within her.

She thrived on this savage treatment. Gradually the purse strings were loosened. It was no problem winning the right to run the plantation as he wished, that was one of the reasons why she had wanted to marry him. The purchase of more slaves from the coast smugglers, the money for tools and materials to clear and extend the plantation, that had taken time. He bartered sex for hoes, for better rations for the slaves, for blankets, for a nursery, for a hospital, for more cabins, for everything he required.

It had been a long, sordid process. Their first night together was a revelation to him. Martha knew things that even he, raised in a brothel, was unaware of. She desired him in a way that shamed him. On that very first night, she had roused him easily with her mouth until he was ready to take her. Then she rolled over and pushed her backside toward him. Her fingers were slippery with snake grease which she smeared on to him while she pressed her body closer.

'No,' he had said, pulling away.

'You'll do as I want!'

'No.'

'Casey!'

'No.'

'Jed taught me this way so I wouldn't have a child.'

'No!'

'It's rather nice. He liked it.'

Casey wanted to puke. He retreated to the edge of the bed. Martha followed him and ran her hands over his body, trying to coax him.

'Come on, you darling creature. Don't you understand? I need you! There, here, everywhere! I need you in me.'

'No.'

'I'll do anything for you, Casey, if you do anything for me.'

'No.'

'Please, oh please!'

The desperate note in her voice gave him an idea. 'What about Tissa?' he asked. 'Can we have him in the house?'

'To do what?' She was suspicious but willing. Her hand seized him and began a slow massage.

'As the houseboy. Lizette, too, as a maid.'

'Oh, Casey!' She sighed and twisted so her back was to him. He was in her hand and she gently placed him between her buttocks. He pulled back.

'Tissa? And Lizette?' he asked.

'Yes, yes!' she said, reaching for him again. He closed his eyes.

When he discovered to what lengths Martha would go to satisfy herself, he found it surprisingly easy to oblige her. First, it was small favors, then larger ones as he resisted her more. Now, after six years, he had got all his requirements and advanced the plantation to the point where it was making a profit. He had his commissions, his brokerage fees, and his percentages; all giving him an income unknown to Martha. He was freed of his dependence on her.

Martha, he knew, was no longer dependent on him. It had not taken her long, once she had discovered the delight of having a buck in bed with her who could be forced to do what she wanted. It began with Tissa. He was a handy slave, clean and obedient, and constantly in and out of the house. He was so pleasing that Martha promoted him to general factotum leaving Hilda, who was getting older and grouchier, to concentrate on the cooking in the kitchen away from the house.

Tissa was moving around the parlor as Casey gazed at him from the depths of his drunken recollection of the early months of his marriage. He watched Tissa help Hollis to his feet, leading the man gently out of the room. He was a good boy and a fine breeder. Casey chuckled to himself as he recalled how Tisa had been so shocked by his first encounter with Martha.

It had happened after one of their arguments when Casey remained obstinately in the parlor and Martha went off to her chamber in a rage. She had put on her best negligee, one with red ribbons that when pulled exposed her breasts. Her bed was huge, with a purple tester and velvet drapes. She had arranged herself on it and sent Lizette to summon Tissa.

The boy, always eager to oblige, had come into the room innocently. When he saw Martha lying practically naked on the covers, he flushed and backed away.

'Tissa,' Martha said coyly, 'I want you to help me.'

'Yas, ma'm' he gulped. Her near nakedness was having an effect on him that he didn't know how to conceal. He clasped his hand in front of him with alarm. Martha's eyes glinted.

'Come here,' she said, 'beside the bed. I need you close.'

He stepped forward, his mouth drying. The door of the room was closed and the only candle was on the dressing table and its light couldn't penetrate the shadows of the bed.

'The bed seems to be shaking a little, Tissa.'

'Yas, ma'm.'

'Put your knees here,' she said, patting the bed beside where she lay. 'Put your weight on it. If it shakes we must do something about it.'

Tissa swallowed anxiously. Martha's nipples were taut under the diaphanous material of her nightdress. He dared not let his eyes stray lower.

'Come,' she said, touching his waist. 'On to the bed.' Her hand, as if by accident, brushed his crotch.

He froze, rigid with fear at what she might do at his condition. Instead of scolding him, she cooed with delight and began to stroke him. Tissa swayed on his feet, his sense of right and wrong blurred by the rise and fall of her breasts as her hand loosened the waistband of his breeches and drew him out.

Casey had been relieved when he found out. It had puzzled him the next day that Martha should be in such a good mood and giggling girlishly without her customary sulky behavior when he refused her. Tissa, in contrast, had such a hangdog manner that Casey's suspicions were immediately aroused. When Lizette confirmed that Tissa had been in Martha's chamber the night before, Casey roared with laughter instead of exploding with outrage.

'She's your wife, Cas,' Lizette had chided him.

Even if Casey wasn't perturbed, Lizette was. She had become Casey's regular bedwench, a status that gave her superiority over all the slaves on the plantation. The arrangement annoyed Martha intensely.

Lizette had her own cabin close to Hilda's and she considered herself the true guardian of Casey's interests. 'How can you let Miz Martha rut with Tissa!' she had exclaimed.

Casey was sitting with her in her cabin. Free, their son, a light-skinned boy with an engaging smile, bounced on his knee.

'Why not?' Casey had asked, shrugging his shoulders. 'I do it with you, and with others to get stock. So does Tissa. If Martha wants him, I don't mind.'

'It ain't right!' Lizette was adamant. The years had turned her adolescent prettiness into the beauty of a confident woman. Casey wondered why she was so vexed.

'If she starts with Tissa, she won't stop there. She'll have the britches off every niggah she fancies.'

'All the better for me,' chuckled Casey. 'She'll leave me alone and then I'll have more time for you.'

'No, it ain't better! It will upset the slaves. It's against tradition. She's a white woman and she ain't supposed to pester with the slaves.'

Casey considered Lizette carefully, removing Free from his knee and standing the boy on the floor. 'Martha has never been governed by convention,' he said thoughtfully. 'Otherwise she wouldn't have taken me. There's not a great difference between me and Tissa.'

'How dare you say that! You're the Bondmaster. It's your fortune and energy that keeps The Drongos going. Tissa is a slave buck with a hard prick and a soft head.'

Casey murmured a few words to console her, reflecting as he spoke on the way he could take advantage of Martha's new proclivity. He resolved to ignore it until the time came when he needed leverage over her and could play on her guilt to get what he wanted. The situation suited him perfectly, a subtlety that Lizette, whose slave sense of propriety was offended, could not understand.

Over the weeks, he watched the relationship between Martha and Tissa reach its peak then drop off as she discovered other bucks. He encouraged her by posting his most virile slaves to tasks close to the house, then spending the day in Bayou Sara or at the compound. He utilized Tissa's own feelings of guilt to bind the slave to him. He set the boy to report on Martha's dalliances.

There was not a slave Martha had without him knowing. He changed the slaves around frequently, so Martha had no chance of forming more than a casual liaison. That was all she wanted. He felt no jealousy, only relief that Martha's demands on him were reduced. The knowledge that really she was under his control and that he had brought a once proud white lady to such depths, gave him an odd satisfaction. She still had control over the money, but he was her master.

Casey's head dipped to his chest and the glass slipped from his fingers. The clatter as it fell to the floor woke him and he opened his eyes, peering around the parlor in amazement. The pain in his head drew him back to the present. He fumbled to get out of the chair, tottering with the effects of the whisky he had drunk.

'Tissa!' he called, unable to raise his voice to a shout. He collided with the table that was upturned since Martha's hasty exit an hour before. He toppled over its legs and sprawled on the floor.

'Damn!' he muttered to himself. Strong hands seized him under his arms and helped him to his feet.

'You drank too much again, Cas.' Lizette held him steady and shook her head. 'Why are you trying to destroy yourself with liquor?'

'Huh?' He jerked his head up and stared at her.

'Every night you drink whisky and curse your wife. Next you'll want to start lashing the slaves.' She supported him as he staggered across the room to the entrance hall. He hiccoughed.

'I'll lash Martha,' he said, 'not the slaves. What buck's she screwing tonight?'

Lizette flushed. 'Let me help you upstairs.' She steered him across the floor. 'Tissa isn't back yet.'

'Tissa? Is he the one?' He felt sorry for himself and hiccoughed again.

Lizette was holding him around his waist. He liked to bask in her concern and sympathy. It was an emotion Martha didn't know. She only wanted him for sex and now, with his own connivance, she might no longer want that. With the insight inspired by his whisky intake, he began suddenly to have doubts. Martha's criticism of him had been more acrimonious lately. Did that mean that she was preparing to dispense with him?

He stopped abruptly on the stairs as the pain increased, driving out the balm of liquor. 'By the devil!' he said. 'What's that woman up to now?'

'I told you it wasn't right,' Lizette said, encouraging him to continue walking. 'Don't neglect her, Casey. She could do things.'

'What sort of things?' He walked up the stairs blindly, knowledge pounding with the pain in his head. It was Martha who had drugged Lucy. If she tired of him, would she seek to get rid of him in the same way? The bayous, an alligator, poison; it was so easy.

Lizette was murmuring in his ear but he didn't hear. Fear sabotaged his thoughts. He had always assumed he could exploit their marriage to his own ends, waiting until he had creamed off sufficient from the plantation to regard his fortune as restored.

'Martha and Tissa took Mas Hollis to his quarters,' Lizette said, hoping to calm him.

'By the devil!' He gripped the door to his own chamber. 'Hollis?' A sudden pang of concern knifed through him. 'The woman can't do that! Wandering abroad at night with the old lecher. It's, it's . . .'

The exaggerated outrage of his drunkeness deprived him of speech. He pushed Lizette aside and galloped down the stairs. She ran after him, begging him to come back. He flung open the door and hurried on to the veranda. Tissa rose up from the darkness where he had been lying on the floor, preparing to sleep.

'Mas Casey!' he said in surprise.

Casey seized him by his shoulder. 'Where's Martha?'

'At de garsonny!'

Casey slapped Tissa's cheek, reeling back with the force of the blow. Tissa stood firmly.

'What's wrong, Mas Cas?'

'I told you to watch her.'

'She dere wid Mas Hollis, sah. Not a slave buck.'

Casey stared out at the darkness. The path to the *garçonnière* was a broad one that the slaves had cleared, tearing up the undergrowth and planting flowering shrubs in place of weeds and brush. The lanterns hanging in the portico of the *garçonnière* and from the boughs of the live oaks gave the gardens a festive air. Casey liked The Drongos and the gardens to be brightly lit to serve as a constant reminder to the slaves of his mastery over them.

His drunken fatigue had left him, driven away by his impulse to find Martha. 'What's she doing with that old scoundrel?'

'Ah sorry, sah.' Tissa tried in vain to humor him. 'Ah t'ought as he yo' friend . . .'

'By the devil!' Casey leaped off the gallery and strode along the path. Tissa started after him.

'No,' said Lizette, calling Tissa back. 'Let him go.' She had tears in her eyes.

'Why he vex' fo', nuh?'

Lizette gazed after him fondly. 'Ah don't know.' She sobbed and tried to hide her tears from Tissa.

'He's a good man, Tissa, but ah fearful dat he don't know what right from wrong, no mo'.'

In the distance he saw Casey swaying as he approached the *garçonnière*. His voice drifted back to them, blown on the breeze that bowled in from the bayou, heavy with the odor of the swamp.

'Martha!' Casey shouted crossly. 'Martha!' He stopped, wondering if he had spoiled the element of surprise. It was impossible that she would cuckold him with that drunken shrimp, wasn't it? Hollis was older than her, but he was handsome and willing and obviously without morals.

Casey's heart sank at the thought of a white man willingly making love to Martha. It was the threat he feared. He ran toward the circle of light spreading out from the portico, blinded with despair.

Martha was standing in an archway, her black hair loose and flying in the breeze, strands crossing her face so her eyes were obscured. Her cloak was open, billowing behind her as she stepped out to meet him. Her dress clung to her body in the moist night air. She brushed the hair from her face with her hand and regarded him coldly, as one does when a child asks an impertinent question.

'Martha?' Casey said softly, checking his stride and holding his hands out to her.

'Yes?' She sounded disdainful.

He touched her hands, trying to hold them, but she pulled back. 'What are you doing?'

'It's no concern of yours.'

'Were you up there with Hollis?' He frowned.

'My god!' she said. 'Are you jealous? Jealous of a spineless cracker whose pecker is so small he couldn't fill a key hole?'

He smacked her cheek. It was a sudden blow that caused them both to stare at each other with astonishment. He saw her gaping at him, about to unleash a torrent of abuse, and he couldn't stand it.

He gripped her wrist and pulled her after him, out of the blaze of light into the darkness at the edge of the courtyard. She hit at his back with her free hand and tried to resist but his strength was too much. He dragged her along without caring what she did.

When they were in the undergrowth, away from the light, he turned and jerked her to him. He released her wrist and seized her around her waist with one hand, holding her chin tightly between his thumb and forefinger with the other. He snarled, his teeth gritted together in anger, and he drew her face up to meet his.

He opened his mouth and crushed her lips in the fury of his kiss, seeking to devour her. He pressed her firmly against him, forcing her to submit until her mouth parted and his tongue entered her.

His hand descended from her jaw, under her cloak, to the top of her bodice. He slipped his fingers between the loose cleavage and seized her breast in his hand, squeezing it. She struggled to draw away. He relaxed his grip then drew her toward him, making her lose her balance so she fell to the ground. He spread himself on top of her until they lay full length in the grass.

He raised her skirt, banging his lips against hers to keep her silent while his fingers caressed the top of her thighs. He paused now, overwhelmed with desire and wanting to make her want it too. He stroked her, priming her with his fingers.

When he mounted a slave wench to get a whelp out of vengeance, it was a brutal, selfish act. With Martha he was lost. He lowered his lips again to kiss her passionately and she responded without the tension that usually divided them. Her hands began to massage the base of his spine, slipping under his waistband and down between his buttocks.

The thought that she might have been in Hollis's arms filled him with remorse and anger. She was his!

She lay under him, waiting, with her hair bedraggled and her bodice torn. Her face was bruised where he had struck her and the pain tingled, bringing tears to her eyes. She quivered and raised her body to receive him, weeping happily.

He stared at her. 'I love you!' he said fiercely. 'Damn you! Damn you!'

CHAPTER TWENTY-FIVE

Casey swaggered down the avenue toward the old stockade. He was proud of his achievements and Hollis's congratulations at the state of the planation pleased him. It was early in the morning; the two men had shared a pot of coffee brought to them on the back gallery of the house by a bustling Hilda. Neither had mentioned the events of the night before and Casey, who had slept soundly in his own chamber after he had brought Martha back to hers, felt at peace with the world.

He waved to Lizette who was sweeping the hard mud in front of her cabin. The children cried with delight at seeing him until Lizette told them to hush. Free darted away from his mother and ran after Casey, shouting 'Master! Master!'

Casey halted and let the boy run into his arms. He lifted him off the ground and raised him above his head. Both of them laughed.

'Fine boy,' said Hollis.

'My first,' said Casey with a father's delight. 'Lucy had a son but he died.' He could say that now without bitterness.

Free was naked, his skin almost white. He was a strong lad with a straight nose, black hair in ringlets, not kinks, and the deep gold eyes of his parents. Casey shook him fondly and returned him to earth, kneeling down to chuck him under his chin.

'You must help your mother today, Free. Do what she tells you.'

'Yes, sir.' The boy's face darkened.

'What's wrong, Free?' Casey remained crouching at the boy's level, trying not to intimidate him.

'I'd like to come wid you, sir.'

'Free, you must say "with you", not "wid". No slave talk from you, boy.'

'With you, sir.'

'Good.' Casey stood up. Free, who was six, came up to his waist.

'Not today, Free. This gentleman is Mr Hollis Pickup. He used to be a famous fighter in the days of the flatboats. He's going to inspect the nigras.'

Free bowed shyly. 'Good morning, sir. My name is Free Todd. I'm the son of the Bondmaster.'

'Very good!' Casey chuckled and Hollis patted the boy's head. 'Now run back to your mother.'

'Will you come tonight, sir?'

'I'll try,' Free ran happily back to Lizette who had been watching from her doorway with a frown on her face. Casey knew why. Sometimes, when he was in a bad mood, he would cuff the boy's ears and send him back crying. He sighed. He would like to spend more time with Lizette, sharing the pleasures of having a son of their own. It was hard because of Martha. Hollis was speaking as they continued their walk.

'What did you say?' Casey pushed the problem of Martha to the back of his mind. 'I wasn't listening.'

'I said you're lucky man to have such a son. Is the girl yours too?'

'Yes.' Casey shrugged his shoulders. His eyes were on the slave line that stretched across the slope of the hill running down to the barracoon. The slaves were hoeing and he watched to pick out the slackers.

'Will you sell your children?'

Hollis's remark made him halt. 'Not those by Lizette; they're special,' he said, stroking his chin. 'The others? Well, it takes a long time before a female can breed. She'll start to earn her keep in the small gang in the fields from about twelve years old, but she won't give whelps until three or four years after that.'

'You have everything thought out.' Hollis sounded surprised.

'I have to. This plantation is a business. Every slave costs money to raise and feed. There's no other animal takes so long to reach maturity. For twelve years, every nigra whelp is a drain on the plantation. He's too young to work effectively. I've got nearly a hundred of them here. I'll have to wait another five or six years to recoup their cost.'

'You'd actually sell your own children?' Hollis persisted.

'Sure!' Casey resumed walking, satisfied by the pace of the slaves working in the field. 'Maybe I'll keep some for breeding. They're from the best stock, what?' He laughed. 'Actually, I'd like to have more wenches. I need as many females as I can get. Most planters can't breed from their slaves.'

'Why not?' Hollis hurried to keep up with Casey's long strides.

'They work their slaves too hard and feed them too little. Feed is important. My herd gets the best corn, meat twice a week, and green vegetables. It costs a fortune in provisions and Martha grumbles, but it's necessary. The nigras have to rut properly for the juices to mix, not be in a panic like worn out rabbits.

'Does Martha really control the finances?'

Casey glanced suspiciously at Hollis. 'Yes,' he said, concealing his resentment. He was reluctant to admit that Martha's handling of the accounts was part of the success of The Drongos. He could raise slaves and treat them right and deal in them for the maximum prices but without Martha's financial acumen, The Drongos would be bankrupt.

Casey was anxious to get off the subject of Martha. He clapped Hollis sportingly on his shoulder. 'You still like a drink, I see, judging by last night.'

'Yes.' Hollis raised his head. 'I can take it. I've had more experience than you.'

'Why do you say that?' Casey clenched his fists.

'It's not good for you, Casey, You're young, you've got your whole future ahead of you. You're not a failure like me.'

Casey relaxed and said nothing. They were approaching a long barn built on a brow where forest had grown five years before. He pointed at the building with its unpainted timber sides and a roof of cypress shingles. It was surrounded by a picket fence.

'That's where the future is,' he said. 'In that paddock.' He led Hollis to the gate and swung it open.

They were facing the barn. It was shaded by trees that had been left when the forest was cleared. The sun was beginning the climb in the sky and the light was bright, giving the compound a cheerful appearance. This matched the cries of happiness from the children romping in the grass and sand in front of the barn.

Children were everywhere, peeping around the corner of the barn, tumbling out of doorways and windows, hanging from trees, racing with whoops of joy around the perimeter of the fence, or simply sitting in groups under the trees.

'It's unbelievable,' said Hollis with a gasp. 'I've never seen so many niggerlings.'

'There's more inside,' Casey said with a chuckle of pleasure. 'Prime stock, healthy whelps, every one of them. Here!' He caught the arm of a young girl as she raced past him to the barn. She was naked. He crouched down in front of her and put his hand around her thigh.

'See here,' he said, urging Hollis to feel the child. 'Strong limbs; she'll be a good field hand.' He passed the girl to Hollis who followed Casey's example and squeezed her leg.

'Fine chit,' he said gruffly, turning the child and smacking her backside.

'One of mine,' siad Casey. 'Or one of Tissa's, or one of the bucks I've sold. I don't know.'

Hollis stood up and the child ran off. 'Why do you raise them like this?' He followed Casey toward the barn.

'Reduces costs, it's more practical and it keeps them healthy. If they stayed with their dams they'd more likely die than survive. Besides, this way the mothers don't know which is which. They aren't attached to their gets and so when I sell the mother, she don't regret anything.'

The inside of the barn was cool, with plenty of air coming from the open windows. On the floor there were three rows of wooden trays with a naked black baby in each tray. Some were crying and others waved their arms. The noise was ear shattering and Casey grimaced. A few older children were tending the babies, bouncing them in their arms and trying to keep them quiet.

Four old women in long shifts and cotton caps moved among the trays, occasionally stooping to wipe a baby or to turn it. One of the women hurried over to the door when she saw Casey.

'Mornin', Mas Cas,' she said, bobbing her head.

'Everything all right, Nancy?' The noise in the barn was reviving his headache. He stepped out into the open and the old woman followed.

'Yes. Mas –' she hesitated, about to speak, and Casey noticed it. He turned back to her.

'What is it, Nancy?'

'Mas Ruffin, sah. He done take six mo' fo' de small gang. Dose chil'n too young fo' de fiel', sah.'

Casey shook his head. 'That's for me to decide, Nancy. They're probably ready for seasonin'.'

'Yas, sah . . .'

'Come on, Nancy, what else?'

'Not'n' sah.' The slave glared at Hollis and bobbed her head. 'It time fo' feedin', sah, if you' 'scuse.'

'Yes, yes.' He nodded his head to dismiss her, puzzled about what it was she didn't want to say in front of a stranger. 'Something to do with Calmes, I suppose,' he mused aloud as they walked back across the paddock.

Ruffin Calmes was standing at the gate of the stockade to meet them. Casey pointed him out to Hollis as they walked along the path. On the left and right, where the path turned sharp down the incline to the Bayou Celeste, the forest had been cut back and slave huts built in lines. They were empty, their doors and windows open to let in the air, because all the slaves were in the fields.

'Calmes is in charge of the work gangs,' explained Casey. 'The drivers and the other slaves live in these huts. He has the new ones under his observation in the stockade. I take care of the breeding and Calmes gets the nigras accustomed to work.' He paused thoughtfully. 'He don't work them hard, just gets them responsive to orders.'

'Does he lash them?' Hollis saw a whip in the man's hand as he waited for them in the distance.

Casey grimaced. 'When it's necessary.'

In the years he had known Calmes, Casey had never felt at ease in his company. Apart from the fact that the man had been bribed into silence, there was an unctuous quality about the overseer that Casey found disturbing. He was mild-mannered and self-effacing in Casey's presence, accepting instructions without a protest and doing his job satisfactorily.

Casey had been obliged to give the overseer a free hand in the disciplining of slaves. He was experienced at breaking in raw bossals and he was effective. Casey's stipulation was that any punishment meted out to a slave should not be excessive. It should be used as an example to others, administered coolly and not out of anger.

Calmes had accepted Casey's authority from the day Jed was killed and Martha had given him gold to enable her to make her deal with Casey. He was a dour man who rarely showed any emotion and Casey was unable to tell if the overseer liked him or not. Their relationship was businesslike. Yet Casey suspected that hidden under the surface of Calmes's dispassionate personality, there was a man of cruel and ruthless mien who would play havoc with the slaves if he was ever allowed to go unchecked.

Casey's suspicion about the overseer was based on no more than a memory from the days when he himself was a slave and he discovered that the mildest white man could become the most vicious. Tissa, who was Casey's eyes and ears among the slaves, never doubted that Ruffin Calmes was just in his dealings. The man was unmarried, not partial to wenches and had no favorites among the slaves. Occasionally he joined his cronies in Bayou Sara for drinking sprees but otherwise he kept to himself. He lived alone, tended by Hannah who cooked for him, and by a succession of boys as his runners.

He greeted Casey with due deference and nodded at Hollis. Casey was amused by the sight of the two men sizing up each other. Hollis was so used to being a scrounger and a tipster, his bearing gave him away as one of nature's inferiors. Ruffin Calmes noticed it and reacted sulkily to Casey's announcement that Hollis wanted to select some slaves to train as fighters.

'When would he like to see them?' he asked, addressing Casey and ignoring Hollis. 'They're all in the fields on tasks now. I don't want to disrupt the routine unnecessarily.

'Quite right! Routine gets a slave through the hardest task,' Casey explained to Hollis, involving him in the conversation. 'I don't interfere with Mr Calmes's handling of the nigras. He does it well. We have three whites under him on a part time basis, the rest are negro drivers. Good men; only use the whip when they have to.'

'The slaves will have it worse when they leave here.'

Casey flinched at Ruffin's remark. He tried never to think what happened to the people he sold. They went to the auction happily, proud of their status and ignorant of the misery they faced. He wanted no doubts to tamper with his own design.

'Not if they work well,' he snapped, glowering at Calmes.

The three men walked across the center of the compound to the overseer's cabin. Casey's rapid glance around the stockade told him everything was in order. The new slaves who lodged in the barracoon had been driven to the fields to get accustomed to working under a driver with a whip. A gang of four hands was weeding in front of the barracoon. Casey saw Hollis eyeing them with interest.

'Who are those boys?' he asked.

'They're my new batch of breeders,' said Casey, sitting down in a chair on the gallery of the overseer's cabin. He accepted without a word the glass of whisky Ruffin served him.

'We keep them penned together at night, isolated from the others, until I assign them a wench each.' He drained the glass and grinned. 'Then they have the sweetest task. They get three months covering the filly. If she doesn't take in that time, I try them with another. If they're no good at that one, I sell them.'

'You tell them who they have to mate with?'

Casey wondered why Hollis looked surprised. 'It's the only way to get good stock. If they rut with any wench they fancy, the lines might get crossed and I'd get a runt. I try to match them with a wench according to their size, their looks and their liveliness.'

'My grandfather was the expert. He knew the tribes his slaves came from. He kept stock books with each nigra's pedigree in it. I can't do that here so I judge by eye.'

Hollis was watching the four young blacks keenly. Under the glare of the hot sun, sweat drained off their glistening bodies into the faded blue osnaburg pants flapping around their thighs like breechcloths. Their muscles rippled as they swung their cutlasses at the weeds. They worked with a strong rhythm, aware of the white man watching them.

Hollis's whisky glass stayed in his hand untouched and his mouth hung open.

'Look at them beauties,' he said, wheezing with excitement. 'I could train any of them to fight and they'd lick the best.'

Calmes snorted. 'Nigras fight to the death, don't they?'

'That's right,' Hollis was slobbering with excitement.

'Shame to lose a prime buck for sport.'

Hollis turned to face the overseer who was standing behind him with the jug of whisky in his hands. 'If I train those bucks, they won't lose, Mr Calmes.' He raised his glass and drained it, holding it out for Calmes to fill again. The overseer ignored him and moved away.

Casey considered the gang. 'It may keep them out of mischief,' he mused. 'The sap's bursting in them but I've got no fillies for them yet. Call them over, Mr Calmes. Let's take a look at them.'

Casey caught the flicker of annoyance in the overseer's eyes before Ruffin leaned over the gallery rail and shouted for the slaves to come. It irked Casey and made him more determined to give Hollis a free hand to produce a fighter who could become a champion. It would boost the fame of Drongos stock and push up his slave prices.

The slaves trotted over obediently and stood in a line facing the gallery. They seemed to know what was expected of them and stood at ease, their chests heaving with exertion and their faces alert.

'Britches,' said Casey snapping his fingers. The boys grinned and in seconds loosened their baggy slave pants and kicked them off. They waited for Casey to inspect them, unabashed at being naked in front of the white men. One boy was already so excited, his penis began to rise at the thought of his master's hand holding it.

Casey laughed and stepped off the balcony. 'See this one,' he said, grasping the boy in his hand. 'Isn't he perfect?' He pulled back the prepuce and exposed the head of the boy's penis, purple like a bright bougainvillaea petal.

'Makes you jealous, Hollis, doesn't it?'

Hollis's interest was elsewhere. He lay the open palm of his hand flat across a boy's chest and measured him by its span. He pinched the slave's muscles and made the boy raise his arm and flex it.

Casey watched the process with interest. Out of the corner of his eye he saw a boy, probably not more than twelve years old, peering from the doorway of Ruffin's cabin.

Hollis was enthralled by his inspection of the four negroes. The slaves themselves were accustomed to having their bodies examined. White men often visited the plantation to see what negroes Casey had ready for auction, and the inspection was a ritual the slaves expected.

Hollis's examination was more thorough than most, and the boy with the erection soon lost it as Hollis got them dancing. They ran to retrieve a stick that he threw for them. He put them into two pairs and showed them how to push against each other in a trial of strength. The boys obeyed him instantly and Casey was relieved that Hollis showed he could handle such lusty stock.

'He'll need a whip,' said Ruffin, 'if he's going to train those colts properly.'

'No I won't,' said Hollis. 'Get them interested in being champions and they'll do whatever they're told.'

'That's the way,' Casey gloated at Ruffin's discomfort. 'Get your boy to fetch another whisky, will you.'

'My boy?' Ruffin turned in surprise and his face darkened with anger when he saw the boy standing in the doorway. 'Get inside!' he shouted.

The display of temper was unusual for Ruffin and Casey looked at him curiously. Hollis finished drilling the negroes and returned to the gallery, his eyes shining. He sank into a chair beside Casey.

'What a pack! I'd give anything to be able to train them.'

Ruffin disappeared into the cabin and returned with the whisky jar. Casey looked around for the boy as he held out his glass to be filled.

'Do you hear that, Mr Calmes? Hollis here likes our stock. He wants to train them to be fighters. What do you think of that?'

Ruffin had regained his self control although his hand shook as he poured Hollis's whisky. He put the jar on the floor in front of them. 'Makes no sense to lose a nigra for sport,' he repeated dourly.

'Right,' said Casey with a grin. 'You can have these four. Take them to the *garçonnière*. They can sleep in the portico there. Train them for me, Hollis. Get me a champion for The Drongos.'

'Is that wise, Casey?' said Ruffin, his mouth twitching. 'They're lively bucks. They need watching.'

'That's what Hollis will do. Tissa can help him.' Casey saw someone move inside the cabin. 'Who have you got in there, Mr Calmes?' He pointed to the door and saw Ruffin's eyes flicker with displeasure again.

'Some brat from the nursery.'

'Oh yes? Took him from Nancy, did you?' Now Casey knew what Nancy was too scared to tell him. She didn't like the idea of the boy being with Ruffin.

'I need a new runner,' he said.

'Have him out here. Let's see.'

'Boy!' Ruffin called reluctantly. 'Come here.'

The child kept to the doorway and hesitated, his eyes wide as he glanced from Ruffin to Casey.

'Come,' said Casey in a softer voice. 'You know me, don't you?'

The boy licked his lips, his pink tongue vivid against the jet black of his face. 'Yas, sah,' he said nervously.

'Good, good, he's got a tongue.' Casey beckoned and the boy came out on to the balcony, blinking in the sunlight. He was naked and pure black, his hair a cap of tight curls above his young face. His nose was pressed flat to his high cheeks and his ears were small and lobeless. He was sturdy, his young limbs thick and muscular from running wild in the jungles of his native Africa.

'He's ebony,' said Casey, captivated by the boy's color. 'Where did he come from?'

'The last shipment,' said Ruffin, a trifle sulkily. 'I gave him to Nancy to season. He's straight from Africa. Friendly little chap, speaks English already.'

Casey became aware of Hollis pulling his sleeve. He turned irritably. 'What is it?'

'That boy,' said Hollis. 'Is he yours?'

'He's mine,' said Ruffin. 'I bought him myself.'

'Indeed?' Casey put his hand on the boy's shoulder and scowled. 'I think you'll find he's included in my bill of sale. I don't know of any private treaty.'

Ruffin lowered his eyes and Casey knew he had lied. 'What do you think of him, Hollis?'

'He's pure Batutsi, I'm sure. That's a royal tribe, best blood in Africa. They grow tall and strong, fine bodies, not scraggly like your mixed breeds. He'll be better than any of those.' He gestured at the four youths who squatted in the shade from the eaves, waiting to be told what to do. 'He could be a champion in five years.'

Casey pulled the boy to him. 'He's dark, all right. Do you know your name, boy?'

The child shook his head. Casey understood. The boy's name was his own secret, the only thing he had left to link him with Africa.

'I'll call you Ebony, that's your name from now on.'

'I thought Apollo was appropriate,' said Ruffin.

'Too fancy.' Casey stood up. 'I'm, taking Ebony to the house. Happens I need a new runner too if Tissa is going to help Hollis with the four colts. Any objections?'

'But I need –'

'No, you don't, Mr Calmes. You can find another boy to bugger. This one stays pure. He's mine.'

CHAPTER TWENTY-SIX

'Isn't he black,' said Martha when Casey brought Ebony back to the house. 'I've never seen a nigra so dark.' She sounded wistful and Casey, who stood beside her on the back gallery watching as the boy walked with Tissa to the kitchen, glanced at her uneasily.

'His balls haven't dropped yet, Martha,' he said to make a joke of his jealousy. Perhaps he should have left the boy with Ruffin Calmes after all. No, he was too young for Martha. 'He's a pure blood Batutsi, an aristocrat among Africans.'

Martha raised her eyebrow. 'How much did he cost?'

Casey grinned. 'No need to worry. He was part of a lot in the last shipment they sent up from the coast. He's bright, he's learned a little English already. I'll quarter him with Lizette and her children. He can help in the kitchen and pick up tips from Hollis when he's training the fighters.'

Martha demured. 'I don't like this new scheme of yours.'

'Why not?' He was on guard for one of her attacks.

'It doesn't seem very practical. We are supposed to be raising nigras to sell, not to have them battering one another to death.'

'I agree, Martha.' He put his arm around her waist and squeezed. She wriggled away and he smirked, aware that she was willing for him to convince her. It was his reward for his violent display of affection the night before.

Curiously, the hypocrisy in his love for her had vanished. The suspicion that Martha might have been consorting with Hollis had made him realize how fond he was of her. It had surprised them both.

'If we produce a champion, it would enhance the value of our stock,' he said, gently stroking the back of her neck. 'Besides, Hollis's training will keep the bucks out of mischief.'

Her eyes narrowed as she turned her head to look at him. 'You don't have wenches for them?'

He stopped caressing her, alarmed by what he read in her mind. 'No, I don't. Wish I had three fillies for every colt, then we'd breed much faster.' He stepped back. 'Martha, what does that gleam mean? Those bucks are for Hollis to train, not for anything else.'

He lowered his eyes as a feeling of despair swept through him. Lizette was right, he thought. He had let Martha's dalliance become an obsession.

'By the devil!' he said, clenching his fists. 'I'll not have it.'

'Have what, dear?' Martha reached over and toyed with the hair at his neck. Her voice lowered and her eyelashes fluttered. 'Don't get upset.'

'I'm not –' He was going to shout, irked by the mockery he suspected Martha intended. But when he raised his eyes and saw her lips close to his, parted slightly with the tip of her tongue peeping out, he stopped.

Her hand slipped under his shirt which was open to his waist, and she began to massage his chest. 'You have a powerful body, Cas. It's you who should be the fighter.'

He was puzzled by Martha's attitude and searched for the sarcasm. 'So I could get killed, I suppose?'

'No,' she said softly. 'To be a champion.' She raised her finger to his nose and traced it down over his lips.

He snapped at it playfully and she made a moue of mock concern.

It was mid morning, the sun was at its height. There was no breeze and the veranda was stifling. From the kitchen came the clatter as Hilda prepared dinner; slaves ambled across the lawn carrying water, and in the house Lizette supervised the cleaning and polishing of the rooms, her loud voice drifting through to them as she chivvied her helpers.

Despite the time and the place and the noise, Casey was affected by a stronger instinct, one he thought had died with Lucy. Desire welled within him when Martha twisted her hands in the waistband of his breeches and pressed her body against his. They were both sticky with sweat and the heat made his pants stick to his thighs. Martha's pink dress showed patches of perspiration under her arms and breasts. He squeezed her firmly.

'Stop it!'

'Yes,' she replied, rubbing his crotch.

He glanced around the veranda. Lizette was cleaning in the dining room and the sight of her at the window almost made his enthusiasm for Martha die. The house was full of slaves and he sensed there was no time to take Martha upstairs to her bed. The lust was overpowering. He turned back to Martha and leaned her against the railing, a wooden banister unpolished and worn by the weather.

She ran her fingers rapidly up his spine to his neck where she tore at his hair. 'I love you,' she whispered, tilting back her head.

He lowered his mouth to her throat and kissed her hungrily, gnawing at her flesh while his hands raised the voluminous folds of her skirt.

She clung to him and his fingers found her. He opened his pants and pushed forward. She gasped, supported behind by the banister, and by his rough hands clutching her bottom.

He kissed her on her lips as he lifted her with his hands and entered her.

Their bodies were united in a desperate coupling that stirred Casey more than he had ever known. Martha was dependent on him, supported by him as he stood upright, his feet braced on the veranda with her legs wrapped around his waist. He held her in his arms and with his body, feeling like a shaft buried deep within her. Nothing could separate them as they moved to a climax more intense than either had experienced before.

Their sweat ran together. Blood streamed down his back where she clawed at his flesh, and his thighs trembled. Desire had driven out all reason and Casey was astounded when he opened his eyes to find the sun beating down so brightly. Martha's head rested against his chest with her chignon unravelled and strands of her hair sticking to him.

He gazed around the veranda in wonder that such passion should have flowed in that place after so long and at such a time. He glanced at the dining room and he saw Lizette watching them, and his joy faltered when he saw the sorrow in her eyes.

'Tell the bitch to get on with her work,' Martha said harshly, pulling Casey back to her.

The training of the four slaves continued throughout the summer. It was a humid and oppressive time and the youths' natural inclination was to loll in the shade. Ruffin Calmes reduced the amount of work he expected each day from the slaves under his authority. Hollis, however, refused to slacken the pace he set the four youths.

'If an out of condition man like me can do it, so can these boys,' he said to Casey and Martha. Since Hollis had taken charge of the boys, they rarely saw him. He took his meals at the *garçonnière*, had sworn off whisky and was in bed by eight every evening. 'I'm training too,' he explained.

The youths – Harbud, Scully, Dexter and Wayne – were billeted in a cabin close to Hilda's kitchen. They couldn't have had a stricter guardian. She entered into the training regime with enthusiasm, locking them into the cabin in the evening and not letting them out until four the next morning when Hollis led them for a run along the banks of the Bayou Celeste.

Tissa had shown so much interest in picking up Hollis's techniques, he was allowed to train with them as well. Even the new houseboy, Ebony, was drawn into the group whenever his duties at the house gave him time.

Martha had remained skeptical about the scheme. She chided Casey for this distraction and if it weren't for his renewed interest in her, she would have forbidden it.

Casey feared what might happen. Hollis was no longer the clapped out acquaintance of his past. Regular meals and exercise had toned him up into a jaunty, handsome man. His leadership of the four slaves had helped him lose his fawning manner, replacing it with an appealing cockiness. He was, Casey realized when he saw Martha ogling him, a threat.

Casey was determined that Martha would have no need to consider Hollis as anything more than a hired hand. There was too much at stake. Even though he was a drifter, Hollis had the advantage of being white, and Casey could not compete with that. To compensate, he monopolized Martha. She thrived under his constant attention, and softened. At his suggestion, she agreed to attend this display by the four boys. She had warned Casey that she didn't approve and that she was doing it just to please him.

They sat together under the portico, protected from the sun. It was the stuffy heat rather than the sun's rays that caused discomfort at that time of day. The four slaves were limbering up on the grass in front of the *garçonnière*.

'I don't know how they stand it,' murmured Martha sympathetically as she watched Harbud and Wayne rolling over the grass together. The boys were naked, dust and dirt caked with the sweat of their bodies. Their heads had been shaved and their skulls gleamed darkly in the sun. They panted while Hollis stood in the shade and shouted instructions.

'I didn't expect Hollis to keep at it,' Casey said. 'The slaves are young and privileged. They get extra feed and they'll get a fine virgin when they've proved themselves. Hollis gets nothing.'

'Yes, he does,' Martha nodded wisely. 'He's changed. He's got back his self respect. See how bronzed and fit he is. Quite a man.'

Casey bit his lip at the pang of jealousy rising in his breast. It was foolishness. The whole of that sultry summer Martha had only to mention Hollis to rouse him. He was like a lion with a new mate. The intensity of their need for each other had been maintained throughout the hot months. Martha responded with a feeling for him that only made him want her more, and he became frightened that he would lose her.

'I don't approve of this fighting,' Martha told Hollis. 'It's all rather silly.'

Hollis had a twinkle in his eye. 'You'll see,' he said. He clapped his hands and the boys sprang apart, leaping to their feet and standing alert.

'Right,' Hollis called across the clearing. 'Go'n prepare.'

The four boys ran off to the bayou followed by little Ebony. Martha watched them go, her eyes on their backsides as they disappeared into the bushes. Casey frowned and looked quizzically at Hollis.

'With your permission, Casey, I'd like to have a real fight.'

'Here?'

'Yes, here and now.' Hollis spread his hands to silence their protests. 'They've been fooling so far. They need to taste blood.'

'Will they hurt each other?' Martha's voice sounded husky. 'I can't allow that. Mr Calmes told me these bucks are very valuable stock. We'll lose money if they're injured.'

'Calmes has nothing to do with this,' said Hollis angrily. 'Casey put these boys in my charge.'

'Maybe,' said Martha, 'but they are Drongos stock and my investment.'

'Your investment will increase, Martha, if they become champions.' Casey smiled and squeezed her hand. 'Let them fight. You'll see what it's like then and it will prepare them for a real contest.'

Martha's eyes glimmered at Casey's touch. 'Oh, very well,' she said. 'To please you. After this, perhaps you'll give up this silly idea of naked men brawling in the dust for sport.'

'Mint julep?' Tissa was at her side and proffered a glass on a silver tray. Martha accepted it gratefully, wielding her parasol in her free hand to keep the sun's light, as it slanted across the clearing, out of her eyes. Casey took a glass and Tissa offered a third to Hollis. He declined with a curt shake of his head.

'I swore not to drink until one of my boys is a champion,' he said. 'Then I'm going to have me a bust to end all busts.'

'Tell me about your fighters, Mr Pickup. Which is the best?' Martha's tone suggested to Casey that she had something in mind. He watched her warily.

'They're all good. Wayne is the quickest. Dexter's more thoughtful and waits for the right chance. Harbud's got the strength and the height. Scully is faster with his feet.' Hollis drew himself up proudly.

'Even Tissa here is good,' he said, clapping the slave on his back. 'Pity he's too old.'

'Too old?' Martha's eyes widened. 'Why, he's only twenty three.' She drained her glass and glowered at Hollis.

'A fighter has to start young,' he explained. 'Look at that boy.' He pointed at Ebony racing along the trail toward them, followed by Harbud and the others at a more leisurely pace.

'He's probably nearing fourteen. He's beautifully proportioned and he's picking up techniques naturally. In a couple of years he could be the best fighter on the Mississippi.'

Casey observed Martha's eyes pass over Ebony to the four youths with him. She studied each one carefully. They were all naked and their bodies shone with the snake grease they had smeared over themselves after bathing in the bayou. Their muscles bulged and with their shining bald pates they were an awe-inspiring pack of sable brutes.

'Are they all going to fight?' she asked a little breathlessly.

'Only two of them,' said Hollis. 'Tissa can be the judge.'

'Can we choose which two?' Martha squeezed Casey's hand. 'I'll pick one and you pick the other, dear.'

'I thought you weren't keen on them fighting.'

'I'm not, but since we're here . . .'

Hollis was smiling broadly, but to Casey his sunburnt face had creased into a sinister smirk. 'That's the idea, Martha,' he said. 'Choose a buck to be your champion.' Hollis rubbed his hands together.

Martha gazed at the four blacks, her tongue passing from one side of her lips to the other and back again. Casey coughed but she wasn't going to be distracted. He imagined the thoughts racing through her mind and scowled. He was surprised when she beckoned Ebony to her side. She held the boy's hand, gazing into his eyes which were level with hers where she sat.

'Ebony, who do you think is the best?'

Ebony swelled with pride at being called to his mistress's side. He gazed back at her unflinching, ignoring the pressure of her fingers on the palm of his hand and the feeling of blood rushing to his loins.

'Harbud,' he said without hesitation. 'He de meanest.'

'Then I choose Harbud,' said Martha with a smile of triumph. She released the boy and turned to Casey with her challenge. 'Who is your champion?'

'Oh, anyone,' said Casey, puzzled by her game. 'They're all the same.'

'Ebony doesn't think so.'

'By the devil! You want to make it a contest?' He was riled now. 'I'll choose that one.' He pointed at Scully. 'He looks a nimble lad.'

'Mr Pickup?' Casey turned to see Martha lay her hand on Hollis's arm. 'Do they wager at these fights?' she asked.

'Of course!' Casey answered before Hollis could. 'That's how we will increase our profits. By backing our own fighters.'

'There's also prize money for the owner of the winner.' Hollis's smile into Martha's eyes was dazzling.

'Then I'll give a prize of a hundred dollars for the winner of this bout,' said Martha giggling coquettishly. 'I'd love to wager on Harbud. Will you bet against me, Mr Pickup?'

'I will!' said Casey. 'A hundred dollars says Scully will win.'

Martha dropped her hand from Hollis's arm and turned back to Casey. 'Now where will you get that amount of money?'

Casey sank back, startled to realize that he had nearly revealed he had funds of his own. The rocker propelled him forward. 'Why don't you lend it to me, Martha.' He grinned ruefully, ashamed at his loss of face in front of Hollis.

'Very well.' Martha bristled with efficiency. 'We'll open a new ledger for those four boys. We'll see who is the real champion, yours or mine.' She glanced at Ebony. The boy smiled, cocked his head on one side, and winked.

Harbud and Scully trembled like pedigree stallions as they pawed the ground with their bare feet and faced each other across the top of Tissa's outstretched arm. They both knew the prestige a win over the other would give them. A hundred dollars would make the victor the richest negro on the plantation. He could have any wench he wanted without the Bondmaster's consent. It was a prize worth fighting for.

Tissa drew back his arm and the boys hurtled at each other. Hollis groaned. 'Too fast!' he shouted. 'Feel out your man first.'

Ebony leaped up and down, yelling at Harbud. ''Queeze de bossal!'

Casey, not to be outdone, shouted encouragement at Scully. Martha leaned forward in the rocker, her hands grasping the arms of the chair and her parasol forgotten at her feet. Her mouth was open with excitement and her bosom heaved rapidly.

Harbud held Scully in his arms, then the small negro slipped away and danced behind his back, leaping on his shoulders and locking his neck in a pincer movement with his legs. Casey gaped at the speed. The two fighters toppled to the ground. Harbud fell heavily, catching Scully under him and using him to break his fall. Scully was winded and Harbud wriggled away.

'Kill him!' screamed Martha suddenly. 'Kill him!'

Casey was astounded. 'I thought you didn't want to lose stock.'

'Never mind that,' Martha snorted. 'My nigra's going to beat yours!'

Harbud hesitated at Martha's shout. Scully darted in and tweaked his testicles. He roared with pain.

'Unfair,' cried Martha, jumping to her feet.

Casey shook his head in amazement. Hollis winked at him. 'I think we've got Martha's support,' he said. 'Shall I stop them?'

'No, don't stop!' shouted Martha. 'Let them fight to the death.'

Harbud smashed his fist into Scully's jaw. The smaller slave friend to the right then dived to the left, plunging his shoulder against Harbud's massive thighs and knocking him off balance. He jabbed him in his throat then scampered out of range so that Harbud couldn't squeeze him.

'The boy's using his speed properly,' said Casey. 'I'm afraid your buck's too slow, Martha. You picked brawn over brain, dear.'

They both looked at Ebony. He was crouched on the ground with his head close to Harbud's. He said something none of them heard. Tissa waved him away and asked Harbud if he was quitting.

'No, no!' said Martha, standing up. 'We're not giving in.'

Scully rushed in as Harbud rose slowly, but the bigger fighter stuck out his foot and tripped him easily. He waited for him to rise, catching his breath, then repeated the performance. Scully sprawled on the grass and Harbud leaped on him, crushing the air from his body. Scully tried to throw him off, wriggling like a pig, but he couldn't. When he had exhausted himself, Harbud calmly rose to his feet. He looked at Martha. She nodded. He clenched his fist and smashed it down sharply to the side of Scully's head. The slave twitched twice then died.

Martha pursed her lips thoughtfully.

'Well, I'll be danged,' said Casey.

'Absolutely,' Martha smiled but her eyes were hard. 'Now we have a killer. Come,' she called to Ebony. The boy left Harbud and ran to her side.

'You're cute,' she said, squeezing his hip. 'You brought me luck.'

'It's technique,' said Hollis shaking his head dolefully. 'I told Scully that dozens of times.'

Tissa dragged Scully's body away by his ankles and Martha watched with amusement. 'You owe me a hundred dollars,' she said to Casey. 'Never mind. You can get your revenge another time.'

Casey was puzzled. How much of what Martha said was harmless, and how much carried a hidden threat?'

CHAPTER TWENTY-SEVEN

Willard Wadey threw his arms around Casey and hugged him. The door to the tavern owner's office was closed and Casey was standing by Wadey's desk in the center of the tiny room. From the tavern came the sound of a piano being played in a losing battle with the shouts, laughter and curses of the patrons.

The bar was packed. There were two steamboats tied up at the landing. Their sporting passengers who had seen the broadsheets advertising Wadey's entertainment swelled the crowd of regulars. St Francisville planters and wealthy young miscreants from all over the country in search of devilment made up the rest.

'You son of a bitch!' declared Wadey, squeezing Casey's shoulders. His rotten breath wafted over Casey's face.

'You may be yeller, but there ain't a man in Bayou Sara can beat you when it comes to making money. See this!' He released Casey and plunged his hands in the mound of coins on his desk. 'They've gone crazy out there.'

Casey remained silent, watching Wadey shovelling the money into a tin box. He was talking all the time.

'To think it would come to this! I'm doing more business tonight than a bagnio in Nuorleans. Have you seen who's here? Some of the biggest cut-throats in Louisiana. Oh my lord!' he exclaimed happily. 'They'll be a few dead bodies on my floor by morning.'

He pushed the box in the safe behind his desk and closed the door, locking it and pocketing the key in his vest. He buttoned up his coat and patted his large stomach. He gazed at Casey and scratched his head in bewilderment.

'Look at you, boy,' he said, and Casey grimaced. Wadey put his hand up to stop his protest. 'I know you don't want me to call you boy but what do you expect me to do? You're dressed worse than a nigra. To my knowledge you've been wearing that same suit for the best part of five years. Casey, you're my partner. You can afford to dress better!'

Casey shrugged his shoulders without saying a word. He had just finished checking his accounts with Willard Wadey. The bar owner was right. He could afford to dress like a riverboat gambler. The money in the box was his, over five thousand dollars from recent commissions, not including his share of the profits of this evening's enterprise.

'Why, Casey? Why don't you relax and enjoy yourself too?' Wadey waved his hand at the din coming from the other side of the door. 'You can't take it with you, you know.'

Casey's eyes flickered with annoyance. 'I got my plans,' he said softly so Wadey had to lean forward to hear him. 'And you got yours. I hope my money is well protected in here tonight.' He jerked his head at the bar.

'Sure it is.' Wadey tapped the holster at his waist. 'I hired some of the biggest scoundrels in Bayou Sara tonight. They're spoiling for a fight so ain't no one going to run off with the profits.'

Casey nodded. There was nothing else he could do. In the morning, he would remove the box to his hiding place at The Drongos. By that time he hoped to have doubled the amount through wagers on his fighters.

He had brought the three of them, Harbud, Dexter and Wayne. Wadey had contacted his cronies in New Orleans and three fighting bucks had been brought along by their owners. Broadsheets had been distributed in every hamlet and town along the Mississippi and the event was awaited eagerly.

Strangers had begun to arrive a week before. All the rooms at Wadey's and in every lodging house in town were occupied. Some had as many as three men sharing a bed. The whores were working overtime and the pickpockets and footpads were doing so well, they could afford to retire.

'This is all because of you, Casey!' Wadey strode toward his office door and flung it open. The noise almost bowled them over. The enormous hall of the tavern was packed with men standing twelve deep from one end of the bar to the other. The air was thick with smoke and the stench of men who thought bathing was for nancies. The crowd surged as more customers pushed through to be served and slaves wormed around to collect empty tankards and glasses.

'Never seen a night like this,' said Wadey, rubbing his hands together. 'Your nigras'd better put on a good show. They ready?'

Casey peered through the gloom to the stage at the end of the saloon. Hollis was standing close to it, talking earnestly to Ebony. Casey grinned to himself. Hollis had developed a fondness for the boy and took every chance to teach him new things. Ebony saw him watching and told Hollis. He waved his hand at Casey.

'I guess so,' said Casey with a nod to Wadey. He pushed his way into the throng, grateful for the smoke and the dim lighting that concealed him.

Casey's desire to remain inconspicuous was part of his plan to recover his fortune. If he dressed in the manner Wadey expected of him, Martha would wonder where the funds came from. He was supposed to give her all the income from the slave sales. She didn't know about his partnership with Willard Wadey and he didn't want to draw attention to it by dressing fancily.

It had been difficult to persuade Martha not to come to Bayou Sara for the fights. For over a year they had been planning the boys' debut with Hollis. At least once a week, she and Casey watched the three boys training. She took special interest in 'her' nigra, Harbud.

Three weeks before she had visited Wadey's to satisfy herself that everything was in order. She wanted to rent a room so she could sit and look down on the stage from the balcony while the fights took place. Fortunately, Wadey's insistence that he wouldn't have women in his rooms unless they were whores, forced her to stay at The Drongos.

Casey elbowed his way to the front of the stage, causing resentment among the patrons who thought he was stealing their vantage points. He reached Hollis's side, cuffing Ebony's ear as the boy moved away to give him space.

'Are the bets placed?' He had to shout to make himself heard above the hubbub.

'Sure,' said Hollis. 'Don't worry. Only evens though. They've never fought before but The Drongos stock is valued so highly that most people expect them to lick the city nigras.'

'What do they look like?'

'Not much.' He sniffed. 'One's supposed to have won a couple of bouts and there's a new colt. The other's got bile in his eyes, must be an Ibo. They ain't good fighters.'

'Who's going first?'

'I'll put Wayne in against the Ibo, then Dexter can have the new colt, and Harbud will take their champion. I only wish I had funds of my own to back 'em. Our bucks are good, Casey. They'll all win.'

Casey smiled and reached into the pocket of his coat. 'Here, Hollis,' he said, pressing a wad of notes into his hand. 'You've won for me before, now win something for yourself.'

Hollis took the money and winked. 'You're a sly one, Cas. I'll put it all on Harbud. He's got the taste.'

He watched Hollis sidle over to a corner where two men were taking wagers. It was odd, he thought, that after all the time Hollis had been on the plantation, he still didn't know anything more about him than he did when he arrived. The man had dedicated himself to making fighters out of the three bucks and seemed little interested in anything else. Ebony was his closest companion which suited Casey as the boy was being seasoned all the time he was with Hollis. He would fetch a higher price if he remembered half the things the trainer taught him.

It had taken Casey some time to realize that Hollis did not present a threat to his own position at The Drongos. He wasn't sure if his jealousy had been misplaced, but Martha had shown no signs of interest in him during the past year. Whenever she spoke to Hollis, it was to enquire about the progress of her champion, as she called Harbud. Casey knew she had given Hollis money to wager on her behalf, and he had too, to preserve his own anonymity.

As Hollis handed over his stake to the men in the corner, another man with his back to Casey pulled his hat down low over his eyes and moved away. Casey wondered why he didn't want to be recognized. He shrugged. There were all types in the crowd.

River men had a lust for gambling. The chance to wager dollars on fighting negroes instead of on cocks was a rare one. These bouts usually took place under the most secret conditions so as not to attract the attention of the authorities. Bayou Sara was unique that its reputation bequeathed by the notorious flatboaters who founded the settlement kept it immune from official interference. As a consequence, the hamlet and Wadey's tavern were the haunt of all kinds of pirates, brigands, thieves and those who wanted to remain unrecognized.

'Take good care of our winnings when you collect them,' said Casey to Hollis when he came back. 'I can see a lot of shady characters here.'

Hollis laughed. 'You take care, Cas! I *know* these people.' He looked up as Ebony poked his head around the curtain in front of the stage and beckoned him.

'At last,' he said, 'they're ready to begin. I'll go back with the boys to see that Tissa's greased them properly.' He clambered onto the stage and disappeared into the wings.

The slave auctioneer had been appointed Master of Ceremonies for the evening. He was a hearty fellow with a bushy black beard and a scar from a duel across his forehead. Like many of the spectators, he had been a river man before opting for the hazards of life at Bayou Sara. He scratched his crotch comfortably as he stood in the middle of the stage and began a patter of bawdy stories to get the attention of the crowd.

He called the combatants on stage and made them walk around it. 'See here, see here,' he shouted rapidly. 'We have the champion of the French Quarter of New Orleans, one black-hearted, black-assed, black-balled blackguard by the name of Black Devil!'

The crowd hissed the champion. He was a giant compared with Casey's boys. He was a showman and stomped across the stage to glare angrily at his detractors. His huge thighs shook and he grinded his hips obscenely, letting his penis twirl in the faces of the men who were jeering at him. The crowd loved it.

Tram, the auctioneer, shouted the fighter's praises without pausing for breath, the way he called slave prices. He introduced Harbud next and Casey felt a surge of pride when his boy ran up to cheers from the crowd. He was in perfect condition, slimmer and lighter than the Black Devil, and his eyes shone with eagerness at the coming contest. The other fighters stepped forward. The Ibo seemed an indifferent specimen, far inferior to Wayne. Dexter was nervous beside his partner, a young negro without an ear and the stripes of a severe beating etched across his back. Casey was confident his boys would win.

'Ladies and gentlemen,' Tram sang out, building up to the climax of his introduction.

'The only lady here is you!' yelled a gruff voice. There were howls of laughter and someone fired his pistol into the air.

Tram waited for the noise to subside. 'Seems there ain't no gentlemen here, either,' he retorted. 'Only pricks.'

More hoots of laughter and gun fire greeted this, the smell of cordite mingling with the stench of unwashed flesh and bad whisky. Casey grimaced, studying his fighters carefully. Tissa and Ebony were poking their heads out of the wings, anxious not to miss anything. Tissa was stripped to his waist. He grinned at Casey.

'It's a fight to the death,' shouted Tram. ''Less the nigra gets yeller and gives in first. Then I reckon we'll lynch the bugger ourselves.'

'Yeah!' There was a great shout from the crowd and Casey noticed Dexter blinking nervously. Tissa patted him on his shoulder and led him off stage with the others.

The first bout was between Wayne and Ibo. Wayne swiped at his opponent eagerly and felled him to the ground to the delight of the crowd. Casey wished he had Martha with him to share the excitement. The fight looked like being a good one despite the sickly appearance of the Ibo. He had been coached well and had holds Wayne didn't know. Wayne's merit was his speed and he grappled the Ibo without hesitation, breaking away every time he was down and leaping up immediately to renew the fight.

There were no intervals in the contest. Wayne began to tire after excessive dancing around the Ibo and being unable to wear him down. He was getting frustrated and clouted the Ibo across his nose with the back of his arm. This stirred the Ibo's temper and he lashed out with his fists at Wayne's head in an angry burst of energy that had Wayne tumbling backward to the floor in a daze.

'Get up!' yelled Ebony from the wings. His voice was drowned in the shouts from the crowd. Casey clutched at the edge of the stage and willed his boy to rise.

Wayne groped on the mat and tried to stand up. The Ibo roared and jumped on his back, cracking his knees across Wayne's spine. Wayne fell. The Ibo crawled off him and began to kick him in his waist. He rolled him over and pounded his fist into his testicles. Wayne didn't move.

Tram strode on to the stage and announced the fight was over.

There was a shout of dismay from the crowd and Casey wondered what had gone wrong. Tissa was on the stage, kneeling beside Wayne. He touched his chest to feel for the heart, shrugged his shoulders and dragged the lifeless slave off by his feet. His face wore an expression of disgust.

Casey sensed the bitterness of those who had backed his fighter and lost. The end had come too suddenly. The crowd felt deprived of the spectacular death they expected with one fighter screaming in agony as he died.

Tram was on stage listening while Hollis explained something. He called over the trainer for the visiting slaves who nodded his head indifferently. Tram stepped forward.

'Now hear, now hear, now hear,' he shouted. 'The next entertainment will be in thirty minutes. Time for y'all to fill your glasses and place your bets. It's the fight of champions, or the battle of the bastards. Black Devil from the Vieux Carré versus the ugly giant, Hercules Harbud from The Drongos.'

There was a surge in the crowd as drinkers fought their way to the bar for more whisky. Others exchanged money and promisory notes hastily scribbled on scraps of paper. Casey glanced around. The man with his large cloak and hat to his ears was passing more money to the two men taking wagers in the corner of the room. He wondered whether the strange man, whose face was hidden in the shadow, was backing Harbud or the Black Devil.

Two negroes bounded on to the stage and faced each other. Black Devil was a hand taller than Harbud and had thighs that seemed they were chisled from granite. His chest was massive and he swung his arms at his side like a bear. There was a flurry in the crowd as last minute wagers were placed. Casey sensed Harbud was expected to lose, especially after the dismal showing by Wayne. The two began to circle each other. Casey was surprised to see Hollis jump off the stage and edge into the crowd. Ebony followed him.

Casey pushed through and caught up with Hollis, holding his arm. 'What's wrong?' he demanded.

Hollis looked startled. 'Er, nothing.'

'Why is Harbud fighting now and not last as we arranged?'

Hollis gulped. 'It's Dexter, he won't fight. He's shit himself with fear. Too clever that one, always said so.' He pulled his arm free.

A shout rose from the crowd as the big negro picked up Harbud and hurled him to the stage. The boards shook.

'Where are you going?' Casey tried to hold Hollis but he slipped out of his grasp.

'I need a shoot of whisky!' he called back, pushing away from the stage and beckoning Ebony to stay with him. The boy looked from Casey to Hollis then squirmed through the crowd after the trainer.

Casey spat with disgust. He wanted to chase after Hollis to bring him back but it was pointless. If Dexter did not fight, there was going to be trouble. Money had changed hands on the outcome. The mood of the crowd was already ugly and people would soon wreck the tavern if they did not get the third fight. It had to be a good one too. Perhaps Hollis deserved that whisky.

Casey wondered nervously about his own position. If the crowd knew he was the owner of a slave who refused to fight, he might even be lynched himself. There was no one meaner than a Bayou Sara man who felt he had been cheated.

The problem robbed him of his enjoyment of the fight taking place on stage. Black Devil was using his greater reach to his advantage. Whenever Harbud dived in to punch him or to pound his huge stomach, the negro spread his arms wide and embraced Harbud. He squeezed him in a bear hug and released him so he flopped, winded, on to the mat. The crowd tired of that after three moves and began to jeer.

Black Devil thrived on the abuse and turned on Harbud like he was a small boy, picking him up by the scruff of his neck and flinging him into the wings. Tissa was there and pushed Harbud back, shouting something at him which none of the crowd heard.

Harbud hurtled at Black Devil's throat, his arm chopping across his larynx as he darted away. The huge negro choked and stumbled when Harbud attacked him from the rear and slapped his shoulders against his broad back. Suddenly the giant howled and the spectators watched in amazement.

Harbud's hand was gripping the giant's testicles from behind, pulling the scrotum back through his thighs. Black Devil tried to swing around but he could not shake off Harbud. The more the giant moved, the greater the pain he was in and the louder he shrieked with rage. The crowd loved it; planters hooted with delight and pistols were fired in the air.

Harbud was spurred on by the acclaim. He released Black Devil and kicked the giant with his knee into his backside. He lunged forward to grab him again. Using both hands, he tore at the giant's crotch and clawed at his anus.

The giant was wild with agony and rage at the attack coming from his rear. He fell backward and Harbud deflected him so he landed heavily on the boards. Harbud fell on him, pounding his fists relentlessly. Black Devil doubled up with pain. Harbud moved in, pressing both thumbs on the negro's larynx.

He squeezed and the crowd began to count in unison, 'One, two, three . . .'

Casey felt sickened as the big fellow fell limp with the life choking out of him. He toppled over with Harbud on top of him, still clinging to his throat. He was dead.

The crowd was happy, even those who had lost money. 'Next entertainment in thirty minutes,' called Tram.

Casey looked around for Hollis and Ebony at the bar, but Tissa was calling him. He clambered on to the stage and followed him into the wings.

'Dexter can't fight, Mas Cas,' Tissa said.

'Why not?'

Tissa snorted with disgust and waved to the corner. Casey was dismayed. Dexter was lying on the floor with his arms clutching his knees up to his chest. He was weeping softly, like a baby, and sweating with fear. The Ibo and the colt he was supposed to fight were standing over him, laughing.

Casey saw the Ibo hold his penis out over Dexter and start to urinate. He leaped forward and smashed his fist into the Ibo's jaw. The negroes turned on him. Tissa pushed them away.

'Forget it, Mas Cas!' He thrust himself between Casey and the Ibo. 'Dat niggah hoodoo'd Dexter. Ain't no way he gwine fight now.'

Casey bit his lip. Harbud joined them and glared threateningly at the Ibo. 'You did well,' said Casey, swallowing rapidly.

'Ah done it fo' Mistis Mart'a, sah. She proud me nuh?'

'Yes, yes, I'm sure.' Casey wondered what to do. Judging from the noise of the crowd, people were growing impatient for the next bout. He walked with Tissa away from the corner leaving Harbud to comfort Dexter. Tram saw him in the wings and rushed over.

'That sure was sweet, Casey. Your nigra ready for the last fight? They want to see blood this time, spilling over the stage. Oh yes, siree, your boy must give it to them.'

'I haven't got a boy,' said Casey. 'He's been hexed. He won't fight. You'll have to tell them the bout's cancelled.'

Tram gaped. 'I can't do that. Three men have been killed in here already. They'll shoot me.'

Casey found he was surprisingly calm. He turned away from Tram to walk on to the stage. 'Then I'll tell them myself,' he said.

Tram held on to him. 'You don't know these men! They'll lynch you.'

The roar of resentment at the delay was getting louder and more menacing. 'Give them the boy,' Tram said. 'We'll raffle him so you get his value. They can tear him to bits themselves. Anything so they get blood.'

'No!' Casey was adamant. For eight years he had managed to survive in this white man's world. If they turned against him now it was no more than he expected would eventually happen. He glanced around the back of the stage. There was no window or door to escape from. Dexter was still cowered in the corner with Harbud squatting beside him. The Ibo and the colt were laughing together, pointing at Casey and scoffing at his failure.

Tissa was pulling off his breeches. When he was naked he went up to the auctioneer with a broad grin on his face. 'Mas Tram,' he said, ''nounce de fight. Dat white trash don't know one niggah from another. Ah'm gwine take Dexter place.'

Tram grunted with relief. He pushed Casey aside and walked out on to the stage. The crowd jeered.

'I won't let you do it,' shouted Casey.

'Ah got to, Mas Cas. To save yo'. Rub me wid grease nuh, sah.' Tissa pressed the container in his hand. The colt eyed Tissa with new respect and listened as the Ibo spoke anxiously into his ear.

Casey annointed Tissa hurriedly, fretting about him. 'It's to the death, Tissa. You've never done this before. You're not fit!'

'Sah!' Tissa laid his hand on Casey's shoulder. His eyes were clear and unafraid. 'Yo' 'spose to 'courage me.' He grinned and turned his back on Casey so he could continue to apply the grease.

'Ah does be fit, sah, an' ah ain't too old. Ah run every mornin' wid Harbud an' ah fight too.' He waggled his shoulders, loosening up. 'Dat colt done a terrible t'ing to Dexter. Ah gwine ring his neck fo' yo', sah.'

A lump rose in Casey's throat. He couldn't speak as he finished greasing Tissa. The boy was in fine shape. His body was hard, his shoulders as broad as Harbud's and his muscles firm. Casey slapped him on his buttocks and took a deep breath before he spoke.

'Thank you, friend.' He watched him march on to the stage.

When the two negroes were facing each other, the difference in them was obvious. The colt was young, maybe seventeen, with the gangling limbs of an adolescent. He was cocky and bounced up and down, taunting Tissa. Casey groaned. Beside him, Tissa looked sedate, lacking the energy of the younger one.

The crowd spotted the contrast in the two and a hubbub of excitement broke out. There was a rush with last minute wagers. A hush fell over the tavern as the two moved in to make the first contact.

'They like it!' hissed Tram into Casey's ear. 'They see youth against experience. Good match. Thank old horny we're off the hook.'

'He ain't experienced,' said Casey glumly. 'He's a fool.'

'He sure looks gutsy enough for a fighter,' Tram chuckled. 'I'd wager a hundred he'll win.'

'I'll take it.'

They both turned at the voice. The man Casey had seen earlier with his hat pulled down so that his face was hidden, stood beside them. His cloak was wrapped around him and Casey still couldn't see the man's face.

'Want to make it a thousand?' The man's voice was high pitched and mocking.

Casey stared for a second then tore off the man's hat. Dark tresses blurred in front of him and dark eyes blazed furiously. 'Martha!' he gasped. 'What the devil are you doing here?'

'Same as you,' she said with a sneer. 'Watching Tissa get his neck broken.'

'He'll win,' said Casey.

'A thousand dollars says he won't.'

'Done!' Casey bit his lip. The colt and Tissa grappled,

feeling out each other's strengths and weaknesses. He handed back the hat to Martha and she clamped it on her head, tucking up her hair to resume her disguise.

Casey frowned at this extra complication. 'You must go,' he said. 'The crowd might turn rough. You shouldn't have come. I told you not to come.'

'Shut up and watch the fight!' Martha glared at him.

The thud of a body hitting the mat stopped Casey's retort. Tissa had flipped the colt over his shoulder and he fell in an awkward heap at his feet. The crowd loved it, howling with delight. Some cheered the colt to get up, others shouted at Tissa to stamp on his neck.

'Where's Hollis and Ebony?' asked Casey, gazing out at the crowd. 'They should be here.'

'How should I know? Get up, get up!' Martha shrieked.

'Keep your voice down, Martha. People will hear.'

'I want that black bastard to hear. What's he grovelling on the floor for?'

Tissa was obviously puzzled by the colt's apparent reluctance to rise. He was tempted to leap on his back and finish the fight. Instead, he bent down to turn the boy over. That was what the colt was waiting for. He grasped Tissa by his wrists and toppled him on to the stage. He somersaulted over him and slammed his body across Tissa's throat, knocking him back to the floor as he tried to rise.

'Bravo!' shrieked Martha, clapping her hands wildly. 'You must buy me that nigra, Casey. He's wonderful.'

Casey gawked at her. 'He'll be dead in a few minutes,' he said. 'Don't you care about Tissa?'

Martha ignored him as the fight progressed. What Tissa lacked in speed and surprise he made up for with determination and calculated moves. He fought doggedly, hoping to wear down the colt's eagerness with solid muscle power. He remembered what Hollis had taught him about technique, grappling with the colt when he was near and taking advantage of the boy's lighter weight to throw him about the stage.

Casey's confidence grew as Tissa showed he had staying power. The colt tired slightly but he wasn't hurt. Every time Tissa threw him, he landed on his feet and sprang up ready for the next hold.

Tissa fought hard and the colt retaliated, smashing his fists into Tissa's face with a speed Tissa couldn't avoid. He took one dreadful punch above his eyes, then another. Blood spurted out from a cut under his eyebrow, streaming down into his eye and smearing his face with blood.

The shouts from the crowd were thunderous, shaking the walls of the tavern. More shots were fired and empty bottles sailed through the air from one end of the bar to the other. The blood confused Tissa and he had to wipe it away.

The boy rushed in, pitching his weight behind his punch. Tissa sensed him coming and sidestepped, checking the colt's headlong rush with his knee into his crotch. The boy's angry grasp silenced the crowd. He fell onto the floor clutching himself. Tissa wiped his eye.

'Get him now!' shouted Casey. 'Oh, why doesn't he finish him off?'

'He's too slow,' said Martha. 'Always has been.'

Tissa hesitated, wondering how he was supposed to kill this boy who was as slippery as a watersnake. He jumped up to stamp on him. The colt rolled away, leaped quickly to his feet and socked Tissa another blow in his eye. His finger nails clawed at his flesh and raked his hand down Tissa's cheek. The pain angered Tissa. He lashed out blindly, trying to grab the boy in his arms. The colt was too quick and danced around the stage laughing as Tissa lumbered after him.

'He'll break yer maid,' yelled a voice. 'If he catches yer.'

'Hold still, boy, let the brute have yer.'

Tissa closed with the colt and grappled with him, showering blood across the stage and on to the spectators. His superior strength gave him the advantage, and his anger added a new impetus. He held the boy and fastened his fingers around his neck. He began to squeeze but the boy wasn't caught properly.

He smashed his forehead into Tissa's nose, at the same time gripping his penis. As Tissa fell away blinking at the pain, the colt held on to him. The boy's nails, which were filed to sharp points, sank into Tissa's flesh, tearing his penis from the root. In his haste, Casey had neglected to grease it. The colt's fingers pulled away strips of flesh as Tissa tried to escape.

Tissa's howls of pain and anger thrilled the spectators. Blindly,

Tissa thrashed at the boy with his fists. He broke away. Blood streamed from his eye and penis. Casey couldn't believe it.

'Kill him, Tissa,' he begged. 'Kill him!'

'He doesn't know how,' said Martha. 'That's his problem.'

'He'll do it.'

With a bellow of rage, Tissa seized the boy's neck in both hands. He fell to the floor with him and began to bash the boy's head on the boards. At the same time, he tried to throttle him. This was what the crowd wanted: blood and murder and shrieks of pain and anger.

Casey nodded. 'He's got him now.'

The boy's fingers pinched Tissa's chest as he tried to get a grip on him. Sowly his nails sank into Tissa's flesh, drawing blood. Tissa released one hand from the colt's throat and slapped the boy's fingers away. It was enough for the boy to wriggle out of his grasp. Instead of darting away, he flung himself at Tissa and knocked him off balance back onto the mat.

The colt, in a desperate lunge, threw himself on top of Tissa, tearing at his penis with one hand and gripping his neck with the other. He pushed his face close to Tissa's and opened his mouth. His teeth sank into Tissa's jugular vein. Blood spurted on to the floor.

Tissa jerked with a spasm then, as the crowd crowed with excitement and the blood gushed out, his eyes froze, his body went rigid, and he died.

Hollis hurried around to the back of the tavern, pulling Ebony after him. He carried a leather saddle bag in which was stuffed five thousand dollars in single bills, the money won by Martha and Casey, and by himself, on Harbud's victory. It was not a poor reward for a year's work, he reflected, although it should have been more if Wayne had won and Dexter hadn't got into such a funk.

'Come on,' he said to Ebony, 'We ain't got much time.'

'Yo' shure, Mas Hollis?' the boy asked doubtfully.

'Of course! You want to go to Nuorleans, don't you? You want to be free?'

'Yas, sah.'

'This is the only way. I'll help you.'

The noise from the tavern was deafening. Hollis found his horse where he had tethered it earlier that evening. He patted the animal's neck to calm it and checked the harness. Satisfied, he hitched on the saddle bag and mounted, pulling Ebony up to sit in front of him. He dug in his heels and the horse reared. Gently, he coaxed him out on to the highway and turned toward St Francisville.

He chuckled. He had won at last. Casey and Martha would never see him, their money, nor their favorite slave again.

CHAPTER TWENTY-EIGHT

Free sauntered on to the back gallery with a dish of eggs and ham in his hand. The ham was chopped into chunks, juicy with gravy; the eggs, fried soft in butter and steaming hot from the pan, were piled on top of the meat. Free eyed the dish, his mouth watering and his nose twitching at the delicious aroma. He raised his eyes briefly to guide himself through the door into the dining room. He did not see Casey who was standing quietly in the corner of the veranda gazing out at the fields.

The smell of breakfast stirred Casey and he waited for Free to return. From inside the house came the clatter of plates as Lizette laid the table. She was singing softly and stopped when Free entered the dining room.

'Put dat dish on de table, Free,' she said. 'Ah done finish.'

'Is Casey going to eat all that ham?'

'That's right, son.'

'That's more than a slave in the quarters gets in four weeks.'

'Maybe so. Marse Casey de Bondmaster so he 'titled to what he want. Now you run back to de kitchen an' see what Hilda has for you. Ah gwine upstairs to call de mistis.'

Casey heard the sound of Lizette ushering Free out of the dining room. He strolled to the veranda railing and leaned against it. Free did not come as soon as he expected so he glanced back through the dining room window. He saw his son had returned to the room and was helping himself to a piece of ham from the plate. He stuffed the ham into his mouth and ran out.

''Morning, Free,' said Casey as the boy stepped out on the veranda.

Free halted and stared at Casey. His mouth was bulging with the stolen ham.

'You must say "Good morning" when I address you, Free.'

Free nodded his head vigorously.

'Come on, son, let's hear you.'

Free glanced sidways then lowered his head, working his jaws rapidly to reduce the chunk of ham so he could swallow it whole. He covered his mouth with his hand, pretending he was going to sneeze.

Casey laughed. 'You'll choke yourself, Free. Take your time and chew the thing properly.' He was amused when his son's gratitude changed to an expression of horror as he realized that Casey knew about the ham.

Free gulped it down, juice spilling from his lips and drooling over his chin. 'I'm sorry, sir,' he stammered. 'It smelt so good . . .'

'Really?' Casey hitched himself up so he was sitting on the railing. 'Maybe it did, but it wasn't yours. Are you getting like a common slave who steals from his master?'

'Oh no, sir!' Free stood meekly with his head lowered and his hands behind his back, the way his mother had taught him. He waited.

He was smart in the black breeches and white cotton shirt that Martha had chosen as the livery for their house boys. His feet were bare and his hair, Casey saw, had been freshly combed. His face, except where the ham juice glistened on his chin like a pearl on velvet, was scrubbed and shining.

Casey was thoughtful as he appraised his son. 'You are growing into a fine young man,' he said. 'No wonder you're so big if you are eating from my plate every day.'

'Oh no, sir. Not every day.'

Casey snorted. He ought to get angry with the boy, lash him a few times across his fingers then tell Hilda and Lizette. They ruled all the slaves and would soon see that he didn't steal from his plate again. He had a soft spot for Free. The boy was lively and obliging with an independent spirit that showed he refused to be cowered. Casey was proud of his son, even though he was born a slave.

'Don't let Hilda see you taking my ham, Free,' he said, chuckling. 'She'll paste your behind from here 'til Sunday.'

'Oh, yes, sir.' Free looked rueful. 'Hilda sure can wallop.' He rubbed his backside and his eyes gleamed mischievously at being let off with a caution.

Casey slid down off the railing and cuffed Free affectionately around his ear. It was two years since he had brought the boy into the house to aid Lizette and the slave girls after Tissa's death and Ebony's disappearance with Hollis. He was developing rapidly, giving an impression of the man he would become.

'By the devil!' exclaimed Casey, 'You're the best young colt I've ever seen. Fine body, pure blood lines. As soon as you're old enough, I must find you a wench so you can get me a whelp, Free, eh?'

He chucked the boy in his crotch, fondling his small penis in his fingers. Free's face turned to scarlet but beneath his embarrassment he was proud.

'I'll give you good Bondmaster stock, sir,' he said.

'That's the way, boy.' Casey laughed. 'Go to Hilda now.'

'Yes, sir.' Free bowed his head politely and trotted off the gallery.

'You spoil that boy.'

Casey turned from watching Free kicking up his heels like a high spirited race horse as he ran across the grass. 'You sound like Martha when you say that.'

'Hah!' Lizette grunted. 'Martha would agree with you. I've seen her ogling Free with that devil's look in her eye.'

'No!' Casey was scornful. 'Free's too young. He's still a child. Martha's not like she used to be.'

'Thanks to you.' Lizette's lower lip trembled. 'I don't see much of you now. You spend all your nights with her and with the wenches. I didn't know it would be like this. I'm still a slave.'

Casey moved to Lizette's side and put his arm around her waist. 'Don't cry, Lizette. We'll go home together some day, I promise. But you know how it is.' He frowned. 'I'm the Bondmaster here. I have my duties . . .'

Lizette's eyes glimmered with tears as she gazed at him. 'You're a slave too,' she said.

'No.' He felt her doubt and sadness and tried to draw it from her with his embrace. Her heart thumped against his chest.

'I know it's difficult for you,' he whispered. 'I'll come to you tonight. We'll make love.'

'It's not your loving that I want!' She pulled away. 'Why must you always think like that? It's you I want. Before it's too late.'

'What do you mean?' He held on to her hands and searched her eyes.

'So we can make a life together. You're supposed to be the Bondmaster and I'm supposed to be your slave. Hah! It's Martha who owns us both. No, don't say I'm wrong,' she added as the anger flashed into his eyes.

'One day, you'll have to decide, Casey. You can't have us both. You can't be white and black together.' She tore herself away from his hands and ran off the veranda in tears.

He stared after her. He was baffled. He had thought Lizette was content and that she understood his situation. It took time to get Martha under his control so she wouldn't disrupt the plantation routine. Lizette had wanted him to do that. He scratched his head, jerking it up in surprise when he heard Martha's voice behind him.

'That girl gone again? We must get a new maid, Casey. She's never here when I want her.'

'Lizette? I sent her to the kitchen for something.'

'You see!' Martha sounded triumphant. 'She forgets things too.'

'No. It was to see Hilda.'

'Trust you to stick up for her!' Martha pouted.

'Don't say that, dear.' Casey put up his hand and touched her cheek tenderly. 'She's nothing to me, you know.' He wondered how long she had been standing watching them together.

Martha slapped his hand away irritably and walked back into the house. He followed.

Hilda brought in the coffee pot and fussed over them as they ate their breakfast. She had increased in size over the years and moved slowly, her heavy breathing filling the strained silence in the dining room.

Martha scowled and banged down her cup. 'For heaven's sake, Hilda, do you have to make so much noise? Leave us to eat in peace.'

'Yas, ma'm.' Hilda sniffed loudly.

'Where's Lizette? She should be here.'

Hilda rolled her eyes to the ceiling and folded her pudgy arms across her bosom. 'Ah don't know what got into de gal dis mornin' –' she began.

'That's enough!' Casey pushed his plate forward and stood up.

'I'm going to Bayou Sara today, Martha.'

Martha scowled and said nothing.

'I won't be back until nightfall.'

He moved around the table toward Martha. She was regarding him with a glint of excitement. He bent to kiss her and she turned her face, presenting her cheek to him. He brushed it with his lips while she closed her mouth around a forkful of ham and egg, yolk dribbling down her chin.

He forgot the devilment in her eyes as he strode out of the house. He knew that when he was away from the plantation, Martha spent hours in her office studying her ledgers. Occasionally she sent for Ruffin Calmes to have dinner with her and to keep her company until it was time for Ruffin to call up the slaves at the end of the day.

Lizette, who waited on them, reported to Casey on all that the two discussed. It was plantation business, about crop yields and cotton prospects. What Lizette didn't tell Casey, and so he neither knew nor suspected, was how Martha treated her.

That morning, as soon as he boarded a pirogue in the Bayou Celeste and a drongo began to skull it down stream, Martha walked out on to the back gallery and shouted for Free. The boy popped his head out of the kitchen doorway, saw Martha's stern expression, and scooted across the grass at top speed.

'Yes, ma'm?' He bobbed his head, grinning obligingly.

'Tell Mr Calmes to come here,' Martha snapped.

'Yes, ma'm.' Free backed away.

Martha tossed her head angrily and her hair, which no longer had the luxurious sheen of her youth, fell lankly on her shoulders. She walked back into the house and paced through the twin parlors inspecting the furniture and the floors and the mirrors carefully. She was looking for signs of dust, of housework not done properly. Everything was immaculate, spotless. She sat down on her favorite chair on the front piazza and sighed.

It was years, she reflected, since she had been to New Orleans. She longed to escape from The Drongos but she was a prisoner. If she took Casey, there would be the inevitable ostracism to face. If she went without him, she expected he would rob her and disappear. She had less illusions than Casey about their relationship. Habit made her fond of him and she would miss him.

The price of slaves was soaring, keeping pace with the increase in the cost of cotton. In another two years, Casey would begin selling their own product; slaves born and bred on the plantation and raised for slavery. What a price they would fetch! That would be the time, thought Martha. When she had all the proceeds at her command, she would be ready to dispense with Casey. Her plan then was to enjoy the sweet life of a woman of independent means: perhaps a grand tour of Europe, a mansion of her own in London. Two years, that's all . . . not long, not long.

Lizette coughed, startling Martha out of her reverie. She looked up at the slave and frowned. Lizette was the bane of her life. The slave irritated her beyond measure. She had a condescending manner; a sneer hidden under her smile that seemed to mock her. Martha gripped the arms of her chair and sat up.

'Where were you at breakfast, Lizette?'

'Ah ax Hilda 'tend yo'. De chil'un.'

'Speak properly to me, for heaven's sake! You don't use that slave talk when you speak to Casey.'

Lizette arched her eyebrows and said nothing which infuriated Martha more than if she had sassed her.

'I've been inspecting the house. It's filthy. There is dirt everywhere. I want you to scrub the place from top to bottom. Polish all the floors and clean all the rooms properly.'

'Yes, ma'm.' Lizette seemed unmoved by the preposterous command. 'I'll bring some girls from the quarters to help so we will get the job done while Mas Casey is out.'

'No, you won't! You can do it yourself. It's about time you did real work around here.' Martha glowered. 'Do you refuse?'

'No, ma'm.'

'Then get on with it.' She clapped her hands and stood up, shooing Lizette away. 'Seems like a tanning wouldn't do you any harm. That will get rid of your queenly airs.'

'Yes, ma'm.'

Martha slapped her face. 'How dare you be insolent with me.' She sneered as Lizette's light brown cheek flamed to red under the blow. 'Just because you have a couple of whelps by Casey! Don't think that makes you any better than you are.'

'No, ma'm.' Lizette tried to keep silent but the provocation was too great. Her eyes flashed and she fell into the trap Martha had set.

'I know I'm no better than I am, Miss Martha,' she said haughtily. 'But I'm the one with Casey's children, not you.'

'How dare you!' Martha swung at her again and Lizette's hand caught her wrist. She struggled to break away but Lizette wouldn't let go.

'Damn you, Lizette! You'll pay for this.' She pulled at Lizette's cap with her free hand, dislodging it and sending her hair tumbling around her shoulders. She stared at it jealously.

'You hussy!' she said. 'You whore. Let go of me.' She grabbed a handful of her hair and pulled.

Lizette released her wrist and tried to pull Martha's own hair. She got both her hands on it as Martha screamed.

At that moment, Ruffin Calmes walked around the corner of the house with Free, exactly as Martha had planned.

'Help, help!' Martha shrieked when she saw them. She stopped attacking Lizette. 'I'm being murdered.'

'No, you're not,' said Lizette, withdrawing with horror as she realized the enormity of what she had done. 'I'm sorry.'

Martha wailed loudly with sham tears as Ruffin jumped onto the veranda and stared at them both. Free crept to Lizette's side and reached up to put his arm around her waist.

Lizette whispered something to him in patois, the creole language of Dominica. He stared at her and she pushed him away. He dashed off the veranda before Ruffin could stop him.

'Did you see that?' Martha screeched at Ruffin. 'She attacked me. Hold her, hold her.'

The overseer looked from Martha to Lizette and his hand tightened around the stock of his whip.

'The bitch! You saw it, Ruffin, didn't you?'

'Aye.' Ruffin stroked his chin. 'I saw what I saw.' He breathed deeply. 'What do you want me to do, ma'm?'

'String her up and stripe her!' Martha's face was set in a hard glare of determination. She felt the sore patch of her head and began to weep again. Ruffin hesitated.

'If Casey was here, he'd know what to do,' she sobbed. 'The girl's nothing to him, you know.'

Comparison with Casey was sufficient to get Ruffin to do what she wanted. He looked apologetically at Lizette.

'Don't worry about me,' Lizette said dully. 'I'll go with you.'

She brushed past the overseer and walked off the veranda.

'She'll escape,' screamed Martha.

Lizette turned and tossed her head defiantly. 'I can take my punishment,' she said proudly. 'I hope you can take yours.'

The punishing of Lizette took place in the afternoon while Casey was at Bayou Sara and the slaves were in the fields. Lizette was popular and Ruffin advised that the punishment be carried out before the field hands knew about it in case they decided to make trouble.

'We ain't got enough white men for a big whipping,' he said. 'We need them to deter the nigras. They can get mighty uppity these days.'

Lizette was led, unbound, by two drongos into the center of the stockade where a gallows had been hastily erected. A new rope hung from the pulley suspended from the gallows' arm. It was tied in a noose with a slip knot at the end.

Martha was ensconced on the veranda of Ruffin's cabin, feeling hurt and justified in the action she was taking. The pleasure of it was robbed by Lizette's refusal to protest or beg for mercy. She carried herself proudly across the compound, casting a scathing glance at Martha when she stood, naked, under the noose.

Martha fidgeted, disturbed by the sight of Lizette's superb body, trim and firm in the sunlight.

'Get on with it!' she said impatiently to Ruffin who was on the balcony beside her. 'Tear the flesh off her!'

Ruffin arched his eyebrows unhappily. He had absolved his own conscience by reasoning that Lizette was Casey's wench and therefore deserved what she was going to get. He was pleased that Free had disappeared because he didn't want to have to punish the boy too if he tried to interfere and protect his mother. He was a cute kid. He raised his hand above his head and brought it down to start the lashing.

One of the drongos slipped the noose over Lizette's head, honking happily. He widened the loop and brushed it down Lizette's body, rubbing the rough rope over her breasts, abdomen and thighs. He tightened it around her ankles. He nodded at a second drongo who was holding the rope.

The drongo pulled and Lizette toppled over, her ankles being dragged skyward by the noose and her head scraping along the ground. The second drongo helped the slave with the rope and together they pulled until Lizette was suspended in the air, head down with her hands reaching for the ground to support herself. She spun wildly.

Ruffin walked over with his whip; it was heavy at the stock to give the lash more force. He flicked it in a trial thrash and it tickled Lizette's ankles. Martha grumbled loudly. He steadied himself, feet apart, and drew back his hand for a proper blow. The tongue of the whip cracked through the air and its plaited leather thong sliced into Lizette's flesh. She gasped with shock.

'Not hard enough!' called Martha, 'make her scream.'

Ruffin scowled, recoiled the whip and lashed again. The blow caught Lizette as she spun, cutting into her breasts and sending a trickle of blood dripping into the mud below her. Still Lizette did not cry out.

'Again,' shrieked Martha. 'I want to hear her beg for mercy.'

Ruffin curled the whip up in his hand and walked back to the cabin. He offered the handle to Martha. 'You do it, ma'm. I ain't got the taste for it like you.' He spat on the mud at her feet.

'I will!' she cried, snatching the stock from him. She flashed it first in his face, thrilling as the leather snicked across his cheek and drew blood. Then she tucked the whip under her arm, raised her skirts in both hands, and hurried across the compound.

Lizette was still spinning upside down from the gallows. Her long hair hung down to the mud and blood. She hauled herself up and grimaced at Martha.

'My turn now,' she said. 'Yours will come.'

'How dare you!' Martha stamped her foot with rage and flicked the whip so it whistled through the air. It fell on Lizette's thighs and Martha withdrew it slowly so it stung across her stomach. She cracked it down a second time flicking her wrist skillfully making the lash fly to its target. It smacked into Lizette's buttocks and she began to spin again.

'Scream, damn you!' shouted Martha. 'I'll humble you yet!'

She poised for another blow, concentrating her fury on striking Lizette with maximum effort. There was the smack of leather in the air and to Martha's amazement her own wrist seared with pain. She cried out and dropped the whip. Another blow cut across her bosom and spun her around.

She peered through the tears that pricked her eyes. Casey was standing a few yards from her, a whip in his hand and a sneer of hatred on his face. Martha swooned at the sight of him.

Free ran across to the gallows and cut down his mother.

CHAPTER TWENTY-NINE

Casey sat in the doorway of Lizette's cabin, his legs hanging down and his feet, which were bare like a slave's scuffing up the dust. He leaned his back against the door jamb and gazed across the lawn and the pond to The Drongos.

In the twelve years he had lived in the house, he had grown fond of it, despite the calamities that had befallen him. It was an old fashioned house, with none of the white columns and wide piazzas the wealthy cotton planters of the county considered essential. Its simple grandeur, dappled with shadows from the live oaks growing close by, suited him. He wouldn't admit that The Drongos had become his home. It was enough to say that he had become accustomed to the way of life, and liked it.

He sighed, wondering whether Martha had ever sat in a slave cabin and looked at the house the way he was seeing it. For a slave, The Drongos house represented the omnipresence of his master. The more magnificent his master's abode, the prouder the loyal slave felt.

Casey had heard slaves in Bayou Sara boasting about the number of columns on their master's house and the amount of slaves he employed in it. Well, the slaves at The Drongos had no such boast. The house had no columns, only the wrought iron friezes at the front, and a few house servants. That was the way he liked it.

He knew that Martha was sitting on the front veranda reading a book while he sat on the stoop of Lizette's cabin, like a slave, gazing at the house. He preferred to spend his afternoons, when dinner was over and the day was drawing to an end, with Lizette, not with Martha. This routine had established itself gradually since the day he lifted Lizette down from the gallows and held her bloodied body in his arms.

Martha had fainted at his feet then and he left Ruffin to care for her. His concern was for Lizette and with young Free's help, he had carried her to Hannah's cabin, the same one he had met her in. Free ran for water and together they bathed Lizette, washing away the blood from the cuts on her breasts and hips. After a while she recovered sufficiently to walk, supported by them both, back to her cabin. She had lain there for two days during which time Casey didn't leave her side although Martha called him hourly.

Hilda prepared unguents and rubbed them in her wounds. He cared for Giselle, their daughter, and for Free. Most of all, he cared for Lizette, showing her the love he knew she craved, and deserved.

No mention was made of the incident when Lizette returned to the house. She resumed her duties, Free helping her more and more as he grew older. Martha was cool toward Casey, and he to her, for several weeks while they learned to live with the traits that they had rediscovered in each other.

Casey had been as shocked by Martha's cruelty to Lizette as she had been by his preference for the slave over her. It was as though both had forgotten the passion of the relationship they had shared during Hollis's year on the plantation.

Inevitably, Casey reverted to his role of stud, instead of lover, to Martha. She responded with the necessary favors whenever he sought something from her. He performed his duties capably although all joy had vanished. Now he was only happy when he was in the cabin with Lizette, Giselle on his lap and Free amusing them with his antics.

It was just as inevitable that Martha should seek to fill the time when he was with Lizette in some way. At first, she sought out the company of Ruffin Calmes. The overseer became a regular visitor to the house. While Casey sat with Lizette in her cabin, Ruffin and Martha drank whisky in the parlor, waited on by Free.

Martha's attitude to Free was puzzling in view of her jealousy of Lizette. She doted on the boy, beginning to treat him as though he were her own son. She explained patiently to him how to serve, how to wait on a lady, how to treat guests and visitors. She showed him books and, in quiet afternoons sitting on the grass under the shade of an oak tree, she taught him to read.

Casey was flattered by Martha's interest in the boy. It helped to bridge the rift between them. Lizette, however, saw only mischief would come out of it.

'Why is she doing that, Cas?' she demanded. He turned away from contemplating The Drongos and looked back into the cabin. Lizette was sitting on a chair, her feet stuck out in front of her in an attitude of exhaustion. Giselle was playing at the back of the cabin, within sight of Casey.

'All day she talks to Free, filling his head with nonsense.'

'What kind of nonsense?' Casey rose from the stoop and walked inside to join Lizette. He patted her hand affectionately. 'Nonsense about you, do you mean?'

'Oh no, she doesn't talk about me much. She tells him about the world and traveling and England and France. She shows him pictures in books and something she calls an atlas. I heard her tell him she's going to take him over the seas one day on a Grand Tour.'

'Well now, that is nonsense indeed.' He squeezed her hand. 'He's company for her and she's educating him, Lizette. It's a crime for a slave to read and write and if she's teaching him to do that, it saves me the task. Free's young yet, he can come to no harm with her. We must let him learn while he can.'

'You don't mind?'

'Why should I?'

'Because he's our son.'

'He's also her slave and it is an opportunity for him.'

'You know what's she's like. She's an evil, wicked woman.'

'She's also white. Free needs to know what she can show him.'

'Why does he need to know?'

'Because he is free, that's why. Sure, he's a slave here but it won't be long before we go back to Dominica. He needs a white education to get on in this world.'

'You don't worry that she's stealing him from you? Educating him isn't to help Free. It's to bind him to her like she . . . well, like she's his mother and not me. She tells him I'm a house slave and he's got brains to be more than a slave.' She sniffed, clasping Casey's hand.

He scratched his head. 'If it's helping the boy . . .'

'When are we going, Casey?' The despair in her voice shocked him. 'It's not only Free, there's Giselle. What's to become of her? You're supposed to be the Bondmaster, can't you do something?'

'I'm doing it. You know I need Martha's consent for everything, in law. And you know what I have to do to get that.'

He walked over to the window of the cabin and leaned out. Giselle was sitting on the mud playing with one of her mother's kerchiefs, trying to tie it in her hair. She had it bunched on her head and gazed up at Casey. The kerchief fell off and she laughed. She was a good natured child, nearly nine years old. In time, she would grow into a very beautiful woman. Was she going to be a slave too? He frowned and pulled his head back into the cabin.

'Why can't we go now?' Lizette's eyes shone at him with excitement.

'I'm not a slave stealer. Do you want to be a runaway? I'll buy your freedom at market rates.'

'Are you going to buy Free and Giselle too? Your own children?'

Casey sighed. 'Yes, Lizette. I have no legal right to them. You're a slave and children take the status of their mother.'

Lizette got out of her chair and kissed him on his cheek. 'Do you have the money to buy me now?'

'Yes.' He put his arm around her waist.

'Then why don't you do it now?'

'It's not that simple, Lizette.' He let her go. 'Jed and Martha stole my inheritance and I'm going to get it back. In a few months, we'll be able to sell some of the whelps from the nursery. They'll fetch good prices and I'll get more commissions.'

'Casey!' She shook her head in exasperation. 'In the quarters, the slaves talk just like you. "We'll run away," they say. "Not now; in a few months." ' She stopped and suddenly her eyes brightened.

'Casey,' she whispered, stroking his cheek with her finger. 'Why don't you steal it back?'

'That's not my way.'

'She did it to you.'

'Is that why I have to do it to her? My way is better. I've done something here no white man has ever done, I'm the Bondmaster in my own right. People respect me, and I've made The Drongos famous throughout the State. If I steal and run away, you know what people will say? They'll say that's what happens when someone trusts a nigra.'

Lizette pouted. 'You should kill her,' she said. 'No one would know. That's what she will do to you one day, when she's tired of you.'

'No!' Casey was angry. 'She saved my life, remember.'

'Only because she wanted you for herself. She'd be easy to kill. I could do it myself with some poison in her coffee. Hilda would tell me how.'

'No!' Casey gripped Lizette's shoulder and shook her. 'Never think of such a thing. I'll get my revenge my way.'

Giselle stepped into the cabin holding her head up carefully to display the kerchief which she had managed to tie in close proximation of her mother's. She smiled happily and pirouetted in front of them.

'What a pretty girl,' said Casey releasing Lizette and bending down to embrace her. Lizette watched, shaking her head sadly at Casey's gullibility.

The slave compliment of The Drongos had drastically reduced over the years. The monthly auction had culled the able bodied males and lately females had been sold off as well. No more shipments had been received from Barataria for months. It was rumored among the few slaves who remained that ships had been stopped from landing Africans and Creoles from Cuba. The older slaves, the drongos, had either died or been sold as well.

Lizette considered these developments when she met some weeks later with Harbud, Dexter and the other slaves in a cabin close to the old stockade.

Harbud was a driver now, in charge of the able bodied slaves who worked in the fields. After Tissa's death and the disappearance of Hollis with the proceeds, Casey had abandoned his plans to raise fighting negroes. Harbud had accepted the change in his fortunes stoically but Dexter, who didn't have Harbud's status, was less amenable.

'Ah tell yo',' he said at the meeting, keeping his voice low. 'Slavery comin' to an end. We gwine be free soon. Dey be people call 'bolitionists workin' fo' we freedom.'

'Dey can come work 'gainst de bollweevil, not de 'bollition,' said Chaucer, a lanky boy with a stupid grin. 'Ah weary dat pesky beetle.'

'Ah doubt ah live to see de freedom day,' said Harbud, fidgeting in the cramped cabin.

There were over a dozen slaves squeezed into the tiny room lit by a stub of candle burning low on the floor. The group met almost every week at night when work was finished in the fields and Ruffin had done his rounds. When the overseer had passed through the lines of cabins the chosen slaves, one by one, gathered at a different cabin each week. Despite their tiredness after a day in the fields under the hot sun, they were eager to discuss new rumors and gossip.

Lizette supported Dexter's view. 'Sure yo' gwine see it, Harbud,' she said. 'Ah hear Martha talk to Ruffin 'bout de troubles at some plantations where de slaves rebel 'gainst their owners. She say it spreadin' an' she praise de Lord it ain't happenin' here.'

'To rebel don't make yo' free,' said Harbud gloomily.

'It does if yo' run away,' Dexter hissed. 'We could rise up and kill Mas Ruffin so he don' search for we. Den we go down de bayou in de p'rogues to de Mississipi.'

'What we gwine do den?' said Chaucer.

The only sound in the cabin was the deep breathing and grunts of the slaves as each waited for another to answer that question.

Dexter felt he would be losing the respect of the others if he didn't provide an answer. 'Ain' necessary fo' dat, anyway,' he said, and the slaves sighed with relief. 'De 'bolitionists gwine do dat for we all.'

'How dey do dat?' Chaucer demanded.

'De white folks,' said Dexter, 'dey know how. De white man know ever't'ing.'

'Dey ain' gwine kill no one, dat fo' sure,' said Harbud. 'Whites ain' gwine kill whites to free we po' niggahs.'

The talking continued aimlessly as it did every week. Lizette slipped out and moved carefully through the cabins back to her own quarters. She was welcomed at the meetings because of the gossip she could bring from the house. She sensed their talk was doomed to remain talk. Resistance was not part of their make up. The slaves who were prone to agitate had been sold. Dexter was the only one with ideas, and he was a coward. Whether Lizette liked it or not, she would have to act alone.

The lights from The Drongos house shone over the lawns and were reflected in the surface of the pond. She stood outside her cabin watching the house. Casey had gone to Bayou Sara for two days and she missed him. Martha had Ruffin Calmes to keep her company, and she also had Free. The boy slept on the floor in the entrance hall and revelled in the importance this gave him. He was a real house nigger now, thought Lizette. A stranger to her.

Carefully she opened the door to her cabin and crept in. Giselle was sitting up in bed.

'Mam?' she said sleepily.

'*Oui, doudou*,' Lizette answered. 'Yes, darling. Why aren't you asleep?'

'Ah waitin' fo' yo'.' The girl held out her hands.

Lizette closed the door and turned down the lantern. She was tired and it was already late. She would have four hours sleep before going to help Hilda in the kitchen with the baking. She lay down beside the child and took her in her arms.

'Giselle, my love,' she said, 'yo' mammy's here now. Sleep tight.'

Giselle was playing with some of the children from the pen when Ruffin Calmes shouted her name. Their laughter ceased abruptly. One child, perhaps sensing calamity, burst into tears.

'Stop that,' said Giselle firmly, rising to her feet. Mr Calmes was beckoning her and she ran obediently over the grass to stand in front of him.

The mistress was walking down the path toward her, accompanied by a stranger. The house was out of sight behind the trees and Giselle wondered why the overseer wanted her. He was glaring as he stroked his whip handle without saying a word.

'That's the brat,' said Martha.

Giselle was used to Martha's coarse voice and knew that the mistress didn't like her. She didn't flinch. The stranger was dressed in black trousers, a black frock coat and a black stovepipe hat. He was peering at her with an odd expression on his face which made her feel uncomfortable.

'Spoilt to blazes,' said Martha sniffing. 'She feeds well, her dam's my housemaid so she gets all the scraps stolen from our table.'

'Indeed?' The stranger crouched down, his knees cracking. He pushed his face close to Giselle's and she smelt the whisky on his breath and saw the red veins spidering out from his long nose. She looked up anxiously at Mr Calmes.

'What's your name, dear?' asked the man, squeezing her thigh. His fingers crept up the inside of her leg.

Giselle brushed the man's hand away and squirmed out of his grasp. She was startled and wanted to cry, but the other children were watching.

'You see!' said Martha with an angry snort. 'What a little lady she thinks she is.'

The stranger was nonplussed. 'She's a pretty little chit, for sure,' he said to recover his composure.

'Just the sort for you, I shouldn't wonder. Eight or nine years old, and a quadroon. You'll make a lot out of her in New Orleans.'

'Well,' said the man frowning and turning to walk back to the house. 'She's not for me, you understand. I'm merely the broker.'

Ruffin sniggered. 'Breaker is more like it.'

Giselle gazed in amazement at the three adults. They seemed to have forgotten about her until Mr Calmes turned back and saw she wasn't following them. His sniggering frightened her and she wanted to run. He caught her hand, squeezing it tightly, and made her walk with them up to the front of the house.

'Where's my mam?' she demanded when she saw the cart. A sense of foreboding overwhelmed her. She dragged her feet and Mr Calmes had to pull her along.

'Hear the chit!' said Martha. 'You'll have your hands full with that little missy, I can tell you.'

The man leered. 'They soon quieten down with proper treatment.' He attempted to smile at Giselle. 'Your mam has gone away,' he said. 'She sent me for you.'

Giselle regarded the man with scorn. 'No, she didn't. I saw her this morning. I want my mam!'

'Oh!' said Martha, clutching her head and groaning. 'I can't stand it any more.'

Ruffin smirked. 'You're lucky that Casey took Free with him to Bayou Sara or you'd have that scamp shouting at you too.'

As he spoke, a white man who had been hiding behind the cart crept up to Giselle. He slipped a sack over her head and bound it quickly. The other man held her wrists and she sank to the ground, kicking and struggling to break free.

The two men were too powerful for her and she was soon trussed up like a chicken and bundled into the back of the cart. The man in the black frock coat took out some money and counted the notes into Martha's hand.

'So nice to do business with you, ma'm,' he said, raising his hat. 'If ever you have any other girls about her age, but they must be quadroon and virgin, call on me.'

Martha glared at him contemptuously. 'No others,' she said. 'You only got this one cheap because she's surplus.'

Ruffin nodded at Martha. He climbed on to the wagon to drive it down the hill to the bayou landing where the men had a pirogue waiting for them.

Martha went into the house, smiling to herself. She walked into the office and locked the money in her escritoire. The house was empty. She had sent Lizette on an errand to get her out of the way.

Slowly, she wandered through the downstairs parlors. It was amusing to think what Giselle had in store. The girl ought to be thankful. She could have sold her to a slave factor to work in the fields, instead of to a pimp.

Martha found the whisky bottle she had been looking for. It was hidden among some samplers in her needlework basket. She took a long draught from the bottle by its neck, then placed it back in the basket. She carried it out to the veranda where she would sit embroidering until it was time for dinner.

CHAPTER THIRTY

Free was fifteen. He had developed apace; his limbs were lithesome and muscular. He was strong, his body compact and showing none of the awkwardness of his age. His skin, lighter than honey in color, was smooth and unblemished. His eyes shone with the sappiness of his youth and he had an easy smile that was captivating with its sincerity and trust.

He was a handsome boy with high cheek bones and a long, straight nose from Casey, and full lips and petite ears from his mother. His face was capped with a tousled mop of ebony black ringlets that made him look like a Mediterranean godling instead of a backwater's slave.

Martha had been conscious of his beauty ever since he began to work in the house as a child. She had watched him avidly as he grew, changing from an engaging infant into a self assured youth with a bloom of attractiveness she found irresistible.

He moved across the veranda toward her with an animal grace that emphasised the lines of his body under the tight black silk of his breeches and shirt. Had he been a man, Martha could have suspected him of flaunting himself deliberately to intrigue her. In one so young, it seemed natural and unaffected.

Martha was moved to muse on Free because, as usual, she was sitting on her veranda alone. She had summoned him to bring another mint julep. As he passed it to her, his hand touched hers and she thought there was a slight lingering of his fingers. Perhaps it was her imagination. She had become obsessed with the boy and looked for every opportunity to confirm that he felt the same way about her.

It wouldn't be unusual, she reasoned, if he did desire her. The age difference meant nothing to a lusty, mixed breed youth. She had always been kind to him, helping him to improve his mind and encouraging him to treat her as a friend, not as his owner.

She had never whipped him, nor reprimanded him, and had taught him to believe that he was rather special. She had hinted at the pleasures he would enjoy as he got older. Perhaps now, she thought with a gasp at her boldness, that time was approaching.

She sipped the drink slowly. Free was waiting within earshot, ready for her call. That he was devoted to her she knew from his smiling manner and the concern he always showed her. Quite unlike Casey. She sighed. It must have been months since Casey had made love to her. She could not remember when, nor did she worry. Theirs had become a partnership based on a mutual need for each other.

She had no illusions about Casey. She knew he was trying to retrieve his fortune from her. She also knew that after so many years, he had become attached to The Drongos and regarded it as his. That sex had left their marriage was a comfort. She no longer had to suffer the hypocrisy of his lovemaking.

From where she sat on the front piazza, the view down to the bayous and to the flat swamp lands beyond was framed by the wrought iron frieze. In the fading light, the fronds of leaves trailing from the branches of the live oaks and the heady scent from the magnolia bushes added a dreaminess to the scene. How romantic it would be, she mused again, unable to push Free out of her mind, if instead of the bayous she was with him overlooking the canals of Venice.

The heavy tread of leather boots striding through the house from the back entrance roused her. She drained her drink to perk herself up and to shake off the pleasant feeling of lassitude. She was ready with a smile when Ruffin Calmes poked his head around the door.

'Late today,' he said bluntly, when he saw she was waiting for him. 'Had to stripe a nigra for laziness.'

'Again?' Martha tilted her head to listen politely to the overseer's account of his day. Every evening, it was the same routine. At times she thought she took more interest in the management of the plantation than Casey did.

'Strange, isn't it?' He sat down without being asked. 'The nigras are getting too tiresome these days. Even here we can't escape the rumors.'

'What rumors?'

'You know, about abolition and insurrection.'

'Hah!' Martha held up her hand to quieten him then raised her head and smiled coyly at Free who had come on to the veranda and stood waiting behind Ruffin.

'Whisky, as usual, I think, don't you, Ruffin? After such a day.' She held out her glass to Free who proffered the tray. She gazed at him, trying to hold his golden, lively eyes with her own.

'Yes,' she said, her eyes glinting. 'You can bring whisky for us both.'

Free bowed briefly and sauntered away. Martha noticed Ruffin was watching him. 'Thank goodness,' she said to get his attention away from the boy. 'I've no trouble with Free. He's perfect.'

'Fine lad,' said Ruffin, pulling at his crotch. He leaned forward. 'It's the house slaves you have to watch, Martha. They carry the gossip that stirs up the field hands. They prepare the food and drinks so they have every chance to poison us.'

'Oh no, surely not!' Martha was shocked. 'My slaves would never do that. Aren't they content here?'

'What about Lizette?'

'Lizette has learned her place since she's been removed from the house.' Martha was definite about that and her chin jutted out as she thought about it. At first there had been a dreadful time after she had sold Giselle. Only Casey could calm Lizette and it was obvious the girl could no longer work in the house. Casey had put her in charge of the wash house where she was out of Martha's sight.

'I've no trouble here now,' Martha continued. 'There are two good girls to clean the house, Hilda to cook, and I've got Free, of course.'

She stopped speaking as Free brought the whisky. He offered the tray first to Martha who took her glass and thanked him with her eyes, and then to Ruffin.

Martha was dismayed to see Ruffin wink at Free and pucker his lips. Did he always look at Free like that? She had never noticed it before.

'Free,' he drawled. 'I have some tasks to do in my house tonight. If the mistress will spare you, I'd like you to walk back with me. It won't take long.'

'That's impossible, Ruffin.' Martha thrust out her bosom and glowered. 'He can't leave the house at night. I need some protection.'

'No problem,' said Ruffin, leaning back in his chair and stretching his legs so his crotch bulged. 'You can come tomorrow, in the morning.'

'Out of the question!' Martha bridled. 'Don't you have enough slaves in the stockade to do your . . .' She hesitated, searching for the words.

'Personal affairs?' he supplied, not in the least bit intimidated by Martha's huffiness. He rubbed himself and took a sip of whisky.

Free was standing at ease at his side, his face alive with interest at hearing himself discussed. He was intrigued by the tensions he sensed between his mistress and the overseer.

'We don't have spare slaves actually, Martha,' Ruffin said. 'And certainly none to trust like this boy.' He gestured at Free and his hand brushed against his thigh. Martha clucked her tongue, clenching her glass firmly in her hand.

'I'm sorting through my effects. One collects so much over the years. Someone intelligent like Free would be a help.'

'No!' Martha's voice was husky and she felt a pang of what could only be jealousy. 'He's mine, Ruffin. You must look elsewhere for your sport.'

'Surely he's Casey's?' Ruffin gloated at Martha's displeasure. He drank. 'Bring another for me, boy.' He let Free take the glass from his hand while Martha scowled.

'I'll have one too,' she said.

Free's smile as he stepped to her side, mollified her. He was such a beauty, it amazed her that she had managed to keep her hands off him herself. Perhaps, she thought, she should speak to him about people like Ruffin before it was too late. The boy seemed perfectly willing to do what the overseer wanted. It was too horrible to contemplate . . .

'I think Casey has oversold our stock,' Ruffin was saying. 'We've only a dozen hands and a pen full of whelps with a few old biddies to nurse them.'

'Casey sold the stock when the price was high.' Martha resented criticism of Casey's management of the plantation because it implied criticism of her. Ruffin knew that she was the one in control.

'We plan to sell all the whelps next year and close up the pen.'

'What will you do then? The Drongos ain't nothing without slaves.'

'Exactly. Maybe some day it will be against the law to have slaves.'

'That's ridiculous.'

'Casey doesn't think it is.'

Ruffin was aghast. 'You share this view?' Martha was silent.

'Well!' Ruffin snatched his drink from Free. 'Listen to me, Martha Barrow. You've done better with Casey than I thought possible. He settled down well here. But don't you underestimate him.'

'You can go, Free,' said Martha. 'Wait on the back porch in case I need you.'

'Yes, ma'm.' Free bowed his head politely. His eyes, Martha was sure, held some hidden meaning when they met hers. She felt weak inside.

'Casey couldn't surprise me,' she said to Ruffin. 'We know each other too well for that. We have the same ends, to make money out of The Drongos. Casey can tell the trends and I rely on him. I'm fond of him, too.' The admission surprised her as much as it did him.

Ruffin was embarrassed. 'Like I say,' he said quickly, 'he's done well. Doesn't it worry you, though, that he spends so much time with Lizette and the slaves?'

'It used to.' Martha gave a resigned flutter with her hand. 'Not now. Lizette serves him better than I do.'

'Consider the time he spends with the slaves. He's thick with them.' Ruffin made it sound a crime.

Martha snorted. 'That should prevent the uprising you're always talking about, shouldn't it?'

'Sure, it should.' Ruffin stood up. 'Unless Casey's leading it himself.'

Martha sat on the piazza long after Ruffin had gone, thinking about his remark. She stared at the night rolling in slowly over the bayous, bringing with it relief from the humid heat of the day. Free padded softly in bare feet across the piazza to hang out the lamps. She waved her empty glass at him and he replaced it without disturbing her train of thought.

Casey, Lizette, Hilda, even Free, she realized, had so many opportunities to destroy her. Her life was in their hands. It always had been. Short of preparing all her food and drinks herself, there was not much she could do about it. She had to trust someone. She was startled by the sound of Casey's voice in the hall.

'Mistress abed?' he asked Free.

'No, sir. She's outside.'

'How many tonight?'

'A few, sir.'

'Hmm.' Casey mounted the stairs. 'See she gets to bed all right, Free. Don't let her have any more whisky. She's been at it since breakfast.'

'Yes, sir. Shall I bring you a night cap?'

Casey chuckled. 'You're a scamp, Free. No, son, I have to rise early tomorrow. I want to go out to the north field and see what Ruffin's work gang is doing there. Harbud tells me Ruffin hasn't been to see them for three weeks.' His sigh carried through to Martha.

'Don't know why we have that overseer. He does nothing but prattle with Martha all day. If I didn't check on the slaves, we'd never know what's happening on this plantation.' Free was silent.

'Don't let the mistress keep you up all night, son.'

'I can handle her, sir.'

'Good. Call me if you need help. Your mother says Hilda left a chicken pie for you in the kitchen. It's good.'

'Thank you, da'.'

Martha slurped at her drink and drained the glass. She was furious. 'Free!' Her voice echoed out into the night like the shriek of a harridan. 'Come here!'

He was by her side in seconds, frowning at her distress. He leaned over and took the glass from her hand as she squinted up at him.

''Nother drink.' She belched. 'Now!'

'Sure, Miss Martha.' Free grinned amiably and made no attempt to move.

She focused on him again and sucked her lips. Was he being disobedient? 'I could have you flogged,' she said suddenly. 'Don't think that I couldn't. Ruffin would do it. Can't rely on Casey for anything.'

Free smirked knowingly. 'Mas Ruffin partial to flogging young boys,' he said.

Martha heard the mockery in his voice and straightened in

alarm. 'What do you mean?' she asked. 'Has he tried it with you?'

'Oh no, Miss Martha.' Free was contrite now the crisis was past. 'The slaves. I've heard them talk about the things he does sometimes. In his cabin.'

'It's disgusting!' She braced herself on the edge of the chair. 'I've never heard the like.' She squinted up at him and his face reassured her. His expression was one of innocence with his eyes reflecting the devotion he had for her.

'Oh, Free!' she said, holding out her hand. 'You are good to an old woman.'

He took her hand and laughed, helping her to her feet. 'Lor', Miss Martha,' he said, still chuckling. 'If you're an old woman, I must be an old man.'

She stopped and stared at him quizzically. 'What do you mean by that?' She clung to his arm and swayed slightly as he turned to her. His eyes sparkled with mischief.

'Because you aren't much older than I am.'

'By the devil,' she muttered. 'Did I teach you flattery too?'

'No, ma'm.' He was serious now, guiding her slowly along the deck of the veranda to the door. 'You taught me English, a little French and Geography. No flattery.'

'Bah!' She giggled and felt a gush of affection for him. 'You're a good nigra, and no mistake. Wiser than your years.'

She hung on to his elbow, relishing the warm, musky odor of his body. It reminded her of Casey so long ago.

'Where's Casey?' she thought suddenly, halting him at the door.

'He went to bed.'

'Really. Do you know, Free, I feel so hot tonight, I think I'll go for a walk.' She let go of him and steadied herself against the door jamb. 'Will you come with me?'

'You're not going far, ma'm?'

'No, Free,' she replied drunkenly. 'Don't worry, I won't fall into the swamp. Just a little walk in the moon . . . moonlight. I used to walk a lot years ago.' She crossed the veranda and negotiated the steps carefully, aware of Free hovering beside her, ready to catch her if she fell.

'I'm not tipsy,' she said, linking her arm under his. 'Not a bit.'

'Neither am I!' His voice was steady, suggesting nothing.

Its very boldness thrilled her and she laughed harshly. In the dark, she could imagine he was a young gallant escorting her after a ball. As a girl, she followed the party circuit until the small hours. It was a gay life until she inherited The Drongos and all its debts. She sighed.

Free drew closer. 'Are you sad?' he asked.

'No!' She was scornful. 'Why should I be when I've got what I wanted?'

'What's that?'

Free's question brought her back to the present. She blinked. The sight of him, with the moonlight playing on his long, curly hair and his straight nose in profile, filled her with an explosive desire to kiss him. She thought of Casey already asleep in his room. Casey had provided the solution to all her problems. He had given her everything she wanted. For a price.

'You wouldn't understand,' she said, quickening her pace. 'I'm not sure that I do.'

'Try me.'

Again she glanced at him. He was her height, his shoulders were broad and his waist where the white silk shirt was tucked in his breeches and secured with a cummerbund, was trim. If she forgot who he was, forgot his age, forgot everything . . .

They were at the *garçonnière*. She hadn't been in it for years, not since Hollis was there. Or was it with someone else? She couldn't remember their names. There were so many on stolen nights when Casey didn't seem to care.

'Do you know this place?' she asked hesitantly.

'Yes.' His voice cracked. 'I was here this afternoon.'

She pulled away from him. 'Whatever for?'

He shrugged his shoulders. 'Sometimes a man likes to be alone. Casey said I could use it.'

'For a wench?' Her heart thumped and she was sure he would notice. She didn't want to hear his reply. 'Take me inside,' she said quickly.

'There's no lamp.'

'The moon is bright enough. I know my way. We can open the windows.'

Her mouth dried as she followed him up the narrow staircase, holding his hand tightly so she wouldn't slip and miss her footing.

She waited at the door while he opened the shutters. It made little difference to the darkness in the room. He returned to her side and she put her arm around his waist. He didn't flinch.

'Free,' she said, 'this is very wicked.'

'Is it?'

His voice sounded so innocent that she swayed against him, wondering if she should turn back. Was it her fault Casey had abandoned her? So many naked black bodies had been flaunted in front of her by Casey, by Hollis when he was training the fighters, and by Ruffin and Jed when they inspected new stock . . .

She could tell Free to take her back now, and nothing would be spoiled. Even his innocence would be preserved.

'Let's sit on the bed,' she said. 'Take me there.'

She leaned against him as he guided her across the room.

They sat down and she put her hand on his thigh. 'I've taught you a lot of things, Free. I want you to listen to me as though this is another lesson.'

'Then it isn't wicked?'

'No.' Martha smiled. 'You do have to learn, don't you? This is just another part of your education.'

'Casey likes you to educate me. He said he can't do that.'

'He's right.'

Martha reached for his hands and placed them on her bodice. 'You can only learn these lessons from a woman,' she said, pressing his palms against her bosom. 'Don't you feel nice?'

She was disappointed when he made no move to hold her in his arms and smother her with kisses. 'Here,' she moved his hands down until they were on her waist. 'You can touch me where you like. I don't mind, I don't –'

She was interrupted by his mouth brushing against her cheek like the kiss of a nephew for an old aunt. She gripped his chin in her fingers and pressed her mouth over his, crushing his lips with a passion she did not believe she was still capable of.

He tried to push her away. She hesitated, dismayed at the ardor he aroused in her; knowing she would not stop until she was satisfied. She trembled and made a token effort to repel him but her fingers brushed instead against his crotch, swollen under the thin shield of his breeches.

He flinched, and tore out of her embrace. He stumbled and

fell with a groan on to the bed.

'Don't be alarmed,' she gasped, melting inside. She flung herself on the bed and took him in her arms.

'I'll show you, boy. Just do as I say.'

CHAPTER THIRTY-ONE

Casey replaced the bricks in the chimney-breast with care, patting in the last one and touching it with his fingers for luck. He stepped back with an air of satisfaction. The candle flickered and he glanced around the cabin anxiously. The door and the windows were all closed and he was alone. He sighed.

It had taken him a long time, he reflected as he reached for the chair and sat down. He was fond of Rhoda's old cabin despite the memories it held for him. When he despaired of ever succeeding in making his money back, he would cross the bayou to visit the cabin where Rhoda used to live.

He spent days at the cabin, replacing shingles, fixing windows, renewing the gallery posts, clearing a path through the undergrowth. He tended his small garden, carrying the produce over to Hilda to prepare for dinner. The time he spent alone at the cabin renewed him, giving him the strength to withstand the assaults to his ambitions perpetrated by Martha.

No one ever disturbed him there. Martha had forgotten its existence, even when she was sober which was very seldom now. The few slaves that remained were frightened of Rhoda's old cabin and refused to pass near it. They had been scared off by Hilda's tales of swamp spirits and they believed jumbies haunted it.

Casey had unwittingly given substance to the legend. Slaves passing through the swamp at night had sometimes seen the weak glow of his candle. The light where no one lived terrified them and fueled their belief in the tale of Rhoda's ghost. Casey encouraged the legend because no curious slave would venture where they thought spirits dwelt. His money was safe.

The hiding place behind the bricks in the chimney-breast was Casey's reason for coming to the cabin at night. When he received his commission payments from Willard Wadey, he stowed the money in a wooden coffer behind the bricks. It had taken many years to fill the coffer and now he had actually done it, he was perplexed.

He stretched his legs in front of him and the candle flickered with the movement. He scratched his head and considered what to do. When he had been hoarding the money every month, the solution seemed simple. It was what enabled him to ignore his shame at raising and peddling slaves. He was getting his revenge.

Now, with enough money to purchase Lizette and Free from Martha, and to return to Dominica to start a new life, he was not sure if he really wanted to leave. By rights, The Drongos was half his.

Twenty years had passed since he had left Dominica as a boy of seventeen. Free was almost that age now. Did he really want to forsake the life he had made at The Drongos and start again?

It was easier in the bleakness of the dark night, to opt for the simple way out. Martha had no heirs and he, as her husband, would inherit The Drongos from her. Yet he could not kill Martha like Lizette often urged him to do. He would have to wait. He was secure for the time being. He was the Bondmaster of The Drongos with a dozen loyal slaves, a fine son and a grand house in which to live. He stood up and snuffed out the candle.

When he opened the door of the cabin, the wilderness was cloaked in darkness. He closed the door softly behind him and paused on the gallery, sniffing the air. It was balmy. There was no telltale scent of a negro prowler creeping through the undergrowth on his way back from a voodoo swamp meeting. He sauntered along the narrow path confidently; the night held no terror for him. There was no moon and he could barely see two paces ahead, yet he found his way easily to the Bayou Celeste. He waded across it, relishing the cold water lapping around his thighs, and emerged dripping wet to gaze at The Drongos.

Lights burned on the front piazza and the back veranda and shone from the windows of the upstairs rooms. In Jed's day, drongos guarded the house. Now there was only Free asleep on a mat on the floor of the entrance hall. Casey knew of the uprisings in other parts of Louisiana yet he had no fear of that at The Drongos. His slaves were docile, easily controlled, and predictable.

He strolled toward the house, feeling proud. He had saved The Drongos even if he had compromised himself in doing it. He was right to value the plantation and the house so highly. It would, he knew, be difficult for him to leave.

When he pushed open the door into the entrance hall, he was careful not to bang it clumsily and wake Free. He looked for the boy. He was nowhere to be seen. That was puzzling. Casey had noticed that Free had been lethargic for months and his usual cheerful countenance showed strain. He smiled to himself, assuming that Free must have found a wench. It was odd, though, that the boy wasn't at his post, in case Martha needed him.

Casey crossed into the drawing room and glanced around. Sometimes the furniture would be in disarray if Martha had got drunk and scattered books and cushions around the room. Since she had taken to drinking secretly, she squirrelled away bottles of whisky only to forget where they were hidden. This caused chaos when she tried to find them. He tried to restrict her drinking although he often wondered why he should bother. She was happier in a stupor.

He heard a sound on the stairs and stepped rapidly to the parlor door. Free was peering down cautiously into the entrance hall. Casey was surprised to see he was naked. He watched Free descend the stairs warily, his ears and eyes alert. When he reached the floor, he entered the other parlor and Casey saw wales leaking blood on his back. They were gory stripes torn into his skin by a woman's nails raking his back in the throes of passion. Casey, too, had suffered similar wounds. He wasn't shocked, or angry, only aware that Free was no longer a boy.

He stepped out from behind the door and called softly. Free halted as though the wrath of god had descended on him. His shoulders began to shake with fear and even his buttocks quivered. Casey chuckled and Free turned hastily, his fear of the unknown changing to alarm at the sight of his father. He gulped with fright at what Casey would do to him.

'Well, well!' Casey drawled. He leaned against the wall and folded his arms across his chest.

Free covered his crotch. 'I heard a noise,' he said lamely.

Casey raised his eyebrow. 'I'm glad you weren't neglecting your duties.'

'No, sir.' Free bit his lip.

'Come here.' Casey scanned Free's body as his son walked toward him. He moved loosely now the tension had passed. There was no fear or resentment in his eye, only curiosity about what was going to happen. Casey liked that.

'Stand with your legs apart,' he instructed when Free was in front of him.

He reached out and made a pass around Free's shoulders, ignoring the blood that smeared his fingers as he pinched his flesh. He slid his hands down his spine to his buttocks then kneeled to continue feeling his thighs and calf muscles. He fondled Free's shins, then his knees, his thighs, and his penis. It was moist and Free flinched.

'Ah hah!' muttered Casey, a twinkle in his eye. 'Tender spot?'

'Not usually, sir.'

Casey nodded, patting Free's abdomen and fingering his chest briefly.

'Am I to be auctioned?' There was a hint of mockery in Free's voice.

'Doubt if I could get your price these days,' said Casey. He walked over to the stairs and sat on the fifth step. He admired Free; his body was perfect.

'The only advice I have to give you, son,' he said, 'is to take care.'

Free's face relaxed into a smile. 'I didn't want it to happen, da'.' He shrugged his shoulders. 'Then when it did, well, I didn't know how to stop.' He sat on the stairs, one step lower than Casey. 'She has a way of getting me when I least expect it. This *tuli* just jumps up and I can't stop her.'

'I know, son.' Casey patted his shoulder. 'I know what she's like. Don't worry. She'll tire of you soon enough and then she'll leave you alone. I blame myself. I should have put you to a wench before now.'

'A wench?' Free looked askance. 'Am I to be a slave stud?'

'You're that already, Free.'

The boy faltered, his annoyance draining away and a tear springing to his eye. He gazed up at Casey who put his arm around him.

'It makes no difference, son. Pleasure her and you'll improve yourself. That's the way it is for us.'

Free tried to squirm out of his embrace. 'I don't want it that way, da'.'

'Truly?' Casey stared at him.

'Yes, da'!' Hope shone in Free's eyes, clearing out the tears of despair.

Casey held him firmly, almost in tears himself as he understood what he had to do. 'You've given me confidence now,' he said.

'There's a place, far away from here, where you can be yourself, be free. There's an island where whites don't reject or manipulate a man because he's not white, and where blacks aren't slaves. It's our country, Free. I'm going to take you there.'

'Please, da'!'

Casey grasped Free and kissed him gently on his cheek. The two of them drew strength and hope from their new found bond.

Above them, at the top of the staircase, Martha watched. The hatred in her heart sparked out of her eyes like lightning in a thunderous sky.

The white youth had blue eyes and fair hair. His clothes were torn and dusty, showing signs of a long journey. He swaggered into the yard in front of the piazza and lifted the bundle he carried slung over his shoulder and placed it down on the flagstones at his feet. He stood with his hands on his hips and stared at the house, a grin of triumph spreading broadly over his tanned face.

'Well I'll be damned!' he said aloud, slapping his thigh. 'I made it!'

Free, who was watching from the veranda, regarded the youth suspiciously. Shacks had begun to appear all along the bayou housing families of poor whites. These people were pitiful misfits who were too lazy to work and showed only resentment for those who did. The slaves distrusted them, and not without reason. Nigger hunting was their favorite sport. They were mean individuals not above tormenting a man simply because he was black. Sometimes these crackers came to the plantation pretending to seek work. Their intention, Casey maintained, was only to steal.

The youth seemed to be a year or two older than Free. His clothes looked bedraggled, and Free assumed he was one of the swamp whites. He reckoned he could lick him in a fair fight. He stood on the top step and watched the youth pick up his bundle and stroll toward the house.

The stranger raised his head and glanced at Free with eyes that took in everything. He grinned. 'Hello, boy,' he said in a bossy manner quite the opposite to the whining tone usually used by the poor whites.

'Here, take this.' The stranger tossed his bundle at Free who responded with the reflex of one used to receiving orders. He caught the bundle then, in dismay at what he had done, dropped it deliberately on the steps.

'I don't take orders from no cracker,' he said angrily.

'Who are you calling a cracker?' The youth scowled and stood one step below Free, facing him.

'You.'

Free did not expect the punch to his midriff and the clout across his ear as he doubled up, winded. He gasped and the youth stepped past him onto the piazza before he could stop him. He bunched up his fists.

'Get off our piazza!' Free shouted, catching his breath and lunging at the stranger.

'What a peculiar way to greet visitors,' the youth said, holding his hand up. 'Surely you're not going to strike a white man, are you?'

Free hesitated, and studied the youth again. He was glancing around the piazza with the confidence of his race. 'You ain't a cracker?' Free asked grudgingly. 'You ain't one of those poor swamp whites?'

The youth grinned again. 'Sorry, boy, if my appearance fooled you. I've been traveling for weeks to get here. Came by the trace, you see, not by the river.'

'Where did you come from?'

'Nuorleans.' He rolled the name together in a casual drawl.

Free was impressed. He looked at the bundle still on the steps and thought about retrieving it. Before he could do so, the youth headed for the open door into the house. He didn't enter but put his head through the doorway and had a good look around.

Free remembered Casey's warning about whites who came to steal and he was suspicious again. He got ready to hold the youth by his shoulder and throw him back down the steps. This time, he wouldn't get punched.

'You keep out of there,' he shouted. 'Visitors wait here on the veranda.'

The youth turned. When he smiled, his face was friendly but without it there was an aura of aloofness. He raised an eyebrow. 'I'm waiting,' he said.

'What do you want?' Free demanded, realizing that he should have asked the question first before making a judgement about the stranger's status.

'I would like some respect from you, to begin with, boy.'

Free flushed. 'If you're worth it.'

'Does your mistress know how you treat visitors?' The youth sat in Martha's rocking chair and stuck out his legs. He surveyed the scene in front of the house with apparent approval. 'Call her for me.'

Free licked his lips, uncertain what to do. Martha had not mentioned that a visitor was expected but the stranger was so much at ease, he clearly believed he had a right to be relaxing on The Drongos piazza. Free needed help.

'I'll tell her you're here,' he said. 'She'll decide for herself if she wants to see you.'

'Oh, ho!' The youth scowled. 'It seems you're the master in this house, boy. That will soon change, I'm telling you. Get her.'

Free backed to the door, frowning at the stranger's tone. 'What name do you want me to tell her? She'll need to know who you are.'

'Says you!' The youth grinned suddenly. 'Tell her I'm a relative.'

'Relative?'

Martha stared at the youth from the doorway and reached for Free's arm. He hoped the stranger saw how his mistress depended on him.

'By the devil!' said Martha, intrigued by what she saw as the youth scrambled to his feet and bowed.

The stranger weakened under her hungry stare and his tanned features darkened with the suspicion of a blush.

'What a pleasure,' Martha said, dropping Free's arm and sweeping across the deck of the veranda with her hand outstretched. The boy clasped it, raised it to his lips and kissed it, his eyes boldly lingering on Martha's.

She smiled, pulling back her shoulders and breathing in so that the flabby lines of her waist weren't so obvious. She sat down in the chair he had vacated and, keeping her back straight and with her most charming smile, asked the reason for his visit.

'To see my relatives,' he said.

Martha didn't hear him at first. 'Free,' she called. 'Bring two mint juleps.'

Free didn't move. 'In a minute,' he said. 'Casey told me to see you are all right when he is away. I'm not leaving you alone with a strange white man who hasn't even given his name.'

Martha scowled but said nothing.

The youth looked outraged. 'Do you let your slaves address you like that? How can you feel safe when you're alone with such an uncouth nigra?'

'Who are you calling a niggah?' Free bunched his fists. 'Let me throw this whippersnapper in the swamps where he belongs!'

'That's enough, Free,' said Martha, feeling faint. She couldn't understand what was going on.

'Are you sure you're a relative?' she asked. 'My father had several children outside his marriage to my mother. Some of them think of themselves as my relatives but I have a different opinion. I suppose you're the son of one of those swamp bastards?'

She glanced at the youth again and fluttered her eyelashes. She wondered idly who would get thrown into the swamp if she did tell Free to put him out. This youth was quite the most attractive man she'd ever seen!

'Swamp bastard?' The youth grinned, showing a perfect row of gleaming white teeth.

Martha flushed with a strange excitement that seeped through her entire body and she felt herself moistening with anticipation. She giggled girlishly, longing for the mint julep that Free refused to bring. The boy really was becoming rather tiresome. How dare he show her up just when she should be creating a good impression on the visitor.

'I was born in New Orleans,' the stranger said. 'I never knew my father. That's not surprising, really, because my mother was his mistress, not his wife. She lived in a tiny house in Rampart Street. Ah!' The youth stopped when he saw the odd expression on Martha's face.

'I see you know about it. I don't remember it because my mother got very poor and we were always moving on. My mother often spoke of a great plantation house somewhere on the Mississippi that was my real home.' He paused and sneered at Free.

'She said that there were obliging slaves and a big house called The Drongos.'

'Go on,' said Martha breathlessly, clutching her bosom.

'My mother died last year. She was a dear, kind soul, always proud, even when we were destitute. She never accepted charity. People said she was crazy, but she wasn't. Her one aim was that I should come here and claim what's mine.'

'Yours . . .?' Martha gazed from Free who was gawking at the stranger with his mouth open, to the youth who seemed so full of vitality and intelligence and courage. Her heart missed a beat.

'There's nothing here that's yours.' She peered at the youth, trying to see some family resemblance. 'It's ridiculous. Who do you say your father was?'

'You know, don't you?'

'Do I?' She smiled coyly, and then began to wonder. 'Perhaps I do. I've heard of those houses in Rampart Street.'

'Who?' demanded Free. 'Tell me! I want to know.'

The youth was disgusted. 'I'm Kit Barrow, so Jed Barrow was my father, boy. He was the owner of this plantation. That means this house, the land and you, yes you, boy, are mine.'

He turned to Martha. 'Isn't that right, auntie?'

CHAPTER THIRTY-TWO

Casey's reaction to the news baffled Free. His father continued whittling a stick while he blurted out the details of the stranger's arrival. Casey was sitting on the stoop of Lizette's cabin. He had spent the morning since dawn riding on the plantation and he was in a somber mood as Free breathlessly related the details.

'Ain't you going to send him packing?' Free demanded, frustrated by Casey's apparent lack of interest.

Casey stopped fiddling with the stick and raised his head. Free saw a glint of amusement in the older man's eyes. 'I ain't sending him packing,' Casey said, shaking his head. 'You told Hilda there's an extra for dinner?'

'No, sir.' Free had run to look for Casey as soon as he had left Martha and the stranger.

'You're neglecting your duties, son.' He rose to his feet slowly. 'We'll tell Hilda together. Then you must see that the *garçonnière* is prepared for our new resident. You won't be able to use there again.'

Free followed Casey, puzzled why his father seemed so unperturbed. Perhaps he was really getting too old. He moved slowly as though his joints hurt and he seemed to have missed the point of what Free was telling him. He tried again.

'He said he has come to claim the plantation, da'. Ain't that worrying?'

'No.' Casey paused. 'Why should it be?'

Free sniffed. 'He ain't a regular fellow, da'. He punched me when I wasn't ready.'

'You should not have sassed him.' Casey shrugged and walked over to the kitchen cabin.

Hilda, alerted by the instinct of a fey slave for sensing a change in the rhythm of the plantation, was waiting at the door. She had grown so huge that she completely blocked the entrance. She rubbed her hands anxiously on her pinafore.

'Wha' happen'?' she demanded, reading the excitement on Free's face.

'We have a visitor,' said Casey.

'He says the plantation and all of us belong to him,' Free jabbered, unable to contain himself. 'He says his name is Kit and he was raised in New Orleans and his father owned The Drongos.'

Hilda gripped the door jamb, her face growing ashen. Free was pleased by the effect his news had on her.

'That's enough, boy.' Casey squeezed his shoulder. 'Are you all right, Hilda?'

'Whoo!' The old lady shook her head, setting off a ripple of trembling through the rolls of fat on her body. She gasped, her vast bosom heaving as she struggled to control it and digest the news.

'Jed did have a wench in New Orleans,' said Casey. 'I knew her.'

Hilda shook her head again and her double chins wobbled from ear to ear with indignation. ''T ain' true!' she said emphatically. 'Marse Jed ain' never tell me 'bou' no son.'

'He didn't know,' said Free. 'The boy's on the piazza now right enough, and Martha damned glad to see him.'

'Ah ain' believin' it 'til ah see de whelp,' announced Hilda. 'Mistis Mart'a so lonely fo' comp'ny, she glad to see de devil heself if he look fancy 'nuff.'

'This one's fancy.' Free shook off Casey's hand. 'He's got hair the color of flax and the brightest blue eyes you ever did see.'

Hilda snorted. 'Jed's hair was black like a niggah's, an' his eyes were gray.'

'Makes no difference,' said Casey with a grin. 'He could take after his mother.'

'Whoo!' Hilda threw up her hands and shooed them away. 'Ah got ma cookin' 'tend to. Ah see dis white boy den ah tell yo' who he is.'

'Why is that?' said Free happily as he walked to the house with Casey. 'Hilda's more concerned than you are, da', and she's much older.'

'What does that mean?' Casey's voice had an edge to it.

'Well, you're acting like some old stick in the mud. I thought you'd show more interest when I ran –'

'Now, listen, son!' Casey caught him by his ear and twisted it until Free howled with pain. 'Seems like you're getting too big for your boots these days.'

Free's eyes watered. 'You're hurting!' He bunched his fists ready to strike Casey in his stomach if he didn't stop.

'Take a hold of yourself, Free.' Casey let go and stared at him sternly. Free lowered his eyes.

'Don't think because you are Martha's buck that you can do what you like. She's a fickle woman, son, and you're no match for her. She has her tricks, so watch for them. Mayhap this white boy will appeal to her more than you. If he does, she'll send you packing, not he. So be careful!'

Free's high spirits sank. 'Yes, sir,' he said sulkily, uncomfortably aware that what Casey said was true.

'I hope it don't happen, Free. Just take it easy. Be patient, don't sass Martha, nor the boy. Smile at them all the time, and do what they say.'

Free was horrified. 'Have I got to be a slave to that trash?'

'You are to Martha.'

'She's different.'

'I know, son.' Casey cuffed him gently with his fist on his cheek. Free sensed the affection behind the blow and took it without flinching.

'It's not for long, son. I've made my plans and this boy could be useful. Let him have Martha and The Drongos. We're going to leave here, you and Lizette and I . . . soon, maybe next week.'

Free bit his lip and gazed at his father with pride. Casey's face was lined and careworn. His hair had begun to recede and his dark curls were thinning and speckled with gray. His eyes were no longer bright, dimmed by the strain he had lived under for years. He had a habit of rubbing the back of his head as though trying to smooth away a pain and he did it while Free watched. He smiled ruefully.

'Run along, son. Look to your mistress. I'll come soon.'

Free touched his father's hand before he turned and ran. He glanced back when he reached the veranda. Casey was standing by a magnolia bush gazing sadly at the house, as if bidding it farewell. He looked a tired figure at the end of a long trail. As usual, he was stroking the back of his head.

Free waved, and was overjoyed to see Casey wave back. He resolved to do what his father said, to swallow his pride and serve Martha without question. It would only be for a few more days . . .

He had the mint juleps ready for when Casey joined Martha and the stranger on the piazza. He hovered in the hall peering through the window and listening eagerly to the conversation while he waited for

Casey to call him. He wanted to impress the visitor with his speed.

Casey climbed wearily up the front step and Martha turned to greet him with a smile.

'Ah,' said Kit before she could speak. 'This is your man, I suppose? Head driver? Overseer? I hear plantations sometimes have colored folk in such high positions. Honest and reliable, eh?' He chuckled to show how charming he could be.

Martha frowned. 'This is my husband, Casey,' she said frostily.

Kit at least had the sensitivity to blush. His chuckle changed to a cough and his eyes showed his astonishment, then dismay. He remained in his seat while Casey offered his hand. He took it feebly, speechless with embarrassment and disgust.

'We've been married since Jed died,' said Martha. 'Casey was such a help.' Her eyelashes fluttered.

Casey had seen Free watching through the window and he snapped his fingers for the boy to pass around the tray of drinks.

'At last,' said Martha, taking hers eagerly. 'Such a surprise, isn't it, Casey? Kit being Jed's son, I mean.'

Casey rubbed his head. 'Pleased to welcome you to The Drongos, boy,' he drawled. 'Ever lived on a plantation?'

'No.' Kit's surliness showed he felt slighted by Casey's attitude.

'Not an easy life, but you'll get used to it. Slaves need to be handled the right way to get the most out of them. You can't be squeamish. When you punish a nigra, boy, do it to correct him, not out of anger. Do it when the other slaves are around so that your stock can see you're serious.

'Never threaten a slave, boy, because if you're serious, and give him time, he'll run before you can punish him. Runaways cost time and money and they breed discontent.

'Don't fool with the slaves, boy, you've got to get their respect. You've got to start now. They'll be watching you already for a weakness. If you show you're weak, you'll be useless as a slavemaster.'

'Oh, Casey!' said Martha. 'Must we talk about handling slaves now?'

'Why not, Martha? If he's Jed's son The Drongos is partly his so he's got to handle the slaves right. Do you think you can, boy?'

Kit appeared to be having a fit. To overcome his anger at being addressed as 'boy' by a man who was clearly a quarter black and thus a 'boy' himself in New Orleans parlance, Kit took a large sip of the mint julep. Its strength made him choke and he was spluttering and retching while Martha looked on appalled.

Casey strode over and slapped him heartily between his shoulder blades. The youth's face reddened and he stared up through watery eyes.

'Thank you, sir,' he gasped. The tension passed. Casey slapped him again, gentler this time.

'Then welcome to The Drongos, Kit. Welcome home.'

Free was piqued by the way Casey and Martha accepted the white lout. They listened to his stories about how he found his way to The Drongos, chuckling at his anecdotes and sympathizing with him for his struggle. Free was kept busy mixing fresh drinks, setting up the table for the extra guest and chivvying the house girl to prepare the *garçonnière* for its new occupant.

He served Kit grudgingly at table, observing how the youth took for himself the best portions instead of leaving them for Martha. To Free's eyes, the youth was a scrounger whose presence at The Drongos meant trouble for him, and for his father. Even if Casey did seem to welcome Kit, he didn't. As soon as possible, he intended to tell Martha what he thought of this interloper.

He had no opportunity to see Martha after dinner. Ruffin had heard the news about Kit's arrival and was an early visitor. Casey left them all together and went off toward the Bayou Celeste. Free watched him walking away from the house with a spring in his step. He could not understand why his father was so happy.

Kit's shout roused him from his reverie and he hurried into the parlor.

'Bring the drinks, boy,' Kit said, gesturing impatiently. Free glanced at Martha who nodded her head.

'That one needs a lick or two,' Kit was saying as he left the room. He paused in the hall to listen.

'Martha's favorite,' said Ruffin with a leer. 'I'd like to strip the breeches off him and tan his backside to ribbons.'

'Stop that, Ruffin!' Martha glowered. 'Free is a good houseboy. We don't have another suitable. And you are mistaken, Ruffin. He is not my favorite.' She smiled at Kit.

'I could paste him myself, if you like,' Kit said.

'Spoken just like Jed!' Ruffin slapped his leg. 'Needed a man like you here for years. I'll be pleased to show young Kit around the plantation, Martha. Teach him a few things. You ever larrup a nigra?'

'No.' Kit leaned forward.

'There's an art to it. If you cut him, you lower his value. I paddle them mostly. Use a leather flap, stiff like a board, shaped like the blade of an oar. Got small holes bored in it with an auger to give it more impact.'

'Lay that on a nigra and it doesn't cut but it sure stings his hide until he hollers like his balls are being nicked. Right nice to hear him yell and it does a power of good to a sulky buck.'

'Sounds exactly the treatment that your boy needs,' Kit said to Martha.

'I'll decide that,' she replied huffily.

Free smirked to himself outside the door, secure in his position as his mistrees's favorite whatever she said to confuse Ruffin and Kit. He controlled his misgivings during the rest of the day and longed for them all to go to bed.

To his surprise, Casey showed Kit to the *garçonnière* that night, talking to him as though he was his oldest comrade, giving him advice on the routine at The Drongos.

Matha retired early, swaying on her feet as he helped her up to her chamber. She dismissed him curtly and he had to go back to clear away the debris from the long hours of drinking. He went for his supper in the kitchen. Lizette and Hilda were there and plied him with questions about the newcomer.

'He's trash,' said Free arrogantly. 'He's worse than a cracker. I don't care if he is Martha's nephew. I don't have to like him.'

Lizette, who was cheerful for the first time in months, warned him to show the guest proper respect. 'It's just for a short while,' she said. 'Until next week . . .'

He realized then why she was so happy. Casey must have told her of his plan to leave.

'Is it true?' he asked, his spirits raised. 'Does Casey really mean what he said this morning?'

'Hush,' said Lizette, glancing toward Hilda. 'That's our secret.'

'Say, Hilda, what do you think of Kit?' he asked quickly to divert the cook's curiosity. She was eyeing him suspiciously over the rim of a cauldron of soup.

'Ah ain' sayin' yet,' she said mysteriously. 'But ah will . . . ah will!'

Free returned to the house, hoping to speak to Martha about Kit and what he thought of him. He went to her chamber only to find that the door was closed. He put his eye to the keyhole but it was covered from the other side. He listened at the door and heard the drone of voices.

'Oh no,' he muttered to himself at the thought that Kit had got into his mistress's chamber. Then he listened again and heard Casey's voice. It had been months since Casey had spent the night with Martha. It was odd. He crept slowly down-stairs to his mat at the door, feeling thoroughly dejected.

The next day he was kept so busy by Kit that he had no chance to speak to Martha until she went to her office in the afternoon. He entered without knocking to see she was making notations in a large ledger with a quill pen.

'What the hell do you want?' Martha said angrily when she looked up and saw him watching her. 'Can't you see I'm busy?'

'I'm sorry,' he said, and backed out of the room, wondering what he had done wrong. She seemed to have changed in her manner toward him. She had never snapped at him before.

That night Free waited until after midnight then walked softly up the stairs and tiptoed across to Martha's door. He pushed gently against it, expecting it to swing open easily as it usually did when she wanted him. It was locked.

He was really puzzled now. Martha had been cool toward him the whole day and he was anxious to know why. He slept on the floor outside her room in case she would open the door and call him in. She did not.

Martha was tired of Free. It had taken the arrival of Kit to show her how much she let Free dominate her. When she considered it, she was amazed that she had ever seen anything attractive in the slave. The lust she once had for his body had changed to resentment and anger for what Free knew of her. She resolved to have nothing more to do with him while she waited for an opportunity to discard him permanently.

Kit was the catalyst that changed Martha's feelings. She was fascinated and intrigued by him. Her lovers had always been slaves whom she could summon and dismiss at will. None of them held her interest for more than a few nights. Casey was the exception because of the bond they shared and that bond kept them together.

Kit was white, fiercely proud and independent with the added excitement of being her own family. It was no matter that he had so far shown no interest in her beyond what she should expect from a newfound nephew.

At nights, when she lay alone in her bed, with the door securely locked, she wondered if she should go to him in the *garçonnière*. She watched every day for some sign that he reciprocated her feelings. Unfortunately, there was none.

Kit was so charming and friendly, he got on well with everyone. Even Ruffin liked him. Martha assumed that Casey had arranged a bed wench for him in the *garçonnière*. It made her furious and wild with frustration.

One morning, ten days after his arrival, Martha and Kit were sitting on the veranda with Casey when they saw Ruffin striding up the hill accompanied by three white men. Martha excused herself before they had time to reach the house.

She darted inside. She wanted to fix her make up which, having a beeswax base, tended to melt in the heat. She had to brush her hair, too, for she wanted the visitors to see her at her best. She recognized them as Bayou Sara's most prominent citizens: Willard Wadey, Tram the auctioneer, and Tom Jakes who owned the hardware store.

'Can I help you, Miss Martha?' Free surprised her when he stepped out of the shadows of the hall.

'No, boy! Why do you always get under my feet?'

'Martha –' Free gaped at her.

She gathered her skirts in her hand and hurried up the stairs. She was pleased when she heard Kit shouting for Free because now he wouldn't follow her.

A new house slave, a girl Casey had sent from the pen, was polishing the floor outside her chamber. Martha ignored her and entered her room.

She sat in front of the dressing table and stared at her reflection in the mirror. An idea entered her mind when she thought of Free's tiresome pleas. It would be an ideal way. Her heart quickened at the boldness of her plan. She brushed her hair quickly, considering how to make it succeed.

From downstairs she could hear the boom of Willard Wadey's loud voice and the chatter of the others. Her mouth went dry and she licked her lips. Slowly, she rose from her chair and went to the door.

She opened it and looked down at the slave polishing at her feet.

The girl hung her head shyly at being noticed.

'Go down the back stairs, gal.' Martha said. 'Tell the young white man, Master Kit that is, that I want to see him here. At once, do you understand?'

'Yas, mistis.' The girl crawled away.

Martha walked purposefully to the front stairs.

'Free,' she called, leaning over the banisters. 'Come here, please.'

Free took the steps two at a time and bounded across the landing to her door. 'Yes, Miss Martha?' he said breathlessly, his eyes showing his gratitude at the chance to please her.

'What are they talking about downstairs?' she asked. She had loosened her corsage and her breasts seemed to be bursting out of her dress. She lounged against the door and fluttered her eyelashes.

Free gulped. 'They want Casey to send stock for an auction because the town's business is slackening off.'

'Ah, yes . . .' She appeared to be thinking. 'Have you given them drinks?'

'Yes, Miss Martha. Can I get you one?'

'Why not?' she said. 'Wait a minute. I'm sure I have a glass here somewhere. Come in.' She stepped aside to let him enter.

Despite her resolution, she felt a surge of yearning sweep through her. His touch as he brushed past her made her gasp. She followed him into the room, shutting the door carefully and pretending to turn the key.

He heard the click of the door and halted by the bed. 'Miss Martha . . .?'

'Shhh!' She put her finger on her lips. 'Don't speak.' She glided over to the bed and sat on it, putting her hand around his waist and pulling him to her.

'No . . .' he said, rooted to the spot. 'I want to talk to you, Miss Martha. Have I offended you? You've been . . .' His voice died as Martha's hand slipped into his breeches and she began to fondle him.

'Please . . .' he gasped, trying to draw away.

Her free hand unlaced his cummerbund and pulled his breeches to his knees. She lowered her head and her lips closed over him, drawing him out.

He staggered forward and fell with her on to the bed. She opened her legs and urged him on to her, locking her ankles together behind his waist, writhing against him. He groaned.

There was a knock on the door.

'Help!' shrieked Martha hastily, opening her legs and scratching Free's face before he could break away.

The door swung open and Kit stared at her.

'Help!' cried Martha. 'I'm being raped,' she added to make sure he understood. 'Help me!'

CHAPTER THIRTY-THREE

'Damn the boy to hell!' Willard Wadey pounded his fist into the palm of his hand. 'Don't worry, Casey,' he said. 'We'll see you're reimbursed. You're lucky we came.'

'Rape of a white woman is a lynching matter,' said Tom Jakes, a runt of a man who toted two guns in his belt. 'That's what nigra 'bolition brings.'

Tram stood behind Casey, his hand on his shoulders. 'I know you're upset, old partner. We'll deal with the buck for you.'

'No,' said Casey, hardly able to speak for the pain pounding in his brain, and the disappointment engulfing him. 'It's not necessary.'

'Yes, it is,' said Wadey. 'The buck rogered your wife.'

'The boy's his son,' said Ruffin, sneering. 'He's soft on him.'

Tom Jakes was livid with rage. 'But he was a slave, wasn't he?'

Ruffin nodded.

'I'll punish him,' said Casey slowly, raising his head and trying to shut out the light. He was sitting surrounded by the four white men on the veranda. Upstairs, Hilda and Lizette were trying to comfort Martha who was having hysterics. Kit was standing guard over Free who had been bound with his own breeches and was laid out on the deck of the back porch.

'No, you won't,' said Ruffin. 'I know you! If we do nothing now, as soon as Wadey and Tram go you'll tell Free to get on with mixing the mint juleps!' Ruffin turned to Wadey.

'Terrible things have happened in this place,' he said. 'I could tell you . . . Look at Casey, he's half nigra himself, ain't he?'

Willard Wadey paused in his restless stride up and down the piazza. 'That's neither here nor there,' he declared. 'Casey has no say in this matter. He's too involved. Damn! This is the clearest case of rape of a white woman I've ever heard. Do you deny that, Casey?'

Casey raised his eyes. They were dull and without fight. He couldn't speak. If he said Martha encouraged Free with his tacit consent, it couldn't change what all of them had seen when Martha screamed.

The white men were outraged, not because they were concerned about Martha. It was the threat to their own shabby lives they were worried about. The freeing of slaves was a daily topic and the most feared consequence of abolition was what the freed slaves would do to white women.

'We'll surely have to punish the bastard.' Wadey turned to the auctioneer. 'Tram, what's the nigra's value?'

Tram stroked his beard. 'He's a mustee, I suppose. Fancy buck, fully house trained, Drongos stock.' He paused and looked around the veranda as he calculated Free's price.

'Could be anything up to five thousand dollars. More if you get the right people at the auction. Some men like slaves that are spunky and pretty, don't they Ruffin?' He leered at the overseer.

Wadey gestured impatiently. 'Average it, Tram. Say he's a field hand.'

'About two thousand. Depends.'

'That's it. We'll settle for two.' Wadey put his hands on the arms of Casey's chair and leaned over him. 'We're going to buy that buck from you, Casey. You can come to Bayou Sara tomorrow to collect the money.' He straightened and looked over the railing to the yard.

'That's a fine tree out there.' He pointed to a large live oak. 'Tram, you take the boat back to Bayou Sara and round up some of the folks. Tell them we've got a special entertainment and it's a hundred dollar contribution for anyone who wants a poke at the nigra. Oh, we'll have such a crowd!'

'When will we do it?' asked Tom Jakes, hopping from one foot to another in his excitement.

'Sun down,' said Wadey firmly. He flung himself back on his chair, ignoring Casey slumped in a rocker with his eyes glazed.

'Are your slaves reliable, Ruffin?' he asked the overseer as Tram made his way down to the boat landing.

'Sure.' Ruffin licked his lips. 'You really mean to do this thing,

Wadey? Seems a big waste of a prime buck. Let me give him a hundred lashes and keep him in the stockade. I could punish him properly . . .'

'Damn! The buck's ours,' said Wadey. 'We've set the price. We'll punish him good and the word will spread about what happens to a troublesome nigra in the bayous. That'll stop their freshness. At the same time, we'll get some sport, eh, Tom?'

'Sure thing.' Tom nodded, spittle drooling from his lips.

Wadey contemplated his empty glass. 'Got more whisky, Casey?'

Casey didn't hear. The only word that was throbbing through his head with the constant pain was: why? There were so many questions and he couldn't answer them.

He knew it was impossible to save Free. Slavery existed because resistance was broken by fear of punishment. A crime required a reckoning. For what Free had been caught doing, Wadey was correct with his Bayou Sara style justice.

Casey's mind was dulled at the thought of losing his only son, the last of the Bondmaster seed. Why? he wondered. Why had it happened at the very moment he was ready to take Free and Lizette away from The Drongos for ever? Why?

A hand shook his shoulder and a voice called him from far off. He ignored it but the voice was insistent. 'Casey! Casey!'

'He's brooding,' said Hilda. 'Let him be.'

'Casey!' Lizette slapped him across his cheek. He turned to look at her.

'There's nothing we can do,' he said in a hollow voice.

He was alone on the piazza. From inside the house came the sound of raucous laughter. Wadey and Tom were in the parlor, their muddied boots propped up on the couch and a bottle of whisky between them. Ruffin was regaling them with stories, none of which were complimentary to Casey.

Lizette was whispering to him. 'Hilda will get Kit off the back porch. We can release Free.'

He sat up and took her hands in his. 'What?' He looked beyond her to where Hilda was standing, sweat pouring down her fat cheeks as she wrung her hands nervously in front of her.

'I said –'

'I know what you said. What do we do when we've freed him?'

'Run, of course.' Lizette stood back and glared at him. 'We can go into the swamp. We'll get away, the three of us together.'

He rubbed the back of his head. The pain didn't ease and he didn't move.

'Hurry,' said Lizette. 'We haven't got much time. They'll be here from Bayou Sara sooon.'

He looked up at her and smiled faintly. 'By the devil,' he said. 'We'll give it a try. Are you willing, Hilda?'

'Sure, Mas Cas. Ah gwine tell Kit ah need help to tote mo' whisky from de storehouse. Yo' go 'roun' de oder side of de house an' release Free den.'

Casey hugged Hilda briefly, kissed her sweaty face and slapped her bottom. Lizette pulled away.

They left the piazza together and walked around the west side of the house where they would not be noticed by Ruffin and the others drinking in the parlor.

Casey peered around the corner and saw Kit sitting on a chair with Free on the floor in front of him. Free was gagged, his hands bound behind his back with a rope and his ankles tied with his own breeches. Kit kicked him as he talked.

'You see what happens to a fresh nigra? Oh, I should kill you myself!' He struck him in his crotch with his foot. 'You're going to be thrashed a thousand licks then lynched. And that's too good for what you done.'

Kit raised his head as Hilda bustled out of the house and asked his help. She was so convincing, he could not refuse. He knelt down first to check Free's bonds, gave him another kick for good measure, then followed Hilda off the veranda to the storehouse.

Free raised his head immediately and looked around, obviously seeking a means to escape.

'Go on!' said Lizette, pushing Casey around the corner. He stepped back hurriedly.

'No,' he said. 'We must wait until Kit can't see the veranda. Let Hilda take him into the storehouse first.'

They watched anxiously as the old cook waddled along the path and Kit strode behind her. He glanced back from time to time to see Free did not move.

'Now!' said Lizette when Hilda and Kit entered the storehouse.

It was too late. The rear door to the house opened slowly and Martha peeped out. She looked both ways, saw there was no one guarding Free, and rushed over to him. She bent down and kissed him on his cheek. He wriggled violently.

'Did you ask her to help too?' Casey turned on Lizette in a rage.

'No,' she said. 'We left her upstairs.'

'I didn't mean it!' Martha was crying. 'Free, I didn't know this would happen. I only wanted Kit to fight you, to get jealous . . . Oh!' She fumbled to release his ankles but the knot was too tight.

Free mumbled desperately behind his gag, shaking his head.

'What? Oh yes.' Martha tried to unfasten the knot holding the gag. 'Keep still,' she said. 'It's so tight. Drat. I've broken a nail.' At last she untied it and pulled the cloth away from his mouth.

'Free!' she said, holding him in her arms and pressing her mouth over his in a desperate attempt at a kiss.

He pulled away angrily. 'My hands,' he pleaded. 'Loose them quickly.' He spun around so his back was to her.

'Oh yes, yes I will.' She struggled with the knot. 'Don't pull your wrists apart like that, dear. You're tightening the knot. Oh, Free, what shall we do?'

'By the devil,' he gasped. 'Loose me!'

'Take me with you, Free. I can get money. We'll go to Paris, to Venice, all those places we've dreamed of.'

'Yes, yes,' he said. 'Anything. Just untie me.'

'You promise? You're not vexed with me?'

'No!' He shook his head, his eyes bursting with frustration that Martha was taking so long. A shadow fell over them and he looked up in horror.

'What have we here?' Ruffin stood with his arms akimbo, chuckling wickedly. Tom Jakes was behind him, his pistols pointed at Free.

'He's mine,' said Martha. 'You shan't hang him!'

'I believe we will, Martha.' Ruffin put his hand under her shoulders and lifted her up as she burst into tears. He checked Free's bonds were still holding and retied the gag.

Kit came hurrying from the storehouse, a jar of whisky in each hand.

'Kit,' said Ruffin sternly, 'you have a lot to learn. Come with me, I have things to tell you about The Drongos and what Casey did to your father.'

Martha reached for Kit and began to cry hysterically, leaning her head against his shoulder as Ruffin led them both into the house.

Tom Jakes sat down on the chair, rested his pistol over his knee and propped up his feet on Free's body. He rocked slowly backward and forward, his eyes scanning the plantation for any sign of movement.

Casey clung to Lizette. He began to whimper like a child as his head seemed to explode with pain.

Tram shouted for quiet. There were a score of white men gathered in the yard in front of The Drongos. Behind them, cowering nervously under the trees, were the slaves. Free was in chains, standing beneath a live oak that had a rope with a noose tied in it slung from a bough.

Willard Wadey, Ruffin Calmes and Tom Jakes stood behind Tram and faced the murderous looking gang of ruffians who were the Bayou Sara gentry.

'Now y'all see this fine nigra,' Tram began in his singsong auctioneer's voice. 'Y'all paid for this nigra so we can recompense Casey who's the buck's Bondmaster. That means now the nigra's ours. Our nigra raped a white lady so we gwine punish the buck.'

'Lynch and bowel him!' yelled a voice from the crowd while others shouted in support.

'You nigras out there!' Tram gestured at a group headed by Harbud who crouched under the trees. The women led by Hannah were keening a dirge that harkened back to Africa with its monotone of wailing and sorrow.

'You can tell every nigra in the swamps and bayous. There's no freedom from slavery in this or any other world. A nigra who rapes a white lady can expect to die like this buck here.' Tram held a whip in his hands and he thrashed it across Free's shoulders. The slaves winced and their wailing swelled louder.

Lizette pushed through the crowd of whites. She was carrying a pitcher. The men let her through reluctantly, some clutching her breasts or grabbing at her backside with their grimy hands.

She walked boldly up to Willard Wadey. 'Please, sah,' she said, tears in her eyes. 'Let me give dis watah to ma son to ease his dyin' gasp, sah!'

Wadey stared down at her pompously. 'So you're the buck's dam, are you?' He winked suggestively and leered at her.

Lizette waggled her shoulders so that her shift slipped down to reveal her breasts. Wadey scratched his crotch.

'All right,' he said. 'I shall come to your cabin later.'

'T'ankyo', sah!' Lizette ran across the gap separating Free from the crowd.

Ruffin was placing the noose around Free's neck, ready to pull it tight. Three whites held the other end of the rope, all set to jerk it up at a signal from Tram. Free was going to be suspended from the bough while he slowly strangled. No quick death for rapists.

Free saw Lizette running toward him. 'Go back, mam,' he said. 'Go with da' to that place.'

Ruffin struck him a blow across his mouth to shut him up. 'What's that?' the overseer demanded, pointing at the pitcher.

'Water,' said Lizette, her eyes brimming with tears. 'Mas Wadey says I can give it to Free.'

'He did, did he? Well I say you can't.'

'It's all right, Ruffin,' shouted Wadey. 'Let him have it. The buck might live a little longer.'

Ruffin scowled. 'Only if she drinks from it first,' he shouted back. 'I know this wench, she's a Bondmaster get and as tricksy as a conjure.' He glared at Lizette and raised his whip. 'Drink, wench, before I lash you.'

Lizette turned to Kit, her eyes wide with an unspoken plea. 'For Free,' she said softly. 'You didn't hate him, did you?'

'No,' said Kit, blushing.

'You first!' said Ruffin, jabbing her between her legs with the stock of his whip. 'Drink!'

'Ah don' wan' to drink,' said Lizette, backing away. 'De watah does be fo' Free.'

Ruffin tightened the noose and Free gagged. Lizette screamed as she realized it was too late. Kit held her and tried to draw her away.

'Free, Free!' she screamed. She raised the pitcher to her lips and took a sip.

'Ruffin! It's only water, for God's sake,' cried Kit. 'Let her give it to the boy.' He led her forward.

'Let's see her swallow it first.'

Lizette swallowed, raising her neck proudly so that everyone could see. She thrust the pitcher hastily at Free, holding it up to his lips. Her hands trembled and Kit had to help her.

'Free . . .' she screamed as her hands went limp and the pitcher dropped to the ground. Slowly, she slid down Kit's legs and crumpled in a heap at his feet.

Ruffin rolled her over with his foot. The whites of her eyes stared up at him. 'Poison!' he said, kicking the pitcher away. It shattered and its contents seeped into the mud. 'She wanted to rob us by poisoning the bastard. I knew it!'

The crowd surged forward and two men seized Lizette's body by her ankles, spreading her legs apart. One man unbuckled his breeches and rubbed himself until he was hard.

'Let the buck see this rape,' he said, falling on to Lizette's lifeless body and ramming himself into her. 'She's warm, she's warm!' he cackled. 'How sweet!' The crowd roared with laughter.

Tram gave the signal. The three men pulled on the rope and Free was jerked into the air by his neck. They secured the rope around the trunk of the next tree so that Free was swinging a foot from the ground, his body weighted down by the chains. He was still alive.

Ruffin gleefully sliced his whip across Free's penis.

'That's mine,' said a man wielding a knife as he rushed forward from the crowd. He grasped Free's penis and slashed at its root until it was a bloodied lump of flesh. He held it up to the jeers of the crowd. Free struggled with the pain, each spasm of his legs serving to pull the noose tighter.

Another man sliced off his testicles and tossed them in the air, catching them as they dropped and pretending to juggle with them.

Willard Wadey stepped forward and drew a long slash with his knife from Free's throat to his gaping crotch. Tom Jakes, not to be outdone, drove his knife into Free's waist, scoring a bloody line from one hip to the other.

Men surged forward, each one of them hacking in a frenzy at Free, blood spurting from his wounds on to their hands.

The slaves melted away in terror as dusk fell, seeking refuge in the swamps before the white man's butchery turned on them.

Kit ran from the scene, Free's blood spattered over his face, until he reached the bank of the Bayou Celeste. He collapsed there and vomited.

Free finally died when Ruffin thrust his knife up through his anus, splitting him in two.

Kit puked until his stomach was empty and he seemed to be retching up his guts. He lay in the mud by the bayou and wanted the earth to open and swallow him up. His clothes were soaked with Free's blood and his own vomit.

He wriggled out of his shirt, pulled off his pants and lay the clothes with his knife on the bank. He stepped gingerly into the water until it was up to his knees. He sat down in it, twisting his body rapidly and sluicing water over him in a frantic effort to scourge himself of the blood and shame, and to wash himself clean. He was almost submerged with only his nose protruding above the water line.

It would be so easy, he thought, to drift down to the bottom of the creak and to lie in the mud and leaves and never be seen again.

A lantern bobbed through the darkness toward the bayou. He watched its progress as it swung through the trees. He sank deeper into the water. He wasn't afraid of spirits but he did not want any of the crazed white men to find him. The lantern stopped at the bayou's edge and he peered out of the water at it.

A figure was bent over his discarded clothes. The shape raised itself up and wheezed.

'Oh my lor'!' Hilda dabbed at her pudgy cheeks and heaved to recover her breath. 'Not another one?'

Kit waited to make sure Hilda was alone before he called her name.

'Whooh!' She nearly fainted with shock, the lantern shaking and threatening to fly out of her hand into the bayou.

'Hilda, it's me, Kit.' He rose out of the water and Hilda's legs collapsed and she fell into a heap, her mouth working speechlessly with fear.

The lantern remained in her grasp and Kit stepped dripping out of the bayou and took it from her. He hung it on a branch and crouched down in front of her.

'I'm no jumbie, Hilda. I was trying to get clean.'

Hilda touched him cautiously. 'Mas Kit, it does be yo' in trut'?'

He grinned and helped her to her feet. 'I apologize for frightening you. I was frightened myself. I thought you were one of those mad men.'

'Dey gone,' she said. 'Dey all gone. Ruffin gone too. He won't come back here no mo'.'

'I'm sorry, Hilda.' Kit felt like crying and he lowered his eyes.

She grunted. 'Why, wha' yo' done do?'

'I feel I am somehow to blame . . . for what happened. I was a fool . . . trying to throw my weight around and pretend I was a big man. Free could have been my friend. I didn't mean him any harm. I'll need someone like him to help me if I'm to do my share on the plantation.'

'Don' worry 'bou' de boy, Mas Kit. It was young Free's time.' Hilda hitched up her bosom, recovering her wits. 'Yo' got Mas Casey to help yo'.'

'Where is Casey? Is he hiding? He wasn't at the . . .' His voice failed him.

Hilda's eyes narrowed and she studied him suspiciously. 'Ah don' know,' she said.

Kit laughed. 'You're lying. You don't trust me because I'm white. Where are you going, anyway?'

Hilda frowned. 'Ah does go to de swamp sometime. Mas Casey don' mind.'

'Take me with you.'

'Why fo'?'

'I don't want to go back to the house yet. Alone.'

'Yo' won' be 'lone. Mistis Mart'a does be dere, cryin' she heart out.'

'Please take me with you,' he said again, his eyes pleading.

'Ah ain' gwine nowhere wid a naked white man.' Hilda chuckled and reached for her lamp, raising it high so she could see Kit clearly. He covered his crotch with his hands and flushed with embarrassment.

'I forgot,' he said feeling foolish. He turned around and bent down to pick up his breeches.

Hilda gasped. 'What dat?' she asked, pointing at his backside. The lantern shook in her hands throwing weird shadows from the trees above their heads.

'What do you mean, Hilda?' He smiled at the old woman's commotion and pulled on his pants. He picked up his knife, sticking it into his waistband, and took up his shirt.

'Dat patch on yo' rump . . . what is it?'

'A birthmark, Hilda. That's all.'

'But it's black.'

'Sure it's black, like a mole. Nothing unusual in that, Hilda. What's wrong?'

'Not'in,' she said, wheezing heartily and gripping his hand. 'Yo' help me cross dis bayou nuh. We got t'ings to do tonight. If!'

CHAPTER THIRTY-FOUR

Casey paced the rickety gallery, talking softly. He was alone, except for the company of ghosts who shambled up and down with him in the darkness as he discoursed gloomily with them. The gallery was not a long one and when he tired of pacing, he squatted on its floor and let the spirits of his imagination hunker down with him.

Darkness was total around the old cabin; the blackness of the night a pall over the murky wilderness, isolating him utterly in his melancholy.

'What else,' he asked for the umpteenth time, 'could I have done?'

The ghost of Mary, his mother, dressed as usual in the gaudy garb of her profession, pouted prettily and tried to dismiss the matter with a joke.

'Yew got two thousand dollars, Cas. That's more than I ever got for a night!'

'But Free was my son.'

'Yew had other whelps and yew sold them.'

'They were my slave get. I had to sell them to make The Drongos profitable.'

'Free was a slave too,' said Mary. 'So was his mother. Don't get vexed for that.'

'They were special!' Casey moaned aloud. 'They were Bondmaster seed, like me. They were my flesh and blood.'

'Ain't wise to get soft with your own kind, boy!' Carlton Todd's harsh voice boomed in the darkness reverberating through Casey's head with the impact of a slap on his ears. 'You've only got yourself to blame.'

'I thought it was for the best.'

'Damn nonsense! You should have quit The Drongos as soon as you knew Martha liked to rut with the stock. Drains the niggers terrible. Women like her are bound to come to a bad end.'

'She kept pestering me.'

'That's what a buck's got a pecker for, ain't it? You were so damn foolish. You wanted Lizette on the side and you neglected Martha. No wonder she turned to niggers.'

'It happened to you.'

'Blaming me now, are you?' The specter of Carlton Todd seemed to grin ruefully. 'It's Ella's black blood that was bad, not mine.'

Could he really blame his ancestors for what had happened, Casey wondered. It was comforting to seek consolation in the idea. With Carlton Todd's rapacity and Mary Gregg's licentious nature in his breast, maybe it was inevitable that his actions would lead to that day's tragedy.

He had accepted Free's dalliance with Martha as part of the depravity of his life at The Drongos. What seemed to whites to be heinous was to him and Martha, in their bayou kingdom where slave breeding was their obsession, a matter of course.

'But why?' he asked aloud. 'Why did Free get caught by Kit just when I was ready to take him to Dominica?'

'That's simple, boy.' Carlton Todd growled at Casey's stupidity. 'What the hell do you want to come back to Dominica for? Can't you let the Bondmaster rest in peace?'

Lucy drifted on to the gallery, her blonde hair billowing like a halo. She smiled seraphically and her caress eased the pain in Casey's head. 'Perhaps you were meant to stay here, Casey.'

He clung to the railing and pushed himself to his feet, chasing away the spirits with a shake of his fist. The memory of Lucy made him angry and he stomped the length of the gallery and back again.

None of this would have happened, he thought, but for Lucy's insistence. Yet it had happened. He had let Free die, and done nothing to save him. He had fled, like a runaway, to Rhoda's cabin, afraid that the white men would turn on him when they had finished with Free. Cowardice and shame were all that was left of the greed and lust bequeathed to him by his heritage of mixed blood.

He stared out at the darkness and listened to the gurgle of the swamp behind the cabin and the snap and whistle of night animals in the undergrowth surrounding it. A dim glow of a light through the trees, radiating from the bayou like a sunrise, seeped into his solace.

He blinked as the brightness spread, then hovered a hundred yards away. One of the spirits seemed to come to life and rushed toward him from the light. He backed to the wall of the cabin, pressing himself against it, ready to resist this charging jumbie with fists flying and legs kicking.

'Casey!' a voice shouted as the shape burst from the darkness and landed with a thud on the gallery. He shook his head, bemused, wondering how the duppies had become real with a musky smell and a coarse shout.

'Casey! I see you there!' The figure crouched in a fighter's stance at the end of the gallery. A knife was in its hand.

'What do you want?' Casey shouted, his voice startling himself. A sleepy bird cawed with fear.

'You!' said the figure. 'Ruffin told me how you killed my father in the swamp.'

'Kit?' Casey peered at the shape. It was real and threatening, moving slowly toward him, inch by inch, crouched like a cougar.

'Yes,' Kit hissed. 'Hilda led me here. Did you kill him, Casey?'

Casey hesitated. He backed along the gallery and was caught in the corner by the railing, unable to move further. He rested his hands on the rail and judged the distance between himself and Kit. He could swing up with his feet and deflect the boy as he attacked. Or he could somersault over the railing and conceal himself in the swamp.

The light from the lantern grew nearer and the blade glinted in Kit's hand.

Casey relaxed. It didn't matter any more. Kit was Jed Barrow's vengeance; his destiny. He was ready for death.

'Yes,' he said, feeling the pain surge back into his head. 'I killed Jed.'

Kit lunged and there was a burst of flame in Casey's eyes. He sank instinctively to the floor, preparing for the long silence of death.

Instead, there was a clatter as a lantern fell near him and its fire spilled around his legs. The lantern had been thrown by Hilda who set up a wail at the side of the cabin, tugging at Kit's breeches as he toppled on to Casey.

The knife slipped from Kit's hand and fell into the darkness.

'Get off him,' Hilda screamed. 'He ain' de one!'

The flames singed Casey's bare feet and he drew them up quickly, pounding his knees into Kit's crotch. The boy gasped at the pain and, as the fire found him too, rolled off and fell over the gallery edge to the hard mud below. Hilda uttered a cry of triumph and flung herself on top of him.

'Take off yo' britches,' she shrieked, tugging at Kit's waistband.

Casey shook his head and watched the flames spreading through the dry wood of the old cabin. He slipped off the gallery and stared at Hilda. 'By the devil!' he shouted, 'this ain't the time to roger the boy. Get him away from the fire.'

'See dis!' Hilda's weight across Kit's shoulders prevented the boy moving.

Kit thrashed his legs but Hilda succeeded in pulling his breeches down to his thighs, exposing his buttocks.

'See dis!' she screamed with excitement.

'You've gone mad, woman!' Casey glanced from Hilda to the cabin as the flames began to creep up the outside wall.

'Look, Cas! Dat black hind quarter!'

Casey ran toward the cabin. If he hurried he would have time to get in before the flames engulfed the door.

'Just like Lucy's whelp,' screamed Hilda.

Casey halted. He turned slowly and gazed at the old slave. The sweat was pouring off her face. She had lost her cap in the struggle to debag Kit and her hair was a patchy mass of gray whorls. She was pummelling Kit's backside and shrieking incoherently. Her face was blotched by the light of the flames flickering close to her.

Casey walked back slowly, leaving the flames licking the cabin door. The blaze lit up the night, sending grotesque shadows leaping at him from the overhanging trees. He reached Hilda and seized her hands.

'Stand up,' he ordered. 'And stop this caterwauling.'

Hilda clasped him and dragged herself to her feet. Kit rolled away, winded, tugging at his breeches. She fought so catch her breath.

'Miss Lucy,' she panted. 'Her baby . . . in de swamp . . . black rump . . . like him!'

Casey frowned. 'The babe died, Hilda!' He glanced back at the cabin as the flames whooshed up to an open window.

'Ah done lie.'

'What . . .?'

'Ax de boy.'

Kit was crouching, preparing to leap at Casey. Hilda pulled her hands out of Casey's grasp and waddled between the two of them.

'Kit!' she cried. 'Listen to yo' da'.'

Her shout made him hesitate, and he glanced with curiosity at Casey, waiting.

Casey gaped at the cabin. The flames were burning the gallery. Soon they would take the wall and the shingles of the roof. He said nothing.

Hilda's whole body shook with indignation at his willful silence.

'Kit,' she cried again. 'What was the name of yo' mam in Nuorleans?'

Kit scowled. 'Rhoda.'

'Aagh!' Hilda gave a strangled cry and staggered headlong into Casey. 'It's him! Kit does be yo' son! Rhoda stole Lucy's babe. He ain' die in de swamp.'

Casey hung his head, hearing the ghosts in the crackles of the flames.

'I don't understand,' said Kit. 'This is just a ruse . . .'

'No, son,' said Casey, turning his back on the fire. 'Rhoda lived in that cabin. She took you when you were born because Lucy, your real mother, died. I am your father, not Jed.'

'You?' Kit buried his face in his hands as the full implication struck him. 'But you're half bl –'

There was a crash as the gallery post buckled and fell into the flames. The fire had a firm hold on the front of the cabin. Casey gawped at it in horror.

'Look after Hilda,' he shouted, thrusting the old cook, shaking with tears, into Kit's arms. He ran across the grass and jumped into the flames, diving through the blazing doorway into the cabin.

His hair was alight and he patted his head to snuff it out. The fire had singed his legs and his arms yet he didn't feel the pain. He ran across to the chimney, tearing off his shirt to use as a mask as the fierce heat engulfed him.

The fire had a hold on two walls of the cabin and was crackling through the dry cypress shingles on the roof as if it was tinder. The blaze lit up the cabin's interior and the shadows danced mockingly like the ghosts of Casey's past.

He ignored the voices shouting his name and tore at the loose bricks in the chimney-breast. He reached inside the hidden cavity and his fingers touched the coffer as the ceiling sagged and bits of burning shingle fell around him. He tugged at the box until it was in his arms. He dodged as a flaming rafter fell, catching his shoulder. The cabin was filled with smoke as flames leaped around him. He staggered blindly, fighting for breath, lost in the inferno with his treasure box cradled in his arms like a baby.

He heard the voice calling. A gush of air rushed to his face and Kit was at his side.

'Take this, son,' Casey said, thrusting the coffer at him. 'It's yours.'

Kit grabbed the box, and also held on to Casey's arm, pulling him to the side of the cabin where he had come in through the window.

'No,' said Casey. 'You go, get out of here. Go north! There's enough money in that coffer for your future. Educate yourself. Get a wife. Get children!' He paused, his eyes staring wildly as another rafter fell, crashing on to his head.

'Kit, go! I'll stay here and the secret of your black blood will die with me.'

Martha woke suddenly. Her mouth was dry, her lips cracked and she had a fire inside her throat that only water could satisfy. Her chamber was in darkness. She staggered out of bed, weaving uncertainly to the door. She flung it open.

'Free!' she croaked. Then she remembered.

The house was deserted and not a lantern burned. She groped her way down the stairs and into the dining room. There was water in the filter and she poured out some into a goblet, drinking it thirstily. The draft revived her and she tried to blink away her headache.

Carrying more water in the goblet, she felt her way to the hall and out on to the veranda. She was puzzled to find the door wide open, and no slaves. In the darkness, across the Bayou Celeste, a red haze lit up the sky outlining the tops of the live oaks against the skyline. She leaned on the rail and tried to recall what had happened. She shuddered.

She remembered Ruffin escorting her to her chamber and Lizette making her put on her nightdress and lie down. Ruffin told her she was still distraught and must not worry because he was going to cleanse The Drongos of the evil that stalked it. She had asked for a whisky and Ruffin had sent Lizette to get it. It was a strong measure and she had sipped it gratefully, listening with only half an ear while Ruffin ranted. Then her thoughts began to bump into each other, sleep seized her brain, and Ruffin's face went out of focus. The whisky had been drugged.

'Lizette!' she had whispered as she fell unconscious.

It was the laudanum that made her thirsty. She drained the goblet and gazed again at the sky reddening with the blaze. She wondered what was burning so brightly. There was only swamp on the other side of the bayou, and Rhoda's old cabin where Casey liked to mope when he was vexed with her.

Casey! Was he dead too?

She wailed with despair and ran off the piazza in her nightdress. She was barefoot. She hurried dwon the path in the direction of the bayou, bumping into trees and tearing her nightdress on the branches. A slave loomed out of the darkness, running beside her. He stopped and blocked her path.

'Help me!' she screamed at him.

'Yas, mistis.' Chaucer put his arm out and held her. His fingers fondled her breasts.

She slapped his face with a blow that was given strength by her pent up frustration. Chaucer cowered away.

'Help me cross the bayou!' she demanded.

The slave obliged.

Kit flung the coffer out of the cabin window and turned back in time to catch Casey as he toppled forward. His hair was on fire and his back was burned a bright red. Kit lifted him up to the window sill and rolled him over out of the window where Harbud and Dexter were waiting.

The two slaves caught Casey and lowered his body gently to the ground. Kit jumped out after him as the roof collapsed and showered him with burning shingles and sparks.

Groups of slaves stood in the undergrowth watching the cabin being eaten up by the flames. Hilda was in the arms of her sister, Hannah, and she was murmuring softly.

'Ah done lie,' she said, gulping for breath. 'Ah done lie.'

Harbud stood over Casey while Kit retrieved the coffer from where it had fallen in a thicket.

'Mas Kit,' said Harbud softly. 'Wha' we gwine do?'

Kit's face was covered with dust and soot. His fair hair was charred, and in the light from the flames, he looked as black as the slaves. He knelt beside Casey and felt for his heartbeat. 'Get some water,' he said.

Dexter passed him a cup and Kit splashed its contents into Casey's face.

Casey stirred. A shadow fell over him as he opened his eyes. He peered up beyond Kit's shoulder. 'Martha?' he whispered.

'Yes, Casey.'

'Kit?'

'Yes.' The boy paused then said, 'I'm here, father.'

Casey struggled to sit up. He put his arms out for Martha. She clung to him, her head resting on his shoulder. She was shaking and sobbing. Casey held her firmly.

'I'm sorry, Cas,' she murmured between her tears. 'I love you, Cas. I love you!'

Casey patted her shoulder, staring behind her to where Kit was standing with the coffer in his hands. 'I told you to take that and go, white boy,' he said. 'Look after yourself.'

'No,' Kit shook his head. 'Not without you, father.'

'I'm staying here, son.' Casey grunted. 'Martha needs me.'

He smiled. The pain in his head had gone.

FLOODTIDE

Suzanne Goodwin

Stella grew to womanhood in a land torn apart by the Boer War, but the thunder and flash of guns on the distant horizon did not trouble her until her sixteenth year. To the battle-hardened British troops the fire at the farm was just another brutal act of war: to Stella it was a blazing beacon burning her past to ashes and lighting the way to a strange new life in distant lands.

Who would not pity a wounded soldier dying in the parched veldt far from his English home? How could Stella fail to nurse the pale, aristocratic Rupert Coryot back to health – to give him her frank young love? And how could she suspect that his summer passion for her, a Boer farmer's adopted daughter, would change in the colder climate of his ancestral home?

Viscountess, lover, actress and mother, Stella flees from the scorn and hatred of Edwardian high society to seek fame in the theatre. But as the Great War shatters the world she knows, she learns that her love will never die.

HISTORICAL ROMANCE 0 7221 3974 8 £1.95

THE PASSIONATE SAVAGE

Constance Gluyas

Lucien Marsh was a loner, a man who wouldn't settle down in any one place with any one woman – however beautiful she might be. And he had two women who loved him with all their hearts and would shatter their lives to lie in his arms –

FLAMING DAWN the fiery Indian princess who broke her people's trust by giving herself to the white hunter and following him into a white man's world.

LADY SAMANTHA PIERCE the sophisticated society lady who broke her marriage vows to possess Lucien, restlessly seeking to capture her true love and desire.

THE PASSIONATE SAVAGE is the unforgettable romance of two magnificent women raging from the untamed American wilderness to the aristocratic world of Victorian London.

HISTORICAL ROMANCE 0 7221 3901 2 £2.25

Barbara Riefe

SO WICKED THE HEART

Snatched from safety and her husband's harbouring arms by the lawless corsairs of Algiers, fiery but tender Lorna Singleton is forced to obey a pirate captain's bold lusts. But Ahmed's animal passion does not lack barbaric splendour. As a Christian slave in brutal Muslim hands, Lorna must find a protector to save her from the torment and degradation that awaits her in the casbah . . . even if the price of salvation is her virtue.

SO WICKED THE HEART is a gale-force story of surging passion and turbulent love, an unabashed tale of a woman's struggle to defend the storm-wracked fortress of her heart against an onslaught of unparalleled savagery and betrayal.

HISTORICAL ROMANCE 0 7221 7363 6 £1.95